"**Keep with the darts**. I'm changin[g] [...] armored men shouted.

Brody took this as his cue to [...] [behind a cubi]cle wall. He listened as the guards switched their magazines, slapping in clips with actual bullets.

Thorp ignored the gas, popping up to fire, with tears running down his cheeks and off his chin, the flesh circling his eyes a deep ruby. He wiped at his eyes with the length of his arm.

"They're switching to live fire," Brody shouted to Thorp. The smoke grenade spun in his direction, and he kicked it away to a safe distance, sending it gliding across the floor, hissing angrily.

The muffled whistle of the fire was now different, a denser, meatier sound. The bullets smacked into the cubicle walls with more punch to them. The air over his head was filled with sawdust, bits of semiburned cubicle upholstery.

Brody remained in his hiding place, feeling useless, still holding the Franklin-Johann.

Thorp noticed him trying to bat the sting of his weeping eyes. "They're going to kill us. You've got to shoot back."

Brody shook his head.

Thorp dropped down into cover and shouted at him, his voice rising to a desperate shriek, "You take out your sidearm and you *shoot*, soldier."

"I can't."

KNUCKLEDUSTER

ANDREW POST

KNUCKLEDUSTER
ANDREW POST

MEDALLION
P R E S S

Medallion Press, Inc.

Printed in USA

For Traci

Published 2013 by Medallion Press, Inc.

The MEDALLION PRESS LOGO
is a registered trademark of Medallion Press, Inc.

Typeset in Lucida Sans
Printed in the United States of America
ISBN 9-78160542493-4
10 9 8 7 6 5 4 3 2 1
First Edition

Acknowledgments

Lorie Jones, Emily Steele, and the entire Medallion Press team. Never before have I met such dedicated folks who show such enthusiasm and genuine love for what they do. And my wife, who was there every step of the way in every definition of the phrase.

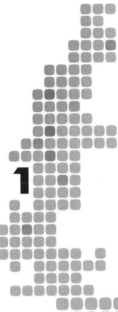

1

Artificial light filtered down through the kudzu of overlapping wires onto the man with orange-stained eyes. The bouncer watched him smoke one cigarette after another, since there was little else to watch. When he checked the time by his phone screen, the bouncer did the same.

At ten to eleven, the man tucked his phone into his peacoat pocket, ground out his smoke on his boot heel, and marched across the littered avenue. Without a line to wait in, he walked directly up to the bouncer, shouting over the bone-shaking bass leaking out through the front doors. It was the music du jour, lonely cowboy country with a mismatched undercurrent of scattered percussion. "Cover?"

"Ten," the heavily tattooed doorman replied for the hundredth time tonight. As the man withdrew his jigsaw card, the bouncer sized him up. Lanky, built like a basketball player. Close-cropped hair the color of mud, a wave in the front made crooked from a cowlick. A long narrow face with a week's worth of coarse black growth. Familiar.

It took the bouncer a second before he remembered him from a month before, asking questions, starting a fight, and beating a man half to death. What was it that he used for a weapon? It was what everyone knew him by. Blackjack? Tire iron? Sock full o' dimes? No, the man used a fist armored across the fingers with black metal—a knuckleduster. But it was in the middle of his name, like a heavyweight's fighting moniker. Something "Knuckleduster" Something.

Something "Knuckleduster" Something held up his jigsaw card between his first and middle finger with a posture that read nothing but impatience.

With inked hands, the bouncer ran the card through his device, waited for the screen to show something other than an hourglass. Before the verification bleat sounded, confirming that the cover charge was accepted, a gust of recollections hit him.

He shot to his feet and extended a flattened hand toward the man, barring him entrance. "Hey, buddy. We don't want any trouble in here tonight. Got a whole slew of guys who wanna just take a load off and not be bothered, okay? Besides, one of you and God knows how many of them. You really think that'd be such a good idea, make trouble?"

The man just stood there. "What's that thing tell you?" he asked after a moment, nodding at the device in the man's hand.

The bouncer looked into his eyes, seeing them close up now. He saw a dark brown hue and confirmed something else he thought he noticed earlier—the whites appeared to be tinted ever so slightly the color of pumpkin skin. Weird.

The man repeated his question, slower this time, about what the device had told him.

"N-nothing," the bouncer said, stammering, coming out of his transfixion on the man's eyes. "The bossman didn't spring for the good ones. This just takes the ten bucks and makes sure you're twenty-one or older"—he shook the device as if that could suddenly improve its engineering— "and it don't tell me nothing about no one who comes in here." Realizing he was saying too much, he shut up.

"So if I were to ask you if a friend of mine was here tonight, you couldn't tell me?" the man asked.

"No."

"And if for whatever reason, something happened here tonight . . ."

"Bossman says this is a place where people shouldn't feel like they're being watched," the bouncer answered, nearly quoting the bar's owner and his vision for this particular watering hole verbatim. It took the bouncer a second before divining what the man with the odd eyes was implying by asking that and just as he opened his mouth to spit a lie to try and cover his tracks, he was cut off.

"Just want a drink," the man said, his voice low and even.

"You're not here to rough no one up? You nearly killed that guy a month ago." He flashed back on that bloody scene—the guy wheeled out on a gurney with a broken arm and a shattered jaw. Ugly stuff.

The man smiled, showing a row of straight, tall teeth, and shook his head. "Quick splash of the hair of the dog and I'm gone. Scout's honor."

Sure, the bouncer could turn away anyone he deemed unfit to drink in the establishment. But times were hard, and his boss had told him that unless they were naked and carving symbols into their bodies with broken glass, let them in. Hell, let the crazies in too; they liven up the place. He gave the man his jigsaw back.

"Fine," the bouncer said, curling his paw until just the thumb stuck out. He waved it over his shoulder and stepped aside. "Go on ahead. But if you start any shit with anybody, slick, those knucks of yours will be going in *my* pocket."

"You betcha." Whatever his name was smirked and entered the bar.

The place was packed.

The noise was overwhelming and claustrophobia inducing. One song went into the next with barely a breath of time between. Heavy club music with obscene lyrics and then more of those remixed country songs. Brody studied the endlessly shifting mass of dancers under the strobes, lasers cutting swaths of colored light over their sweat-slicked bodies. The lights and constant movement of the flailing crowd gave the sensation that the building itself was moving, flipping end over end, spiraling through zero gravity, and the people weren't dancing but fighting to keep stability on an untrustworthy surface.

Brody stood far from the dance floor at the back wall and watched the crowd for fifteen deafening minutes. He grew accustomed to the layout of the place—where the exit was, where the staff were stationed. He took in as many details as possible on every person in an attempt to cross-reference them against what he knew about Jonah Billingsly, which was little. He had a spotty description, something about an old tattoo that was faded to a blotchy mess and he also knew what the man had done, but who looks the part of the abusive boyfriend?

The bar's AI must've gotten wind that someone had been inside for more than ten minutes and still hadn't ordered a drink. A woman, accumulated in translucent blue and aggressively topless, bleated at him: "Hey, sugar, how's about a tall boy? They be only fifteen buckaroos for the next ten minutes."

Brody waved off the holo and the woman disappeared, seemingly folding in on herself, gone to pop up elsewhere to pester and jiggle at someone else.

He moved his gaze from one corner of the place to the next, passing briefly over the lady-boys with their sparkly attire on the dance floor. An angry drunk who beats his girlfriend to unconsciousness weekly probably isn't much of a dancer, Brody assumed.

He watched the group at the bar instead: men

clad in stained overalls. Dockworkers, possibly. They pounded dark beers and slammed shot glasses of stuff that even they, the hardworking manly man consortium, would finish with watering eyes. Brody didn't know what Jonah did for a living—Marcy was foggy on that detail—but he was pretty sure there was a good chance he was among that group.

Brody decided to see if they'd cough up info if he acted like a lonely drunk looking for conversation. Adopting a waver, he made his way to the overall-clad horde, deliberately stepping on one of their steel-toed work boots. He apologized profusely, making sure to let his eyes swivel loosely in their sockets, feigning deep intoxication. "Hey, hey—sorry about that, man," he slurred.

The guy pushed his knitted cap off his eyes to better size up the saboteur of his fun. When the man turned into the blasting pulses of light, a hard face, puffy and ruddy, presented itself to Brody, complete with knitted brow and a thin, splitting set of lips so chapped they appeared burned. He seemed to be actively mulling over whether or not to make the shoe scuffing a big deal. This melted away when another beer was set in front of them and Brody slapped his jigsaw down on the bar to pay for it.

The bartender scanned the card with a handheld device and walked off without ever having touched it.

"Again, I apologize, my man. I do."

"It's no big deal. They're old boots anyway." The dockworker clapped Brody on the shoulder and raised the beer and took a deep swallow.

All the while, the man was unknowingly being scrutinized. Marcy, the woman with the swollen-shut eye who contracted Brody, had mentioned the tattoo on her boyfriend's wrist that once said her name but now looked like an out-of-focus bar code. As the man lifted his stein to polish off the beer with a second gulp that made his throat bulge, Brody saw it peeking out from under the stained cuff of his overalls. It was easy this time. No asking around, no getting false leads, no paying for information. The first goon he approached was the one he was sent here to find. Sometimes things just worked out. It didn't matter what Jonah and Marcy used to be like as a couple, if they'd ever been happy. What mattered was what Jonah was now: a mean drunk, a man who hit women. Brody sometimes thought of himself as the sum of an equation, this plus this equals him, a living result of bad actions.

Brody dropped the impersonation of a happy drunk, regained his posture, and felt his heart stumble into its new rhythm, suddenly awake, pumping fast.

The dockworker noticed Brody still standing there, his demeanor shifting as well, cascading into easily read hostility. He set the beer stein aside, foam still clinging to the inside of the glass. "Not that kind of place, Nancy."

"You Jonah?" Brody asked, ignoring the taunt.

The dockworker squared up the cap on his head. "That's right."

"So you get a kick out of it, then? Is that why you do it?"

"What's that?" Jonah asked and pulled one lumpy

hand from the rubber-lined pocket of his overalls. Bruised knuckles, a swollen wrist—evidence he'd recently been hitting something hard. Like a woman's skull.

There was a boa constrictor that lived off Brody. He wore it day and night. With the sight of Jonah's bruised hand, it tightened. It was looped over his shoulders innocently enough when he met Marcy or any other woman at the community center. Like a lei placed around the neck, an added kiss on the cheek, harmless. But slowly, as he got to know more about this man from the battered girlfriend, the cold skin of rage knotted around Brody's throat.

It reached that point now, the fever pitch of preoccupation. He had even been having dreams about Jonah all week as he patiently bided his time until Friday night when he knew the guy liked to go out for drinks after work with the boys. Which, more often than not, ended with Jonah staggering home and putting a few fists to Marcy.

Not this time, Brody decided. He'd let Jonah drink, let him get good and loose and foggy-eyed. But before he settled his tab and took that angry walk home to dispense some undeserved punishment on the woman he supposedly loved, Brody would detour him, rearrange things, and put him on a new course. Instead of sleeping it off in his shitty apartment after giving his dying girlfriend another few slaps, Jonah would be lying in a hospital bed with plenty of time to think about the downward trajectory his life had taken up to that point.

"She's sick," Brody said.

Jonah's eyes narrowed. "You know my girlfriend?"

"Those three days she was gone? She was at the community center, sleeping on a cot, eating cold soup. We met, talked."

"You a caseworker? Come here to tell me I drink too much, that I shouldn't beat my girlfriend when the bitch is costing me an arm and a leg with all her goddamn medication?"

"No. She asked me to give you this." In one quick motion, Brody pulled his hand from his coat pocket, the knuckles all wrapped in a flat piece of metal, and hammered it into Jonah's cheek.

Jonah's head snapped back, his cap falling off. The man was stunned, drunk enough that his reflexes were poor. He took a step forward and swung with his right.

Brody ducked and gripped Jonah's elbow, using the forward momentum to move him away from his pack of friends. Their attention had been grabbed certainly, but not one of them came to his rescue. They held their beer steins by their glass handles and gaped, wordless.

When those on the dance floor noticed the two men fighting, they ceased their gyrations and shuffled aside. Some continued to dance at a safe distance, apparently too moved by the particular song to give two drunken idiots the time. Others gawked openly. A few took bets with a series of manic hand gestures to one another. A finger on Brody, an open palm representing fifty big ones.

Brody made quick work of Jonah, threw a few punches when he could easily sneak them in, always jabbing with the brass knuckles.

Jonah swung wildly. His sweeping passes pulled

him forward and made him stumble in whatever direction he thought Brody was in. Cursing and hissing and drooling, Jonah was drunk enough to be seeing double. Clearly Jonah knew he would not win this one. Something was fueling him—seething contempt perhaps—even if he hadn't landed a single punch yet.

Brody threw a right hook and connected with Jonah's mouth. The clang of metal on teeth must have been audible to his friends at the bar.

Jonah took the pop to the teeth like everyone did. A punch to the cheek, the gut, the chest—those definitely hurt, but you could take quite a few of them before it dissolved your will to continue. A good blow to the teeth with a knuckleduster? That staggered any man. Jonah covered his profusely bleeding mouth and began coughing. The pink mist was caught in the jittering flash of the club's strobe display, looking like the slow-motion video following a well-placed sniper bullet.

He stood by while Jonah bent at the waist and spat teeth to the floor. The other dockworkers watched, giving each other the elbow and scowling. There was consideration in their eyes: maybe they should get involved. None of them took a step away from the bar and their drinks. Brody read in all their alcohol-pinked faces that Jonah was an asshole, one who very much had this coming.

"Don't do it again," Brody reminded him. To clarify. "Okay?"

"Yeah, okay, fine . . . just don't . . . hit me again, okay?" Jonah slurred.

The victimizer had gotten a taste of his own medecine

and was now repeating lines picked up from those he had beaten. Brody wanted to continue until Jonah was a moaning heap of broken bones on the floor, gripping his belly, his face—hands seemingly moving on their own, unsure where to apply pressure next since *everything* hurt.

But as Jonah bent there, gripping the knees of his pants and spitting blood onto the floor, Brody felt the snake release its binding grip from his neck. It had been sated. It had slowly unknotted and slid off when the final blow was delivered. It had gone and left in its wake a lingering thirst. In the vacuum that the desire to beat and maim left was a conscience trying to sound its call up from somewhere deep. Telling him to stop. Refrain. Think. Resist. Marcy wanted you to give Jonah the same treatment he gave her, his conscience tolled. Not *kill* the son of a bitch.

Brody unclenched his fist. "So we're agreed?"

"Yeah." Jonah choked. "I won't do it again. I fuckin' *promise.*"

"Peachy." Brody removed the sticky knuckleduster from his sore fingers.

Everyone cut a clear path for him as he marched to the door. He stepped outside and immediately fired up a cigarette. As he peered down at the flame illuminated in his cupped palms, *01:59:59* flashed in small red digits in the corner of his eye. He'd have to be home soon.

He noticed the bouncer sitting there on his stool, arms crossed, one eyebrow cocked. Brody took the heavy piece of metal from his pocket and offered it to the burly young man. The knuckleduster was tacky with blood. "I suppose I owe you my merit badges."

The bouncer stared at the reddened object resting in Brody's palm but made no motion to fetch it. "No, thanks," he said, slipping his cell into his jacket pocket. "But I called you a ride."

Just then, mixing with the lights that hung under the awning of the bar, came swinging beams of red and blue. Standing in place, hands in pockets, Brody watched a squad car approach down the desolate avenue.

The squad car parked, and a figure emerged from the passenger seat. Wearing a fedora and a pinstriped slate-on-charcoal suit, Detective Nathan Pierce got one look at Brody and shook his head.

"Boss?" the other officer asked.

"Go get us some statements."

The officer headed inside.

Detective Pierce drew near with a casual stride and announced, "Brody 'Knuckleduster' Calhoun."

As soon as the vigilante for hire's name was uttered, the bouncer snapped his fingers. "*That's* it. *Knew* I knew it."

Ignoring the bouncer having his moment of self-congratulations, Nathan removed the cuffs from the pouch on the back of his belt. "Well?"

Brody sighed and let the cigarette dangle from his lips as he lifted his wrists, bloodied hands palms down.

2

Nathan Pierce took a deep breath before reading from a sheet he found in the dense, rubber-banded file folder. He remained standing while Brody sat at the table in the small, too-bright room. "Ready? Okay, here we go again. Broadwell Alexander Calhoun of Minneapolis, Minnesota, your crimes are as follows. Eleven harassment charges. Two cases of flagrantly disobeying a restraining order. Ten separate complaints against you about malicious threats. Seventeen misdemeanor cases of aggravated assault, all of which were with a deadly weapon, those goddamn brass knuckles we always find on you.

"And a few other misdemeanors, like shoving a man into a mail collection box. Another one says you punched a man in the chest while he was at his job at Tofu Pagoda. Broken noses, broken arms. You gave one man *two* broken hands . . ." He went on and on.

Brody listened and said nothing. He had no way of refuting any of those allegations or previous crimes he had been found guilty of. Each time the police arrived to collect him at whatever venue he had given the men their due comeuppance, he had accepted it without struggle. He struck the classic pose, silent, wrists held out ready for the cuffs.

Any rent-a-cop could scan his jigsaw, see the organized list of his crimes. But his reputation went beyond that. Everyone knew what it meant when Brody "Knuckleduster" Calhoun arrived. Even though they may be part of the citywide problem of dangerous apathy themselves, they knew they should let him do what he wanted. He was an unwavering no when a re-luctant yes was the norm. Unlike many of the averted-eyed masses, he gazed unflinchingly into the vacuous abyss that mankind had dug itself into. Their staring contest held at an unbreakable stalemate.

Nathan threw down the folder. The contents slid out in front of Brody. The files and his old mug shots from when he still wore a beard. The tight text all bundled together on the lines, the reports, the quotes from the officers who had been first on the scene and their observations of what had gone down. Words such as *violent* and *cooperative*, even though the pairing was incongruous, appeared repeatedly.

One of the pages, kept close to the bottom, was

a record of all the community service he had done as recoupment for his crimes. Brody was sure that page went wholly unnoticed. The crimes were much more appealing to fawn over and gape at. Cops didn't like criminals who repaid their debts; they liked them to run. They were the feverish bloodhounds of the city in that way. The chase was all they desired, even if their restrictions kept them from actually doing anything beyond a polite Q and A in a small, windowless room.

"So, what do you make of this? I'll be happy to inform you that the bill's up for switching the law back. We'll be able to stop this fucking around and just put you in a box, throw away the key, say sayonara. You happen to do something like this come January 1, we very well could if we want." He drew in a breath, rubbed his gray temple, slightly mussing his hair. "But until then . . . anyway, we're talking about tonight, weren't we? Today. Number eighteen. Eighteen for you in the breaking-a-man's-face category since we can't call it assault, even though we both know it is. Chiffon's not going to be one bit pleased to hear about this."

Brody remained silent. He was famous for this, being pulled in and stuck in the hot room and not saying a word, ultimately just accepting his sentence, which wasn't even up to the cops. The caseworkers and parole boards held that particular ring of keys with white-knuckled fists. Brody knew it didn't make a bit of a difference. As long as the men he visited continued to carry a pulse, he'd just be pitched back out into the world. They were even obligated to reunite him with his brass knuckles—personal property couldn't be confiscated if he had the receipt from that tobacco shop slash pugilist's accessory boutique, which he did.

Brody, as well as the detective, knew that even the judges who favored the lax state of the law liked him. They didn't see a vigilante but a human coupon. On a monthly basis he was doing what the cops could never do—and it was off the government payroll. And in a roundabout way, justice was being served. To them, a minor auxiliary bonus. Since Brody had discovered the convenient loophole and begun making temporary employers at the community center, the rate at which women were being brought to the ER for signs of battery had halved.

"Let me tell you, it's not just you who gets an earful when you do this shit. *I* have to hear about it, too. And just so it keeps Chiffon off my ass and makes it seem like I'm trying to do something with you, I'm going to ask her to move your monthly visit up to Friday. She'll know what to do with you and how many more hours will finally make you get the message to quit this shit."

Brody thought about his probation officer. Her cramped little office, her constant gospel music. The antique candy dish on the corner of her desk, while inviting, was clearly not there to be sampled from by her "clients" but maybe, as he always suspected, as a symbol of learning to control oneself. What would she have to say about number eighteen? A few hundred more hours mopping floors? Or would this prove to best her patience, causing her to send him to the Minneapolis Penitentiary for a few months to "gain some perspective," as she was always threatening to do one day?

In the corner of his left eye, Brody caught a glimpse of a pinprick of flashing red: *00:59:59*. Only an hour before his lenses would require a charge. It prompted Brody to move this talk to the fast track. After clearing his throat, he spoke for the first time since the cuffs were thrown on. "I have *nothing* to say. You got me. Here I sit willingly, not giving you any trouble. I just did what I thought was the right thing—"

"Yeah. A real knight in shining armor, you." Nathan put the file back together, slammed the end of it against the top of the stainless steel table to straighten the pages. He took the keys out of his waistcoat pocket and gestured for Brody to lift his wrists. He unlocked the cuffs and gathered them up with a clatter of metal. "Hiding behind that adulterer's loophole won't stand up forever. Eventually we'll have to scan you for biological evidence that you were actually screwing these women."

"Maybe in January," Brody dared quietly.

Letting that slide, the detective tucked the cuffs away, stared at Brody. "It's funny how you claim you're actually in relationships with all these women, but when we run you through the sniffer out front, you always come up clean. Figured you'd have picked up something by now, especially since it's at the community center you're meeting all of them—the *last* place I'd expect to find a clean woman. And you always tell me you had absolutely *no* idea the husbands and boyfriends were beating your new friends . . ."

Brody blinked. "It just happens."

Nathan stifled what he was going to say next with a grunt and let it go. Instead, "I know you already have a collection of these, but I'm going to give you another one just for shits and giggles." He removed his business card and flicked it onto the table between them. "Next time some poor girl asks you to intervene, tell her to give *me* a call. Leave it to the paid professionals, Prince Valiant. Now piss off."

Going back out into the processing area, Brody passed a group of hookers chained shoulder to shoulder to the bench and a gaggle of leather-clad hunchbacks, divided by their assumed gender. He went to the counter to retrieve his belongings.

The uniformed cop on the other side of the bullet-proof glass finished the call he was on, hung up, took a sip of coffee, and then finally asked Brody through the intercom for his name—last, middle, first.

As the cop presented the items and dropped them into the drawer, he said, "Wallet: black leather, silver chain. Contents: driver's license, expired military ID, jigsaw monetary and personal account card, Mega Deluxo Mega Savers card, also expired. One butane lighter. Look at this antique: one cellular phone. One pack of cigarettes of a foreign brand. One contact lens case . . . What's this attached to it?"

"The battery," Brody said, impatient. He wanted to get home.

"What the hell do contact lenses need a battery for?"

Brody wiggled a finger next to his right eye. "Carotene lenses." *Let's get a move on here, please.*

"All right, one carrot bean. Carrot teen. *Whatever.* A contact lens case. And one pair of knucks, black." The officer dropped the knuckleduster, the heaviest of the items, and it made a terrific bang as it landed in the metal drawer.

Behind Brody, one of the men dressed in head-to-toe shiny leather gimp attire unzipped his mouth. "Hey, man, that's favoritism. Am I going to be getting my whip back? I doubt it. That's bullshit. You hear me? That's *bullshit*."

The uniform ignored the masochist's protests and slammed the drawer under the partition. "Any complaints about how you were treated during your stay can be sent to us at our website. Please remember that by releasing you, the St. Paul Police Department is not encouraging you to break the law in any way but has considered your unique case and has deemed you satisfactory to be released back into the general populous under the stipulation that you will try your very best not to cause any other problems or break any other laws in the state of Minnesota henceforth. Know that by passing through the front doors, you have agreed to these terms. Thank you and have a nice day."

Outside the precinct, among the row of parked squad cars and night traffic, Brody spotted Marcy standing near a telephone pole, smoking a cigarette with a shiver quaking every inch of her slender five-foot frame.

They met in the middle on the sidewalk. In the dim light being thrown off the precinct's entryway behind him, Marcy's face looked even more battered and swollen than he remembered. He had met her when the injuries were fresh, and now, well into a week of healing, they looked somehow worse. An inky, shallow pit swallowed her entire right eye because the skin of her brow was hardly able to hold in the green and purple knot outcropping it. He made sure not to let Marcy see him staring.

"Hey," she said softly, tucking a purple-and-green-streaked strand of white-girl dreads behind an ear busy with piercings. She looked apologetic, seeing him with his hands red from the fight, his wrists bruised from the cuffs. "I hope you didn't get in too much trouble or anything."

"It's fine," Brody said.

Here came the terribly awkward moment. The job was done, and all had been settled save for the minor detail of payment. Beating up guys for the women he met at the community center was one thing. He tracked them down, gave them what they deserved with a certain enthusiasm, but discussing how much he was owed afterward took the air out of his heroic sails. But a man had to eat, he reminded himself. The batteries for the lens changer weren't exactly cheap, either.

"So, what'd we say—fifty?" she asked, withdrawing her pocket ordinateur.

Brody removed his wallet and extended his jigsaw card, his stomach twisting. This felt wrong, but at the same time the promise of money coming his way was a jolt to his system. He watched her make the tabulations on the touch screen, punching the keys and scrolling up and down in the menu, her fingers bejeweled with gaudy costume rings.

Once through, Marcy looked up at him, her unnaturally crooked smile toothy and bright. It probably hurt to smile, but she did it anyway. "I gave you sixty instead."

"You didn't have to do that," he replied, taking his jigsaw from her hand gently.

"No, it's okay. I got paid today, and with Jonah not living with me anymore, my grocery bill is, like, a *third* of what it used to be." She smiled again, the right hook of her mouth unable to go up as far as the left, but it faltered as if the left side, the frowning side, had succeeded in pulling the right down into the doldrums with it. "You deserve it for what you did tonight. I mean, violence begets violence, right? I think it'll be better this way. Whoever Jonah shacks up with next, maybe he'll think twice before coming home stinking drunk and pissed off."

"How're the treatments going?" Brody asked.

"Good," she said with buoyancy, putting her ordi back in her purse. "A few more rounds and I'll be done. They had to cut out a pretty big hunk of my pancreas, but I guess they got it all. So, yeah—it's a good thing." She sounded unsure.

Before Brody knew what was happening, Marcy took a step forward and put her arms around him. She hugged him tightly, her face mashed against his chest, the scratchy texture of her dreadlocks tickling his chin. Her warmth, both figurative and literal, was surprising.

"Thank you so much," she said. "I know it's bad to want someone to get hurt, but I don't think he'd understand it any other way. I feel better and worse

at the same time. Does that make sense?" She wept—
wetness soaked through the material of his shirt and
touched the flesh of his chest, chilled already from the
late November air.

Marcy released him and seemed momentarily
embarrassed, then daintily wiped at her bruised eye
with the back of her hand. She didn't meet his eyes. She
stood there, obviously unsure as to what came next.

Brody knew from experience that Marcy would
want to extend their friendship, ask him to lunch or
something. After all, they had used the adulterer's
loophole as a way for him to do this for her, so why not
make it official? But he knew that every time she laid
eyes on him she'd be reminded of Jonah, even though
the two men weren't a lick alike. He'd be a bookmark
flagging that horrible chapter of her life, forever
glued in place. There might be good times ahead of
them. Great times, even. But every time they were
asked to hear the story of how they met or perhaps
during her own reflecting on their relationship and its
origin—there it'd be, a blemish that regardless of what
pristine beauty surrounded it would continually be
the most noticeable aspect of that possible *them*. So,
instead, Brody decided to say his line to complete the
transaction. "Take care of yourself."

"Yeah, you too. Thank you again."

"Don't mention it," Brody said, turning to walk in
the direction of the light-rail station.

Once off the train in relative proximity to his apartment building, Brody turned a few corners and walked

the cold streets of St. Paul. He crossed the bridge into Minneapolis and entered the first bodega he found that still had its lights on.

The red digits on his lenses reminded him that he had only twenty minutes before he'd be completely, helplessly blind. Navigating the city sightless would be impossible, and his mind was already fatigued enough that putting on the sonar before he could get a full night's sleep would be an invitation for a migraine. He found the batteries he needed at the back of the store among a jumbled offering of other electronics. They were just a set of two batteries, the size of typical double As, except set into a long security bracket to prevent theft, too wide to be jammed down a pocket on the sly. He took them to the counter, and fifty of the sixty credits Marcy had given him mere minutes ago evaporated from his account with one quick swipe.

"Have a nice night—or morning, I suppose," the clerk said, referring to the clock on the wall.

Back out into the night, he made it to the front door of his apartment building just as the final ten minutes of his lenses began to count down.

Brody's apartment was spread out, one wholly undecorated room, before the elevator doors. It was cavernous with its cement walls, cement floor, cement ceiling. Windows along one side provided ample light in the mornings. In a corner were his television, black pleather couch, coffee table. Next to it, the kitchenette: cupboards with no doors, his meager collection of plates and glasses on display, cleaned and neatly arranged. The bedroom was divided from the rest of the space by a ratty paper curtain he'd bought at a flea market, fixed to the ceiling with duct tape. It contained a mattress thrown in the corner, the nightstand a re-purposed bucket.

He didn't feel like watching any television or re-questing his voice mail—he knew it would just offer the same emptiness that his mailbox downstairs had. Of course, this never came as much of a surprise. He never got anything besides his monthly injury payment from the government, a nice impersonal Army apology printed on yellow paper with the check attached—a perk he gladly cashed.

But he'd spent his October check already and still had two weeks before the next. He considered the ten credits still floating, never touched as actual hard currency, in his bank account. Ten credits. He began arranging lists of combinations of things he could afford with only ten credits as if accumulating an order from a menu of dollar items at a fast-food joint. Toilet paper was always one of the essential items, kind of like the soft drink when ordering off that menu board. Other essentials he thought about were of course food, cigarettes, laundry soap. Paint was unessential, but it still found its way onto the list. A few more bottles of black and gray would be nice. Now he was just mixing a little bit of every color he had to make his own black, but when dry it always ended up looking more cobalt. This reminded him of the painting he left out on the balcony earlier in the day.

He went to the row of floor-to-ceiling windows and rolled a few of them open to let some air in. While he had been out, he had left the dryer going and the loft was sticky with humidity, every glass surface fogged.

Out on the balcony, he looked over downtown Minneapolis. The light-rail expansion had gone up a few months after he had signed the lease, and the crosstown track now ran right by his window, obscuring a good portion of the view. A trio of magnetized cars zipped by soundlessly on the raised track, just the occasional screech when metal met metal on the curves and bends steering between structures. He flicked his cigarette over the railing and watched it trail down, down, down to the street below. It hit asphalt, spraying a puff of embers that only took a strong breeze to snuff.

With the painting still gummy to the touch in places, Brody went back inside, leaving the windows open, and prepared himself a cup of green tea. He collapsed onto the couch and, desiring some sort of noise, asked the television to find a classical music station. It found some. He let the coolness of the pleather on his back soothe him. Collecting the painting and making tea felt like routines of an automaton. He wasn't in his head while doing them. His pulse was still quickened, his mind still choked with the night's activities.

He decided to use the last few minutes of vision to go into his outdated cellular phone and erase the documents he had gathered on Jonah Billingsly since that often helped to clear it all out, to purge it from his life as a job complete. Brody wasn't a cop, so he wasn't allowed any investigative applications on his cell, but he had a few homemade ones that worked nearly as well but operated just outside of legality. Jonah had received what was coming to him, and Brody could delete his homework on the man with confidence that the job was done and he'd never have to track down that particular individual again. Brody knew his type of justice was concise and seldom required repeating.

Brody found himself dozing off during the contestant introduction portion of a *Prize Mountain* rerun. The corner of his left eye flashed *00:00:59* and pulled him completely free from his encroaching slumber. He used the minute remaining on his lenses' charge to turn off the TV, fill a bottle of water, and trudge into the bathroom, the only room in the apartment that had a door and its own walls. He approached the mirror.

00:00:32. Jonah had actually gotten him. On his cheekbone was a trio of tiny scratches, probably from a sleeve zipper or a ring. He dabbed on some salve.

00:00:15. He leaned forward over the sink and spread his eyelids wide with his index and middle finger and fished in with his other hand, pinching the membranous disk off the surface of his eye. With the remaining seconds Brody had before the sight-gifting carotene concentrate petered out and the world before him began to cloud, he gazed at himself. In a moment, the artificial vitamins that the lenses provided would be metabolized, and his eyesight would quickly slide back into darkness.

In the mirror before him, Brody saw someone both familiar and unrecognizable as himself. He saw his age, his scars. With each tired blink the orange stains in the whites of his eyes faded out to a haggard bloodshot. After, they'd cloud over entirely. Naturally, he'd never seen that part of his return to blindness happen, but one drunken night of self-pity, he'd taken his own picture out of curiosity of what a photo of a blind man looks like—and he wondered if he'd possibly, even as blind as he was, see a flash. The next morning he had put the lenses back in and looked. Instead of that set of browns he'd inherited from his mother, just two white disks in their place, like doll's eyes as they'd be found only halfway down the assembly line.

The lens charger clicked on, and the new set of batteries went to work exposing the lenses to a continuous blast of ultraviolet. It helped to both sanitize the disks and restore the microscopic carotene power plants that made up the membrane of the lenses. With shadows starting to litter his vision, he listened beyond the bathroom light's fluorescent buzz: three long notes issuing from the charger denoting the charge's commencement. He looked down at the two dishes labeled with a Braille *L* and *R*. The charge indicator lights winked out just as the blackness ate the last bits of sight, the aperture shutting.

He felt around on the counter for the sonar case, but it wasn't where he usually put it. He checked the shelves of his medicine cabinet. Nope. He cursed and turned around, now fully enveloped in his blindness, and ran his hands along the bathroom wall, slapping and grabbing as he walked out. He imagined his Frankenstein strut looked like a cruel pantomime of a blind person.

His knees bumped his mattress, and he allowed himself to fall into bed. He reached over the sides of it, his fingers patting around over the cool, concrete floor, searching for the sonar. No dice. He rose and carefully moved across the space to the living area and scoured around the couch, the end table. Again, it wasn't there.

Brody followed the beacon of his refrigerator's hum to the kitchen counter. He scolded himself about remembering to put things back where they belonged or at least having the device close at hand *before* he took out his lenses.

After searching the entire apartment, he found the sonar where he should've begun his search—the inside pocket of his coat. He opened the hockey puck–sized case and pulled out the device—the diameter of a soda can bottom and the color of a Band-Aid, flesh tone but not quite—and pushed it onto his forehead where it stuck with an adhesive that never got fuzzy or lost its tackiness.

He pressed the power button on the device's side, and the world came into focus again but this time much differently. He could see maybe thirty feet in all directions, but anything farther might as well be the edge at the end of the world.

The sonar silently pinged and sent out its ringing wave of echolocation. The device used ultrasound and the path from his ruined optic nerves to his brain to catch and render shapes and rough details into a mentally palatable stream. But color—helpful ones like the signs denoting which bathroom was the men's—could not be illustrated with the sonar. Everything in floating pixels, polygons springing up around objects to map their general shape and size. From a distance, everything was simplified to its basic elements and clunky shapes, the details distilling more and more as he neared the object in question.

The curves of a voluptuous woman could be made to look blocky, poorly rendered, an altogether boring representation of what was actually before him if he wasn't willing to concentrate. Some time to focus, a clear mind, and perhaps a little alcohol, and details would begin to sharpen and faces would look more like . . . faces.

Brody went over to the open windows and shut them one by one. The sonar sent out its ping with the last window closed only partway. He could see the city beyond his balcony, the cars collected at the intersection made into rough shapes like soapbox derby cars. The buildings, giant cubes laid out in a pattern, stacked along the street. Textures, like the cracked asphalt, the slickness of a telephone pole covered in stickers, were smoothed down to their simplest three-dimensional shapes. Pages stapled to the pole could be seen but not read, unless their print was embossed or in Braille. Even smaller things—the fruit flies that always found a way into his apartment—were tiny flitting signatures of movement his sonar picked up and coded down for Brody as singular hovering pixels. All of it together, a life-size wire-frame diorama.

He turned the sonar off, sick of wearing it even after just a few minutes because of the fatigue it gave his brain. He stuck it to the wall next to the bed like a kid saving a piece of gum for the next day and lay down on the bare mattress to sleep but didn't for a good handful of hours.

Brody blinked at the darkness in his eyes, listened to the city that, even with closed windows, could never be completely muffled. The constant hum of the interstate, the chirp of the midnight light-rail hitting that bend right outside his window, the heater units going all at once in the various apartment buildings shouldered up next to his, the air filtration systems on the corner of each street purring away, dutifully pulling dust and infinitesimal debris from the air. He listened to the closest sound: the bugs gathering around the lights he had accidentally left on, clinking their exoskeletons against the glass, struggling fruitlessly to get at the warmth within.

He'd wake the next morning to see the lights had been on all night, luring in more bugs trying to find a place to shack up for the oncoming winter, and he'd curse, because that was going to be another pile of credits tacked onto his utility bill that he couldn't pay. He'd have to procure another client among those women who had nowhere to go but the community center and no one to talk to but those who already knew Brody's name, sobriquet and all. Another fist thrown, another transfer of credits, another day marked off the calendar doing what he didn't *want* to exactly but felt compelled to continue nonetheless.

3

It was Saturday—the one day in Brody's tireless week roaming bars and clubs that was reserved for painting. He took his easel out of the corner and set it up in front of the wall of windows.

The painting he had been working on, using a mix of acrylic and oils, was to be a snapshot of the city seen beyond his windows: red curtains flaring in the wind in the foreground and the metropolis in daylight beyond, something of a rarity for him. When he finished it he planned to hang it in the apartment, his sole piece of décor. All his previous paintings were layered under this one, but he had a good feeling about this latest attempt. He wanted to look at it with his lenses in and see a reminder not only of his artistry but that the Twin Cities also existed during the day.

He sat there in a pair of beat-up jeans and a T-shirt and painted for close to two hours before his hands shook from hunger. He took a step toward the kitchen and glanced back at the canvas, comparing it to the real thing behind it. It was looking good. He saw that he had spilled a couple of drops of black and red paint on the floor, but he had the lease on the place for another two years—plenty of time to scrub it out later.

Lunch consisted of a salad with tuna-flavored soy balls and hydroponic cocktail onions, evidence he was scraping the bottom of the barrel as far as the contents of his pantry were concerned. He stood within a few feet of the canvas as he ate, examining his work. At that precise moment, when the light was just right, his painting and its subject were identical. A few more minutes and the light would change, and there it'd be: a painting of an estimation of what his city looked like in the daylight.

09:59:59 flashed that terrible cautionary red only a machine can produce. That was all the new set of batteries could provide, it seemed. He sighed and went to the bathroom to remove the lenses to try to eke out the last bit of charge he could claim from the batteries, switched on his sonar, and slapped it to his forehead.

Exiting the bathroom, he looked at his painting on the easel. Just a flat square, textured with colorless paint. It might as well be a sticky, wet slab of canvas with nothing but black paint. He clicked off the sonar and opted to navigate his apartment in total darkness, smelling paint and faux tuna, listening for his cell to ring about something, anything to occupy his time. A case would be good, a woman on the other end begging him to do something about her awful husband. He wished no ill will toward anyone, but he relied on people doing what they did if he was to ever finish the painting.

Alone in his apartment for weeks at a time, Brody often considered getting an honest nine-to-five job to finance as many batteries as he wanted, but he felt better operating as a freelance problem solver of sorts. It felt appropriate for a war veteran who had a remarkably short fuse. But the longer he remained in the apartment with the silence and the memories of the crying women with bruised faces he met at the community center, he felt a tightening on him, as if he were in the grip of a giant snake, slowly being squeezed.

After he'd gone out and given whomever what was deserved, he could sit in the silence and the looming isolation calmly for two days. No more. Then he'd have to leave—go to the community center, work off a few hours his probation officer scheduled, and inevitably come across yet another woman who required his help. And then he'd be off again, another snake around his neck choking everything else out of his life until nothing but tunnel vision remained. But this time it came quicker; he had just dealt with Jonah the night before and already he was distracted, tight.

Brody rifled through the shoe box of old lens charger batteries in the cabinet beneath his bathroom sink. One pronged cylinder after the next felt solid to the shake. If they sloshed around, their liquefied alkaline was still good. If they felt solid when shaken—no good, used up, dry. He found one that sounded chunky inside, only parts of the fluid congealed. He snapped it into the panel on the underside of the case and looked at the top for the light to flash on. Oh, right. Blind. Strange how easy it was to forget.

Sonar on, he went back out and cleaned up his easel. He put the painting in the corner by the window where it could dry in the afternoon sun. He had a cigarette and chose to put the lenses in even without knowing whether they had gotten a decent charge. The moment his index finger retreated from the surface of his eye, the indicator sprang up: *10:59:59*. Eleven hours. Still less than half a day.

He sighed. "Better than nothing."

Brody pushed through the front doors of the community center to find the place nearly empty, save for a lone older gentleman in the corner playing both sides of the foosball table. Brody approached the reinforced glass and tapped on it with a knuckle.

Samantha, the spritely older clerk who was always there on weekends to sign him in for his community service, looked up from the ordi he was studying in her palm. She smiled, slid aside the partition, wafting out Chanel No. 5, powdery and acidic. "Well, good morning, good looking. To what do we owe this pleasure?"

"Just thought I'd swing by and get a few hours done."

"Let me see what I got for you." Samantha carefully

set the unit on which she'd been doing the crossword aside to get the printed list of tasks.

Brody noticed the ordi was shiny, new. Not like his phone, with the cracked screen and thumb-polished keypad. He found himself compelled to ask. "Got yourself a new ordi?"

"Excuse me?" Samantha said, shooting daggers over her thick half-glasses. Corrective surgery was getting cheaper by the year, but she still wore reading glasses.

"Ordi. Ordinateur," Brody explained but her confusion remained. "Uh, minicomputer? Newfangled abacus?"

Samantha followed his gaze to the handheld ordi on the counter. "Oh, this thing? Pete got me that for my birthday." She flipped to the next page on the clipboard. Brody could see that a majority of the easy jobs—dusting, putting up weatherproofing on the windows—had already been done by the other community servicers, none of whom he had ever actually seen around the place. "All I can do on the damn thing is make calls and do crosswords. But at my age what more do you really need? What did you call it?"

"An ordinateur. Can I see that for a minute?" he asked, pointing at the clipboard.

She handed him the list. "That French?"

"I think so."

"Why are you using French? Is that cool now or something?"

"Not that I know of. I guess whoever makes the gizmos gets to decide what to call them." He tapped an item on the list. "Does that still need to be done, the basketball court?"

"Mopped *and* waxed." She furrowed her brow, clearly still stuck on talk about ordinateurs. "The French make the gizmos?"

"Canadians, actually. And the basketball court would be my pleasure." Brody smiled and handed the list back to her. He removed his keys, cell, and wallet and set them on the counter. That was the rule: one had to leave all personal belongings at the desk during community service. It was pretty hard to cheat court-mandated hours while parked on a barstool around the corner without a jigsaw to settle the tab.

She picked up the ordi and settled an answer into three down on the crossword—*diligent*—and asked, "So that's the word they use for 'telephone' nowadays, huh?"

"And all other electronic devices."

"All others? Whatever happened to the other shit?"

Brody smirked. "Pardon?"

"You know, the laptops and desktops, tablets and web-books, the towers and hard drives and thumb drives and the this and the that. The stuff that every-one just *had* to have or else you might as well be using two cans and a string or making smoke signals to call your neighbor. That shit."

"They're all one big happy melded together family now: ordinateurs."

"That's confusing. I'll tell you what I think. *I* don't like it."

Brody laughed. "I'll be sure to let someone know because I am clearly in charge of deciding technological colloquialisms."

"There you go again, talking nonsense." Samantha collected his things from the counter and put them aside, save for his jigsaw card. That she inserted into the ubiquitous nautilus card reader, a big black conch shell commonplace in the community center and in just about every establishment—government, restaurant, or otherwise.

She waved him over to the body scanner to the right of the office window. "I know you're not carrying anything, but the last time I let you go on through, I really got chewed out."

"It's fine." Brody stepped through the plastic doorway, and no alarms went off. He stepped back through and again nothing went off. He put out his arms as if to say: *Good?*

"Okay, go on ahead," Samantha said.

As Brody approached the elevator, he said over his shoulder, "You shouldn't be so hard on yourself. Did you see my phone? It's ancient."

From the kiosk, Samantha shouted, "The phone I had before this gizmo had a rotary dial, honey. Try *that* on for size if you want to compare old junk."

He laughed, smacked the call button. "Is the floor buffer still in the utility closet up there?"

"You know it is. It'll be right where you left it. Thanks, sugar. Ain't no one but you ever want to do more than a half-ass job round here."

"Oh, it's my pleasure."

The door skidded aside.

"And the court system's," Samantha jibed just before the elevator door closed.

Brody was unable to squeak out a decent comeback. Alone in the elevator going up, he cursed but it was with a smile.

The gymnasium was empty. It reminded Brody of his apartment in its chasmal, yawning emptiness and how each footstep reverberated off the walls. The wood floor creaked and popped with each step upon it. Above, the entire ceiling was a paneled skylight, the glass tinted to keep a majority of the sunlight out, causing everything beneath it to take on a jaundiced look.

After an hour, he had the entire floor mopped. He wheeled out the floor buffer and went to work, patiently steering it around the gym floor in grinding circles.

As the buffer droned, the constant hiss of the scrubber gliding across the wood's lacquered surface forced Brody's thoughts elsewhere. He held the finger throttle down on the buffer and slowly steered it to the right, then the left, and then back again. The sound drilled in, mining the memory best associated with a similar sound.

And just like that, time receded and towed Brody along with it, ten years rewinding.

4

Burning flesh. Popping and sputtering akin to the sound of meat
on a griddle. Hearing it, smelling it but
never seeing it. Around Brody, people
cheering. Laughing, even. Someone cried
out in a foreign tongue, jubilant victory trumpeting all around him. Steeped in the noise
and confusion, Brody lay against the wall of
the bus depot with his eyes dead in their
sockets. His legs badly burned. Shaken
to the core with terror and pain, ears
ringing, and blinded. But still alive.

Hours before, he had been moving with
his unit through a bus station in downtown
Cairo. They had gotten a call from
another unit that a bomb had been
located and disarmed there and Brody's

unit was to follow with a final, painstaking sweep. The entire depot had been cleared; all that remained was the small room at the back reserved for napping. Rows of cots, fans blowing across those in the midst of long travel, pots of iced water to ladle from. It was where insurgents, going from one clandestine base to another, could often be found.

The area they were sent to investigate was around the corner from a bank of pay phones, Brody remembered. The unit marched quickly in a pack. Brody was always appointed tail so most of his steps were taken backward. They paused, crouching in unison at the doorway. Brody checked the rear—all the citizens were on the floor, ducked behind counters and potted plants and bus station directory stands. Clear. He tapped the shoulder of the man ahead, and the tap made it all the way up to the point man. Wordless, they stood and the point man vanished around the corner.

When the man before him moved up, Brody stood from his crouch. While turning forward momentarily to check his footing, he saw it: a gallon milk jug wrapped in duct tape nestled between two garbage cans. A length of fishing line. He had barely enough time to complete the thought, let alone shout before the point man's shin struck the line. The clink of the pin being pulled echoed.

The soldiers froze at the sound, that telltale chime. They broke formation, scrambled, and several incoherent yells made it halfway out of their mouths when the improvised explosive device detonated. Brody expected a concussion blast, some fragmentary pieces flying off, chunks of slag or ball bearings, wood screws. But no, the initial explosion wasn't that strong—it was meant as a cruelty, a humiliation, a blinding burst of ignited white phosphorus. A flash like a magic trick, a blossom of brilliant white leaping at him. And then the bomb's heart itself. Just *hearing* it: a pop followed by an angry whoosh. The heat washing across his face. Then the screams.

Brody would later be told by the corporal that it was basically the innards of a flash bang with half a gallon of lighter fluid and lamp oil. A trip mine Molotov cocktail. Blind and unable to run. Brody, the tail, not quite all the way into that narrow hallway leading to the nap area, was the sole survivor. As he lay in the infirmary tent, unable to see anything before him, the corporal had told him he'd been lucky. Every other man had died on the spot, their skin burned to the third degree, their brains boiled in their skulls.

"You're fortunate you got blinded, son," the corporal said. "Because you sure as hell wouldn't want to have seen how those boys looked when we found you."

It was just as bad, though. Having to listen to them burn as he furiously rubbed his eyes with the backs of his gloves. Hearing them burn as he tore the gloves off and rubbed with his hands. If only he could get what-ever this shit was out of his eyes. They needed him. But all he could do was sit, listen, and stare in their general direction without being able to see anything through his new, permanent blackness.

One of them had screamed for his mother, another

for a woman named Helen. Another cried to God. Despite his injuries, Brody thanked the fates that his best friend had left their unit a week before. Thorp would've been point and that would've meant certain doom for him.

Soon after it became quiet, but the hissing persisted for a long time.

The buffer collided with the wall, and Brody snapped out of the recollection, physically twitching when he did. He buried the horrid consortium of images back in his mind and took a second of quiet contemplation before returning to work. This memory managed to crop up every few days. Especially when he removed his lenses for the day and didn't have the sonar on. That was when the imagination worked best, when there were no visual distractions. The projectionist of his memories was always more than happy to find the reel that carried the bad stuff and offer up a matinee.

He glanced back at the trail he had left in his wake. The polish had long before rubbed off, and he was scuffing the hell out of the clear coat. He shut the machine off and looked at the ten and a half feet of gritty gymnasium floor he'd have to figure out how to repair before leaving for the day.

After Brody managed to cover the damage with a fresh coat of lacquer, he set up the wet floor sign and returned downstairs.

Samantha thanked him for his work and told him how many hours he had left: 295. "Well, you're getting there," she commented, putting the ledger back on its nail. She set his belongings on the counter, and he placed them in their proper pockets.

"What is it?" he asked, knowing she was going to throw some life advice on him whether he asked what was on her mind or not.

"Just you," she said with a sigh. "Coming here every couple of days, picking away at that record of yours. I wonder what you'd do if you didn't get in trouble all the time—if you'd still come here."

"I'd like to think I would," Brody said. He felt comfort in talking to Samantha. She was a kindly old lady he felt a bond with, one he couldn't quite explain. Was she like an older sister to him? A sage grandmother sort who dispensed advice like a mystically possessed vending machine, every piece perfectly suited to the recipient who never requested it but always needed it?

"I wonder why you don't stop trying to fix everybody's bothers and just go about your own business. I mean, the things you do for folks, the messes you get yourself wrapped up in—it's enough to make a person think you're suicidal or something."

Satisfied that everything was put back in the right pockets, Brody began buttoning his coat. "I'm not suicidal," he murmured.

She shot him the I-know-you're-telling-me-stories-young-man look his grandmother had aimed his way countless times.

"What? I'm not."

She took a deep breath and what she said next, she illustrated by talking with her hands in big, sweeping gestures. "It's a never-ending cycle. You get in trouble for roughing up someone, you get sent here to do your work, you meet some other sad soul who wants you to help them, you do, and you get in *more* trouble, you fib to the cops and tell them you're seeing these girls in the romantic sense. But it's obvious there ain't a damn thing going on between you and any of them. And it just keeps going around and around." She whirled her finger in the air. "What do you get out of it?"

"What do *you* get out of it?" he asked, a faint curtness coming into his voice he didn't intend.

"I stay on this side of the desk. Sure, I may get a bed ready for someone, I might microwave a hot dog for some kid who got dropped off here by his good-for-nothing parents, but I'm not walking around looking for trouble. You're going to wind up getting yourself killed doing *that* business. You should meet a nice girl and stop all the shenanigans. Just tell me why you put yourself through so much grief. Tell me what *Brody* gets out of it."

"I don't know, Samantha," he said, using her name to let her know he was serious. "I don't get anything out of it, I suppose. But that's okay with me."

With her stockpile of advice nuggets dispensed to depletion, Samantha just shook her head. "Just remember what I said."

"Will do."

"You coming back later this week?" Samantha called after him as he crossed the entryway toward the front door.

He said over his shoulder as he pushed open the glass doors, the belt of Christmas bells that hung on the door no matter the season jingling, "Probably. If I don't get myself killed first, that is." He smiled and was gone, the door easing closed on its hydraulic, shutting out the cold air with him.

As Brody walked to meet the 3:45 train, his phone began thrumming against his thigh. The caller panel read *You're in trouble now*, a self-appointed message that popped up whenever his probation officer called.

He answered, gritting his teeth, looking southward in anticipation of seeing the train arrive so he'd have an excuse to hang up.

"I have a lot of things to attend to today, so here it is: the CliffsNotes version in easy-to-follow bulleted points. I'm disappointed. That's one. Second, I thought we talked about your little midnight fisticuff trysts."

"It wasn't as bad as it sounds—"

"Third," Chiffon continued without even registering his attempt to interrupt, "another hundred hours have been put on your tab."

"Okay." Brody slumped his shoulders. What could he do, refuse? The train rounded the corner into sight. He sighed with relief. "But I'm actually about to get on the rail here in a second and I—"

"You're fortunate; you really are. If it were in my hands, I'd see to it that you got a little time to cool your jets in one of Minnesota's many fine correctional facilities. But as it stands, until they uncap the Wite-Out again at the capitol building, here it is, my gift to you: one hundred more little opportunities for you to not only make the Twin Cities an ever better place to live than it already is but also an upped dosage of what I've already prescribed to you: perspective."

"Thank you, Chiffon," Brody forced himself to say.

"Miss Doyle is fine," she corrected. "Detective Pierce has asked me to move your appointment up. So mark your calendar. This Friday, the day after Thanksgiving. Bright and early. My office. Are we clear? Understood?"

"Yes. Sounds good. Thank you."

"See you then. Bye now."

Brody hung up and cursed under his breath then again when he boarded the northbound light-rail and saw there wasn't a seat to be had. He gripped the bar and let the gentle tug of momentum pull at his frame in a nauseating rush of speed.

He considered what Nathan had told him the night before, about the loophole law getting changed early next year. He knew how Chiffon—Miss Doyle—felt about him and what he did; many of her other clients were the men he paid drinking hole visits to. Let a fist fly in January, and it was off to jail he'd go. Pretty doubtful there would be a bodega where he could get lens charger batteries in exchange for his wages pressing license plates.

Of course, it might be what she'd choose to do come Friday—just a day shy of a week from now—and throw the lever on the trapdoor he was always tap-dancing on and drop him into a cell. The term *Black Friday* would certainly have a new ring to it then.

5

When Brody returned to his apartment, he immediately got in the
shower to remove the smell of floor
polish and industrial soap. That and the
call with Chiffon always put him in a bad
head space. The woman could instill terror,
make him see barred walls and uncomfortable
prison mattresses and even smell the fires of
a riot—where, he guessed, he'd most likely
be dispatched when the guards were
preoccupied. A shower was the only
cure. Lenses out, sonar off, a makeshift
sensory deprivation chamber to remind
himself he still had the law on his side for
the time being.

Once out and toweled off and dressed,
he could see from across the room that

the icon for voice mail on his screen was blinking.

Could the redaction have changed in the last hour and Chiffon be calling to inform him with unabated giddiness in her voice that he was going to spend some time in an eight by ten after all? For a beat, the smell of smoke from the prison riot fires rekindled, and the thought of someone emerging from the murk, hunched and smiling with a head full of bad thoughts, shiv in hand held low to the side, lumbering toward his open cell made his throat run dry.

He walked over to the mounted screen and read the display: *Thorp Ashbury.* As he stared at the name in plain black text, his mind reeled back to dusty days in the desert heat, heavy body armor on his shoulders, shared laughs in the back of the soldier troop carrier with this man. Miss Doyle's threats evaporated and an elation he hadn't felt in years replaced it, clicking easily in place. He told the screen, "Play voice mail."

Thorp's voice came across every speaker in Brody's apartment. "Hey, it's Thorp. Just wondering if you had a spare couple of days. Maybe you'd want to scoot out here and do a little fishing. Turkey Day's coming up and if you wanted to stick around for that, maybe I could rustle up something. If you don't already have plans, that is. Or just go get our own bird. Pheasant's in season. Currently. Either way, uh, give me a call. And we'll, you know, get something going. Take care, buddy. Talk to you soon. Bye."

Brody asked the screen to play the message again, and he listened closer this time. The first pass he got *what* Thorp was saying, but now he wanted to hear *how* his friend was saying it. The guy rarely talked in clipped sentences like that. He had a cavalier swagger about him, a bravado that came from being the top dog in whatever small town he was originally from, lauded high school football champ or the like. Obviously, something was distressing him.

But then Brody thought about what they had been through together, all the places and disasters and awfulness that had passed before their eyes. Again, he traveled back ten years to Egypt. They had been sent merely as peacekeepers, as contracted policemen with much better firepower. They had been told several times that they were not to use their guns and their presence was all the reassurance the citizens needed. "You're a reminder of what's not to be messed with," their commanding officer had told them.

Brody remembered them trying to help an old man who had gotten his arm caught in a bear trap, right there in the city's alleys. He decided to move along through the memory, dodging the more difficult moments of it. He jumped over what had happened to Thorp, what the guy had been through and dealt with—and then the rest of that peacekeeping effort when Brody finally got blinded and was put on the same list as his friend. Invalided but for two completely different reasons and shipped home within a month of each other.

The projectionist wouldn't let it sit merely at that, though. The incident in that alleyway, with the man caught in the bear trap, unceremoniously commenced play. Piecemeal, it came to him. Turning the corner, seeing the man hunched, his limb in the metal bite of the trap, begging in a scattered, trembling voice for help—eyes wide, his lips peeled back in a feral way.

But that was as far as Brody's mind would allow, and he jumped the edit ahead to when Thorp had become introverted and rarely spoke to anyone about anything. His bravado had been amputated, and grafted on in its place was a staring quietness that could never be shaken. It surprised Brody to get a call from Thorp now. In all the years they'd been stateside, they'd never exchanged anything other than a vague card around the holidays. And now he was inviting him to Thanksgiving dinner? Why now?

Brody put his wariness aside. It didn't matter how long it had been. He decided to just be thankful he had someone who wanted to spend any time with him at all.

"Call back," Brody told the screen, and Thorp's number was dialed.

Over the speakers of the apartment, Thorp answered on the sixth ring with a tired hello.

"It's Brody. How are you, man?"

"Hey," Thorp said languidly, as if he had been woken up. "How's it going?"

"Just returning your call. That sounds like a plan to me. I could stand to get out of the city for a while. Where are you living nowadays?"

Thorp made prolonged grunting sounds indicative of a man stretching, and when he spoke again, it was with a bit higher tempo and levity.

"Chicago. Well, not Chicago proper. It's a good

drive from here. I can *kind* of see it from here; let's just say that. So it's not too much of a trek, really." There it was, that clipped way of talking again. Perhaps it was how the man was now. Maybe he had been placed on medication or had taken advantage of some of the postwar therapy sessions the military offered. Brody couldn't picture it, the big football star sitting in a cramped office with a shrink or organizing one of those pill-a-day containers with the seven plastic lids, but you never know.

"Fishing, huh? Sounds like paradise."

"Yeah, well, I got myself a good chunk of land, some decent woods to roam around in. It's old farm-land and I figured why not, so now I'm trying to do the cranberry thing. Eventually, I might try my hand at selling to Ocean Spray or something when I can get through a season without completely killing my crop."

Brody laughed. It felt good. At first it'd he felt enormously awkward talking to Thorp, but he quickly found himself falling back into the brotherly rapport they'd had so long ago. Brody realized how much he truly missed the camaraderie of friends, of people he knew he could trust and talk to about certain things that only they'd know and be able to relate with.

"What day works for you?" Thorp asked.

He had to be home next week for his scheduled visit with Miss Doyle, perhaps even leaving Thanksgiving night to ensure he'd be back in time. He folded his arms and told the empty apartment, his voice finding the microphone, "Anytime that works for you. You're the host."

"All right, let's say tomorrow. That work? I'll have a room ready for you. That is unless you *want* to sleep in the barn."

"No." Brody chuckled. "That's quite all right."

They exchanged their good-byes and the call ended.

Brody recalled his fonder memories of Thorp, all of which took place before the events in that Cairo alleyway. Thorp was always a troublemaker and a prankster, the gleaming life of the party where only gloom and homesick thoughts riddled their minds. Whenever their company was crowded into the boxy interior of the Terrapin ATV or in the troop carrier Darter launching from one dust-choked spot to the next, Thorp lightened everybody up with a crude joke—or a *really* crude one. Brody recalled how Thorp had acted out a particularly nasty one, standing in the middle of the two rows of buckled-in troops, humping the air and cackling like a madman.

Brody looked forward to his trip.

The train rolled into the station in Minneapolis precisely on time. Brody boarded and found a seat by a window but not before pausing at the steps into the train to take his final breath of city air for what he hoped would be long enough to forget the smell of exhaust and the ceaseless hum of interstate noise.

Being Sunday, not a lot of people were heading to Chicago. He had a booth in the dining car to himself and enjoyed his coffee as they hummed along southeast well over two hundred kilometers an hour on an elevated track that provided a monorail zoo tour in fast forward quality to the trip, albeit one that wasn't remotely exotic since it only featured cattle and the occasional horse intercut with long stretches of farmland after farmland, the occasional autumnal-colored hill, and scraggily patches of trees left to grow unbothered or even manicured in any way. Life that wasn't planted for harvesting but just grew because it was there and always had been.

The television mounted above the bar played to no one in particular. The news was on, expounding last night's Vikings victory. Brody listened absently until the sports scores turned to grave news. A report detailing the cheerless unveiling of a monument at a Minneapolis shopping center. It was in memory of those killed last month on October 20 when Alton Noel, a retired soldier, had gunned down ten people before turning the gun on himself. "The Midtown Massacre," as the newscaster called it, was one of the worst tragedies that had befallen Minneapolis in decades and spurred a new law enforcement effort in upping gun control.

It was the first time Brody had heard the story. He took a moment to go through the roster of men that had been in his unit while in Cairo and decided he didn't know an Alton Noel. Either way, the news was depress-ing—and sadly—it made him think of the man he was going to visit, the lonely ex-soldier. He silently scolded himself for making the comparison to his friend.

The news team immediately turned to a sunnier story, the tremendous winnings a couple had scored the night before on *Prize Mountain*.

Brody welcomed the whiplashing topic change,

sipped his coffee, and watched Wisconsin roll past his window as if it were scenery on a revolving banner.

The train pulled into Chicago a few minutes shy of two hours from when it had left Minneapolis. Brody got out into the crowded station. He knew he was in Chicago immediately. No question about it. It differed from Minneapolis in innumerable cultural ways. Women walked by in veiled hats and evening dresses made up entirely of whisper-thin fiber-optic material. Scrolling text and images of swimming sea life washed around on their elegant, tapered bodies.

Once out of the station and onto the sidewalk, Brody saw the street people and their shock-value wardrobe: the chain-mail tunics with windows cut out of them to display plump, augmented breasts or tattooed buttocks. They flitted by quick as insects on old-fashioned roller skates with swearwords written in black pen all over the white leather. One slapped Brody on the shoulder and called to him in Russian, "Watch it, shit cake." Certainly not something you'd hear in Minneapolis, where the most alarming piece of foreign slang talk was Norwegian.

The rest of the people, those not out to shock, were mostly in suits and ties, one in three wearing a paper mask or a respirator strapped to their face.

Brody weaved in and out among the onrushing wall of people who were so preoccupied with their ordis that they absentmindedly played chicken with everyone coming the opposite direction. He wondered if it just *seemed* like he was going against the flow and broke off onto a side street where the foot traffic wasn't as congested. Here he could actually walk a straight line without having to move out of anyone's way.

He couldn't help but look around, even if it made him look like a tourist. It'd been years since he'd been here, and while he couldn't say it looked all that different, he had forgotten what a strange place Chicago could sometimes seem, depending on the neighborhood.

Namely this one.

Bundled tentacles of cables connected every building, as if some creature had pushed itself into and around every standing structure. Some were repurposed as lampposts, with the lights hanging on the horizontal columns of wires and tubes. In other places, if the tendrils happened to stretch in front of a business's storefront, they simply tacked their sign directly onto it. Brody had seen a newspaper comic online about Chicago's wire problem. It featured a man in safari apparel hacking at dangling cables with a machete in one hand, a briefcase in the other, trying to navigate the sidewalk to work. Now it made sense.

When Brody's father was young, he thought the idea of everything wireless meant that all telephone poles would disappear and repairmen would never use anything but a computer to diagnose a connection problem, the wrench and screwdriver as extinct as the dodos and lobsters. But as nice as advancements can be, the end product had a lot of work behind it and with more wirelessness came more need to make that wirelessness possible, which, funnily enough, resulted in more wires.

Minneapolis had its share of wires but not like this.

And as far as how everything else looked in Chicago compared to his city, well, that differed greatly too.

Here and there were old-style marquees. Others opted—if they had the cash—for signage made entirely of holo. On every street corner, just like back home, were the air-scrubbing units mounted to the sidewalk as commonplace as fire hydrants.

Again, Brody felt the need to step out of the churn of foot traffic to stand apart from it all and get his bearings. He feared if he just went with it, he'd end up walking right into Lake Michigan. He looked skyward at the view through the skyscrapers interlaced with more columns of wires and beyond that black net over everyone's heads, unmanned police aircraft, drifting like paper airplanes being pulled along by strings, on constant patrolling surveillance. He had been in town only fifteen minutes, and already he wanted to leave. *Cab. I need a cab so I can get the hell out of this.*

Four passed him up before one finally heeded his wave. He slid into the back, glad to be able to shut out the noise. Door closed, the self-piloting cab asked for his destination in a sober voice. The question had been recorded years ago most likely.

Brody read the address from the e-mail Thorp had sent him.

"Please insert jigsaw card to verify funds," the cab requested.

Unaccustomed to driverless cabs, Brody looked for the reader on the glass dividing the front and back of the car. He found it and slipped the plastic card in, with its jigsaw puzzle arrangement of black and white, stripes and dots, the bar codes and blocky robot text that only mechanical eyes could decipher.

After a pause, "We will be more than happy to transport you to your destination today, but be aware that your bank account is currently in the negative. Your banking establishment has been kind enough to supply you with the necessary funds for *this* trip, but we're afraid to inform you that you lack the necessary funds to go any farther beyond your requested destination."

"Okay," Brody said, pinching the bridge of his nose. This news came without surprise to him. The train ticket had swept out those last ten credits, and now the cab was reaching a hand down into his bank account's emergency funds. "Thank you for telling me."

"Yes, sir," the cab said.

Brody watched from behind the glass as the steering wheel spun around on its own. The cab gave a single burst of accelerator and wedged itself back into traffic.

On the other side of Chicago, Brody felt the tension ease off him again just as it had when he originally left Minneapolis. The cab rumbled on the desolate two-lane road in the country. Expansive farmsteads and agricultural campuses flourished out from under the gray umbrella of pollution.

In the fields, toiling with bent backs, farmers worked at picking the soil free of any large stones that'd make planting difficult, depositing them into burlap sacks lashed to their backs. Once closer, Brody noticed not a one of them was human. They stood on narrow legs that tapered down into toeless feet, just arrowheads that the robots trundled about on, elegant and weightless as flamingos. Narrow torsos and necks, heads made up of just a set of glass eyes and a round speaker approximately where a mouth should be. Artificials weren't as common in the city, much to everyone's surprise when they first came on the market. They were reserved for hard labor, sometimes cooking and cleaning, sometimes nursing home care, but most commonly in janitorial jobs and keeping the parks, graveyards, and roadsides tidy.

The Artificials—or Arties—stood erect and turned to stare at the passing cab. It was strange how they got distracted so easily, but Brody figured they were a hot commodity in the farming industry and theft was common. If he were to engage in conversation or even humbly approach one of the Arties working in the field, he imagined they'd group up on him and calculatedly break every one of his bones. He shuddered at the thought as he passed the robotic farmers and looked into each set of their reflective glass lenses, unable to read any indication of what they were making of him.

Just as they had raised their heads when the cab was approaching, they collectively lowered them when they saw the cab wasn't going to slow or stop. They returned to work, silently toiling.

The cab continued on, accidentally going through a stop sign at a deserted four-way intersection. After the turn, the road went from cracked pavement with faded lines to a two-lane dirt path, rocky and rutted in two opposing sets of tracks, those going into the farmland and those coming out.

Brody rolled down the window and lit a cigarette. He waited for the cab to ask him to please put it out, but it didn't. Clearly it was an older model. They bumped along for a few more miles and then turned into Thorp's long gravel driveway.

They approached a two-story rust-red farmhouse with dormered windows and a barn off to the side. The whole place needed a fresh coat of paint. The cab eased to a gentle stop, and a crunch sounded as the emergency brake was thrown.

Brody waited, and the receipt fed out of the mounted printer, telling him his overdrawn account had just been shoved down to an all-time low of negative four thousand and ninety-eight credits. He got out with his solitary bag and approached the house.

The cab reversed out of the driveway and started its lonely journey back to the city.

Brody took a deep breath. The air smelled so different. There was something to be said about living out where the constant push and pull of the air on the streets wasn't tampered with hypoallergenic filters or thick with the rank of wastewater and factory runoff. It made his throat itch, his eyes water a little. But it felt good, natural, being exposed to allergens and dust for the first time in years. It was a welcome irritation.

He rang the doorbell and heard a series of thumps inside the house, heavy footsteps on hollow hardwood.

The door opened and Thorp, aged faintly around the eyes and mouth—his laugh lines were more etched in and his crow's-feet sprawled out nearly to his ears— smiled warmly. His hair was nearly gone on top, leaving a shaggy hay-colored mass that went over his ears on the sides and nestled down into the collar of his flannel shirt in the back. His freckled pate reflected the afternoon sun with a polished sheen. "Hey, hey, look who it is," he exclaimed, pushing aside the screen door.

They took a moment to shake hands, get the small talk about his trip out of the way.

The inside of the house smelled like Thorp had just turned the vacuum off seconds before Brody rang the bell. Beyond that smell of vacuum-recycled air was the intoxicating aroma of ham cooking. Real meat. It had been years since Brody had eaten anything that hadn't come out of a plastic wrapper or an aluminum can. Even America's Favorite Automat joints that had sprung up all over Minneapolis and St. Paul only offered food that was made elsewhere, states away, freeze-dried and vacuum sealed only to be popped open and microwaved. Just like Mom used to make. Right. But here, this was something different—something *amazing*. He felt magnetically pulled by the aroma.

"What's that smell?" Brody asked, wide-eyed.

His friend grinned—making the wrinkles he'd developed all the more obvious—and told him it was ham. Brody had to ask for confirmation that it wasn't the fake stuff he was smelling, that minced mushroom and soy stuff pressed together like particle board to make fake ham. It smelled too good, he added.

"Nope. Real thing. Guy up the road apiece raises pigs."

Brody hadn't been exposed to allergens or eaten actual meat in years. It was beginning to feel like this wasn't just a different state he had traveled to, but a different time. A time detailed by his grandparents.

"So, how was good old Chicago?" Thorp asked, guiding Brody upstairs.

"Congested," Brody said. "Loud. You know, the way it always is."

"Well, that's the city for you. You should think about coming out this way, buying one of these plots before the developers turn them all into highways. You could get lucky like I did and have them put some wires over it and you'll be *made*, my friend. Hark Telecom pays me ten grand a *month* just to have those wires going over my property."

"No kidding?" Brody said.

He hadn't noticed any power lines or wires running over Thorp's property. It made him pause because he considered himself more observant than that, but power lines looping overhead was beyond a regular sight in Minneapolis or Chicago.

Thorp opened the door to a small bedroom with a bed and a three-drawer dresser. He threw out his arm in a grand gesture of presentation and allowed Brody in.

Brody looked it over, nodded, and set his suitcase down on the floor.

"Coffee?" Thorp asked.

Brody nodded.

"I'll go get it on the burner. Make yourself at home. I'll give you the tour whenever you're settled." Thorp clomped back downstairs.

Brody changed out of his peacoat into a pair of jeans and a sweatshirt. As he stepped into the bathroom, red digits reared their ugly numerals. *02:59:59.*

He sighed. He'd have to squeeze a charge into the lenses sooner than he had thought. He had a collection of the batteries with him, but all of them were nearly solid to the shake. He knew that while he was going to enjoy his vacation, it wouldn't be without the constant worry about money and how seeing in color might have to wait a few months. Brody decided he'd wear the lenses until they counted out the very last second. He hadn't seen Thorp in a very long time and wanted to enjoy the stay—and all its colors—for as long as he could.

He came downstairs to the smell of not only the ham in the oven but fresh coffee. When he turned the corner into the galley kitchen, he saw that Thorp was making the coffee on the stovetop. The coffeepot had a glass bubble, and percolating into it was the warm brown liquid. With an oven mitt, Thorp took the coffeepot from the burner and put it on a trivet on the counter.

"Quite a place you got here," Brody commented.

"Thanks," Thorp said, obviously distracted by the roasting pan he now had out of the oven and was diligently trying to scrape the ham from the bottom of.

Brody looked around the walls. Medals hanging by their silk bands from nails, a few framed plaques, a couple of photographs of their unit. He found himself and Thorp standing side by side in the middle, their arms over one another's shoulders, cigars in the corners of their mouths. The photos were printed on standard ink-jet paper, pixelating the images around the edges and slightly mussing the colors from an apparent shortage of blue in the cartridge when the picture had printed. The men in the photo appeared to be wearing yellow camouflage, and their faces were redder than an Egyptian sun could've ever rendered their flesh without actually . . . broiling them.

The thought happened before he could catch it, and he made himself turn his thoughts elsewhere. Instead, he concentrated on the image itself, the men before they'd been burned alive, the people they were.

It had been taken the day before the ambush in the Cairo alley. They had just gotten news that after their final sweep of this particular quarter of the city, they could go home. They were prematurely in celebration, unfairly ignorant by the blindfold of fate, that the following day would prove to be something that would forever stain the two men's minds. For Brody, though, it would prove doubly worse—being struck blind would be waiting for him a week beyond the tragedy.

He studied himself in the photo, young, the crew cut, the cigar—smiling like he had something to smile about, some victory achieved. He wanted to step closer to the photo and hiss at his past self: "You fool." That kid with the body armor, holding the assault rifle like some sort of hero, was totally unaware of the curveball headed toward him just a few hours later.

Brody wanted to ask Thorp if he ever thought about that day but decided not to. It was a dumb question after all. Of course he did. Brody knew the events of that day probably passed with more frequency in Thorp's mind than his own. He moved away from the photograph, blinking away memories.

"Out here all alone?" Brody took a seat at the

kitchen table. It was an easy estimation. The place was decorated like a man lived here—no curtains, just venetian blinds, no framed pictures besides the ones that featured military guys. In the living room there were no decorations save for a mounted buck head on one wall.

"Yeah," Thorp said, still struggling with the ham. It was really glued in there. "I got my profile on a few sites advertising that I'm a single guy with a big old farmstead all to myself and a steady income. But no bites. I guess young women like to sow their wild oats in the city before retiring out to the sticks with a jabber jaw like me."

Brody smiled. "Mind if I smoke?"

"Not at all. Hell, you can have one of my cigars if you want. One good thing about Illinois, you can still smoke out here. I don't know how you do it in Minnesota with their goddamn nonsmoker initiative." Thorp still struggled with the ham, one hand gripping the roasting pan, the other wedging a spatula under it. He looked over his shoulder with sweat on his brow. "Can you even smoke on the sidewalks?"

"You can, but if a cop passes you, you get dirty looks." Brody passed on his friend's cigars and smoked one of his own cigarettes instead. "They're just itching for that law to get passed all the way, so they can club you over the head the second you light one up."

Thorp got the ham free with a clatter of metal on the stovetop. The ham nearly flew out of the pan. He cried, "Whoa!" as if saddled upon a disobedient horse. He put the steaming slab of—*real!*—meat on a ceramic platter and brought it over, still steaming, to the table. He opened the fridge and filled his arms with three different assortments of mustard, a salt grinder, a tub of margarine, and a stack of bread slices. "Beer?"

"Yes, please. Say, you need a hand with all that?" Brody asked, starting to stand when he saw Thorp nearly take a tumble with all the things he had gathered up against his chest.

"No, no, you're a guest. I got this." He put everything down on the table and sat.

They ate roasted ham, and Brody tried all three of the different mustards Thorp had made by hand. They were quiet for the majority of the meal.

When they finished, Brody picked up his bottle of beer and looked out the window behind Thorp. The Artificials were now toiling in the patch of land directly across the road. "You got any of those?" he asked.

Thorp threw his arm over the back of his chair and twisted around to see what Brody meant. He caught a glimpse of the Artificials and turned back around. "No. And the owner of those goddamn things needs to learn how to set the property line on them better. I came out front last week and saw them picking apart my garden. Had to go to his house and tell him to shut them off because when I took two steps toward them—on *my* property, keep in mind—they all turned toward me with their hands out like they were challenging me to wrestle." Thorp took a slurping pull off his bottled beer, which apparently he had also made himself. "If it weren't for the pork chops and ham he brings this way, I might've just snapped on the guy. Should probably mosey on down there sometime tomorrow, see if he's got any birds he'd be willing to part with."

"What all do you grow out here?" Brody asked.

"Cranberries, mostly. Some carrots, too. Potatoes, strawberries, sunflowers. Just whatever I feel like doing that year. I grow most of it for myself, can what I know I won't get to before it spoils." Thorp reached over to the humidor on the counter and took out a thick cigar. "Here, I want to show you something." He opened the heavily tinted sliding glass door that went out into the backyard.

Once it was open, Brody stood next to Thorp and saw all that lay beyond. What at first glance he took to be metal sculptures were twisted wrecks of old military aircrafts positioned around the backyard like shaped hedges on display. A few of them he recognized from their own tour, certain models of the Darter troop mover and the Terrapin ATV. Big holes blasted out of them, jagged as shark bites in their metal flesh. Parts missing, the rudder of the Darter was entirely gone, in its place, a sooty amputated nub. Brody felt a pang of sympathy for his friend as they walked into the yard and Thorp showed off his collection.

"You remember this one, don't you?" Thorp asked, nodding at the Darter.

Named after the Darter species of dragonfly, the vehicle resembled the insect in structure if slightly exaggerated in places. The bulbous head with the four jump seats—two pilots and two gunners. The abdomen could telescope out thirty feet to accommodate an entire unit of soldiers or contract like an accordion to make itself a smaller target when the soldiers had been dropped off. Four wings on the back made of lightweight titanium membrane doubled as solar panels when the mechanical beast was at rest. Two places for sentry turrets, the housing having been welded over with blank metal plates in the decommission process.

The back door ramp of the fuselage abdomen was open, and Brody bent down to look inside. The cramped interior was smaller than he remembered. The lap bars were all up, the dangling belt buckles swinging in the wind. Inside, it smelled like disinfectant, mud, gunpowder. He stood up, tried to stifle a sigh. This wasn't what he had in mind by visiting an old friend. He felt phantom pains peck at his back and chest—that terrible punch one felt when taking fire, even through body armor. The clatter and heat of a rifle vibrating with discharge in his arms, kicking against his shoulder. Incalculable carnage.

"Got this one after the war. They were selling them online for a song. Got this one, which is mostly intact, and this other one here for even *less* because, as you can see, it's in a lot rougher shape. Kind of a hobby of mine."

"Impressive," Brody said, knowing Thorp had been searching for his approval.

Thorp pointed with his beer toward the hill at the far side of the property. They strolled that way under the shadow of willows. They went past the barn. Through the open doors, Brody glimpsed a couple of horses standing in their stalls.

At the end of the hill, overlooking Thorp's fields, Brody gazed at the rows of rich brown soil, recently tilled. The land divided up into different sections for different crops. The sunflower heads on their long necks bumped against one another in the breeze. Beyond the first collection of fields was the cranberry bog. It appeared to be just a pond, but there was a smattering of crimson beads off to one side, floating berries held collected by bolted together two-by-four planks meant as a corral. Even from that distance, Brody could see the carrots on the inverted glass planters lining the far side of the property, their color reminding him of the whites of his own eyes. And against his best efforts, he remembered how most of his visit would be seen in black-and-white polygons and pixels. He studied the beautiful scene of crops before him and tried to commit as much of the color and idyllic display of agriculture to memory as he could.

They stood for a while in silence, looking at the land. It soon became obvious to Brody that Thorp was slowly edging into a reflective mood. Brody was accommodating, even though he didn't want to talk at length about the military. He took a sip from his beer and washed it over his teeth and let it settle, crackling in a pool on his tongue. He waited for the inevitable conversation to begin.

"It's a shame what they put us through out there. It really is."

"Yeah," Brody said, kicking at invisible rocks at his feet.

"We shouldn't have seen the things we did. Especially at our age. Man, we were really young. Over there, doing that shit, taking orders from guys who probably had no idea what the hell they were doing themselves." He paused, contemplative. "Bunch of bullshit." He seemed to be having the conversation entirely on his own. Brody kept quiet and nodded when appropriate.

After Thorp had nattered about the service to exhaustion and grew quiet, Brody felt like he was being rude and decided to contribute a small amount. He said, "Glad that's all behind us."

Thorp didn't respond, didn't nod, didn't do anything for a moment. Then he turned and looked into Brody's face, squinting at the gleam of the setting sun.

Brody didn't think he was going to like what came next. Inevitably, this was when Thorp would say something he'd had on his chest for a very long time, really open up, and they'd undoubtedly end up crying or really getting into an hours long conversation about everything they experienced. Truly, Brody wanted neither. He wanted some time out of the city, maybe go fishing and hunting as the initial call had promised, but he didn't want to revisit ghosts that he had no trouble finding on his own.

Thorp chewed his lip. They stared at one another for a few beats of silence, the crickets beginning to play their music in the surrounding wilderness. Brody waited for Thorp to unravel completely. He tried to steel himself for it as best he could.

Thorp said, "My sister's joined up."

6

"Nectar?" Brody said.

She was ten years younger than Thorp and just a sprite, almost elf-like in her appearance. She was topped with a head of golden-laced strawberry blonde hair and sparkling green eyes that made any-one looking at her take heed. Brody had met her only once and had forgotten all about her until this moment in Thorp's backyard over-looking the cranberry bog.

He and Thorp had practically been kids themselves, fresh out of basic, new friends, with Brody tagging along out to middle-of-nowhere Illinois for a family picnic. Brody recalled Thorp calling Nectar over from the swing set, and once she had come over, not really sure what to do, Brody stuck out his hand for her to shake. She took it with reluctance and confusion. That'd been before the firebomb that rendered him blind and well before his decade of working as a pay-per-use vigilante. Back when he was just twenty-three, Thorp twenty-four, both men stepping into the combat boots as a way to jump-start rudderless lives.

Now, ten years on, Brody and Thorp were in a similar rural backyard again, talking about a girl, someone he unfortunately had entirely misplaced in the clutter of stuff he wished he could forget.

"Yeah. She's all"—Thorp waved his hand around his head wildly—"confused and shit. I mean, the service is a good thing to get into when you're young, but the way they treated us and how we came back and everyone was pissed at us and everything—when we'd just been doing what we were told. I can't imagine how she'd take it, how she'd *survive* over there."

"It's a different time now. It's Cuba again. That whole mess'll probably turn into something in a few weeks. We're no longer in Egypt. People's attitudes have changed. Toward the military, toward the uniform. I don't think she'll go through the same things we had to."

Thorp turned away. "I don't want her involved in that."

"Remember how your folks questioned your decision to join? Remember how you told me you fought with your dad about it and how you signed up anyway? It'll be the same thing with Nectar; I'm sure of it. The more you tell her she shouldn't do it, the more she'll *want* to."

"I thought if anyone you'd be on my side about this.

Christ's sake. Here we are, both of us fucked up from all that bullshit they put us through—you blind and me messed up in the head—and you're talking like you've still got the fucking fatigues on."

"I'm just saying that your sister can make her own choices. You may not like them, but they're hers to make. If it were up to me, sure, I wouldn't want her to go, either, but there's not a lot we can do about it, is there?"

"Saint Brody," Thorp scoffed. "All hail Saint Brody, patron saint of bullshit. Goddamn it. What is with you, anyway? You never could have a goddamn opinion on anything. Every time the CO would tell us to go some-place, you never questioned it. You just went right along. Now you're—what? Roughing up wife beaters and drug dealers in Minneapolis? Jesus."

"You looked up my record?" Brody didn't even think Thorp would own a screen, let alone go to the trouble of paying for a public records search and digging into police reports. He felt his neck and cheeks flush with warmth, anger causing his voice to waver. "I know they're public files, but don't you think it's a bit nosey doing that, especially to a friend?"

"*Friend*," Thorp spat. "That's a good one. I haven't talked to you in *how* many years? And don't play in-dignant with me. Your record's out there for anyone to see. Who cares. You want to know my record? Since we've been discharged, I've gotten three DUIs and my license taken away. I was in a couple of bar fights, and I punched a cop about a year and a half ago and they still won't put me away because I'm considered 'troubled' due to what fuckin' happened to us over there. Do you know what it's like to not even have to spend a night in the drunk tank because I'm considered fragile goods and how I'm—apparently—emotionally distressed? You call me a friend, asshole. You go ahead and call me that one more time, and I swear to God I'll knock your teeth out."

"Hold it," Brody said, wanting nothing more than to reel the conversation back. "I just want to know what the hell is going on. You're clearly upset about Nectar signing up. Have you told her any of the stories? She may not even know how you feel."

"Oh, I've told her. I've told her *all* about it. She doesn't listen. She has no idea what it'll be like. I mean, she's delicate, and she's just a kid. She thinks she'll be playing crossing guard for some Korean kids, but it'll be gunfire and carpet bombing and the whole fucking thing. What if she doesn't come back?"

Brody continued Thorp's train of thought. If Thorp thought of himself as fucked up in the head now, imagine what he'd be like if she died over there or came home paralyzed, breathing and eating out of tubes for the rest of her life. That news story he'd heard on the train about the ex-soldier gunning down all those people in the shopping mall came back again, and as before, Brody gave himself a mental slap on the wrist for thinking it.

Brody considered asking Thorp if he wanted him to speak to his sister about it, but he realized it had been the whole reason he'd been invited here in the first place. He had an inkling there was a motive behind the visit, but he never imagined it would be Nectar joining the military.

He stared at Thorp, who had now fully melted down. He stood there, aged and balding, holding his bottle of homemade beer to his chest while his other hand gripped the bridge of his nose. His cheeks were red, and his shoulders rose in ragged pulls and fell in jerky sobs.

Brody took a step forward. He placed a hand on his friend's shoulder.

"I can pay you. Whatever you want." Thorp looked up, tears making his eyelashes glom together. "I got money. Like I said before, Hark Telecommunications. They're paying me boatloads for these wires." He gestured above his head, and Brody finally saw insulated wires as thick as wrists above them. "Whatever you want, just as long as you get her to change her mind."

"Has she gone to basic yet or is there still time?"

"She has to go through the class work stuff first. At Fort Reagan. *Remember*? Will you please go and talk to her in Chicago?"

At the mention of the nearby city, the one Brody dreaded having to revisit any sooner than he had to, *00:09:59* began blinking in the corner of his eye, impossible to ignore. As if by kismet, it helped cement his decision.

"Yes," he answered, forcing eye contact with Thorp, "I'll go and talk to her."

Brody listened to the crickets outside the window. Occasionally, one of the horses in the barn whinnied and the sound would alarm him—he was not accustomed to sleeping in complete silence. He was surprised to discover that there was such a thing as it being *too* quiet. Added to it, he couldn't sleep in any bed that wasn't his own, and he now had Nectar Ashbury on his mind.

He listened to the contact lens charger beep every few minutes, indicating that it was charging the battery, which he knew would be minimal. He didn't want to go into Chicago with the sonar; he saw that as a formula for catastrophe. He'd be some blind guy asking everyone coming in and out of the base if they knew Nectar Ashbury. She could pass right in front of him, and he'd never know it was her because everyone would appear in black-and-white wire frame.

Brody considered asking Thorp if he could have an advance. Just as a means to get another battery. But asking for money right off the bat didn't look good so he decided against it.

He'd wear the sonar on the trip to Chicago and put in the lenses at a gas station bathroom once he got there, get as much legwork as possible done on the remaining battery, have the chat with the girl, and swap the lenses out for the sonar on the ride back that night. It wouldn't take long, especially since he knew where the base was located and which building her classroom as a greenhorn would be.

Brody wasn't sure what he'd say to Nectar or how he'd even approach her. Certainly, she wouldn't remember him. He'd have to remind her who he was, then slowly slide in the detail of why he was there. He hoped she'd be willing to go somewhere else to talk, because he knew from experience that anyone, veteran or not, who tried to talk a new recruit out of signing the final release would be met with nothing but hostility.

He remembered attending that exact classroom compound himself, and when one parent came to try to talk some sense into their son or daughter, the promise of war on everyone's mind, the instructors all but took the man by his coattails and threw him off base. A few of the students even shoved the man out through the front gate, calling him names. Communist, one. Bleeding-heart pacifist, another. Brody thought about this, getting ganged up on by a bunch of muscled young men he wouldn't want to fight.

Deep into the night, after Brody finally managed to doze off, he heard gunfire. He roused from sleep, alert, snatched the sonar from the headboard, and fixed it to his forehead. The framework of the bedroom spiraled out before him, then the hallway and the stairs. He listened intently, sitting halfway up in bed, then reached down to fetch the knuckleduster from the back pocket of his jeans on the floor. It wouldn't be any match for whatever made that racket of a three-round burst, but it was better than going down there with nothing at all.

Brody descended the stairs, cringing with each creak the steps elicited. At the bottom, he peered with the sonar into the living room. There was a shape of a human body splayed out on the couch. Judging by the shape of the skull, the heavy brow, and the long, wide chin, it was Thorp, sitting comfortably with a handheld device propped up on the coffee table by a stack of old *Field & Stream* issues. It was a newer, expensive unit: a Canon Gizumoshingu—literally: Gizmo Thing.

"Oh, shit. I'm really sorry," Thorp said, straightening up when he noticed Brody. He sat forward and clicked the Gizumoshingu's monitor off and unhooked the cable connecting it to a small cylindrical device, a unit Brody recognized immediately.

"No, it's fine. I heard whatever you're watching and it surprised me is all. I didn't see a TV or anything in here earlier."

Thorp wrapped the cord around the textured cylindrical unit and tucked it under the couch cushion, of all places, then closed the ordi's lid. "I just have this one. Sometimes I mount it on the wall. Other times I don't—I worry about getting robbed, being out here all alone and everything."

"What were you watching?" Brody asked, already knowing.

"Some of the old gun-mount footage from the firing range and stuff," Thorp said.

Brody knew the gunfire wasn't from the firing range. It was too scattered, no time between bursts for careful aiming. It was footage from the war. He also knew from the self-help audios he had bought when seeking refuge from his own memories of war that watching this kind of footage was unadvisable.

"They let you keep your gun-mount footage?" Brody asked.

"I asked for it," Thorp said, reclining again. "It took a while, but they mailed it to me a few weeks ago."

Brody leaned against the doorjamb. The living room was cold, the hardwood floor making the bottoms of his bare feet numb. The sonar picked up a few logs in the wood-burning fireplace through its louvered hatch. Everything inside was burned down to cinders. He asked, "Did they give you everything that was on it?"

Thorp hesitated, then sat up. "Yeah, everything's on there."

Brody remembered the day he was handed the cylinder. The tech guy behind the glass partition at the armory had to explain it to him. "Underside the barrel . . . Yeah, the bracket there . . . Yep, just like that. Every time you switch the safety catch off, that camera will start—everything you shoot at, it all goes onto the cylinder, your rifle's black box." The man added, "Just in the event there's a mishap."

Brody wanted to press further, take another step along that road. Given what Thorp had done with his rifle during their time in Cairo, he wondered if anyone surveyed what was on the footage before mailing it out into the world, where it could be seen by anyone, duplicated, and put online to confirm the suspicions of everyone who detested that unpopular war and what the troops had done while in Egypt. He decided not to ask. It was late and already it was going to be hard for both of them to get any sleep, having scratched even that far into the wax enveloping their memories.

Thorp felt ashamed at being caught watching the gun-mount footage. But old habits were hard to break, and he was unaccustomed to having company. Something in him had lost the capacity to understand that sound travels, or perhaps his hearing was starting to go. He had no idea that Brody could hear what he was watching all the way upstairs. It must've been loud because Brody managed to get all the way downstairs before Thorp had even noticed him standing there.

Now, Brody loomed in the living room like one of the shrinks, playing the silent game, not saying anything at all so you'll just go on and on and on and unload all of it. Thorp knew better. He kept his mouth shut and waited for the other man to say something first.

"I wouldn't worry about her," Brody said.

"How can I not?" Thorp spoke into the darkness, straight ahead toward the fireplace. Brody had that thing on, the sonar, and when he did, his eyes clouded over and only cleared when he put the lenses in. It was hard to look at him like that, his eyelids blinking over those useless orbs in his head, his head cocked to listen. Couldn't he just close his eyes? After one glimpse, Thorp had to look away from Brody and his dead eyes.

Something knocked against his thoughts, like the hull of a boat suddenly colliding metal flotsam just below the water's surface. If he had just stayed in for a few more months, maybe he could've seen that goddamn thing that blinded Brody before it was tripped. Maybe his friend could still see without the aid of lenses or that sonar thing if he had *just fucking stuck with it.*

Brody didn't respond.

"Sorry. I'll keep it down. Go on back to bed."

Brody lingered in the room. The sound of him moving from foot to foot, his bare heels sticking to the lacquered wood like something being peeled up, continued for a few silent moments. It was as hard being in this room with him now as it was getting up the gumption to call him for help. Torturous.

"We'll get it figured out," Brody said but not until he was halfway up the stairs, as if he wanted to drop the statement, then evade the scene so Thorp couldn't lure him into another debate.

Thorp knew he could go on and on and sometimes he got a little wound up about things, and as much as he wanted to chase Brody up the stairs and ask what he was planning to say to his sister, Thorp left it alone.

He waited until he heard the upstairs bedroom door close and the squeak of bedsprings before reaching under the couch cushion for the cylinder. He uncoiled the wire around it and plugged it into the side of the ordi and continued watching, tallying mistakes like a coach reviewing last night's game. He paused only to make sure the noises he heard were the wind, never going outside without a gun in hand. Just like any other night, except with company trying to get some sleep upstairs, Thorp had to do it quietly.

7

The morning came and Brody stuffed the lens charger in his pocket with no idea exactly how much time had been put into them overnight. He removed the battery from its housing and gave it a shake near his ear. Solid. He tossed it into the bathroom trash as he went downstairs. Before he was halfway down he knew that Thorp had coffee on the burner and bacon and eggs in the pan. Again, the smell betrayed it as the real deal. Despite the day he had ahead of him of trudging around Chicago in the cold trying to talk a young woman into dropping out of the military, he was allowed a glimmer of happiness.

Brody stepped into the kitchen and

in the pixelated representation of it saw Thorp still in his robe as he turned around with a sizzling pan.

"So that's what they make you wear, huh?" Thorp asked. "Son of a *bitch*, look at that thing. Christ, you look stupid."

Thorp had seen it last night—well, more like just a few hours ago since it had been nearly three when Brody had been awoken by long-ago gunfire pushed out of tinny ordinateur speakers—but apparently Thorp didn't feel like commenting on the sonar until now. It was odd, how different he seemed from last night. Shielded behind this chipper outgoingness, reminding Brody of his father's friend who was on emotion-stabilizing medication. Gruff and canted forward, hands in pockets one moment, then laughing about everything after one shake of a pill bottle and a glass of water. Perhaps that was the case with Thorp. Maybe he was on some kind of pill that smoothed him out. Or perhaps this was just who his friend was now and it was Brody who would have to get used to it.

"Thanks," Brody scoffed, walking to the table and carefully having a seat. He had decided to wear the same clothes he'd worn on the train yesterday, his starched button-down shirt, tie, and slacks, because he knew people were a tad more cooperative when he wore a tie. And since he was going to Fort Reagan, where it was unlikely that answers would be handed over to even the most well-dressed of men, Brody decided he'd at least try to look his best.

Thorp scraped two strips of bacon onto Brody's plate. "It really kills me to see you wear that thing."

"I could take it off." Brody smiled. "But that won't make eating breakfast very easy."

"'Enlist now. Serve your country. Become a hero.' My ass. More like, 'Enlist now, have something terrible happen to you, get mailed back home with all kinds of shit wrong with you, and—"

"All right." Brody put up a hand. "Don't get me wrong. I'm sore about what happened to us, too, but let's not start with that shit again. Let's just have our breakfast, and I'll be on my way to go talk to your sister, okay?"

"I'm sorry," Thorp said, setting the pan on the stovetop. "I don't mean to get wound up about it. But it just kills me what happened to you. I should've been there. I should've bucked up and dealt with— you know—and gone with you, waited until after the shit cooled down before I started talking about post-traumatic stress."

"Forget it," Brody said, his voice stern, and took up his fork.

Thorp stood by the table and watched Brody chase his bacon and eggs around the plate. Suddenly, he shouldered on a coat and went outside with a cigar.

Brody remained at the kitchen table, eating what he could catch. He wanted to look up to see where Thorp went, but the sonar couldn't see through glass, even though it had been polished to an invisible sheen. He upended his coffee, tasting the bitterly sweet silt of half-melted sugar that had settled to the bottom, and removed his phone to call a cab. While he listened to the phone ringing he went so far as to actually cross his fingers that they'd send a cab that was driven by someone with a pulse.

When asked for his name and jigsaw number, he hung up. He had forgotten that he was completely broke. He went outside and paced through the grass that he hadn't been able to tell was moist with dew until he felt its cold sting on the tips of his toes, even through his boots. He got to Thorp standing by a tree on the crest of the hill overlooking the fields.

"Hey, buddy," Brody said, tightening his coat around his neck. It was a chilly morning, and he wondered if what he was stepping through in the grass was frost and not just dew.

"Sorry about that," Thorp said. "I get kind of nutty sometimes about all of it. You're the first and only guy I knew in the service that I've had out here, and I guess I wasn't ready for it. Normally, I deal with it all right—it's just with Nectar and having you here, it's pretty hard *not* to think about the grunt days."

"Understandable," Brody said. He glanced down at his feet, then looked into Thorp's green eyes, picturing them how they were supposed to look instead of the shifting white orbs he saw with the sonar.

"What is it?"

"You know what?" Brody said. "I'm just going to come out and say it, because there's no real easy way around it. I'm flat broke. And I need to get a cab into Chicago if you want me to talk to Nectar. Could you spot me a ride?"

"Yeah, yeah. Of course. No problem." Thorp took out his cell and called the cab company.

They walked back to the house and waited in the living room for the car to arrive.

Brody stood at the window, staring at the lawn. If he had to endure asking his friend for money when he hadn't even been here a full day yet, at least the fates could see to it that the cab was driven by a human. *Give me that at least.*

Brody wasn't so lucky. As soon as the cab pulled into the gravel driveway he could tell it was being piloted without an actual driver. He didn't even need to see that the windshield had no one sitting behind it. The damn things slowed to a crawl before making a turn ever so carefully, the way a small dog might go down darkened steps—with overwhelming hesitance as if the very next step could spell certain doom. Brody sighed.

The cab put itself in park. Once Brody was in the back, he heard the casual electronic prompt, "Where would you like to go today, sir or madam?"

He answered, "Chicago," with a voice weighted heavily with reluctance, hoping the robotic cabbie would detect this and decide to do him a favor and *accidentally* take him somewhere else. The one and only time Brody would've been happy if technology decided to be uncooperative.

During the ride, Brody turned his cell back on, and a series of beeps sounded, alerting him that he had an abundance of voice mail waiting. They were all from his probation officer. He immediately called her.

"Mr. Calhoun," Chiffon said as if she had been waiting for his call for hours. She probably had been.

Her voice was pleasant, upbeat despite the underlying streak of impatience.

"Just returning your call from earlier this morning." Brody bit his knuckle and winced, expecting the worst.

There was a beat of bitter silence.

"I see you've left the state," she said plainly.

"Visiting a friend." *Too fast*, Brody scolded himself. *You answered that too damn fast.*

"This doesn't happen to be like most of your friends, I hope. You seem to have a lot of friends who are always asking favors of you. I sincerely hope you're not breaking your probation by leaving the state to visit a friend like *that*."

"I should've told you that I was leaving the state. I'm sorry. I'm here to see one of my friends from the service but it's just to Illinois and I'm steering clear of any big cities."

"Don't lie to me. I can see you're in Chicago right now as we speak."

"I know but there isn't a grocery store nearby. A man has to eat, right?" *Again, too fast. Do you* want *to go to prison?*

Chiffon sighed. "Listen to me. Do I have your undivided attention at this moment? We could just as easily have this conversation in person, say, in a holding cell."

"You have my undivided attention, I assure you," he said.

"I have a nose for malarkey, and the stuff you're trying to sell me is rotten. You and I made an agreement. As far as the law is concerned, it's being bent to its very limit with you. For everything you've done, all the noses you've broken—literally—and toes you've stepped on—figuratively—you *should* be in jail right now. Time and time again, I let you off easy. Not to say that what you do is right. No. But if you don't behave yourself while you're out of state, I'll have no choice but to reevaluate your case. January is on fast approach, I'll remind you."

"I understand," he said, then switched on the speakerphone and tossed the cell to the seat next to him. He pulled the sonar from his forehead and tucked it in the map pocket of his peacoat. He put in one lens, blinked until color faded back into the world, then the second and waited until he could see out of both eyes. Immediately thereafter, the low charge indicator sprung up, blinking as bright and terrible as the hazards of a burning, overturned car: *01:59:59.*

"Don't tell me what you're up to or where you're going or why you're in Chicago. I don't want to know. You visit your friend, go to the top of the Willis Tower, have a hot dog and see a ball game, have your day of thanks if that's what you want to do, but just make sure you're on the first train home, with all the citizens of that city just as you left them—unharmed. Understand?"

"Yes, ma'am."

"All right. We have an appointment . . . when?"

"Friday," Brody replied at once. "I'll be there. Don't worry."

"Don't misbehave. See you soon, Mr. Calhoun."

"Yes. Thank you. Good-bye." Brody closed his cell and felt the tension he had momentarily escaped from with a decent breakfast reassemble itself. He hated calls from his probation officer anytime, but today every single word the woman said felt like one bad diagnosis after another, every syllable and terse pause midsentence a slice across the throat. He held the phone to his chin and absentmindedly chewed on its corner. When he felt he'd chip a tooth if he bit it any harder, he put it away and wrung his hands.

As if his conscience wasn't screaming loudly enough, there was the undeniable fact: if he got in trouble again, that was it. He'd be out of options. No more community center and Samantha, no more charges for his lenses. He'd be a blind man in prison with a serious lack of friends.

He ignored the No Smoking sign staring him in the face and lit a cigarette. The cab pulled up to the curb out front of the gated military base nestled between two high-rises. He donned a pair of sunglasses, the carotene still itchy and causing his eyes to water even from the soft glow of the white morning light cutting in between structures.

"We hope you enjoy your destination," the cab told him.

Brody wasn't sure how he was going to get back, but it was something he'd deal with later. He got out, and the cab merged with the bumper-to-bumper rush-hour throng.

He stood outside the tall cement wall of Fort Reagan for a few minutes, finished his cigarette, and approached the front gates. He was hoping that security had been loosened since he was last here, that maybe there wasn't a guard booth and the striped arms that had to be raised to permit a vehicle past. But just as it was when he got off the bus nearly a decade ago, the guard booth stood as it always had been. He knocked on the glass.

The helmeted guard looked up from his personal screen, and his eyes narrowed at the sight of Brody, dressed in dark clothes, a black silk tie flopping in the wind.

Brody removed his sunglasses to be polite. He remembered that it was a positive must in the military. If you were speaking to someone—civilian or not—out of courteousness you removed your sunglasses or goggles. It didn't matter if the sun was in your eyes; courtesy came first. He winced at the morning sun. It felt as if it were burrowing into his skull one claw at a time. "Hi, I'm here to talk with a friend of mine. She's a new recruit."

"Visiting hours for civilians are between noon and three, sir."

"Yeah, but this is an emergency. Her brother is sick," Brody lied and considered for a fleeting second how it hadn't *felt* like one.

The guard looked Brody up and down again, leaned back in his folding chair, and pressed a button on the intercom next to him. He spoke into it with a hushed voice, received an answer almost immediately. The guard leaned forward again, the front feet of his chair slamming hard against the floor of his tiny booth. He slumped with his elbows on the desk before him and said, "What's the new recruit's name?"

"Nectar Ashbury."

He clicked a few times on his screen, got out of the movie program he had been watching, and selected a roster of new recruits. He asked Brody how to spell the last name, and he did. The guard went through the roster a second and a third time. "Sorry, no new recruits here by that name. Is she married or did she change her name? That seems to be pretty common, especially when they don't want anyone to find them and try to change their minds." He glared at Brody.

"That's all right. Probably just a miscommunication on my part. Thanks for checking, anyway." Brody stuffed his numbed hands into his coat pockets and strolled away. He was sure that even if he managed to walk a whole block from the base, their cameras would still be watching his back.

He turned a corner, then another, cut down an alleyway, and went into a coffee shop. He didn't have the means to order anything, but he went into the men's room and locked the door—they couldn't deny him that.

The toilet seat made a surprisingly loud clunk as it hit the bowl, as did the lid when he threw that down as well. He pulled his coat tight around him to prevent it from rubbing against anything filthy—which was to say just about everything in this bathroom stall—and sat there running his hands up and down his face, the sound sandpapery whenever they crossed anywhere below his nose. He would've liked to have had this moment to think elsewhere, but it was just too cold outside and too much sensory overload. Between the flashing signs and the yelling people crowding all around him and everything else noisy, smelly, and loud of this unfamiliar world—that of morning, daytime—he needed somewhere as close as he could get to home, here in

Chicago. It still wasn't good enough. This cramped little stall provided some comfort, but it wasn't complete. The buzzing florescent lights and the sound of all the people out in the coffee shop talking and the light jazz they always play in places like these . . . he had to create an impromptu shelter from it all, here and now.

He left the stall, made sure the door was still locked, and clicked off the light. The most noisome of the sounds, the buzzing lights, disappeared from the fug of noise, but the other layers persisted. He returned to the stall and cupped his hands over his ears and, even with it already being dark, pressed his eyes shut until it nearly hurt.

Now he could think. Process.

He was certain the security detail would be raised at Fort Reagan because of the stunt he'd just pulled. He wondered if the police would be notified, if they possibly had a holo-capture unit going out front at all times as well as cameras to not only catch someone's picture but their exact measurements of shape and size. It wasn't that uncommon anymore at banks and certain government building lobbies. Why not there? He foresaw the police picking him up at Thorp's place, Thorp going off the deep end, and more messes coming out of it. But with cameras all over the city, wouldn't it be easy enough to track him from place to place? What about right here to this street, this coffee shop, this bathroom? And what then? . . . *Where is all this coming from?*

Brody released the pressure he was applying to his ears with his palms. He stepped over to the wall and felt around for the light switch. He had never considered himself a terribly paranoid person before, so why was this coming out now? Did Chicago have that kind of effect on him?

He splashed some water on his face. He disregarded all panic-stricken thoughts and exited the bathroom, crossed the dining area, and pushed out into the cold. But with each step he took, he couldn't help but think that every bit of this—every swing of his legs, every flick his tie scribbled in the air—was being watched. He told himself to stop, and for the time being, whatever it was making him think that way did.

8

Using the reflection of a storefront display loaded to the brim with Christmas trees and other decorations all of red, gold, and green, Brody carefully pulled the lenses out of his eyes as the time remaining flashed ten minutes shy of one and a half hours. He reapplied the sonar to his forehead and carried on down the street, feeling better to remain on the move for reasons beyond him.

After a few steps in darkness, the street reappeared. A building here, cubic and dull in design came first, then the sidewalk, and then the marching snowman-like shapes of fellow human beings. He donned his sunglasses so as not to attract stares at his eyes and the pearlescent appearance they developed when the lenses were out, then removed them when he reached a fiberglass bus stop shelter. He let the ping settle to a comfortable circumference around him. No focus was needed for that. He could just sit here and see all around him, provided no one moved too quickly.

Brody took out his cell but couldn't read anything on its screen, a blank space of the touch pad. The only way he could tell the thing was even on was when he began to dial Thorp's number; each keystroke made its trademark bleep.

He hoped he dialed correctly and brought the phone up to his ear, each pulse as it rang hard to hear with the wind pounding in through the open front of the shelter. One ring led into the next and the next. Just as he started considering the prospect of hitchhiking back to the farmhouse, Thorp answered.

"Sorry it took me so long. I was out in the garden."

Brody pictured Thorp sitting in the soot-stained cockpit of the Darter, gleefully riding shotgun to his violent flashbacks, supplying the gunfire sounds himself—*chunga-chunga-chunga*. "Listen, Nectar isn't on the new recruit roster at Fort Reagan. Are you sure this is where she signed up?"

"Last I talked to her, she said she was going to sign up there. It was the one *I* signed up with, and that was the one she wanted."

"Now be straight with me. Did you actually speak with her, or was this something you picked up through the grapevine?" Brody snapped. It was bad enough he had to be in Chicago, but he was on a fool's errand, half-blind, and without gloves. He was in no mood to beat around the bush.

A long boxy shape, gurgling like a whale stuffed into a coffee can, sidled up to the curb in front of the shelter. Brody waved the bus on, and only after it had gone halfway up the block could he hear Thorp again.

"—I *am* being straight with you, man. She told me she signed up at Fort Reagan. I'm not bullshitting you. I wouldn't do that."

"Well, they told me she's not on the roster. Is there somewhere else I should look? Besides, I'm already here and have no means of getting back to your place."

"Where are you? I'll have a cab sent to you prepaid."

"Forget it. I'm out here. I want to at least make a *little* progress," Brody said.

He could feel the grip contracting. He often didn't feel it until he had a lead, a scent to follow. But already, possibly due to the personal circumstances, the fixation was taking fastidious steps at him. He saw his future, a wall of his room in Thorp's house, photos of Nectar everywhere, pages of notes, recorded phone calls. Normally, his cases were more of the open-and-shut sort, but he could tell this one was going to be different.

"What are you going to do?" Thorp asked.

"I don't know. You tell me. Where does she live?"

"Apartment in Wicker Park, apparently."

Brody closed his eyes, but he could still see every-thing around him. The blocky representations of the coffeehouse patrons navigating the charted wire frame of white laid over darkness—archaic arcade game visuals at best. He rubbed his temples, and the image twisted slightly and then corrected when he lifted his fingertips. "Got an address, or should I just start knocking on every apartment door in every complex in Wicker Park?"

After twenty minutes standing out on the curb with his nose running and his fingers losing feeling even further, he finally saw the cab arrive. Brody allowed Thorp to pay for it since he certainly wasn't going to walk all the way to Wicker Park. And if he knew one thing about Chicago it was to never use the train. Not unless you enjoyed having sharp things stuck into you.

He was relieved to see it had an actual living, breathing driver.

The driver twisted the rearview mirror and peered back at Brody. "Where to, bud?"

Brody recited the address from memory. Thorp had offered to send it to him, and Brody impatiently told him not to bother. Thorp asked why. Brody reminded him that with the sonar on, he couldn't read anything unless it had raised or embossed lettering. Something on a screen or a piece of paper didn't show up whatsoever. "Oh," Thorp had said, his voice low and morose.

"You got it," the driver said and cursed as he nearly sideswiped a truck. He had to jerk the car toward the curb, where he all but sent them into a newspaper print-on-demand kiosk. Maybe keeping fingers crossed for human drivers wasn't such a great idea after all.

Brody lit a cigarette and cracked the window and watched the pixelated smoke drift out in the frigid vacuum. It took nearly an hour to get across town to the apartment building. Traffic in Chicago never ceased. To Brody, it seemed like every hour of the day all people with a car made it their sole mission to collect at intersections and create a disjointed orchestra by honking their horns at random intervals. The cabbie seemed to be the musical sort as well, because he added his own soprano blats to the cacophony at each and every four-way stop they came across, commenting between his staccato honks that Mondays were always the worst.

"You know," the driver said when they got there, "I can't stand you rich boys paying for cabs ahead of time because I don't ever get a goddamned tip. It all goes to the fuckin' cab company."

Brody apologized insincerely and got out, slamming the door.

Nectar's apartment building was massive, easily thirty stories high, and it took a few seconds for the sonar to see all the way to the top. He stood out front for a moment and allowed the sonar to search for anyone hanging out on the stoop. There was no one around.

He mounted the steps and found the buzzer, but nothing was in Braille. The names were on printed plaques that had no texture to them. He chewed the inside of his cheek and considered putting in his lenses, but he had just touched the cab's door handle, seat belt, and seat with his bare hands—God only knew how filthy they now were. On a lark, he tried the door without pressing any of the buzzer buttons. Locked.

Brody returned to the sidewalk and looked up and down the street. Cars, people on the sidewalk, steam rising from the grates. He had another cigarette and kept it dangling from the corner of his mouth so his hands could remain buried in his pockets.

He stood in the sun's warmth along the face of the apartment building and wondered what the hell he was doing out here, risking serious jail time by jumping states while on probation. He thanked his good fortune that Chiffon was understanding. Well, maybe "understanding" was a bit generous, but still. He wasn't in prison. So there was that. If Brody had gotten assigned to any other probation officer, he would've been thrown into the system and outfitted with a wardrobe of powder-blue correctional facility attire, each item with his prisoner number stenciled on the back. For a ghostly and horrific moment, he could almost feel the punch of a shiv entering his belly.

January. Not long at all. Just the name of that particular month crossing his mind prompted his legs to move.

He threw his cigarette into the gutter and went back to the buzzer and punched a button at random. No one answered. He tried another and another. No one answered. It was Monday; most people were probably at work. He considered pushing all the buttons at once and seeing what that got him but thought better of it. Systematically, he went down one column after another, trying each button.

Finally, someone answered. The voice was over-amplified and stung Brody's ears with its surprising volume: "Yes? What do you want?"

Brody said he was a repairman and was buzzed in. He rushed inside and blew into his cupped hands to warm them.

The lobby was sparse, with only a fake tree and a series of elevator doors. He walked to a plastic-coated frame that hung between two of the elevator doors and let the sonar feel its smooth surface. It could just as easily be a framed painting of a sphincter as the tenant listing.

He cursed, went over to where the warm air was blowing up from a vent and stood over it. This was ridiculous, using a faulty device for the visually impaired while *looking* for someone. He might as well march up and down the sidewalk and ask for each individual's name. It would probably be as productive as hanging out in the lobby with no idea if Nectar Ashbury even lived here or not. He cursed Thorp's addled mind. Brody thought of being home, with the windows closed and the heater on full blast and his paints out and a pan of prepackaged lasagna in the oven that he had to share with absolutely no one.

Brody heard keys jingling. The door opened, and he quickly removed the sonar from his forehead and put it in his pocket. He stood facing the general direction of the person who'd entered the lobby, with what he hoped was a plaintive look on his face.

He said to the darkness before his eyes, "Can you help me? I'm looking for my daughter. She lives here and I'm blind and there isn't any Braille on the nameplates."

"What's your daughter's name?" The woman had a sweet voice, and he knew she would help him. Her boots clicked over toward the tenant list on the wall between the elevator doors.

He followed but was sure to keep a respectful distance. She smelled like a bakery—sugary and nice.

"Nectar Ashbury," he said. Of all the dumb luck,

what if he was speaking to Nectar right now? How would she react to this blind guy with a bad haircut and a terribly out-of-fashion coat asking for her? Would she utilize some of that close-quarters combat training she may have learned and deliver a heel to his face that he would never see coming?

The woman murmured the name over and over, and he could hear the squeak of the pad of her finger as it trailed down the plastic on the tenant list. "Apartment 644."

"Six. Four. Four." Brody was still playing helpless. If the tenant listing didn't have Braille, the buttons in the elevator car certainly wouldn't. He hoped the woman would help him just a little bit more.

She offered to get him there, and he let a wide smile spread across his face.

They rode in the elevator in silence. He held on to the railing and listened to her click keys on her ordi as they rode up to the sixth floor.

The doors opened and she wished him good luck. Her generosity apparently expired there. That was fine. He didn't want her to escort him all the way to Nectar's apartment door anyway.

As soon as the elevator doors were closed behind him, he replaced the sonar to his forehead. The hallway spread out before him in both directions. He looked at the nearest apartment. Beside the door was a small plaque with numbers—they were raised digits that could easily be read by the sonar. He made his way to Nectar's door. He knocked a couple of times and took a step back and listened for any noise inside the apartment.

Nothing.

He tried again and this time stepped *closer* and turned his ear toward the door. A faint purring inside, a refrigerator or a space heater. He hunched down and let the sonar feel around the door. The door fit the frame flush, and the sonar's ping couldn't quite probe underneath the door more than a couple of feet. The floor was a jumble of wildly thrown together shapes, nebulous. Either it was covered in sawdust or she had shag carpet.

Getting up from all fours, he wondered why breaking in had suddenly become a consideration.

This is just a favor for a friend, he reminded himself. Nectar wasn't someone on the run. Hell, she probably had no idea anyone was even looking for her. If anything, she was at the supermarket, living her life, the idea of signing up for the military kicked to the back of her mind. Perhaps she had been lulled by the call of adventure the commercials promised, just as they had done to Brody all those years ago.

Brody took out his cell phone and dialed Thorp.

As before, it took a while before he answered. "Yeah? Did you find anything?" Thorp asked hurriedly without even saying hello.

"I'm at her apartment and there's no one answering."

"Shit, she's already overseas, then."

"She isn't enlisted. This is kind of stupid to be totally honest with you. If you don't mind, could you get another cab for me?"

"Can you jimmy the lock on her door?"

"Are you serious?" Brody asked. "Do you *want* me to go to jail? Is this some elaborate prank of yours or something? I know you could always be counted on for a semidangerous practical joke back in the day and all, but even for you—this is a little beyond your typical flaming bag of dog shit."

"Come on. This is important. If Nectar's not enlisted and she's not home, where the hell could she be?"

"Have you tried *calling* her? Have you tried sending her an e-mail?" Brody said through gritted teeth. "Just because she's not home right now at this very second and she's not on some roster at the base doesn't mean she's been kidnapped or sent overseas."

"Kidnapped," Thorp echoed. "I haven't even *thought* of that."

Brody groaned. "Listen to me. We're friends and all, but consider this a serious test of my patience. Anyone else, I'd be giving your money back and saying forget it."

"But I haven't paid you yet," Thorp said softly.

"I know. That's what makes this particular circum-stance different. When I get back, you're going to pay me and I'm not going to refund it like I would with anyone else when their problem is a particularly huge waste of my time." Brody walked toward the elevator and slapped the call button. "I'm serious. This is really a huge pain in the ass."

Thorp said nothing.

"Hello?" Brody said and looked at the screen, momentarily forgetting that it would appear blank to him. He had no idea if Thorp had ended the call or not. Brody hung up and tried again, but Thorp didn't answer. He went down to the lobby and tried calling one more time.

I should've saved that rant until after he paid for the cab to get me back to the farm.

He stood in the lobby on that same heating vent for a few more minutes and tried a third and final time. Again, no answer.

Brody tucked the phone into his pocket, staring ahead at what he assumed was a window but appeared to be only a stark expanse of blackness. The noose reduced itself by another tiny wrench. It was still there, no denying it. The questions and the possibilities and the repetitious demand to know, to end, to seek, to find, to finish—to follow the trail.

"Shit." He pulled at the collar of his shirt, hoping that the act would release the sensation of being garroted. It didn't. Not in the least.

9

Brody knew that once he was out the front door of Nectar's apartment building he wouldn't be allowed back in. Everyone was overly cautious—mostly rightly so—and someone buzzing in a person claiming to be a repairman was a fluke in the armor of suspicion that people, especially in Chicago, had built around them- selves. Brody didn't want to chance someone calling the police.

He pushed back out into the cold and listened as the door eased shut and electronically locked. He stood at the top of the stoop and looked around at what he had available to him as a place to set up camp until Thorp answered his phone. Feeling over the signage for the nearby storefronts, he discovered most of them were scrolling texts—those he could not read. But directly across the street, with an old-fashioned sign made up of blocky neon letters, was America's Favorite Automat. So they *did* exist in Chicago.

Being a bachelor who had little idea how to prepare anything that didn't come from a box, Brody considered America's Favorite Automat—a chain of twenty-four-hour cafeterias—a second home. In an AFA he could order a meal that tasted something akin to homemade, even though it didn't fool his taste buds because in his youth Brody ate only made-from-scratch meals prepared by his mother.

The AFA in such close proximity to Nectar's apartment building was like fate dropping a crumb in his lap. He triple-checked both ways for oncoming traffic and sprinted across the two-lane street and went inside.

It was reassuring that the AFA let him in. There had been many a time that he approached a burger joint, and the doors locked as soon as he put his hand on the glass, a soft voice saying: "We're sorry, but our services cannot be rendered to customers who currently have a deficit in their credit account. Be sure to stop by when your financial troubles have been rectified. Thanks and have a pleasant day." It was one thing to be told off by a person, quite another by an entire burger joint franchise.

It was empty of patrons as many AFAs were during the day. They were mainly a place to get a cup of coffee while on the road or a slice of pie in the middle of the night when sleep was being an elusive little shit.

He took a seat at the counter, and a woman immediately strolled out from the back on soft-soled shoes until she came right before him, turned, and looked into his face with a warm, welcoming smile. The smooth, calculated motion of the woman in the sundress and apron made Brody think of the clock on his grandmother's kitchen wall. On the hour, two little figures came out of their respective doors and slid along on tracks where they met at a bell in the middle and took turns hammering it with tiny wooden mallets. This fluidity of motion and the somewhat unsettling nature of her unbreakable eye contact told Brody that this woman was an Artie.

His sonar felt around the soft rubber over her mechanical facial musculature. The eyelids clicked closed to mimic blinking. "Well, *hello* there, dear," the woman said in an equally warm prerecorded voice that sounded like countless TV mothers Brody had grown up with. "Welcome to America's Favorite Automat. What sounds good to you on this cold, cold day?"

"Uh, just a cup of coffee, please."

"Dandy. Would you like that with cream and sugar, just cream, just sugar, or black?"

"Black, please."

"Would you like to try any of our flavored nondairy creamers?" She rattled off a list of foreign and domestic creamers, some of which he had never even heard of.

"No, thank you."

"Okeydokey. Be right back in two shakes of a lamb's tail." She smiled, turned, walked away, thumped through the double doors without putting her hands out before her, just slammed right through face-first.

Brody was a little disturbed by the transaction. He didn't really like ordering from an Artificial. Who knew what she was doing in the kitchen? He hoped it was organized, with everything sterilized, but there could be a dead body on the floor, swollen and blackened with decay, and an Artificial, unless it was programmed to notice, would stroll right past it.

Shaking the thought away, he looked around for a bathroom. He wanted to put his lenses in so he could watch for anyone resembling the grown-up version of Nectar head into the building across the street. Toward the back, beside the constantly rotating clear plastic shelves that displayed the dessert offerings, was a set of doors. He figured that was the bathroom, since each door had a plaque on it. He stood up and headed in that direction, unbuttoning his coat as he did.

He paused, wondering if the server would come out with his coffee and see him not there and figure he left. Did it have the common sense to know that human beings needed to use the can from time to time? He considered shouting into the kitchen to tell her where he was going but decided against it, fearing it would just cause confusion and delay his coffee.

Brody found the door at the back of the Automat was the bathroom. Noticing the urinal fixed to the wall, he felt proud of himself that he had guessed correctly and gone into the men's. It wouldn't be the first time he accidentally walked into the women's restroom with the sonar on.

Once he was satisfied his hands were clean enough

that he could perform open-heart surgery if he had to, he removed the sonar and put the lenses in his eyes. His reflection slowly emerged out of the gloom. He peered into his own brown eyes and blinked a few more times to get all the clinging motes of blindness out of them. He had a few seconds of perfect vision before the flashing digits came into his view, reminding him that he had only an hour and a handful of minutes before the lenses lost their charge completely.

He replaced the sonar and the lens case into his pocket and went back into the cafeteria.

The server stood at the counter where he had been sitting, a cup of steaming coffee in her hand. She had a quizzical look on her face, as if he had played some cruel joke by turning invisible on her. She detected him approaching and swiveled around. Now, with the lenses in, he could see her eyes were painted to look like a disarming shade of sky blue. The smile hitched up again, servos audibly whining in her cheeks. "Oh, there you are. I thought you skedaddled on me."

"Nope. Just had to use the restroom." Brody removed his peacoat and dropped it onto the next stool and saddled up to the counter.

The server set the cup down before him with surprising grace. She released the loop on the mug, straightened her finger, and withdrew it from the ceramic C on the side of the mug without ever nudging it. After she smoothed her apron, she put her hands on her hips and cocked her head, like a dog hearing a distant whistle. "You look familiar. Have you been in here before?"

Brody hissed. The coffee was scalding. He dabbed at his burned upper lip with a paper napkin. "Not in this one before, no," he managed.

"So you have visited another franchise in the America's Favorite Automat family of restaurants before? Because we have locations all over the globe, even one in Tibet. That may be hot, by the way."

He knew exactly where this was going. Back when the AFA was first introduced as a futuristic chain of eateries with their Artificial servers—that in itself a novelty at the time—there was a craze in personalized service. Whenever you entered an AFA and used your jigsaw card to pay your tab, the AFA put your order into a databank at their corporate headquarters. So whenever you visited another AFA, the connection was made and the server would suggest what you ordered last time. But because Brody often liked to use cash and the Minneapolis–St. Paul AFAs mostly had human servers, the Artificial was confused. It had partial data on him, knew he had visited but didn't have a record of what he ordered.

"I have been in other AFAs, yeah," Brody answered, going with it for as long as his patience would withstand. He had a lot on his mind after all. He was penniless and stranded in Chicago, for starters.

"How would you rate the overall service at America's Favorite Automat on a scale from one to ten?" the Artificial asked.

"What's this about?" Brody said.

"Excuse me. I didn't catch that."

"Why are you asking me this?" Brody said a degree slower.

"We just want to know how we can improve our already renowned service at America's Favorite Automat to provide the most stellar experience anyone could ever want."

"Are you asking me whether or not I prefer human servers over Artificials? Is that what this is about?" Brody asked, holding the cup of coffee within range of his burned lip for another sip. He was in a playful mood, if a somewhat malicious one. It was a shitty day, and talking in circles and confusing a robot was a way to blow off some steam. What would it do? At most, it would reduce the friendliness factor in its personality matrix and fuck off and go wash the dishes.

"We, as a family company, just want to get the everyman's—and every*woman*'s—point of view. We want to know how we can provide the best service we can and—"

Brody interjected, "If you'd like to put this on my record and never allow me in another AFA the rest of my life, fine—or as you'd put it: *dandy*—but I just want to have a cup of coffee and take a load off for a minute. All right?"

The servos in the Artificial's cheeks whined again, and the smile returned. "Certainly, dear." She turned and paced away, slamming through the double doors face-first again, and was gone.

Brody finally took a second sip after blowing a few times. It was then that he noticed the music playing. "What a Wonderful World" came down from overhead. He tried his best to ignore it since today he did not agree.

He lit another cigarette and swung around on his stool, eyeing the constantly twirling wall of desserts.

Pies he could now see the actual color of, not just wire-frame estimations of them. He watched them rotate past—dark, dark cobalt of the syrupy innards of a slice of blueberry. The gory red of strawberry à la mode. The peaked tips of the meringue atop the key lime, browned ever so delicately at their summits. The absolute peerless desserts only a robot could make.

His phone jingled and he answered, never taking his eyes off the everlasting dance of the pies.

"Hey," Thorp said, languorous.

"Thanks for calling me back. Thought I was going to have to get in the soup line here in a minute."

"Sorry about that. I can't take real intense conversations anymore." A second flicked by. "Did you try the lock?"

"As a matter of fact, I didn't," Brody said with mock levity as he watched that slice of blueberry pie slide by for the third time. Three bucks. Oh, to have three bucks right now. The sugar high could last him months.

"No?" Thorp said.

Brody turned on his stool to look out through the front windows of the Automat. He glanced at the stoop across the street. No sign of activity. "No, I didn't break into your sister's apartment. Because that is against the law, as if I needed to be the one to remind you of that. And jail ranks up there in first place, followed only by the DMV as far as places I try to visit as infrequently as humanly possible."

Thorp sighed. "I just want to know what the hell's going on."

"I know you do, but I honestly think you have nothing

to worry about. Nectar probably signed up, maybe filled out a few forms, got her physical, and went home and changed her mind. When I first enlisted, after that hellish physical with the guy tugging on my nuts, *I* sure as hell considered never going back." He kept watching the stoop.

"But it freaks me out. She's not at the base; she's not home. Where the hell is she?"

"She's probably out with friends. I mean, she's— what? Twenty-four? I'll still find her and ask her to call you. Don't worry."

"I-I tried calling her a minute ago, and she didn't answer," Thorp stammered.

"Like I said, she's probably out, has her phone off."

Sighing into the receiver, Thorp blew a gale of static on Brody's end. "All right, I'm just going to come out and say it. And you might be pissed at me, because this sort of changes things in a way. So, here goes. Nectar came by exactly twenty-two days ago."

Brody considered asking him if he was sure about the number of days, but something in Thorp's voice stopped him. He imagined Thorp staring at a calendar with the days Nectar had been missing crossed off.

"She told me she was going to enlist, I told her she shouldn't, and we argued. It got a little . . . heated."

Brody wondered if this was the point when his friend was going to confess to murdering his own sister.

Thorp continued, "I told her about the shit you and I went through in Cairo, and she *still* wanted to do it. She was adamant. The next day and every day up until you arrived last night I've been calling her a couple times an hour. Constantly, man. I even tried last night after you went to bed."

"Well, there's your answer. She blacklisted your number," Brody said, thinking it best to say something encouraging even though he knew it truly didn't sound good.

"I've gone to her place. I've e-mailed her. I even went to her job. She's *nowhere*."

Brody groaned, feeling the whole thing folding itself around him. The grip constricted around his neck, cutting circulation to everything else. Chiffon, his rent, his mountain of community service hours— all of it bled away, automatically shoved off as wholly unimportant. The only thing that remained was the foggy image of Nectar at that backyard barbecue ten years ago: freckled and awkward with a polite smile.

"Have you called the cops?" Brody asked, grave.

"No."

"You should've."

"I *know*."

"This isn't good. This is missing persons. They have people, entire departments, devoted to this stuff, and now that I'm involved, poking around at her apartment, at the base—I'll be the number one suspect. Hell, my probation officer even knows I'm here. We take this to the cops now, my goose is *cooked*. Probable cause, my record, courts backed up, they'll put me on the fast track. I won't see a courtroom for a year, and the prisons aren't exactly full of friends of mine."

"I'm sorry."

Brody took a minute to ponder it. "Where does she work?" he asked, his voice solemn. There was no shrugging off the hold this thing now had on him. The scent, while faint, was on the air—he had to keep sniffing. There was no way to shut that part of himself off anymore. Each sniff caused another foot to step forward involuntary, and that step would give him another deeper, clearer layer to the scent. If he allowed it.

"Well, she has this part-time job at Mama Wash dry cleaner."

"Address. I'm not from around here, remember? Mama Wash could be on the fuckin' moon for all I know." He looked over his shoulder for the Artificial. Bad language in an AFA? That was grounds for getting kicked out. He was sure she'd take him by the scruff of his neck, and when he was out on his ass on the cold sidewalk she'd clap her hands of his dirt and remind him with a smile that America's Favorite Automat was *not* a place for potty mouths.

"Division. It's on Division Street."

"Okay," Brody said. "I'll give you a call with what I find out."

10

Two blocks up and one over. The
sun made a temporary appearance,
then fell behind ominous grayness. It
smelled like snow.

Mama Wash was easily missed if one
didn't know what to look for. The scrolling
marquee was all in Russian. Brody could
speak it enough to get by. He had taken it
in high school since it was rapidly rivaling
Spanish as the second national language after English.

While crossing the street, he tried
to recall those lessons from school on the
rather difficult Slavic language since he
figured if the marquee was in Russian,
the employees would be more than
likely to speak it as well. He pushed in

through the fogged-over glass doors and was hit in the face with humid, perfumed air. He removed his sunglasses and approached the counter, behind which no one stood.

There was a constant clamor coming from the back, banging machinery and the cling and clang of clothing with zippers and buttons making a disjoined, weird music in the rotating drums of the dryers. As he waited, he looked at the services the dry cleaner provided. Steam press, a folding service, alterations.

A middle-aged woman wearing a narrow sweatband lumbered out, her cheeks ruddy and her massive breasts hanging unbridled behind a thin cotton tank top. She dropped an armload of clean clothes onto a folding table and asked him in broken English, "Yes, sir? Maybe I help of you?"

"Yeah," Brody said. "Do you have an employee named Nectar Ashbury?"

The woman's already disgruntled demeanor turned a fraction more dour. She put her hands on her wide childbearing hips. "*That* girl. She has been gone two weeks—no call, no show. She is fired as far as I am of the concern." After turning her head partly away, she kept her sharp eyes narrowed while asking, "Are you police officer?"

"No, just a family friend," Brody said, trying to sound matter-of-fact, as if there weren't more to it than that.

00:45:59.

He changed his tack; he needed to get what he could out of her while he could still see her face in color. She could blush or the color could wash out of her face during a lie, and he wanted to be able to see that change happen.

The woman raised a finger. "One moment." She turned and yelled through the door behind her, "Paige!"

There was some clanging, a wet slap of damp clothes being pitched to the floor. A younger woman emerged. She resembled Mama Wash in a way, stocky and short, with a square face and close-set eyes the hue of warmed caramel. She, too, was braless and in a tank top. Brody couldn't help but notice her breasts, unlike Mama Wash's, still retained some of their elasticity and hung from her chest with resilience.

Paige looked at him, put her hands on the hips of her printed skirt in the same impatient way, then folded her arms over her chest. She grunted, "Name?"

"Excuse me?"

Paige turned to a rack of hanging, bagged garments. "What is your *name*, mister?"

"He look for girl," Mama Wash informed her. "Fired girl."

Paige turned away from the rack of clothes. "You a cop?"

"No." Did he *look* like a cop or something?

She unfolded one arm to wipe sweat from her forehead with the back of her hand. "I haven't heard from her in a couple of weeks. Sucks, too, because without her I have to do all the pressing myself."

Her mother glared at her. "I do press."

"I know you do," Paige said dismissively.

"Did she happen to mention anything about the military or going somewhere?"

Paige nodded. "She's what you'd call a *searcher*.

She talked about signing up all last month, but I didn't think she'd actually go through with it. The month before that, she talked about joining a convent, so who's to say what her aspiration of the week might be. Are you an MP?"

"Family friend," Brody said, sick of the guessing game.

Mama Wash looked back and forth between the two like a tennis ref watching the ball bounce from one side of the net to the other. Finally, she gathered up the armload of laundry she had dumped on the folding table. She asked Paige in Russian if she would be okay alone with this man. Paige nodded and Mama Wash went back to work. Immediately, Paige's demeanor loosened, but she kept her arms folded over her ample bosom.

Brody had to give her something, a little insight to what this was all about. Honesty was the best policy when trying to pry information out of people. If they knew you weren't a stalker boyfriend and your intentions were seemingly good, they'd be willing to offer a little bit more. Brody told her he was an old friend of Nectar's brother.

"Thorp," Paige said, shaking her head. "That was the *last* motherfucker Nectar should've been going to for advice. I mean, no offense or anything."

Brody smiled. "None taken."

"I guess he must've talked her out of it if she didn't sign up, so he can't be all bad, right?"

Brody felt the trail getting cold. Paige was meandering, the urgency in her voice tapering. He asked, "Are you and Nectar friends?"

"Yeah, we hung out pretty regularly. We'd go to the movies, hit the bars." Paige stepped forward and unfolded her arms.

Brody noticed tiny blue bruises on the insides of Paige's arms. Track marks. He met her eyes again so she wouldn't get suspicious of his staring. "Did you ever happen to notice someone watching her when you guys went out? Any calls to her cell she wouldn't take in front of you? That sort of thing?"

"She had guys falling all over themselves to get her number or to buy her drinks, but she never really kept a boyfriend. And the guys she hooked up with were always into whatever interest she was currently taking on. If she was in the I'm-going-to-join-the-convent mood she was all about those cue ball–headed monks in the orange robes. If she was in the itching-to-make-the-Bears-cheerleading-squad craze, she'd be all about the jocks. But never did I see her with any black eyes or anything, if that's what you mean."

"You don't seem too concerned that she's missing," Brody said. He hoped this might upset her if she were hiding something. Bluntness, like honesty, was a skeleton key to people with information. But Paige took him for a surprise: she wasn't offended at all. Instead, she smiled.

Paige, showing crooked white teeth, "If you knew her, you wouldn't be, either. She's probably down in the tropics, taking lessons to become a hula dancer. Give it a couple of days. She'll be back."

Brody felt as if there was more to unearth with Paige, and he knew he wasn't going to be able to with her wanting to get back to work. He checked his watch. It was noon. "Do you think I could possibly convince you to get a cup of coffee with me?"

Paige refolded her matronly arms. "Okay. That sounds pretty good, actually. One second." She went into the back, and Brody listened to her talk to her mother in Russian. When she reemerged, she was wearing a long cotton jacket and a stocking cap that had a couple of round teddy bear ears sewn onto the top. She pointed at Brody as she came around the counter, sliding on mittens. "You're buying."

Paige guided Brody halfway up the block to a diner that was retrofitted out of an old train car. The outside was rounded and covered in panels of stainless steel, seemingly patchworked together haphazardly. Inside, the smell of fryer grease and artificial meat on the griddle made Brody's stomach twist. After the ham he had last night, the real ham, not the soy protein byproduct most places featured, he felt spoiled.

The diner was old-fashioned, and he was thankful it wasn't equipped with front door scanners to verify he had the credit to pay. It was crowded, but a booth in the back corner opened up. Brody and Paige slid onto the vinyl seats, and a human waitress came to their table. Brody ordered a coffee, and Paige ordered an egg white omelet with cheddar cheese and mushrooms, hash browns, toast, a strawberry milk shake—and coffee.

Brody glanced at the scrolling menu on the wall at their booth and did some quick math: her order plus his coffee would come out in the ballpark of ten credits. He smiled at the server as she walked away. He'd worry about paying for it later when he had the information he wanted.

"You and Nectar are close, then?" Brody asked.

Paige shrugged. The teddy bear ears on her knit cap made her incredibly hard to take seriously. "As close as you can be with the girl, I suppose. She's always changing her hair or clothes. She'd push all of these books on me, too. Shit about living with your spiritual side at the forefront, only taking baths on Sunday, or how to build a freaking birdhouse. It was always something. You could see her do the hippie thing with the puka shell necklace on Monday, and by Friday she's wearing cut-up fishnets and rape paint."

Brody grimaced. "Rape paint?"

"Yeah, you've seen those chicks who do that, right? They draw a line of red with henna down the inside of their thigh to look like they've just been raped or had their period or got a back-alley abortion. Sick, I know, but Nectar's always looking for the next thing she can temporarily sink her teeth into." Paige talked loudly. He assumed she had hearing damage from spending so much time among loud washing machines.

She cracked her knuckles, looked around. "It's pretty dead in here," she commented, despite there not being a single booth or stool open. He wondered if she was referring to the clientele. Almost every patron had a suit and a tie on, no one else with her youthful cut-and-paste style of dress worthy of acknowledging.

"Have you ever visited her place?" Brody asked, trying to get her back on track.

"I crash there when I don't have money for a cab or if I might puke if I got on the train." Chuckle.

"Did you ever notice any pamphlets or literature on any sort of hobby or anything? Any indication of what she might be trying to do with her life next?"

"Like I said, she's always reinventing herself. She's like the Material Girl or whatever her name was. You know who I mean; you're old. That singer who was someone different every time she put out an album. That's Nectar, the Material Girl." She turned away. "Fuck, what was that chick's *name*?"

"Madonna," Brody said curtly. "Listen, this might be more serious than you think. She might be in trouble."

"Why? You don't know her. You're just her brother's friend. He's probably filled your head with that conspiracy bullshit he was always filling *her* head with and set you loose on a snipe hunt. She'll be back. With a new haircut and maybe a tattoo, but she'll be back." She frowned. "Was that it? I thought it was like Madam Google or something . . ."

The server slid a cup of coffee and plastic plates of steaming fake eggs, toast, and hash browns in front of Paige and set a cup of coffee down in front of Brody. "The milk shake's gonna take a minute. The machine is on the fritz," the server said, didn't wait for a reply, and walked off.

Paige unrolled her silverware out of her napkin and picked at the rubbery mass of what was supposed to be an egg white omelet but resembled a puddle of melted packing peanuts.

Paige forked up some of the hash browns, talking

toward her plate. "I think—and this is just my opinion here—you should milk whatever you're getting out of her brother and wait it out till she gets back."

Brody cut to the chase. "Did she ever give you a spare key to her apartment?"

Paige's expression turned hard, with a small twist of disgust reading in her pursing lips. "I don't know what your game is, but breaking into someone's apartment when they're out in the world trying to find themselves isn't very cool." She pointed her fork at Brody. "I don't think that's right."

Brody sighed. "If I could get in touch with her, even if it was on the phone for a minute, it would make all the difference. Did she have another cell she used when travelling? The number Thorp's been trying Is still active, but it always goes straight to voice mail."

"The number she gave me is the same number she gave my mom when she first started working for us. I've tried calling her to see if she could come in to help me out, but like I've already said how many times, this is pretty common for her."

Brody wondered if Paige, someone who apparently knew Nectar pretty well, was feeding him lines. Maybe Nectar was trying on different walks of life to see what she wanted to explore next. He thought about Thorp and his paranoia-riddled theories and hysteria when a new possibility of what happened to his sister cropped up into his balding head.

Brody sipped his coffee and thought for a moment. Paige ate as if she were alone in the booth, humming to herself.

The bells jingled on the door, and the server told whoever had walked in to sit where he pleased.

The man said, "No, thank you, ma'am. I'll only be a moment. Just looking for someone."

Paige ducked slightly, her eyes widening, visibly shrinking like a crushed squeezebox.

"What?" Brody asked.

"Shit," Paige said, pulling her stocking cap down over her eyebrows. "Shit, fuck, shit." She hunched and scooted over toward the wall of the booth, folding herself up.

Brody heard heavy footsteps approach. Behind him, the conversations at the surrounding booths momentarily quieted.

A looming figure stopped at the end of their table. Brody had to crane his neck to look all the way up at him, the top of his head nearly hitting the ceiling of the diner. He had a chiseled face with sunken cheeks, a plain slice of a lipless mouth, a set of round, bovine eyes that on anyone else would look welcoming but on this man just looked like portholes cut through a wall that peered directly into hell.

He glared at Paige, ignoring Brody entirely. "Miss Tolsky," he said, his voice as flat and hard as waste metal being dumped on stone. "What, may I ask, are you doing here?"

She wouldn't meet his eyes. "I'm just having lunch."

"In your favorite little feed bag, I see. Good thing I'm not here to kill you because all a hitter would have to do is follow you for one day and get your routines down pat." He put his massive hands on the tabletop and leaned forward.

Beneath the table, Brody slid his hand into his pocket and found his knuckleduster. He placed his fingers through the loops and fanned out his hand to allow it to slide all the way down his fingers. His fist balled around it.

The man still hadn't looked in his direction. He was leaning halfway over the table, the end of his leather tie dipping into Paige's plate of unfinished hash browns. Brody studied the man's profile; he bore a striking resemblance to the stone heads of Easter Island.

"Your mother tells me she can't make her deposit this month. And since I'm not typically in the business of slapping around old, dried-up cunts, I figured I'd pay *you* a visit instead."

Everyone in the place was now listening. All that could be heard was the golden oldies station playing "Mr. Sandman" softly from the retrofitted Wurlitzer in the far end of the room.

Brody looked at what he had at his disposal. Paige's silverware, the fork and knife. His knuckleduster ready in his pocket. His own hands and feet. The swaying length of black tie that hung from the man's neck like a flaccid, boneless tail.

"Seb, if you let me get to the shop, I'll give you everything in the register," Paige whimpered. "Please don't make a scene. I like to come here. I want to be able to come back. Please."

Seb leaned closer to her, his voice lowered into a rumbling purr. "I'll make a scene if I want to make a scene. I'll beat your ass in front of all these fucking people if I want to. Don't *tell* me what to do."

"Leave her alone," Brody said, his voice even.

The massive man shifted around so his face was mere inches from Brody. They were nearly touching noses. This wasn't anything uncommon for him, going toe-to-toe with big galoots who didn't know when to stop. The tie was now hanging directly over Brody's cup of coffee.

"Excuse me, friend. I didn't catch that." Seb turned to Paige, who was smashed completely against the wall and trembling. "Who is this dap, anyway? Your lard ass finally land a boyfriend?"

This was his opportunity. Brody grabbed the man's tie. Seb immediately had a fist ready. Still sitting, Brody ducked the punch, brought his brass knuckles out of his pocket, and delivered one strike into Seb's lantern jaw.

The vibration radiated down Brody's arm, and Seb reeled, lurching and stumbling backward a few feet from the booth, holding his bleeding mouth. He made muffled gasps behind his hand and looked entirely surprised. Not hurt, not offended, but almost appearing impressed.

Brody told Paige, "Go. Now."

She scrambled out of the booth, knocking her plate of uneaten lunch onto the floor. She stepped through the faux eggs and was out the door in a flash.

Brody stood but walked backward, facing the giant.

Seb kept his distance. His eyes flared even brighter, the lower half of his face clamped underneath his massive paw. Blood dripped off his wrist to the floor. In a strange display, Seb lowered his hand and allowed his face to bleed freely.

Brody saw this sometimes. Men who would rather bleed right there in front of him than cover it up or rub at a sore spot while he was watching. Even though it might hurt, they didn't want him to know that he had caused them any pain. Brody, too, remained where he stood, opening and closing his fist, waiting for Seb to come closer. He wouldn't go to him. He didn't *want* to go to him.

The server, from behind the safety of the counter, shouted: "Take that shit outside!"

Brody took another cautious step backward, his hands out and ready if Seb thought otherwise and decided to charge. Brody removed the knuckleduster from his hand and put it back in his coat pocket. He glanced at the server and said, "Sorry," then bolted for the door.

Outside, Paige was nowhere to be seen. Brody looked up and down the street, searching for a hat with ears sewn onto it. He picked a direction and started running to the corner, heavy blasts of steam shooting out of his mouth with every breath. He came to within a few yards of the Mama Wash storefront, but Paige wasn't heading toward it. He looked the other way and saw no one. Seb was not pursuing him.

A rusty Ford Fairlane pulled up to the curb next to him, and the passenger window shuttered down in dysfunctional, squeaking jerks. "Hey!" Paige shouted with a trembling voice from the driver's seat.

Brody didn't think twice; he clambered into the car. She got back into traffic just as the light at the intersection turned green. He looked into the passenger side mirror and saw Seb exiting the diner, still holding his face. He glanced around at the collection of cars in the parking lot and started kicking at the air. Inhuman roars, a mishmash of every curse ever uttered.

They were a few blocks away, moving quickly with luckily timed lights. Brody's heart rate was calming, and he surveyed his hand and saw red marks the knuckleduster left on his palm and fingers.

Paige had a locked hold on the wheel. Her eared hat was askew, some greasy curly hair loose and hanging in tendrils.

He regarded the inside of the car, the set of what looked like meatballs on a string hanging from the mirror, both encased in hard, clear plastic. The dashboard was covered in bumper stickers for various heavy metal bands, with images of skulls and zombies and screaming faces. Something didn't add up. "This is his car, isn't it?"

"Fucker deserves a whole lot worse than this." Even though her face still held the expression of fright, her voice was bitter with rage. She checked the mirror as if expecting Seb to sprint up and dive headlong through the back windscreen.

They stopped at a red light, noon traffic now in full swing. The car was a beater, and it made sounds of automobile indigestion when idling. The whole interior of the car vibrated when the gas wasn't pressed. Brody worried about it dying right then and there and the lummox catching up to them and crushing both of their heads with his bare hands.

"What the hell was that about? And why was it necessary to steal his car?" Brody was once again thankful that the diner didn't have scanners. No one knew he had been there. Without a doubt, the server was calling the cops and everyone on the premises would be questioned. Chiffon would be none the wiser for the time being. He lit a cigarette with shaking hands, slid down on the cracked vinyl seat, and exhaled clouds of gray. "Jesus Christ."

"He owns the storefront me and Mom rent. He owes money all over town, and he pays off his own debts by *adjusting* our rent whenever he feels like it. The guy is a piece of shit." Paige stopped at a red light and let go of the wheel to get the phone out of her pocket. "Excuse me a minute," she said and dialed.

Paige started breaking down as she recounted the events to her mother in Russian. From what Brody could make out, she told her mother to close and lock the front doors immediately and get back to their apartment.

"Do it! He's probably on his way there now!" Paige exclaimed in English. She hung up and sobbed.

The light turned green, and the traffic ahead of them moved along. Someone honked behind her, and she screamed and floored the gas, lurching them forward and nearly giving Brody whiplash.

"Where are we going?" Brody asked. *00:19:59.* "I don't think I want to be trolling around Chicago in a stolen car."

"I don't know. I don't know," Paige squealed, turning right and cutting someone off. They honked. She shrieked again and stomped the accelerator. When the traffic stopped at another red light, she had to slam the brake to prevent them from rear-ending the car ahead.

Brody lost his patience when his forehead nearly bounced off the bumper-stickered dashboard. "That's it. Next chance you get, pull over. I'm driving."

"I'm so sorry," Paige said. Her tough-cookie bravado was gone. She was a sobbing wreck. Her face was redder than when she had first walked out of the back room of the steamy dry cleaner's, a line of drool hanging off her crimson bottom lip, her eyes bloodshot.

Brody pointed at a 7-Eleven. "Stop here."

11

Paige parked crookedly in a space in front of the convenience store, and as soon as the car was shifted into park, she completely crumbled. She held the wheel and dropped her head down so far her forehead touched the soft pad in the middle of the wheel. Her teddy bear hat slid off her head onto the gritty floorboard.

Brody picked it up and dusted it off, placed it on the seat between them. He looked around for possible on-lookers, anyone in the windows of the store giving him the stink eye. People would immediately assume he just broke up with her or slept with her sister. He dropped his cigarette out the window and closed it. The vacuum resealed, and he felt like he was inside a coffin with a crying woman, her noise unfiltered by the urban racket outside. He let her get it out, but all the while he wanted her to switch places with him so they could get the hell out of the city.

This was nothing new to him. More often than not, when he met a battered woman at the community center and she told him about all the times her boyfriend had beat her and the reasons he did it, which never seemed to Brody like valid excuses to hit anyone, she'd fall apart into a sobbing mess. He wondered if it was the simple act of purging what they had been carrying around with them that brought it on. He considered maybe it was simply revisiting times when someone had gotten violent with them.

Either way, it made Brody's blood boil to see Paige, whom he had already come to know as a strong woman, undeniably shaken to the core. It was obvious that the giant at the diner had done far worse than verbally intimidate her in public. The abrasive way she had about her was an indication of that and how she regarded Brody when they first met. A woman who had experienced violence looked at every man like just another possible deliverer of black eyes. For a moment, he thought of Marcy and how she would probably adopt that shell soon.

Finally after her sobbing had quieted, Brody asked, "Are you okay?" He considered putting a hand on her shoulder but decided against it.

It took her nearly a full minute to say she was all right. She sat up and wiped at the corners of her eyes with her index finger. Her face was swollen, her eyes puffy, and her bottom lip still had the occasional quiver to it.

He looked away; he couldn't bear it.

"This has never happened before. Normally he comes into the shop and yells and maybe punches the wall, and we go to the safe and pay him. I've never"—she chuckled—"stolen his fuckin' *car* before. Where are we going to go?"

00:14:59.

"I know a place," Brody said and opened his door. She moved over into the passenger seat without getting out, and he slid behind the wheel. He started the car and got back on the road. They'd have to pull over shortly after leaving the city limits so he could take out his lenses and put his sonar on, but there was no way he was going to let her drive until then. His neck was still sore.

The edges of Brody's vision were beginning to cloud when they reached the farmlands. He pulled the beige Fairlane to the shoulder, nearly dipping into the ditch. They had ridden in silence up to that point, and when Paige asked why they were stopping, her voice was still racked from crying.

He flipped down the sun visor, and a pile of Seb's parking tickets fell into his lap. He tossed them into the backseat and opened the mirror and got a look at himself with his failing vision. He appeared blurry, his reflection obscured with patches of shadows. He removed the lens charger from his pocket and took out one lens, then the other.

"You must be rich," Paige commented.

He looked over at her with one eye completely blind and the other overcast as if thunderheads had rolled into the interior of the car with them.

"Those things aren't cheap."

"They were a favor from an optometrist friend of mine," he said and removed the second lens and put it into the case, operating by touch alone.

"So, you're completely blind without them?" Paige asked.

He got out of the car, slapped the sonar to his forehead. He leaned into the open door, showing her the silver dollar–sized not-quite-flesh tone disk stuck to his forehead. "Not entirely. But you have to drive. That is, unless you don't mind riding with the windshield broken out."

She moved into the driver's seat. She was calm enough now to be trusted with the car.

Brody went around to the passenger side, and with the final ping before he opened the door, he detected a quick flash behind him, what appeared to be a crudely mapped skeleton just out of range. He turned and there was the pack of Artificial crop pickers slowly approaching with smooth, effortless strides. He looked down and saw that he had a foot on the loose, crumbly soil of someone's property. He apologized but it did no good. They continued moving toward him. He climbed into the passenger seat quickly and they were off. The knot they could easily fold his limbs into made him shiver.

His pack of cigarettes was feeling light, but still he fished one out and lit it. He might have to take an involuntary hiatus from the bad habit if things continued like this, being broke all the time. He felt around the interior of the car with the sonar, cocking his head this way and that even though it was kind of unnecessary. He waved a cloud of smoke away, since the sonar didn't really know what to make of it—just a swirl of cubes. It was hard to process, and other things around it lost resolution with having to reallocate processing power.

He rolled down the window a crack, and the visage of the Fairlane's interior immediately improved. He could see nothing beyond the inside of the windshield. He could see Paige—in a stack of wire-frame cubes and polygons—with both hands on the wheel and driving with her back held straight, not even touching the seat. Brody switched on the radio to occupy the space, which to him felt claustrophobic and dead.

"So we're going to Thorp's place?" she asked.

"Yeah, do you know the way?"

"She took me out here a couple of times. Mostly when she needed to borrow money and brought me along for moral support. Me and him don't really get along that well, but it was good to see that she had family she could turn to—even if he is kind of a screwball."

"He means well," Brody said, getting comfortable and pulling the tail of his peacoat out from under him. "And I hope you're right, that Nectar's just out finding herself and all this worry Thorp is going through is simply paranoia."

"You went to Fort Reagan then, I take it?"

"Yeah, no dice. She never enlisted."

"Well, that's good." Paige chuckled. "Don't tell Thorp I said that. Actually, he'd probably agree with me, but he's kind of flip-floppy about the whole Marines thing."

"Army," Brody corrected.

"Oh, right. Army. Sorry."

A beat passed where the sweet melodies of some ancient opera song played through the terrible speakers.

She continued, "You and him met in the military?"

"Yeah, during orientation."

"Was he always so . . . ?" She twisted a finger at her temple. "I'm sorry. I shouldn't talk about him like that, you guys being friends and all."

"No," Brody said. "About him being that way, I mean. He wasn't like that before. We went through some stuff over there, and he hasn't really been quite right since. He took it pretty hard."

"Did he throw the pin and drop the grenade or something?" Paige smirked.

Brody decided to be direct since he didn't appreciate her attitude. "He shot a kid."

"Jesus." She stifled a gasp. "I'm really sorry. I had no idea. Oh, my God. Was it an accident or . . . ? How did it happen?"

"The kid was a soldier. They train them young over there. We were just keeping the general order. We had gotten a call about a man who was caught in a bear trap. We thought it was a joke, another platoon playing a prank on us. We went anyway and saw just that. We pried the trap open and saw that his arm was fake. We knew it was an ambush. There was a kid at the end of the alley with an assault rifle."

"Why would they do that to a kid?" she asked, aghast.

"It'd be a simple flush on us. They never wanted us there, anyway." Brody took a moment to draw in a deep breath. "I hesitated; Thorp fired."

"Did the kid die?"

"Not right away. After we had the whole situation under control, we took him with us back to base and got him to the infirmary. Thorp never left his side. Just sat there and watched the kid take one breath after another. He didn't eat or talk or go for drills— even when our commanding officer told him he'd be brought up on insubordination charges. He refused to move, like he was rooted in that seat. He stayed until a week later when the kid's heart gave out and he died." It was all in Brody's mind every hour of every day, and speaking it aloud felt dreamlike in its ease.

"I feel really bad for treating Thorp like I did," Paige said after a moment. "I used to give him all kinds of shit when he wouldn't let Nectar borrow any money, especially since he's sitting on a gold mine."

Brody had nothing else to say. He listened to the half second of silence between songs on the radio, hoping the next one would be a little more optimistic.

12

They turned into Thorp's gravel driveway and parked beside the house. Brody stepped out and his sonar spread over the property. Not only could he see Thorp riding up on a horse; he could hear the gritty clip-clop of its hoofs on gravel.

Thorp's face was twisted into confusion. He reined the horse to stop a few yards from the stolen car. "Where did you get that thing?" He turned as the driver's side door opened and Paige got out. The map of Thorp's face morphed into a mix of anger and bitterness. He slid off the horse and held on to its lead, keeping his distance from both the car and Paige. He turned to Brody. "What's she do-ing here?" he asked, not even trying to mask his distaste for her.

"We got into some hot water," Brody started and stopped himself. "It's a long story, and it's kind of pointless to even attempt to explain."

Paige stood in the open door of the car, remaining behind it like a shield. She looked at Thorp with newfound sympathy written on her face. "Hi, Thorp."

He ignored her and came closer to Brody, the horse moving forward as well. "Does she know where Nectar is? Is she pulling something with you? Because she's *not* trustworthy."

"Stop," Brody pleaded. "Relax, okay? She thinks Nectar just left town for a while to do some soul-searching."

"You know where she is," Thorp shouted.

At first, Brody thought he was yelling at him. But then he noticed Paige flinch. Brody stepped between them. "Come on. Relax. She's on our side."

Thorp sighed. "I'm going to put Maribel back in the barn."

Watching him go, Brody could tell by the way he walked—his gait almost taking on a stomping quality— and how he shook his head as he guided the horse away that Thorp had a lot more to say.

When he was out of earshot, Paige groaned. "He hates me. He thinks Nectar gets her wanderlust from me."

"Let's just go inside," Brody said, not wanting to hear any more of it.

Paige collapsed onto the living room couch and turned on the screen as if she owned the place.

Brody went into the kitchen. The table was full of

electronic parts, circuit boards, spools of wire, and a soldering gun. Thorp had been an avid amateur electrician and general tinkerer in the service, but he didn't think the pastime would've made it out on the other side with him. He wondered if the compulsive hobby had developed before Thorp enlisted.

He let the sonar probe around the refrigerator. Mapped on all the glass shelves were several bowls with tinfoil over them. He picked one at random and lifted the corner to see what was inside. Food, with the sonar, looked the same. A bowl of olives could just as easily be tiny robin's eggs or what was hanging from the rearview mirror of Seb's car. He grabbed one of the tiny round spheres out of the bowl and squeezed it gently. It was soft, wet. He gave it an inspective sniff. Olives. He ate one and then took the bowl out of the fridge and bumped the door shut with his hip. He hadn't eaten since breakfast, and it was nearly two in the afternoon. He picked at the olives one by one.

Rubber boots stomped on the back deck, the sliding glass door opened, and Thorp entered smelling of manure and soldering.

"Trying to find a way to steal cable?" Brody nodded toward the table covered in electronics.

"Actually, I was thinking about something. Can I see that lens charger of yours?"

Brody set the bowl of olives aside. "It needs batteries. There's no way you can do the right charge with some jerry-rigged RadioShack parts."

"Come on." The colorless plane of Thorp's face folded into a grin, and he gestured invitingly by sweeping his hand toward himself. "Let me see it."

Brody took the lens charger from his pocket and held it out. Thorp gripped it, but Brody didn't release it until after he had said, "You break this thing, it's your ass. You're my friend and I love you like a brother, but if you fuck it up—I will be *seriously* pissed."

"I won't break nothing. Calm down." Thorp went to work at the table.

Noises from a television show in the next room found their way into the kitchen. Paige.

Brody saw Thorp stiffen. Before Thorp could shoot to his feet, Brody moved forward, essentially trapping him in his chair at the table. Brody was close enough that the sonar was able to scribble in more details upon Thorp's face. Enough to detect him mouthing the words: "Is *she* in there?"

Brody nodded.

Thorp put the soldering gun back in its holder before it had even begun to warm up. He gestured at the cellar door next to the refrigerator and started tromping down the creaky wooden steps. Brody followed reluctantly.

Down in the basement, Brody felt the urge to duck every few steps. Thatches of insulation hung from the open floorboards above in thick, pillowy fingers.

Thorp guided him past the laundry area, then into another room through which Thorp had to use a key.

Momentarily, Brody thought about the possibility that Nectar was in there, locked in her brother's basement, gagged and bound to a chair. He banished the disparaging thoughts of his friend and followed him into the next room. The walls, the floor, and the ceiling were brick. As the sonar felt along the walls, he began to see the shapes of guns hanging from Peg-Board coming into focus. At the back wall, a large gun safe the size of a refrigerator. A worktable and a setup for molding metal into bullets.

The smell of gunpowder, striking his nose with the pungent ferocity of sulfur, made Brody a little uneasy. He hadn't smelled gunpowder since the service, hadn't held a gun since the service, hadn't even been in the same room as a gun since the service. Minneapolis-St. Paul police had cracked down on firearms, and it seemed they were the only folks allowed to carry one. Maybe Illinois laws were different, but Thorp's armory was in his basement behind a locked door so he guessed not. At the same time, he didn't find the contents of the secret room much of a surprise, given how Thorp had decided to decorate his backyard.

Thorp closed the door behind them and spoke again at a normal volume. "Paige can't hear us in here," he reassured him as if Brody, too, had been worrying about such a thing. He stepped over to the workbench where a disassembled assault rifle was spread out in ten different pieces.

Brody remembered that sight. Drills by the ever-ticking stopwatch, taking the rifle apart, putting it back together, cleaning it, and basically treating it as an extension of the soldier's body. Brody knew that once some lessons, sights, experiences, teachings were in a person, branded onto their minds, they never went away. They could be set aside, boxed away, but they still quietly took up space in whatever attic or basement they were stowed. Like riding a bike.

"You seriously don't have to worry about her," Brody said.

"How do you know? Maybe she wanted to come here so she could get information on me or find out *exactly* how much I get from Hark every month. Yeah? Ever consider *that*? If we want to find Nectar, we have to think outside the box and consider every possible lead a death trap. That's all anyone wants anymore: money. By the end of the night, I guarantee she'll be telling us she has Nectar strapped with a bomb somewhere and unless we pay her *x* amount of money—"

"Let me explain," Brody interrupted. "She's here right now because we stole some asshole's car that was threatening her. It wasn't even her idea to come with me. We just sort of paired up and headed this way."

"Why didn't you call and ask me? I could've told you she was up to no good. She's a fucking *schemer*, man. You can tell just by looking at her. That ridiculous hat, the mittens. She's trying to put shit in your head. Make you think of her as some wayward kid with an abusive boyfriend. All those charity cases have really dulled your soldier's intuition."

"That's good because you know what? I'm not a soldier anymore and neither are you. You can't go around thinking everyone's up to no good."

"And you can trust her? The girl with the stolen car?"

"If you saw her after that asshole talked to her the way he did, you'd know she was trustworthy. For my sake, please calm down. Leave the people reading to me, okay? I do shit like this all the time. I can tell when someone's trying to pull a fast one."

Thorp put his hands on his hips and sighed for what felt like a full minute, really pushing every ounce of air out of his lungs. He let his hands slap at his sides. "Okay, fine. I trust you."

"Good. Thank you. Jesus."

But without a moment's peace, Thorp asked, "So, what do we know so far?"

While drawing a deep breath, Brody organized his thoughts. "Well, I think Paige has a key to Nectar's apartment, but she wasn't going to cough it up when we first met. Now I think she'll be more inclined to let me have it. Of course, we should consider the fact that she may be right."

"No," Thorp said thoughtfully, rubbing the stubble on his chin. "I don't think she's out of town."

Brody groaned. "Give it a minute, okay? She's a searcher, apparently. You can agree with that, can't you? You know your sister. Paige says Nectar's always trying to find the next thing to get into, fashion or lifestyle or career or whatever. Think about it. Doesn't this seem kind of routine?"

"She hasn't been that way for as long as I can remember," Thorp said.

"Before Nectar talked to you about enlisting, when was the last time you spoke with her?"

Thorp didn't respond right away. This told Brody it hadn't been only a couple of days or weeks. "Last summer. August, maybe. She came by to ask for some money."

"And what do you suppose that money was *for*?"

Brody said leadingly. He continued when Thorp didn't pick up on the tone. "She was probably going to go out of town for a while. Give it a few days. I need to get back to Minneapolis anyway."

"You're going to leave?" Thorp took a step forward.

"I have to. I need to check in with my probation officer and complete my community service *sometime* before I die." He winked. "Otherwise they make you work it off in the afterlife, sweeping God's floors and doing St. Peter's laundry." He tried to bring some joviality into the air, but he knew it wasn't working.

Thorp came closer, his breath rife with the last meal he'd eaten. "We have a lead now. You can get the key from Paige and check out Nectar's apartment. This is what you do, isn't it? The problem-solver man? The gumshoe Sherlock Holmes thing?" He gripped the lapels of Brody's coat.

Brody put his hands on Thorp's and gently peeled them off. Brody looked into his friend's eyes, which to him appeared to be colorless spheres swiveling around in their sockets. But he could still clearly see the desperation in Thorp's mug. "Do you really want me to check out your sister's apartment?" he said with weighty reluctance, trying to make it sound like a ridiculous request.

Thorp's face softened, a certain plunging relief coming across his forehead and laugh lines. "If you would, please, yeah. That'd be great. Even if you just find ticket stubs or something, at least then I'll know for sure."

"Maybe you can come with me this time?" Brody

suggested. Perhaps if Thorp was there to see for himself what Brody thought he would inevitably find—the plane tickets, the reservation of a rental yurt at some Iowa commune—he'd be less prone to fly off the handle with a barrage of questions.

But the suggestion was barely past his lips before Thorp got an exaggerated look of panic on his face. Standing this close, the sonar could see Thorp's eyes widen into saucers.

"Actually, I don't think that's such a good idea. I mean, I'd like to go with you and see . . . that you're right, that everything's fine—because I'm sure you're right—but I got a lot of stuff to do around here." He broke eye contact and stared into the middle distance. "I should stay here. Hold down the fort." Nod. Nod. "Yeah, I think I'll just stay here."

"Maybe some time away from here would be just what the doctor ordered," Brody went on, careful not to gesture at any of the guns hanging from the walls around them. "It'd be good to have two sets of eyes when we're looking around her place. It'd get done faster."

A strange chuckle escaped Thorp's throat. It had a hitch in it, like the laugh itself was stumbling and fighting to retain balance in its convincingness. "No, no, that's quite all right. I'm fine here. You go. Yeah. I'll . . . I'd be better here. I won't get in the way here."

Brody decided it would be fruitless to press it any further. "Okay. Your call. And when I find the receipt from the airline, you'll let me go home?"

"Yeah, yeah," Thorp waved a hand at him. "You make it sound like I have you chained to the radiator or something. But if you find out for sure where she's gone, I'll be happy and leave you alone. I'll calm down. I promise."

"All right," Brody said with finality. "Let's go upstairs and see what you can do with this lens charger theory you're cooking up and I'll talk to Paige about that key."

They exited the basement armory. Brody was relieved. Being around those guns and ammunition made him feel like at any moment his old drill instructor was going to burst out of the woodwork and order him to get down and give him thirty.

13

The afternoon brought colder winds, more promise of snow-storms peeling across the Great Lakes with their eye set firmly on Illinois. Up to this point, the general mood of the house had been uncomfortable, but when Brody looked outside and saw the road was rapidly being blanketed in snow and not even the fields across the way could be seen through the onslaught of flakes, he asked Thorp how often plows came through here. Thorp just laughed.

When Thorp headed outside to the roof to make sure snow wasn't collecting around a section of shingles he claimed to already be in sorry shape, Brody took the time alone with Paige to ask if she'd be all right with bunking down here for the night. She agreed, and when her gaze flicked to the front window, Brody estimated she was considering the risk of driving back or surrendering to spending the night and sleeping in the car.

He offered her the bedroom he was using. She seemed reluctant but took him up on it and went upstairs.

For the remainder of the night, it was quiet. He kept Thorp's ordi off and listened as Thorp moved the aluminum ladder from one part of the house to another. He heard Thorp struggle up the ladder and the careful scrape of a shovel on shingle. Despite not wanting to be out in the cold any more than he already had been today, Brody went outside to see if Thorp needed any assistance checking the roof's weak spots.

Silhouetted against an overcast evening sky, painted there on his two-story stage, Thorp seemingly took clumps of snow at random and flung them from the roof. It was like watching a squirrel overturning clumps of dead leaves in a patient search of hidden caches only he could find.

"We're going to stay the night," Brody shouted to his friend. He hoped using the word *we* would avoid any aggression toward Paige.

Thorp stopped his strange dance of launching *this* snow pile, then *this* snow pile. He leaned on the handle of the shovel and peered down over the gutters at Brody. "Okay. Where is she going to . . . ?"

"I gave her my room."

"But what about you?"

"I can take the couch. No big deal."

"Did you want dinner or anything?"

"I'm all right. You need help up there?"

Thorp looked over his shoulder. "No," he said, drawing the word out, "I think I got the big spots. Gonna go around to the other side in a minute and check over there."

"Well, I'm going back inside. Just stomp or something if you change your mind, okay?"

Thorp smiled, nodded. "I got it under control. I go through this every year."

Brody waved at Thorp and went inside, brushing the snow from his shoulders and hair. He flopped down on the couch and lifted the lid on Thorp's ordi. He craved a separation, a mind-numbing sitcom to jam a wedge between the day's events and what he hoped could be a restful night's sleep.

Unable to see anything on the monitor, he used voice commands to start the video streaming app. He found himself not paying attention to the show. He had to rewind it three times to catch a punch line, and even when he understood the joke, he didn't laugh. Soon he just stared at the screen that appeared blank to him, pretending he could see the people talk and fling one-liners at one another, not even attempting to comprehend what was going on. Laugh track, segment bumper, ad for toothpaste, more unfunny obvious setups and bad punch lines. Still, it was better than silence.

When sleep started to creep in, he rolled over and his elbow collided with something beneath him. He stuck his hand down into the crumb-filled recesses of the couch, and it glanced across the bothersome object and froze when the message of what his finger-tips were feeling made it to his brain. He withdrew the cylinder, the wire coming uncoiled from around it and the plug landing on his chest.

Brody held it before him and ran his fingers across it. Just a piece of heavy-duty plastic, with a roughened exterior for easy handling, a plug on one end for a USB connection, and a place where a hard drive could be unscrewed and slid out.

He wondered where his cylinder was. Dropped into a drawer in some unmarked building, the repository for every recorded second of warfare. He wondered if it picked up all sounds or just that of gunfire. On the far end of the cylinder was the microphone, safely fenced in behind a thick layer of metal mesh. Would his voice be on his? He imagined what it might sound like ten years ago, if it would be higher than it is now, a few thousand cigarettes ago. If his screams sounded afraid and cracked . . . or if he hadn't screamed at all. He couldn't remember if he had. He remembered pain, heat, and other sensations, but he would never know for sure without going over his own cylinder's contents.

Brody aimed the cylinder so the narrow end was pointed down and shoved it back into the couch. He kept pushing until it was successfully buried, where there were only crumbs and shadows. Where it belonged.

In the morning, Brody showered in the downstairs bathroom, got dressed in his slacks and white button-down shirt, and while getting his tie straight, headed upstairs to see if Paige was ready to leave. He knocked, then eased the door open. The sheets had the form of a body pressed into them, and the pillow was dented.

He went downstairs and stepped outside to ensure she hadn't taken the Fairlane back to the city without him. The sonar found the car, painting it onto the black landscape before him as its rudimentary shape, and then found Paige on the front porch swing, smoking a cigarette, her legs pulled up to her chest.

"Thought I'd ditch you?" she asked.

"Honestly, I wouldn't have blamed you if you had."

She sniffed, a tiny laugh that didn't say if she agreed or disagreed.

Brody stepped closer to her, his boots knocking on the planks of the porch. He leaned on the railing and studied every blade of grass tall enough to stand above the snow that'd fallen through the night. Beyond the road, the automated farming equipment was back to work. The seeder made its pounding rounds slowly around the field, leaving a cloud of carbon in its wake and seeds shot into the earth that would wait out the winter and germinate when they were good and ready come spring. Arties followed to make sure all was going to their owner's specifications.

"Do you have somewhere to go that'll be safe?" It was a question he had asked countless times to many, many other women. It was a collection of words that came out of his mouth with such frequency that it may have been as mundane as saying hello or good morning.

"Seb doesn't know where Mom and I live." Paige brought the cigarette to her lips, took a quick drag, and let it go without inhaling. It drifted away from her mouth quickly, scattered by the cold wind. "I'll go back to the apartment, wait it out a couple of days until he cools off. We'll pay him like we always do, apologize, and maybe give him extra to forget about what happened at the diner," she said as if she regretted Brody doing what he did, that she would've preferred to take the beating from Seb.

Brody felt a minor jolt of anger tighten in his chest but let it go by way of concentrating on the roaming seeder machine. He had to choose his words carefully around her. He still wanted something out of her that in all likelihood she wouldn't give up easily. *Tact*, Brody reminded himself. *Forget the anger.*

Nathan's voice and the advice it had imparted to him the last time they had a little chat came to him. "I think you should call the police," Brody said. "Seb isn't going to lose interest in money if he knows he can get it out of you with the use of a few choice words. He'll keep going to that vein as long as it consistently pays out."

"I know. Eventually he might say the wrong thing to the wrong guy at the wrong bar, and he'll get his. But guys like him rarely ever get their due when they should. Odds are, he'll end up living forever."

"Do you have a key to Nectar's apartment?" he asked again. From what Paige had just said about Seb, he figured now was the time to strike. It felt kind of low doing it when she was vulnerable, but he wanted her to consider that her friend could be in trouble. And if so, she should cough up the keys so her newfound protector could snoop.

"Yeah," Paige said, making no motion to reach into her pocket for her key ring.

"Do you think I could borrow it?"

Paige leaned forward to glance in the front window of the house. She lowered her voice. "Something's weird with Thorp. You should go home, put his number on your block list, and forget about it. With him, it'll just be something else next week. He's out here with all those things in the backyard . . . I mean, it's so obvious that . . . Look, I know he's troubled and I'm not making fun of him, but this is going to turn ugly—for you too—long before it gets better. Of course, that's just how I feel about the whole thing." She shrugged, eyes closed. "I don't know. I'm in a weird mood today."

"Listen. I'm not going to steal anything or go through her underwear drawer. I just want to see if there's an airline stub or something." Brody lowered his voice as well. "If I find something like that, Thorp will lay off and I can go home with a clear conscience."

"So you don't really care where Nectar is?" Paige sneered. "You're only doing this as a favor to your war buddy because he saved your life?"

"No, I *do* care where she is. But I'm like you. I don't think she disappeared or anything. As soon as I can convince *him* that, the sooner this will be over and we can all move on with our lives."

Paige leaned to one side and wedged a hand down her jeans pocket and pulled out a large, jangling collection of keys. She found a square brass key and rotated the ring until it came free. She held it by the very end, extending it toward Brody.

He took it, looked at it, seeing Nectar's apartment number stamped onto one side. He removed his own keys, which were minimal in comparison to Paige's collection, and slid it onto his key ring. "This will get me not only into her apartment but through the front door?"

Paige nodded, pulling her legs back up to her chest.

He felt a strange stirring. The key was progress, sure, but at what cost? Another step into Thorp's rabbit hole, another cinch tighter around his neck that would never let up until he knew the truth and everything was put back in its appropriate place, resolved.

Brody stuffed his hands into the pockets of his peacoat. It was overcast and it felt like snow, even more than it had this morning. "Do you need to get home?"

"I should to check on Mom."

"I'll give you a ride," Brody said, turning on his heel. "Just a minute, okay?"

Paige lit another cigarette and said with surprising levity, "Take your time."

Brody searched the house and found Thorp wasn't upstairs, on the ground floor, or in the basement. The kitchen table was still cluttered, but it had fewer pieces of random electronics on it. He went out the sliding glass door, through the collection of decommissioned military vehicles, and out to the barn.

As he crossed the backyard, a gust of wind tore by, the promise of impending snow even more evident. But it wasn't a chill that drove a frigid finger trailing up his spine, just a general vibe of something malevolent. He actually stopped in his tracks and turned around and glanced over his shoulder. The vehicles all stood with their broken glass, hanging-open doors, dangling straps, buckles clinking. He continued the rest of the way to the barn, ignoring the unsettled feeling.

Inside, the warm, dusty stink of animal and hay overwhelmed Brody, causing him to stifle a cough. The particles of dust in the air could be seen drifting in the glow of the hanging overhead lights. He took a second to look at the horses, mapped in crude polygons like an early video game. Of the four stalls, only two had horses in them. The remaining stalls were piled to the ceiling with electronic junk, old appliances with faux wood-grain housings, the green-on-black primordial examples of digital displays, analog dials, bulky monitors of the cathode ray tubes variety, and a heap of circuit boards corralled by miles of spooled wire. Some things he recognized from the service, but a vast majority of it he did not.

He got to the back area where a rustic workbench assembled from two sawhorses and a plank of stained plywood was set up near a collection of stable-clearing shovels and spools of thick rope and chain. Seeing the stockpile of gizmos in such close proximity to the farm tools was a strange contrast, even for Thorp. Brody got a glimpse of his friend's mind here, the way Thorp sorted things, how *all* tools belonged together regardless of their intended use.

Thorp stood next to a machine the size of a freezer chest, repeatedly kicking down an L-shaped lever jutting out from its side. With each kick, the machine lit up temporarily and then darkened, giving off a cough of tiredness. Thorp noticed Brody standing in the doorway and stopped.

Brody spotted his lens charger atop the machine, a new wire hanging out of the side. It was plugged into the face of the large machine that he now realized was a generator. "A kick-start gas genny? Haven't seen one of those in a while."

Thorp stood doubled over at the waist, catching his breath and glaring at the uncooperative machine, the dials of which were dark again. "No outlets in the house and there's no way to wire your lens charger to the main wiring since the electric company has to set up any appliances, even in a farmstead. So this is the best option we have for a nonapproved electronic device."

He kicked the bar, his boot slipped, and the foot pad of the bar sprang back up, in what Brody thought looked like retaliation, and caught him on the shin. Thorp cursed and gripped his skinned leg. Without a moment's hesitation, he kicked the bar down again and again, now with more ferocity driven by annoyance. Each time the generator gave a series of clicks, a whirring as if it were attempting to hold the charge, then slowly it would fade out again and the lights on its face would die once more. Thorp kicked the generator hard on its side, nearly overturning the hundred-pound machine. "Goddamn thing."

Brody removed his coat. "Let me try."

They took turns trying to kick-start the generator. When Brody had broken a sweat, he stopped and let Thorp take over. The two men worked, the cold air rushing in through the open doors, for half an hour before Paige appeared behind them. She leaned over the stall door and petted one of the horse's snouts.

Brody wanted to drive back to Chicago, but he couldn't without his lenses. When Thorp was too out of breath to continue, Brody gripped one of the support beams along the wall, jammed his boot down again and again. The generator looked like it considered turning over but refused.

Finally, when Thorp's turn came, it started with a puff of black exhaust, then a distinct rumble from its engine. The generator vibrated, Brody's lens charger kicking around on top, tethered in place only by its newly grafted-on cord. Thorp opened one of the windows to allow the exhaust out and looked at the generator proudly.

Over the noise, Brody hadn't heard Paige step close to him. She tugged at the elbow of his shirt, and when he turned to her, she had her hand cupped next to his ear. Her breath was hot and moist. "When do you think we can get out of here?"

"Soon," Brody whispered.

Paige, seemingly satisfied with the answer, strolled away to the stalls to pet the horses again.

The lens charger beeped twice, indicative that Thorp's electronic wizardry was a success.

Thorp pulled the plug on the lens charger and wrapped it around the device and presented it to Brody like someone who was displaying a diamond he had cracked out of coal by sheer will alone.

"How much time do you suppose I'll get out of them?"

Thorp shrugged. "Hard to say. Didn't want to overdo it and cook the resistors. You'll just have to put them in and find out, I guess."

"Good work, handyman." Brody clapped his friend on the shoulder.

Handyman. *Handyman.*

Handyman had been Thorp's nickname in the service, and no one had called him it since. Thorp watched Brody walk through the front door of the barn with Paige, glad he could be of help. Up until then, Thorp felt like a helpless idiot who was just hampering his friend. But helping Brody see in color again gave him a surge of self-assurance. It was good to use his hands, to get out of the house and away from his thoughts.

As he took a seat on the still-warm grille of the generator, he couldn't help but notice the crashed Darter in his backyard—and all of it came flooding back, ripping the temporary pride away.

14

Stepping out of the upstairs bathroom, Brody saw the world coming
into focus. He waited for the charge
indicator to come on, and when it did
he was pleasantly surprised that it read
any charge at all. *04:59:59*. It would be more
than enough time to drive into Chicago, drop
off Paige, head to Nectar's apartment, and
get back. He decided to keep Seb's car for
the time being and dispose of it at the
train station parking lot when he went
to catch the train home later that day.

As he tromped down the stairs, he
realized he felt calmer in Thorp's farmhouse,
but there was something to living with
Thorp that he couldn't deny: a certain
contagious mistrust. Whenever he got

a spare moment to himself, he mulled over the idea of Nectar being held hostage somewhere, a car battery hooked up to her. Weeks of endless torture. It was getting harder and harder to shake those images from his head. He displaced the undesirable delusions with the fantasy that when he entered her apartment, she'd be sitting on her couch wondering who the hell he was. With relief, he'd explain the whole zany story, sweeping Thorp's suspicions cleanly aside.

In the car heading back to Chicago, Paige was quiet. They had the radio tuned to a talk show. The topic was the new liposuction clinic that recently opened at the Mall of America. Paige turned it to her favorite station, suggesting that even Brody might like it since they played what she *called* modern rock. To Brody, it was all distorted noises and screaming, but it was better than what they had been listening to so he made no argument.

The song ended, and after the station identification a news brief came on, detailing more about the massacre. The newscaster referred to the killer as Alton Noel, ex-Marine. They were going to release the names of the murder victims, and before the first one could be uttered, Paige switched off the radio.

After a few minutes and further silence between them, Brody glanced over at Paige. She was selecting names from her contact list on her cell and deleting them.

"Don't you need those?"

"Not if you don't talk to them anymore. I don't really keep up with people much. I might exchange numbers with some guy or girl and go see a show with them.

After a while, I'll give them a ring and maybe they won't answer or they'll say they have plans—pretty much telling me they think I'm boring. Most people will keep the numbers, just in case they're throwing a party. Me? That's it. I erase them. Good-bye. Have a nice life, dick."

"I see," Brody said. The road returned to pavement, and the farms began to thin out in favor of new neighborhoods and the odd gas station and greasy spoon.

"Here I am, going down my list and who do I come to? Nectar. After all this with you and Thorp and I don't even get to *see* her? And on top of that, she won't even know I was worried about her. She'll come back with her head shaved and talking in a British accent none the wiser of what kind of disturbance she's had on *your* life. No, I'm deleting her. Fuck it. And her keys? You keep them and give them back to her when you find her."

"Okay."

"With Nectar—it's so fucking irritating. She's a cool chick and has a good head on her shoulders, but she doesn't *get* it. She lets people tell her whatever they think is the undeniable truth, and she goes along with it until she gets bored. And then I have to hear about how Mateusz said this or Abby said that."

"Those friends of hers? Happen to know their last names?" Brody asked.

"No, I mean, when she talks about them it's a flurry of stories, and I only remember the names she mentioned the most. Abby is apparently Nectar's new role model, and Mateusz is just some guy, one of her various maybe-boyfriends. I didn't really want to know so I didn't ask. I'd be surprised if even she knew his last name or *any* of their last names." Paige glared out the window as they entered Chicago's city limits.

Brody made a mental note: *Mateusz. Abby.* He wanted to ask Paige more but figured she had reached her limit. If Nectar had a boyfriend or any close friends worth looking into, there'd be evidence of them at her apartment—phone numbers, dates to meet up scribbled onto a calendar somewhere, something.

They drove in silence for a while, the road rumbling under the battered Fairlane's wheels.

Paige smirked to herself and said, "Nectar's a little strange, but for the most part, she's really sweet. Kind of a mischievous monkey at times. She kind of moves imperceptibly between the two. She's just as likely to bring you soup when you're feeling like shit as put death kisses on your favorite shirt for shits and giggles."

"Death kisses?"

"You never did that to someone when you were younger? You take a drag from a cigarette and find some piece of your friend's clothes, right? Preferably something white. Then you blow the smoke through the material, and it leaves this nasty yellow stain. A kiss from death. It washes out, but it's kind of like putting a hickey on someone's clothes."

"And what's the point?"

"It means you have a secret for that person. At least that's why she does it. Look." Paige pulled down the collar of her coat.

There, faintly, was a small oily yellow smudge in the oblong shape of a pair of puckered lips. Nectar's lips. A death kiss from Nectar's lips. Brody felt as if

he had just been presented with cemented proof that
ghosts existed.

They turned the corner and passed the railcar
diner, made another corner, and arrived at the curb in
front of Mama Wash.

Paige stared out of the passenger window for a few
moments at her mother's business. The windows were
foggy with steam, but there were no shadows beyond.
The sign hanging on the door read Closed, but Paige
informed him they often forgot to flip it when they were
open so apparently it didn't mean much. She asked
Brody to wait and she got out before he could refuse.
She went to the front door and tugged. It was locked.

She came back to the car and leaned down in the
open door. She smiled. "All right, well, I'm going to
head in to work on some stuff that I should've gotten
done before all this fun and adventure."

"Are you sure you don't want me to take you to
your apartment?" Brody asked, hands on the wheel.

"Yeah. Mom won't be coming in today, not after a
scare like yesterday, so I'll have to finish our orders for
tomorrow. Got to keep the customers happy, right?" Paige
smiled again, but both times seemed forced. The waver in
her voice had returned. She was scared, but he'd learned
there was no changing her mind on anything.

02:59:59 blinked, prodding him.

It would be dark soon, and already tiny flakes were
falling, soft and small as pinched tufts of sparrow
down. Despite all that, he wanted to make sure she was
going to be safe. She had been crucial in this whole

process, and he was more than appreciative.

"Good luck finding those receipts," Paige said.

"Thanks. Call me if Seb comes looking for his car," Brody said.

"Oh, I'm sure he will. But fuck that guy. Take care," She closed the door and walked up to Mama Wash.

He waited until she was inside with the door locked before he drove away. The snow alighting on the windshield shifted from those tufts of down, easy to ignore, to genuine clumps. When he flipped on the windshield wipers, only one worked—and it was on the passenger side. Before long, Brody found himself nearly lying across the middle seat to see where he was going. He was glad Nectar's apartment wasn't that far, and after a handful of lights and intersection music, he was there. He had to circle the block twice to find an open space only to realize the massive car wouldn't fit, so he circled another couple of times until a pickup left and he could steal its spot. He now remembered why he didn't own a car.

Back inside Nectar's apartment, he closed the door behind him and threw both dead bolts. He stood there for a full minute, slowly taking the whole place in. From TV cop dramas he knew how basic police work was done. Look for signs of struggle, notes or letters, stuff out in the open that someone else may have been looking for. He didn't see anything out of the ordinary. Nothing looked ransacked or pilfered. The apartment was uniformly tidy, clean.

He stepped inside on the soft beige carpet and glanced at the lime-green vinyl couch and set of chairs.

On the coffee table—just some magazines ranging narrowly in subject from fashion to celebrity gossip.

A wink of green near the far wall of the apartment caught his eye. He bent down and found a thumb-sized router tucked against the wall with a knitted tea cozy draped over it. From the ceaseless flickering lights, it was apparent the unit was still connected. The router was old, reminding Brody of his own phone as well as the heap of stuff in Thorp's barn. There was no need for a personal router anymore; the wireless connection blanket went online across the country about the time Brody was in third grade. A personal wireless router— generally picked up on the black market and tweaked with the added ability to encrypt anything received or sent—was about as incriminating as owning a pager or using pay phones once were.

Still, this was a sign that Nectar hadn't embraced the entire flower child mind-set and abandoned all electronic devices. She had an ordi somewhere, and that would be the best place to find personal information. He saw this as spoor indicating a potential pot of gold waiting to be found somewhere in the apartment and began looking for the stashed ordinateur.

He opened a storage closet along the wall of the kitchen, and a set of lights flickered to life. Under them, an impressive display of tiny oak saplings in individual cardboard pots, all withered and yellowed. Beyond their crumbling leaves, Brody could see a partly obscured banner. As he pushed the saplings aside, their stems snapped like dried, ancient bones. The banner, hand-painted on a length of burlap, read: *Every New Life Is*

Another Step Forward. This Is the Way of The Mothers was written beneath it in smaller print that was nearly illegible because of the painter's crude handiwork.

He searched the bottom portion of the closet. A large bin of potting soil with a plastic scoop in it, a watering can, a few spare unused cardboard pots. When he opened the bin a deep, musty smell came out. He rolled up his sleeve, drove his hand down to the bottom of it, and flexed to find anything with solidarity to it. Nothing. He dusted his hands off and closed the closet door and moved on, repeating the banner's mantra aloud until he had it memorized.

The Mothers.

The bathroom was immaculate. The toilet looked recently cleaned, and the shower curtain was throwing off a rubbery smell which told Brody it was new. The linen closet was full of neatly folded towels. Each one he gently karate chopped to make sure nothing was folded up inside. He pulled the lid off the tank of the toilet and peeked inside. Everything was as it should be. No ordinateur or collection of spare brass knuckles sealed in waterproof bags like in his apartment. The washer and dryer in the bathroom closet were both empty, the lint trap clear. He went into the bedroom next and found the bed made, with throw pillows and a folded comforter at the foot.

Everything Nectar owned was in muted shades of green and brown. The color palette made him think of someone who was environmentally minded, someone who liked nature and spending time in it, someone who might go so far as to chain herself to a tree or spend an entire weekend planting saplings in public parks, a task she was obviously prepared to do.

Brody started going through her drawers but stopped, wrist-deep in blouses, and withdrew his hand. *Why am I going through all her things like this?* Airline tickets or stubs, purchase agreements printed off the Internet—that was what he was here for. He left the bedroom, wondering what had gotten into him. He thought about how he'd taken the lid off the toilet's tank. *What the fuck was I looking in there for? What did I expect to find?*

At the foyer, with a recalibrated sense of what he was seeking, he found there was nothing readily out in the open that he could go through, no mail holder or anything by the front door. He took a deep breath and held it, cast his gaze at the set of windows over her living room—the sheer curtains drawn, the gray light of the overcast afternoon filtering through. Brody took stock of what he was feeling. He slid two fingers into the collar of his shirt, loosened his tie, even undid the top button of his shirt as well as his coat. It didn't help. The tension was still there, the scaly skin ever present.

He turned on his heel and paced the carpeted hall to the bedroom. He opened her drawers again. As he peered inside at the neatly folded collection of under-garments he said, "She's out of town. She's finding herself. She's just out soul-searching."

The next drawer contained a collection of socks in different colors, a silky nugget of balled-up panty hose in the corner. He pushed on the oblong shape to make sure nothing was hidden inside.

He muttered, "I have to find her."

Brody closed his eyes and grimaced at the slip of the tongue. He withdrew his hands from the drawers a second time and placed them in his pockets. He gazed up and caught his own reflection in the dresser mirror. Orange eyes, held at half-mast out of frustration.

He told himself, "Don't. Just look around, find her ordi, an airline receipt, a bus pass—and go."

But as soon as he no longer held eye contact with himself, his hands dove back into the dresser on their own. He heard himself mutter the same claim it had made before. He didn't stop, knew by struggling the grip would just tighten more. He sighed as he watched his hands open the next drawer—jeans and dress pants. Some looked new, and others looked like they'd been worn for decades due to their ragged holes.

Next he went to the closet and threw open the double doors. Paige had been right; it looked like a wardrobe for someone with multiple personalities. Every style of dress one could imagine, ranging from the dark fishnet assortment to the silken classic mermaid cut to the evening gown to the saucy miniskirts. When he activated a fiber-optic cocktail dress, it displayed the phrase: *We Only Get One Earth.* After upending each shoe box and turning out every pocket of everything hanging in here, he clicked it off and closed the doors.

Brody exited the bedroom, shutting off the light as he went. He stopped in the doorway and thought about his own apartment, where he kept his secret things, his accordion file of important paperwork. His social security card, the first laminated jigsaw card he got when he was ten, all the mail from the Army, the carbon copies, and the like. Under the bed.

He dropped down onto all fours and reached under the bed and found a plastic container. It took some effort to drag it out; it was filled to the brim with paper. He flipped open the lid and sat on the floor. The first pages were payroll stubs from Mama Wash, a few doctor bills for birth control, a release for her medical history. Beneath that, he found several envelopes from bill collectors and credit investigators.

One envelope jumped out at Brody. It bore no company logo, and the return address was local. He pulled the trifolded piece of paper out of the envelope. The letterhead had a lock and key symbol hanging above Probitas Security Firm in clean sans serif. It was a company he'd never heard of.

It was a cease and desist letter, but Brody had seen enough in his own mailbox to know this one was different. It wasn't in polite lawyer-speak but a concise, if mildly bellicose, paragraph. After addressing Miss Ashbury, it went on to say that she had apparently been harassing several of the security firm's clients and that to save time they were sending her one letter representing them all. It instructed Nectar to discontinue using "foul language" with their clients' employees and being "antagonistic" with their clients' receptionists. It was signed in a darting, illegible signature below which was printed *Jennifer Sullivan, Lead Risk Assessment Engineer*.

Brody continued to dig to the bottom of the container, looking for anything that would denote Nectar was travelling, even though a dark cloud had just passed over Brody's mind that she hadn't gone anywhere voluntarily. He swallowed and imagined that the simple act was difficult to do, as if his esophagus were under the heavy band of cold, reptilian flesh.

A knock came at the door.

Brody froze, holding his breath.

It came again, three solid knocks.

Brody returned the papers and the lid to the plastic container and kicked it under the bed. He bounded as quietly as he could into the living room. Still holding his breath, he pressed his eye to the peephole. Through the smeary glass he could see two big men in matching blue overalls on either side of a squat man with neatly combed powder-white hair. The old man removed a pocket watch from his tweed vest and stared into its face.

Brody took his chances and opened the door, his hand sliding into the loops of his concealed knuckle-duster. He kept one foot behind the door just in case they tried to rush him.

The old man looked at Brody with mild irritation. "Is Nectar Ashbury here?"

Brody glanced at the two men standing next to their apparent leader. He noticed the patches stitched to the chests of their overalls: O'Malley Moving Company. "She's out for the moment. Can I help you?"

"She's ten days late on her rent," the old man said. "That means I have to kick her out, clear the unit for someone who might be willing to actually *pay* their rent. Are you here to get her things? Because I got these two for the day, and if you have a truck ready, I'm sure if you asked very nicely they'll help you load it.

Otherwise, it's all going on the curb."

"I'm just collecting a few personal items," Brody said. "One minute?"

"Make it fast," the old man said.

Brody closed the door in his face. He raced to the bedroom and grabbed the tote. As much as he didn't want to take the heavy container, he hoisted it into his arms and waddled into the living room.

He stopped, wondering if Thorp wanted any of Nectar's things. He looked around for photos and noticed there weren't any.

The knock came at the door again, and Brody answered. The men moved forward as if Brody was going to allow them in, but he rushed out first and headed for the elevator with quick, short steps, the bin held against his stomach.

The old man shouted, "Do you have a truck ready or not? All this shit's going on the curb otherwise. Be a shame for your friend to be out a sofa just because she didn't feel like paying her damn rent."

Brody didn't answer. He got into the elevator as soon as its doors parted.

15

Brody considered going back to the car to read what he had just collected, but his adrenaline had subsided into a fierce hunger gnawing at him. That's the way it always was with him. In the aftermath of a particularly harrowing ordeal, a reminder to eat came calling.

He carried the heavy container of papers and documents across the street to the Automat.

The place had a few patrons at the counter, a couple blue-collar men with their rubbery waders squeaking each time they shifted on their stools.

Brody went to the back of the Automat and sat in one of the booths with high walls. He pried open the container and started at the top again, taking one page out at a time and setting it aside face-down when it was fully extracted of information.

The Artificial server was at his elbow, her hands folded neatly before her. "Hello there, dear. Welcome to America's Favorite Automat. What can I get for you today . . . Mr. Calhoun?" The transaction yesterday had registered, and now she knew his name and how he preferred his coffee. She asked if he wanted a cup, black, the way he liked it.

"What can I get for . . . ?" Quick math. "Let me rephrase. What's the cheapest thing on the menu?"

The Artie appeared to study him. For a moment, when all was quiet in the cafeteria and all conversations unintentionally paused at the same time, Brody could hear the hard drive deep inside the Artie's head spinning. "Toast," she said. "Two slices of buttered toast and a coffee, our On the Go Special, is only—"

He said yes, that was what he'd like, without looking at her, and she hummed away.

He reread the letter from the security firm. Jennifer Sullivan's signature had been pressed into the paper so forcefully it looked almost carved into it.

There were no dates on the letter; the postmark was smudged beyond recognition. Nectar could have gotten it years ago when she was going through a protest and boycott phase—or as early as a few days before she split town.

She had been busy since the letter listed eight separate places she had been identified picketing, but not one of the incidents had been given a specific date. Another strike against Probitas Security's professionalism, Brody thought. Judges liked specificity, so a list of incidents without known dates would be the same as walking into court and calling eyewitnesses to the stand as "that guy, what's his name."

He put the letter in a separate pile he was reserving for things worth looking into, then continued to dig through the container, reaching the bottom where he found Nectar's social security information—but, sadly, still no ordinateur—and a handful of her expired plastic jigsaw cards.

It was there that he finally got a picture of her. Her first jigsaw card.

She was as he remembered her all those years ago, freckled and strawberry blonde. Next, Nectar at fifteen—freckles more prominent and her hair was short and painstakingly haphazard. A first experimentation with rebelliousness, he assumed. The most current jigsaw was from when she was twenty. The spiky hair was gone, and it had grown back to how she looked when she was younger, long with a faint wave to it. The freckles concealed under a generous layer of foundation. Her eyes were encircled with black eyeliner and mascara, making the vibrant emerald of her eyes shine even more so.

"Doing some homework?" the AFA server asked. She was programmed to say something along those lines, as if to a child toiling at work sheets in a booth alone, that she couldn't quite articulate with her limited prerecorded set of phrases and questions.

Brody twitched, looked up, and saw her looming there, cup of steaming coffee in her hand. There was no place to set it down without leaving a brown ring on his papers. He removed his coat from the seat beside him and threw it over the mass of papers, then carefully took the cup from her, the handoff awkward and resulting in a scalded thumb.

The Artificial was still peering at the table, as if able to see through the thick navy-blue wool of his coat. Her gaze switched back to him.

He didn't like the mildly inquisitive look she had on that rubbery face. Who knew what she could pick up and zoom in on with those eyes, never saying anything about it, but sending the information back to corporate, where it could be scrutinized by a team of bigwigs with too much time on their hands? He stopped himself before his Thorp way of thinking could progress any further.

"Will there be anything else, Mr. Calhoun?" she asked, folding her hands on her apron front and smoothing the material.

"No, thank you," he said and she scooted off. He didn't even need to see her slam through those double doors; he could hear it clear across the joint.

He removed his coat, gathered up the most recent expired jigsaw, and wiped some grime from its bar code. He thought about the pirated applications on his phone that liquor store clerks used on their handheld scanners to verify someone's age, criminal history, or if they had a court-appointed do-not-sell mark on them. His app was altered, though, and he could tap into personal files and police reports if he wanted to, going beyond what was in the realm of legally researchable by the public—without paying.

He took a chance and started the app. He ran Nectar's jigsaw card under its reader, and his cell's screen displayed an hourglass slowly emptying from top to bottom, one grain of sand at a time.

By the time Brody finished his coffee he had gone through Nectar's lease agreement, a gym membership form, and a few recent pay stubs from Mama Wash.

His cell toned, and he snatched it up to see what results it had gathered. Even though the jigsaw itself was expired, the number associated with Nectar Ashbury was the same number she carried from birth to death. The program had fetched a series of files on Nectar, including her arrest record which was surprisingly lengthy.

In the last month she had been given two warnings via phone, and then the hard copy cease and desist letter was sent when another "incident" occurred—or conduct discontinuation packet as the letter called itself. The calls and the letter were from Probitas. The letter didn't mention who or what she was harassing or who had asked Probitas to intervene on their behalf.

He flipped through her other arrests and found a few for being drunk in public. She spent a weekend in women's lockup for making a public nuisance at the Bait & Tackle Bar and Seafood Grill. The farther back they went, the less related they became, ranging to her first arrest when she was fifteen, the same age as that spiky hairdo, when she had rendered a fellow student unconscious by bludgeoning him with a lunch tray, because the concussion receiver in question had ceaselessly bullied one of her friends for an entire semester up until that fateful day.

Brody got out of the list of arrests and chose the other files the program had found. There was the claim her landlord had made against her for back rent that was to be taken out of her paychecks by collections whenever she decided to set up the payment plan. Brody scrolled and saw that no arrangements had yet been made. He went into the other case in the group labeled *pending* and found that she owed a tab to a nightclub called The Glower for precisely ninety-eight credits that was well over six months overdue. That, too, was to go through collections.

Due to his phone's memory carrying such a hefty app as the ID scanner, it left no room for him to be able to fetch maps or directions. He had no idea where The Glower was, and he was reluctant to call Thorp since he had nothing that his friend would enjoy hearing.

The toast had arrived sometime and he hadn't noticed. Now it had gone cold, the butter long soaked into the bread and making it soggy. Still, he ate it, both slices at once as if it were a waterlogged sandwich, drained his coffee cup, and motioned for the server to bring the Automat's nautilus over so he could pay. He gathered up the files as she made her way over, not wanting her to take any more interest in what he had been doing.

After his jigsaw had been scanned, she handed it back to him with the receipt for the scant meal. "Your account has been drained, Mr. Calhoun. I advise you to make a deposit or ask your banking institution for an advance of credits if you want to continue to offer America's Favorite Automat your patronage." He was

Mr. Calhoun now, not sugar, not sweetie.

"Lovely, thanks," he said, returning the files to the bin. "I'll look into it."

Across the street was a pile of Nectar's things. Her couch, with armloads of her clothes piled on top of it, now covered in a fine layer of snow. Her dresser and TV pulled from its wall mounting lay mercilessly next to her vanity on the curb among the row of trash cans. The movers were maneuvering her box spring down the front stoop as Brody passed.

A pang of sadness harpooned him at the sight of all her stuff getting cast out on the curb and casually preyed upon by neighborhood thieves like an unmanned yard sale. There was no way he was going to be able to tell Thorp about it.

He walked the length of the block to where Seb's Fairlane was parked and found it just as he left it. He heaved the container of files into the backseat and got inside. He fiddled with the screen on the car's dashboard and located an archaic version of GPS. He talked at the screen to find The Glower nightclub a few times before he realized it didn't take voice commands. With the touch pad, he typed in the name. It fetched no results; the car's particular version of MetroTab GPS apparently had been installed before The Glower had set up shop.

Desperately wanting a cigarette, he searched the interior of Seb's car and discovered a pack in the glove compartment. Stale and menthol. He opened the window and lit one.

He wanted to call Thorp and tell him what he had found, but he knew it would just throw his friend into a deeper spiral of suspicions and theories. The news hadn't been good, and the leads weren't that great. He stared up the street to where he could just make out the corner of Nectar's vinyl couch sitting on the sidewalk, rapidly rounding at the edges with the steady accumulation of snow. He flicked the ashes off into the cup holder.

Everything he had just read recycled in a ceaseless loop. The warnings from Probitas seemed like the only possible lead, but with Chiffon carefully watching his records of which restaurants he had been scanned at and keeping a spotty trail of his movements, he didn't want to stroll right in through the front doors of any-place, Probitas or otherwise.

He finished the cigarette and dropped it out the open window, exhaling the last drag slowly. Dead end.

A man walked down the sidewalk in full winter regalia, with a stocking cap and earflaps, trying to operate his cell phone with his gloves on. He stopped mid-stride, removed the gloves. He continued on, holding the phone to his ear. As the man passed by the Fairlane's window, Brody heard one snippet of what the man said: "Hey, relax—I don't think making one little phone call is going to hurt anything . . ."

The man with the earflaps was right.

Brody took his phone out and searched for the security firm. There was only one listing.

"Probitas Security Firm. How may I direct your call?"

"Uh, hi there. I was wondering if I could speak to

Jennifer Sullivan, please."

"May I ask what this is in reference to?"

"I'd like to steal a moment of her time to talk to her about something," Brody said, trying to sound innocent as if he were dating Miss Sullivan and the call was to schedule a lunch date.

"Are you currently one of our clients, sir?"

"Actually, I'm not. I want to speak to her for a second about my friend."

"Any risk assessment requests should be made via e-mail," the receptionist said. "If you're trying to contact her regarding the current status of a conduct discontinuation packet for an ex-employee, spouse, or relative, again I encourage you to contact her via e-mail." She then said without taking a breath, "Okay?"

"Can I ask who it is you represent?"

"I'm sorry, but our list of clients is strictly confidential."

"I got this letter that said I should leave somebody alone, but if I don't know who it is, what am I supposed to do? Never talk to *anyone* again?"

"You were issued a conduct discontinuation packet?"

"Yes, yes, I was and I would *like* to know who it is from."

"We're sorry, but unless the requestor has been cited on the packet, we can't give out that information. We list specific incidents in our packets so the receiver will be able to recognize who the letter is from without saying as much. We consider this the best way to remain as tactful as possible to all concerned parties."

"Look, lady. I speak my mind. I put my foot in my mouth so frequently I'm surprised that I'm not getting these letters by the hour. I just want to know who it was who sent it, so I can discontinue my conduct."

"If the requestor has not been cited, then I'm afraid they have chosen to remain anonymous. Perhaps now would be a time to reassess your personal interactions with others. If you go to our website, you will find that we offer a list of references to many psychologists and self-help professionals who may be able to steer you to a more productive and peaceful relationship with the world—"

"How much would it cost to become a client with you guys?" he interrupted. "Do you represent just anybody?"

"What is the name of your business?"

"I don't own a business."

"I'm sorry, but the Probitas Security Firm doesn't take on individual clients."

"So you only represent companies or businesses?"

"That's correct."

Brody took the phone away from his ear and scrolled to pull up Nectar's priors. Only two cases named businesses as the prosecutor. He brought the phone back to his ear. "Do you currently represent"—he double-checked—"Bait & Tackle Bar and Seafood Grill?"

"I'm sorry, but we cannot give out that information, either."

"What about The Glower?"

"Again, we're sorry but—"

01:29:59.

"Sorry, have to run." Brody pressed end on his phone.

He punched in Bait & Tackle on the Fairlane's touch screen, and the GPS found it immediately. He started the car's rumbling engine and pulled out into the snow-slick street. Navigating the city by the firm, female voice of the car's navigational computer, Brody began his approach toward the north side.

Bait & Tackle was a squat brick place set off to the side of a strip mall, the storefronts of which were all vacant save for a Big Lots. Brody parked in the lot and looked over the restaurant's aesthetic. The front was made to look like the open toothless mouth of a fish. The bar and grill's trademarked logo featured bobbers and hooks melded into the name.

It seemed ostentatious and overly themed but appropriate given that this appeared to be a section of the north side where a lot of tourists would be funneled in, clear by the number of hotels, department stores, and faded signs suggesting a bus or boat tour would be a great way to see the city. Now, in the off-season, the area brought to mind images of closed amusement parks, bankrupted roller rinks with nothing but weeds populating their parking lots, and probably all that remained of those boat tours now were blurry photos on an ordi monitor's screen saver.

Brody stepped through the front doors. There was a young lady in tight pants and a polo shirt with a menu ready, asking if he wanted a table for one or if he wanted to sit at the bar. A couple of admonitory beeps sounded from a device hanging on her belt loop.

He explained before she could begin her prepared speech. "Wait, I know I'm broke, but I just want to ask some questions is all. A friend of mine apparently made a fuss here a while ago, and I was wondering if you knew what it was about."

The girl looked new. She held an unbendable smile that hadn't wavered even when her hip-mounted jig-saw reader alerted her to the staggering bum standing before her looking for a handout. "Would you like to speak to the manager?" she asked brightly, another thing she had obviously been trained to say.

Brody agreed to speak with the manager.

The girl led him into the kitchen that threw off a fishy aroma of stuff that wasn't fresh but would smell a whole lot better once battered and fried. The employees all talked at once in a rabble of Spanish and Russian. They got to an office area that doubled as a storeroom, the shelves overloaded with giant jars of mayonnaise and cocktail sauce. The girl knocked on the doorframe, and a man looked up with a phone wedged between his shoulder and ear. He raised his index finger, turned in his office chair, and finished his conversation.

The hostess left Brody there in the heat and noise.

Brody heard the plastic clack of the phone being slammed, the squeak of the office chair as the man got up. He was tall and muscular with an ill-fitting shirt complete with screaming buttons. Brody couldn't decide if the sheen on his forehead was brought on by the heated conversation he had just gone through or having to work in such close proximity to the kitchen. "Mickey Wright." He stuck out a hand.

Brody introduced himself and they shook, the man's grip firm.

"Come on in." Mickey waved him in and remained

standing, crossing his arms across his barrel chest and giving Brody the inquisitive eye, his patience visibly short.

Brody closed the door behind him and said before his hand was off the knob, "I'm looking for someone."

"All my employees have their immigration papers up to date."

"Actually, I'm looking for someone who made a scene here. Nectar Ashbury, midtwenties, reddish blonde. I don't know the specifics of what happened, but apparently your establishment pressed charges against her."

"Oh, *that*." Mickey smiled. "That shit happens from time to time. See, we're one of the few places in the area that features real fish anymore, and the vegetarian groups get a bug up their ass when we put out a new commercial advertising it. They picket and tell us that fish have feelings and all that bullshit. We wanted it to stop because naturally it hurts our business, and we wanted to make an example of them. Worked. Hasn't happened since."

"So there were others arrested at the same time as her?"

"Yeah, four or five."

"Is this restaurant locally owned or is it part of a chain?"

"My dad opened it twenty years ago."

"So it's the only one? You don't answer to corporate?"

"Unless you call the bank corporate, then no. What's all this about?" Mickey asked.

"Okay, forgive me if it comes off as intrusive, but do you have a contract with Probitas Security?"

Mickey laughed. "Three words: *yeah, fucking right.*"

"Why not?"

"Probitas is expensive as hell. Only the muck-a-mucks high-rise caviar-and-champagne crowd can afford that. We're more of the fish sticks and pale ale sort, if you catch my drift. Two for one bottles on Tuesday nights, by the way."

Brody regarded his cell. Scrolling down, he came to the tab Nectar owed in her pending file. "Do you happen to know the owner of The Glower?"

Mickey's demeanor shifted drastically. He raised his hands in surrender. "Sorry, pal. You want to know anything about *that* place, you're asking the wrong fella." He tittered. "Can't help you out there."

"Why? What's the story?"

"The apparent owner—Titian Shandorf, keep in mind—doesn't give a shit and drugs are okay and bringing in your own booze is okay and there's prostitution and porno swaps, gun sellers in one of the basement rooms and . . . It's just one rough joint."

"Titian Shandorf?"

"What, are you not from around here?" Mickey asked.

Brody shook his head.

Mickey cleared his throat and said, "Titian Shandorf is this sick fuck—pardon my French—that the cops have been trying to catch for years. The guy's a murderer and a rapist. Why are you asking, anyway? You a private eye or something like that?"

Brody smirked. "Something like that. Do you know where The Glower is?"

"Down on Dunmore. I'll offer you some advice,

ANDREW POST ● KNUCKLEDUSTER

okay? That area isn't exactly somewhere you'd want to go walking around with anything in your pockets. I can see you're a good, clean guy and you probably don't want to start any shit with anyone, but if you go there, you'll encounter a healthy dose of it regardless."

"Thanks. I'll keep that in mind." He turned to leave.

"Hey, you come back on Thursday. We got karaoke and all-you-can-eat popcorn shrimp that night. I'll set you up real good, okay?"

Brody smiled, waved, walked back through the kitchen.

A rat-faced kid, wan and bent as a warped broom handle, glared at Brody and slid a tattooed hand into his pocket.

Brody returned the glare.

The kid removed a red onion he was in the middle of reducing to dice and went back to work.

Brody eyed the kid's nametag: *Rice*. "Ain't going to deport you," he said, again dusting off his Russian.

Rice nodded as if being deported was of no consequence to him.

In the dining area, Brody thanked the hostess and set back out into the cold.

As Brody made his way downtown toward Dunmore Avenue, he couldn't help but admit that the train station looked inviting. As the Fairlane thundered past it, he saw a train was leaving the station heading west. He wished he could be on it. The light turned green and he pulled ahead, shifting the rearview mirror with the dangling testicles up and away, so he wouldn't have to see that passenger train bullet out of the station. He tugged at the collar of his shirt again, unthinkingly.

He drove another few blocks and found himself in the part of town where most shops had a fiber-optic sign in the window, inviting patrons in iridescent squiggles to get their checks cashed as well as assuring them there would be no questions asked when hocking a valuable or lien. Soon there were liquor stores and head shops, tattoo parlors, and the like. This, he figured, was the neighborhood Mickey was referring to, just as he saw the dented street sign for Dunmore Avenue.

He took a few corners, circled the block to dive back in through the particularly grimy collection of storefronts, and slowed at an alleyway. On either side stood a free clinic and a tobacco and pipe shop. He could see all the way to the end of the alley, where there was a large steel door that looked like it belonged in a butcher shop.

On the street corner, a very poor holo of Santa Claus with only about a hundred frames of animation to him and a tinny and out-of-sync loop of the bell he rang stood next to a Salvation Army collection bucket. Viewed from a certain perspective, the street corner scene painted Santa as an asshole—only ringing his bell to draw attention to the fact that his bucket didn't contain donations but a small smoldering trash fire, something which he clearly felt was *ho-ho-ho-larious*.

Someone behind him honked, and he moved along, drove into a parking garage, and took note of the sign: Under 15 Minutes—No Charge.

I won't even be that long.

Brody left the Fairlane in a cramped spot, not bothering to lock the doors, and went down the sidewalk with his hands in his pockets and his chin tucked into the collar of his buttoned-up coat. The wind was in his face, snow cutting at his eyes.

He passed the free clinic and stood at the mouth of the alleyway, looking down the narrow brick passage to the end where the meat locker door stood. The odds were slim that the nightclub would be behind that door, but Brody knew there were strange nightclubs springing up all over the Twin Cities, even some located in the boiler room of a wastewater treatment facility and the basement of a closed elementary school.

Brody glanced around to make sure no one was waiting for a chance to bottleneck him in and approached the door. Looped through its massive handle was a rusted padlock. He yanked on the lock, and despite it being crumby with a layer of rust, it held secure. He searched for some sort of coded message, maybe *The Glower* spelled backward or upside down in chalk.

On the ground he spotted trampled cigarette butts, broken syringes with bent needles, and a shattered glass pipe, mossy resin still clinging to its winking shards. A small envelope fluttered, nestled among the trash. Brody followed the source of the breeze causing it to shimmy like that. He knelt down and felt warm air coming out from underneath the large door.

Someone had a heater going.

He considered latching on the sonar and prying the rubber tracking along the bottom of the door out so he could reach in there with the sonar's signal, but after touching the bottom of the door he didn't want to risk jamming his fingers into his eyes to remove his lenses.

Seeing inside the club was vital, but he didn't want to risk getting caught breaking in—or worse, shot, if the owner was as dastardly as Mickey had made him out to be—if there was actually nothing worthy of the effort inside. He had probably already burned up five of his fifteen minutes on the parking garage's clock standing here in the grip of indecision. *Think*, he told himself. *Think.*

It came to him, something he had once considered but up to this point had put out of his mind when he'd read the warning the sonar came packaged with. It read in bold that anyone who still had the ability to see or wore carotene lenses should not put on the sonar for fear of irrevocable brain damage, death, stroke, death, blindness, and death. He looked at his filthy hands in the suffused sunlight that managed to eke through the gray clouds above. Too little time to go and wash them, too much potentially here worth investigating. Worth the risk?

He undid the knot in his tie and yanked it out from around his neck with a zip. He tied it over his eyes like a blindfold and waved his hand in front of his face to make sure he could see absolutely nothing. He pinched his eyes shut as tightly as he could and reached into his pocket for the sonar. He felt the momentary conflict with his optic nerves. Unable to decide which incoming information to take, they issued Brody a roaring headache, ringing ears, a runny nose, and a tacky and dry throat—all at once.

Brody worked quickly with his head viciously throbbing. He could feel his pulse gushing one thud after another in his temples, in the crooks of his elbows—sluicing like a pretempest tide in his ears. He put both hands under the rubber tracking of the door and pulled upward as hard as he could. The sonar's next ping reached under the door and spread out into the room beyond.

In white wire frame inside the theater of Brody's mind: an entryway, a barred window, a hanging sign he couldn't read. Next to the barred window another doorway with a half door beyond where he found several coat hangers on a metal bar. Backing up, he felt around the floor. Dried mud, more trampled cigarette butts. A band, like the one received during a stay in the hospital. Possibly they had to be worn when you entered the club.

He came to another room, this one much, much larger. All empty, no movement save for a couple of scampering rats and cockroaches represented to him in the sonar's ping as scattering cubes. Chairs, tables, a stage. A dance floor littered with garbage and more discarded wristbands. Mounted lights, a smoke machine.

Scratches in the varnish of the bar. Repeating, angled columns. It took Brody a moment to realize they were barstools flipped up and lining the bar like stoic pedestals displaying a thousand, tiny nothings. Behind the bar the sonar ping found the cash register, its till open like a tongue ready for the placement of a pill or communion wafer. Shelves for liquor bottles, all empty.

He backed up and found a doorway, open with a rubber stopper. Stalls, sink, tiled floor. Bathroom.

Then stairs. An upstairs hallway. A series of doors, all closed. Brody was unable to feel around them, and there were no keyholes to slide through. One door, the last one at the end on the right, open. Inside, a bed. Nightstand. Lamp with a broken glass shade. Dresser. On the dresser: a cheap assembly-line aluminum ashtray, a pack of cigarettes.

Moving on. Doorway next to the bed. Bathroom. Shower curtain. Bathtub. Foot?

He focused even harder, even though the echolocation ping was getting weak at that distance. A foot, a leg. A thigh. A patch of neatly trimmed pubic hair. A flat stomach, ample breasts, shoulders, neck . . . No head.

Brody stifled a gasp but forced himself to focus. One last push. The neck, ragged, as if the head had been sawn off. He felt around for any distinguishing markings or jewelry. The body was naked save for a band around one wrist. Fingernails were fake; he could feel the layer of glue rising up around the edges.

In the alley, he knelt and felt the soft, warm splat of a droplet of blood escaping his nostril and landing on the back of his hand still gripping the rubber gasket surrounding the door. "Just a little farther." He squeezed his eyes tighter behind his silk blindfold and pressed on.

He felt around the floor of the bathroom for the head, the tool which was used to remove it. No dice. As far as he could tell, the floor was clean. He imagined it was covered in blood, though, something he couldn't detect with the sonar. He backed up, then all at once let the stretching, whisper-thin signal collapse. He pictured it like a tentacle, an ethereal boneless finger ceasing its reach, becoming solid, and shattering like glass. This image was defeated by the onslaught of his headache doubling, then tripling, in severity.

He ripped the sonar from his forehead and gripped his temples, falling to his hands and knees. If he had woken up with this degree of a headache, he would swear someone had just driven a railroad tack through the back of his head. He loosened the silk tie from around his eyes but found even the overcast sun cutting through the snow clouds to be too much. He wrapped the tie around his head again. He kept it on for a moment to let everything settle.

Remembering the grace period at the parking garage, he decided to tough it out and pulled the tie from his eyes. He exited the alleyway and walked as quickly as he could, each step sending a vibration up his spine and into his brain that made him want to scream. He slapped himself down for a cigarette, found none, swore.

He stuffed the coiled tie back in his pocket and opened his eyes. Everything was bleary, overly bright as if captured before him by a camera with a broken shutter. He blinked a few times, and the striped crosswalk in front of him cleared up. For a second he thought the snowflakes falling in front of him were new debris floating around inside the orbit of his eyes, a promise of an oncoming seizure, coma, death.

He found Seb's car and got in and gave the attendant his ticket just as fourteen and a half minutes passed on the meter.

He barely managed to turn a corner, pull the car alongside the curb, and open the door before emptying his stomach into the snow. A majority of the fast onslaught of nausea had been the result of attempting to use the sonar while he had the lenses in, but it was also seeing a corpse up close. Certainly, he had been almost a full city block away in person, but with the sonar it was like being there, seeing and feeling. It was an altogether unique sense, somewhere between touch, sound, and sight—a comingling of the three made palatable to his mind, with all the awfulness and unflinching detail in whatever he desired to aim it upon. Even without color and definite shape, the horror was evident.

Brody hadn't seen a dead body since the service, and the jagged wound, the ripped neck muscles, and the serrated edge of skin around the exterior trunk of the neck were beyond disquieting. His mind swam. Even when he closed the car door and dropped his head to stare at the carpeted ceiling of Seb's car, dotted with cigarette burns, everything still felt like he was at sea on choppy waters. He breathed in and out, trying to distance himself.

The mounting possibility that it was Nectar in the bathtub rapped on the door of his mind, but he needed a second to let the splitting headache subside before he could deal with it. His throat was raw and greased with acidic coffee puke, and he just wanted to wash out his mouth. He reached under the seats and found an empty beer can and nothing else.

He tossed the can into the backseat where it bounced off the lid of Nectar's files. The desire to rinse out his mouth vanished when he was reminded of the plastic tote. He ransacked the container to find the expired jigsaw he had scanned at the AFA. He scanned it a second time to get Nectar's files that were considered pending. He reread what she owed The Glower and thought it was pretty unlikely the owner would take a steak knife to her neck for only ninety-eight credits and some change, even if he was the scourge Titian Shandorf.

Nonetheless, he wanted to know who the body in the bathtub was. He clicked out of his jigsaw-scanning program and started another very small app that coordinated with the former by way of lifting fingerprints and pinpointing them to the owner in the legislative files.

As the sickness finally drifted away and his mouth tasted less like bile with each burning swallow, he felt the *need* to know come onto him. He thought about Thorp, about Nectar with her spiky hair, just a kid with a rebellious streak. If it was her, then it was a lead. As grim as that was to think about, it could be progress in the waiting. It was murder and well beyond a woman simply out soul-searching.

But in order to know, Brody knew he'd have to scan the decapitated woman's fingerprints.

16

Treading through the neighborhood
out of the safety of the car, Brody
couldn't help but compare the area to
the one in Minneapolis that housed the
community center. All of it seemed familiar,
if structurally different. The faces were there.
The conglomeration of homeless, the bearded
men in their found clothes, hanging out in packs
all shushing each other as Brody approached.
He smiled and nodded at them but knew
with his coat and his bloodshot eyes,
he undoubtedly looked like just another
yuppie junkie who was only on this side of the
tracks to sniff out his next hit.

   He pulled his coat tighter and
wished that the empty space between
his black button-up and the satin liner

of his peacoat could be filled with military-grade body armor. There were times when he confronted a wife beater in a bar that he wished he had been permitted to take his dinged-up service armor home with him. There was a certain mental comfort in wearing it; he knew he could take even a .44 caliber slug to the chest right over the heart at point-blank range and survive, if a little bruised.

Brody considered an anonymous call to Detective Pierce instead of breaking into a shitty nightclub and scanning a dead body for prints. The anonymous tip was sadly a thing of the past, especially with pay phones. Making a call on one of those, one might as well state his name and address before discussing whatever nefarious thing he was up to; save the cops time. Brody decided against it. If and when it came to that, he'd find a way to carefully toss what he knew over the fence, so to speak, and scram before anyone knew it was him. As long as it wasn't Nectar.

This is what he prayed for as he passed the free clinic and hesitated a second time at the darkened maw of the alleyway. As nonchalantly as he could he looked up the street and all around. "Please don't be her," he muttered. "Please."

00:45:59.

He'd have to make it quick.

Brody went down the alleyway and examined the padlock. He gave it another couple of tugs with his bare hands and received nothing but dirtied fingers. He patted himself down for something hard to smash the lock off with.

He thought of all those guns in Thorp's basement. One bullet and the lock could be off in a flash. But the notion of having a gun's weight in his hand, the coldness of the metal, the texture of the grip needling against his palm—*no*. It wouldn't be necessary. Not here, not ever. He brushed the idea aside.

Brody took out his knuckleduster and slipped it onto his fingers. He tried to size up how he'd hit the padlock, since a miscalculation could result in a skinned knuckle. He gave it an awkward punch and did just that. He glared at the scaled-back flesh on his middle digit. Not bleeding but still annoying. He mused about the free clinic up the way and if they offered tetanus shots.

The only other thing of remote solidarity on his person was his sonar case made of high-grade plastic. He removed the sonar so as not to damage it and brought the case down on the head of the lock. It swung around on the handle noisily but stubbornly held tight. He hit it again and again and finally it gave. He took the lock off and cast it into the clutter and trash of the alley.

He stepped inside to total darkness and left the meat locker door open to allow light in. All over the entryway was a dizzying mishmash of colors and varying artistry of clashing, innumerable styles. A theme sprang forth: sharp tribal designs overlapping portraits of faces in agony, smiling horned demons with blank, red eyes.

Brody pulled out his cell and selected the flashlight. He closed the door behind him and saw there was no way to lock it from the inside. He was only going to be a minute, he reminded himself, and walked through the doorway into the open nightclub. Now he could see *The Glower* painted on the dance floor in scrawled letters meant to look like they were etched with fingernails into the floor. He walked among the empty chairs and tables, careful not to disturb anything. The flashlight's beam from his phone, as weak as it was, provided sufficient light.

He went to the bar, looked at the empty shelves, the cash register drawer hanging open and cleared of cash. The club's nautilus, much like the one the Automat used, stood under a patina of dust with the receipt tape band pulled out, all physical record of tabs gone.

Brody realized he was dragging his feet. It was true; he didn't want to go upstairs. Even from the bar's ground floor, he could smell the corpse. The putrid, bitter stink of rot emanating from the narrow staircase made his stomach—despite its emptiness—turn.

He took a deep breath and mounted the steps. The walls upstairs weren't like the entryway and the bar itself. There were no leering demons and fanged vampire mouths painted on the walls. Here, decorative floral wallpaper had been painstakingly applied to match at the edges perfectly. It would be unnoticeable that it wasn't cut from one giant sheet if the edges weren't curling up from water damage.

At the open doorway to the upstairs bedroom where he knew the body to be, Brody had to latch his arm over his face because the smell was so powerful. He ran the flashlight over the dresser with the ashtray and cigarettes. Over to the bed, which was covered in a white down comforter soggy and heavy with blood that had dried to a rusty brown. He turned the flashlight beam to the floor and noticed the plain black-and-white checkerboard floor was also covered in streaks and long wipes of dried blood. He stepped toward the bathroom, the smell finding its way around the wool of his coat, despite him clamping his arm around his face so hard he thought he might break his nose. He gritted his teeth, fought the persisting urge to gag.

There she was, one leg up on the rim of the tub like she was just lounging in a hot bath. He looked in the toilet, in the sink: more dried blood.

He took three deep breaths with his eyes closed and forced himself to turn and look at the remaindered trunk of the woman's neck. The cutting had been slow and tedious. The cut wasn't smooth but jagged and messy, and flaps of tissue hung off to the side looking torn, as if the killer had gotten most of the way through and ripped the final portion out of impatience. The wound didn't look remotely fresh; the bruising and the severity of how shrunken and dried it appeared indicated decomposition steadily taking its toll. The woman's chest, as well as the rest of her, was washed in flaking, dried blood.

The sight disturbed him more than anything he had seen in the service. There it was gunshot wounds that pumped thick deluges of blood, the occasional shattered limb from a bomb or a land mine, maybe a head half-emptied from an expertly aimed shot—nothing this barbaric.

Brody cursed, muffled through the sleeve of his coat. He knelt down without letting his knee touch the bloody floor. He looked at the screen of his cell. He couldn't have both the fingerprint scanner and the flashlight going at the same time—it would kill the battery instantly. He'd have to operate in the darkness, nothing he was unaccustomed to, but a necessity he didn't wish to perform while in the same room as a dead body.

He turned the flashlight off and selected the fingerprint scanner. He reached out for the woman's wrist, touched the cold flesh, and a sick wave pulsed through him. Bringing the phone to the woman's limp fingers, he pressed the scan button.

The room was awash for a moment with red light. The scanner track passed back and forth over the woman's hand. Looking down, he watched the light slipping out between her fingers, as if she were an oracle, spinning a spell from beyond the grave using her corpse as some kind of conduit.

The scanner track leapt forward, a series of rays cutting out from between her limp, lifeless digits and slowly reeling back.

Brody waited, all the while breathing through his mouth.

The cell beeped. The hourglass appeared, draining from top to bottom. He'd let it do its calculations and search the databases on his way out. With care he lowered the woman's wrist to rest on the bathtub rim and stuffed the phone back into his pocket.

In the darkness, he fumbled through the bathroom

door, across the bedroom, and out into the hall. He nearly fell down the stairs and had to grip the railing to keep from tumbling the rest of the way.

It was at this moment a notion hit him. During the whole time he was on a journey for fingerprints he had been leaving his own. On the padlock in the alley, now on the railing. Around the dead woman's *wrist* for Christ's sake.

At the bottom of the stairs he inventoried everything he'd handled since coming in. He removed the tie from his pocket and used it to wipe down the railing as he went back up. He switched the flashlight on while crossing into the bathroom. He looped the tie around the woman's wrist and ran the silk band back and forth the way one would shine a shoe.

The dreadful job done, Brody turned away from the body for what he hoped would be the last time and went downstairs. Halfway across the empty dance floor, each footfall making a deep, resonating clack, he stopped as he heard something—a sound, a murmur, a constant buzzing thrum beyond the walls of the nightclub.

It was a sound that summoned so many memories for him of breathless thankfulness but now only fear. It was the beating wings of a Darter. He knew all the Darters had sat in various military bases around the country for close to five years following the end of the war. But due to budgetary reasons, certain big city police departments gave them a new paint job and used them to easily move a lot of police officers at once. He recalled the first time he had seen a Darter in police use. Hovering, giant, like the extinct insect it had been named after, looming with a pregnant belly full of armored special tactics police officers over the rooftop of a building known to house several drug labs. Repurposed.

Brody took another few steps across the dance floor, hoping the Darter was in the neighborhood innocuously to hover over the rooftop of the adjacent free clinic for surveillance reasons, but he knew better.

He got to the front door and edged it open with his foot. The alleyway was empty, but the squawk of police walkie-talkies and the terrible droning of the Darter were audible. He snatched up the broken padlock from the alley debris and deposited it into his pocket. Using his hand with the tie wrapped around the fingers, he shut the door and hesitated, remembering that there was no way to lock the door from the inside.

He darted across the dance floor to the stairs. He went into each room in search of an escape route. One opened into an office area, with a desk and a filing cabinet, a screen affixed to the wall with its glass panel shattered. A small narrow window was located up toward the ceiling. He climbed atop the filing cabinet, pushed and tugged on the window. The glass was frosted over, just the midday light shone through gloomily into the room, filtering through the stifling dust.

Brody's heart thundered in his chest, sweat pushed through his forehead, and his headache returned. Without shame, he felt the urge to piss his pants. He knew this was the flight-or-fight instinct tipping the scales in favor of flight. He took out the sonar case and beat at the painted-over lock on the window to get it open.

The Darter was moving, the buzz rising into a brighter yet thicker tone. They had dropped off their passengers and were going to lift up a good fifty yards off to keep a bird's-eye view on things.

Brody slammed the sonar once more and was rewarded with an audible crack when the thick layer of paint broke away from the lock. He opened the window and realized it came out on the roof of the free clinic.

Directly in front of him were police officers dressed head to toe in heavy riot gear.

Brody stared momentarily as they took their gun stocks to shoulders before he withdrew from the window. He dropped off the filing cabinet just as glass exploded into the office with a clatter of gunfire.

Without a doubt a setup, he deduced. No two ways about it.

He stuffed his tie and sonar case into his pocket and ran into the hallway. There was shouting all around, and on the roof he could hear the steady tramp of boots. He looked down the stairs and on the dance floor noticed a triangle of light cutting inward from the alleyway entrance.

He rushed to the end of the hall. The last door that might yield a possible way out, the only one he hadn't yet checked. Careful not to touch *any*thing, Brody charged into the room and aimed his flashlight at its contents. A countertop that ran the length of three walls, a display of knives and cutlery on pins. He considered what he had at his disposal. Cabinets, a basin sink, a few plastic aprons—The Glower, it seemed, was an operating front for a rich sociopath who liked to watch from the top of his stairs and handpick his victims from the club's attendees below.

Brody's mind raced. He was trapped. The Chicago PD had a shoot-first rule; he would be displayed on the news being carted out of The Glower on a gurney, peppered with holes, using the photo from his jigsaw to show the citizens of Chicago the face of the infamous Titian Shandorf. Justice unquestionably served, all tidied and under the rug. Brody pictured Lady Justice, blindfold and all, clapping her hands of his dirt in contented completion.

He looked to the one wall of the room that didn't have a counter on it. A blank wall, with that same flowery wallpaper—orchids and their stems, in a crisscrossing pattern of freeze-framed growth. Here, far worse than in the hallway, the wallpaper was curled at the edges. Moisture. Mold. It weakened drywall, made a house or building's construction crumbly and dangerous.

Brody decided to take a chance, knowing that running full bore at a wall could result in one of two things: crashing through to whatever hazards lay beyond or slamming into the brick wall underneath. For a second, he thought about the Automat server, seemingly never even aware that those kitchen doors lay ahead of her as she charged through them with her ever-present smile.

Brody backed up until his heel banged into the cabinet behind him. He bolted forward, threw his arms out in front of him, and crashed through the wall. He tumbled into the next room, which upon standing and wiping the black, moldy drywall from his eyes, he saw was the attic above the free clinic. He steered around air-conditioning units and ducked bands of wires, treading only on the beams and not on the insulation between. He made his way past a complicated twist of ducting, then dodged another mass of cables.

He could hear people beneath him asking: "What is that?"

He came to a wall and found himself teetering on the narrow metal beam. He glanced at the wall he had crashed through. On the hanging cutlery he glimpsed flashes of white light—the cops were storming The Glower now.

Brody looked all around him. It was the end of the free clinic's attic. There were no more walls to charge through; everything around him was unpainted cinder block and ducting. He looked down at the fluffy cotton candy of the pink insulation. Before he could talk himself out of it, he stepped forward and let gravity pull him down through the ceiling of the free clinic. More dust, more clatter and noise. People screaming.

He landed on an exam room table just eight feet down from the ceiling. Covered in dust and clumps of black mold stuck in his hair and on the forearms of his peacoat, he jumped off the table and opened the door to the waiting room.

People jumped up and screamed. The poor and the despondent—they didn't deserve a fright like this when bringing their sick kids to get a checkup and a flu shot.

He moved through the hacking crowd of startled people to the front door and was back on the sidewalk. He ran as fast as he could.

The engine and blurred-with-motion fiberglass wings of the Darter above were never that far away. It was a block or more over, and due to the height of the buildings he ran along the face of, they couldn't see him unless they hovered directly over the street he was on.

He turned the corner, checked the sky for the Darter. Traffic and people on the street stopped to gawk at this dust-covered man running around visibly panicked. He cut across the street before the light changed, a car nearly clipping his heels, then returned to where he had left the Fairlane. He slipped on the ice that the snow had become since the sun had gone down, struggled back into the stolen car.

Brody pulled into traffic, where he tried to drive slow. His mind was spinning, various parts of himself hurt, and he felt something wet on the inside of his right thigh. He had either actually gone and pissed himself or he had cut himself somewhere in the scuffle. He obeyed the rules of the road, made frequent turns, and took stretches of road that had few traffic lights, all in an attempt to put as much distance between him and the police, with the most crooked line, as possible. His heart continued to pound so hard that when he came to a stoplight he could actually see the rhythmic throb in the veins on the back of his hands gripping the steering wheel.

He didn't know where to go, so he left town on the first on-ramp to the interstate he came across. He looped around the city on the expressway, where he could see the street where The Glower was based, the free clinic, and the tobacco shop. The Darter, hovering and monitoring resolutely, shoved the falling snow away from it in dusty, ringing waves.

Brody drove until he saw the exit to head toward Thorp's place. His lenses flashed: ten minutes. He drove as far as he could see, finally having to pull over nearly exactly where he had to when driving out to the farm with Paige yesterday.

He parked along the field and sat there for a long time, just breathing—the penumbras shouldering their way in before his eyes took over and everything developed a gray cast over it. Nothing had focus. The last ten seconds on the lenses ticked away.

The radio was on but he didn't hear it. The blood rushed in his ears louder than he had ever heard it. The faraway whine of the gunshots and the alarmed shrieks of those people in the free clinic echoed in his mind. Brody felt parts of him regain feeling as the adrenaline sapped out of his bloodstream—his legs, especially his ankles, his forearms, his face, and his chest. He tightened his grip on the wheel to fight the shakiness. His head spun; he felt both ill and anguished.

When he remembered his cell phone was still searching databases, the sickening sensation doubled and the blade sunk in his belly issuing a fast twist. He withdrew his phone from his pocket. With the remaining seconds of carotene concentrate being supplied to his eyes, he saw the top half of the digital hourglass was only halfway drained. Then his eyes went dark. He was still sixteen miles from the farmhouse. His results were in the ether, darkly en route.

17

Brody wiped his hands on his pants, took off his coat, and used the satin liner, which felt clean to the touch, to dislodge any grime and mold from his fingers. He removed the lenses from his eyes and reapplied the sonar.

Just as he had expected, there was no way he could see outside the car, not with all the windows intact. He tried rolling down the driver's side passenger window, but the ping just shot out the sides of the car—a massive blind spot lay directly in front, which would make driving particularly challenging.

He was tired and didn't feel like being out in the cold anymore. Being shot at wasn't exactly a mood lifter, either.

Rolling up the window and securing

the isolation of the car, the sonar felt out and only found the smooth inside of the Fairlane's glass.

He reached down beside the seat and popped the trunk. "Let's see what ol' Seb might have."

Brody went to the back of the car with the trunk lid flopping in the wind and looked around inside. The sonar felt across the contents of the trunk: some more forsaken empties, the spare, which was flat, a pneumatic jack. No tire iron. He slipped the handle out of the jack and returned to the front of the car and climbed atop the wide hood.

He hesitated, jack handle in hand, to let the sonar ping up and down the desolate country road. The last thing he needed after barely escaping the cops in their raid of The Glower was for some small-town sheriff to tool along and find him standing on the hood of a stolen car, bashing the windshield out like a lunatic throwing his own one-man riot in the middle of nowhere.

Satisfied no one was around, he started beating on the glass, digging a series of craters in along the edge. He palmed the glass, tried to shove it down and out of the bracket, but it held firm. He stomped on it, and finally it came loose and fell into the car in a floppy, crackling sheet.

He slammed the trunk lid, tossed the jack handle into the backseat, shoved the panel of cracked glass aside to ride shotgun for the remainder of the drive. Even going so far as to use his blinker, Brody steered back onto the rural tarmac and continued on. The cold wind tore in over the hood and hit him directly in the face, but he was able to make out the definite shoulders of the road and any oncoming traffic.

Brody wondered if he had just come upon an unrelated incident, if Nectar's disappearance had nothing to do with the dead body at the club. How many people visited that club in a month? Hundreds probably, given its size. All those cigarette butts in the alleyway. How many of them had Nectar smoked? If she smoked at all.

He followed the two-lane road, unable to see anything behind him, and because of that, Brody pictured the Darter—with its shiny new police-issue paint job—following his car on whisper mode. Just as he had done with his unit when they got onto a trail of an individual of interest. For days they followed them through the desert along twisty dirt roads that were barely distinguishable from the countless miles of empty, brown space on either side, across rocky ranges, until they could lead them to a possible headquarters, where they could watch, electronically eavesdropping, creating a measured plan of neutralization.

Brody ignored this suspicion and lobbed it into the pointless paranoia file and forced his mind to other more productive topics. He adjusted the radio so it could be heard over the gale-force wind roaring through the open cavity where the windshield used to be. He wished he hadn't smoked that last cigarette, because he could've really used it right then, just as his nose began to lose feeling.

Brody turned into the driveway to find the farm under even more snow. Earlier he could see the individual blades of grass peeking up through the white with the sonar, but now it was smooth, impregnable to the device's ping. He drove the Fairlane to where he had parked that day and paused. He decided to pull up, to get it out of easy sight from the road. He parked it behind the house, among the decommissioned vehicles. The car looked at home there.

Thorp was outside before Brody had managed to fetch the plastic bin of files from the backseat. He approached Brody with hesitation, his hand out. He curiously touched Brody's powdered shoulder and, looking at the white film on his fingertips, mumbled, "Don't tell me she was involved in cocaine production."

"This?" Brody tried to act like he was covered in drywall dust merely for the sheer giddy thrill of it. "This is nothing." He turned with his arms weighted with the plastic bin, kicking the car door shut.

Thorp held the back door to the house for him and made doubly sure that it was locked securely after they were both inside, checking the dead bolt twice.

Brody set the bin down on the cleared kitchen table. "You're just going to let that be my explanation for why I'm covered in drywall dust?" He peeled off his peacoat, hissing with the painful effort. "No third degree about where I've been all day or what I found out?"

Thorp shrugged. He seemed serene, pleasantly thankful to see Brody was still just continuing to fill his lungs. Brody detected a faint whiff of home brew coming off his friend but said nothing. At least he was mellowed out a little now, something Brody wasn't about to argue with. Thorp pulled a chair out from the table and stared at it, not bothering to sit. Perching, leaning his upper half over the chair back as if he were confused on how the wooden contraption was supposed to be used.

Brody let his coat fall to the floor with a wet slap.

Thorp, bent over the chair, eyed him, a look of tepid, indifferent curiosity on his face. He started at Brody's head and stopped when he reached the top of his leg. "Looks like you had a close call there."

Brody felt the spot and discovered it was tender to the touch. He glared at his fingers, unable to see anything, no color. He smelled them instead. Blood. He paced over to the kitchen sink and ran the water until it got warm.

"You seem pretty calm," he said, splashing water on his face after washing his hands, careful not to get any on the sonar.

"I've been drinking since you left." Thorp sighed, finally taking a seat. He did so slowly, easing himself down like a man twice his age. "Honestly, since you've been gone so long, I've just been sitting here preparing myself." He swallowed. A dry chuckle, then, "Preparing myself for you to come back and tell me the worst, that is. I've gone through every possibility there is and prepared myself for it. She could be dead, kidnapped, raped and stuck in a drum and dumped somewhere . . ."

"It's probably hard to believe with how I look, but I really didn't come up with much," Brody said, ignoring Thorp's morbid listing. "And no news is good news, right?" He patted his face with a towel. The warmth in his pants was slowly touring its way over the summit of his kneecap. It wasn't profusely bleeding nor did it hurt all that much; he could tend to it in a minute.

Once his hands were dry, he stepped over to the container of files and pried the lid off. He turned to Thorp whose interest was already piqued. "Somewhere in there's a letter from a security firm claiming Nectar had been hassling someone's employees."

Thorp got up and thumbed through the files. "It doesn't say who?"

"Not in there but her record lists a few different businesses she had been badgering, the ones that pressed charges anyway."

"About what?"

"Did you—?"

"Yeah," Brody cut in. He told him about Mickey at Bait & Tackle but skipped the hubbub at The Glower. He stressed that Probitas's client had never actually pressed charges since that would've shown up on Nectar's record. And if it wasn't Bait & Tackle, it had to be someone else.

Thorp asked why Probitas's client would want to remain anonymous.

Brody nodded at the only tenuous thing linking Probitas to Nectar. Or, rather, the thing linking who was speaking *through* Probitas to Nectar. "Doesn't say. It just said she should stop being hostile toward their clients. Tell me what you make of them. I'm going to take a look at this." He pointed at the wound on his thigh.

"You got it."

Brody patiently took the stairs one at a time, making full use of the handrail, and went into the bathroom. He removed the sonar and showered in the balmy darkness, unable to ignore that beyond the smell of soap was the coppery tang of his own blood.

Over the hiss of the showerhead, Brody could hear his phone on the counter make a bright, declarative beep. Either it had just received a text message from Detective Pierce informing him that, yes, in fact, they had lifted his prints from the free clinic doorknob and they'd be seeing him shortly, or the fingerprint analysis had found who it was in the bathtub.

He shut off the water and felt where he had been injured. A small slice just right of his scrotum in the tender alcove where his crotch connected with the inside of his leg. He imagined it was from when he dropped through the tiles of the suspended ceiling with the plastic brackets. Brackets that when broken didn't just snap but shattered into daggerlike shards, like glass. He had a scar on the inside of his left forearm from just such a thing, another on his knee—evidence of a summer spent doing remodeling work for a set of brothers who had discovered flipping houses could be lucrative. After the second altercation that required stitches, Brody was told in stereo not to give up his day job.

When Brody stepped out of the shower, he felt the hot finger of blood trail down the inside of his leg. Pushing past the pain, he ran his fingers around the wound. It was bleeding but not profusely enough to be his femoral artery. He unrolled some toilet paper and pressed it against the wound.

He had to sit. His head was swimmy after his terror-filled day, and he realized that taking a shower at the near-scalding temperature he had while still spinning with adrenaline probably wasn't such a bright idea.

Wincing, he peeled the mass of bloodied toilet paper away from his wound and saw, nestled in the crook of his inner thigh, a tiny raised thatch of skin. It came alive with pinpricks when the humid air trapped in the bathroom lapped across it. He sucked air through his teeth.

In the cabinet beneath the sink he found only an economy pack of electrical tape rolls stowed amongst the folded towels. Remembering he was in Thorp's house, he wasn't surprised. But with nothing better as an option, Brody looped the tape around his leg to secure the makeshift bandage, contemplating all along that removing it later to change the dressing would prove to be another delightful highlight of his already ruined day.

Returning downstairs in the remaining set of clean clothes he had packed, a navy gabardine shirt over a long-sleeved thermal and a pair of insulated jeans, Brody stepped into the kitchen to find Thorp diligently studying Nectar's collection of files. Everything else had been removed from the container, but it was the Probitas letter he had in his hands. Brody could tell what it was just by the way the paper had been folded.

In his pocket, Brody had his cell phone loaded with the identity of the woman in the tub at The Glower. It sat there against his thigh, heavy. Even the slightest possibility of it being Nectar and not checking was driving into his conscience. If it was Nectar, prolonging the inevitable news to her brother was cruel.

"What'd you find?" Brody asked, stirring up some conversation just to distract himself. It was unlikely

Thorp would find anything in the files he had missed, but he had to direct his thoughts elsewhere. To busy his hands, he went over to the coffeepot. Cold. He poured some into a cup and drank it anyway, his hands shaking.

"These Probitas people are awfully fucking vague," Thorp said.

I found a dead girl in a bathtub. She might be—and probably is—your sister. It was right there, waiting to be said. Something goaded him. *Say it. It's the truth. Tell him. Break him further. The fissures are already there. Split him open the rest of the way. Insanity might be a comfort for him. A place to just fully give up and surrender and be gone from it all.*

Brody interrupted his own plagued thoughts. "She's an environmentalist," he said, recalling the closet full of dead saplings. "Maybe we should start calling up the factories and plants in the area that produce chemicals or dump their refuse locally."

Again, the cell in Brody's pocket chirped. Impatiently reminding him that he had important information successfully fetched waiting to be read. He reached into his pocket and thumbed the side of the phone to mute it.

"We need to find something," Thorp continued, his voice squeezing to a frustrated whine. "We're wasting time here. We need results. We need progress."

"I'm doing what I can," Brody said, sipping bitter black coffee. "It's anybody's guess what's going on."

Thorp lowered the letter. "So, what, you don't give a shit anymore? You're the one who tracks people." He stood up, nearly overturning his chair.

Brody put a hand out, halting him. "Don't start. I

didn't mean anything by that. I'm just *expressing* that I'm as lost as you are."

His phone hadn't been set to silent; it had been set to vibrate. It hummed a few pulses in close enough proximity to his wound to make it impossible to ignore.

"You need to bring it down a notch and not take everything I say out of context."

Thorp apologized insincerely, found his chair, and read the letter for the umpteenth time. He stared into the page as if the answer were somewhere between the lines.

Brody retrieved the sodden mess of his peacoat from the floor and wrestled the lens charger from inside the damp wool. "I'm going out to the barn to charge these lenses." It would be the only way he'd be able to see the screen of his phone—the only way he'd be able to look at the news to know what to tell Thorp. He tried to keep the gravitas from his voice as he said this, but it was impossible.

Luckily, Thorp was too preoccupied with trying to find the hidden messages in the dead space between the arches and sticks of the Probitas's choice of font to notice.

Brody stood in the barn, kicking the generator when the phone vibrated in his pocket. He cast his gaze to the rafters.

"Yes, yes, in a minute, all right?" Brody gave the generator a final kick, and its engine clattered to life. He plugged in the lens case. He retrieved the phone and stared at the screen displaying the information he could not see.

There it was, being shown to him—possibly, yes, that Nectar was dead. But to him, in the wire-frame puppet show the sonar gave him as a shitty stand-in for regular sight, the screen of his phone was as blank and smooth as a river stone.

Disgusted, he shoved the phone into the recesses of his coat pocket. He frisked himself for his cigarettes and remembered once again that he had none left.

He exited the barn, crossed the lawn, and got in Seb's car. In the glove box he discovered a wad of carbon copy which Brody took to be more parking tickets, a tin of mints, a replacement taillight still in its blister plastic, and—thank the Lord—a second unopened pack. He ripped the cellophane and fired one up, then sighed blessed tar and nicotine and listened to the silence of the Illinois countryside.

He was down to the filter when he heard the generator in the barn choke, sputter, and finally die.

Brody struggled to his feet, the electrical tape giving the hairs in his nether regions a nagging tug, and made the dreadful march through the snow to the barn.

He couldn't tell if the charger was complete or not by sight, but when he heard its magical little beep indicating a full charge, he felt a large piece of his reluctance drip away. It was a strange sensation to feel nothing but trepidation toward the results for the entire trek back to the barn, and now here he was seconds away from confirmation, and he felt an entirely unexpected giddiness swell in his chest.

Under the curious stares of the horses, Brody removed the sonar and put his lenses back in and blinked until he could see. Taking a deep breath, he removed the cell from his pocket and looked at the screen that read: *complete.*

He pressed his index finger to the screen, and it obediently displayed the photo from the headless woman's jigsaw.

It wasn't Nectar.

He gasped a breath of relief, letting his head roll back on his shoulders and the gnarl of anxiety in his chest untangle. He shook his head, feeling woozy. He lit another cigarette, needing it.

Despite the disbanded tension, the impetus in the scare lassoed him again. He felt the pressure returning, building once more. The thought, on autopilot, formed: *Okay, so it wasn't Nectar, but nonetheless, who the hell was she?*

He read on. The body belonged to Abigail Schwartz, a local entrepreneur who owned a gardening shop in Chicago called Mother Nature's Womb, now defunct following a rash of rubber checks. Recalling Paige mentioning an Abby as well as the The Mothers banner in Nectar's closet, Brody scrolled down to see that Abigail was also kind of a troublemaker. She had gotten arrested for protesting against animal testing at a medical research lab in northern Illinois. She had gone into a pet shop in St. Charles, Illinois, known to carry genetically altered dogs, while wrapped in a belt of fake bombs. She had been found guilty of tampering with the local wastewater system when maintenance workers discovered her trying to set up electronic feeders for the rats that called the sewers home.

Brody reached the end of the document where the

list of misdemeanors ended and the notes of interest on her permanent record began. Abigail Schwartz had ties with a group of radical environmental activists known as The Mothers. It came as no surprise to Brody, since it didn't appear to be much of a hidden fact given the name of Abigail's business. Regardless, the mantra he had been muttering to himself earlier rang even clearer in his short-term memory. Abigail and Nectar had known one another.

Brody crushed out the cigarette on the hay-strewn floor and took the cell, loaded with information that he was glad he could share with Thorp immediately, back to the house.

"So, you think Abigail Schwartz was friends with Nectar?" Thorp asked, holding Brody's cell and going up and down through the document.

"I assume they at least knew of each other. Paige mentioned that Nectar was friends with someone named Abby. Either way, I can't imagine a group like that would have a lot of members. They'd want to keep it small and personal, close-knit with people they could trust."

"And this woman is dead?" Thorp asked, holding the cell delicately as if he were cradling the dead woman's hand itself.

Brody solemnly nodded.

"What do you think happened? They got into some kind of tiff amongst themselves and some hippie psycho killed Nectar and this . . . Abigail Schwartz chick?"

That was the military talking, if Brody ever heard it.

"I don't know." Brody wanted to change the subject.

"So, you didn't have your Gizumoshingu on all day today?" He wondered if the raid at The Glower had made the news, if they had his prints or if the unsmiling photo from his jigsaw was displayed on every sidewalk-mounted screen and cable news affiliate in Chicago with *Wanted: Killer* pasted below it.

Thorp shrugged, not looking up from the phone. "I had it on, yeah, just for noise. But nothing really came up." He stopped, his hands lowering. "Why? Is this why you were all dirty? Did something happen?"

"On," he told Thorp's ordi in the next room and it obliged, the Gizumoshingu springing to life, slowly focusing the image. He faced Thorp. "I was in the nightclub, trying to get Abigail's body scanned for prints, and the police showed up. Someone tipped them. I don't know who, but it seems a bit coincidental to me that I barely get in there when they arrived."

He omitted the fact they had a Darter, because that would undoubtedly lead Thorp on a different path. Their shared history with the vehicle would surely come up, and Brody wanted to stay on topic. "I barely made it out. I mean, thank God for that rusty piece of shit out there because if I had to call you to send a cab, I really would've been screwed." He stopped when he saw Thorp's furtive expression, which meant he had a prank lying in wait for Brody or he was trying to find the right words to say something he didn't want to say. "What?"

"Okay, so don't be mad, but I went to the Probitas website."

Brody steeled himself. "And?"

"There's nothing outside of forms to fill out if

you're looking to hire them, really. A place to sign into if you're an employee. I tried Jennifer Sullivan's name with all the common passwords. You know, one-two-three-four and—"

"And?"

"Well, it's nothing I can do anything with, but I looked online for some software and e-mailed the guy, the app's author, and asked how much he'd take for it."

"What does it do?"

"It's called CITC—chisel in the cake."

"So it's a hacking app."

Thorp nodded.

"What'd you find out?"

"Nothing yet. The guy hasn't gotten back to me. Once I get the chisel, I think I'll be able to get in and see if maybe these numbers on the letter they sent to Nectar are like a code or something. Maybe it'll tell us who sent the letter and who knows where she is."

"All right. I think that might get us somewhere." Brody turned toward the living room. The ordi was still on and *Prize Mountain* was giving away an entire house to a lucky couple, but the sound of the cheering audience was momentarily replaced with a double beep. Brody stepped into the living room and bent down to read the news alert as the small text crawled along the bottom of the screen.

"—is believed to be the dead body of Abigail Schwartz, Chicago resident. Her body was discovered during a raid on The Glower. SWAT units discovered an upstairs area investigators are calling the lair of a serial killer. One unidentified man was seen at the club, but police officers were not able to apprehend him. He is believed to be Titian Shandorf, the proprietor of the nightclub. Shandorf is a registered sex offender, a murder suspect in more than six cases, and he is wanted for the rape of three women in the Chicago area, drug running, and leading a prostitution ring. If you have any information about Titian Shandorf or the murder of Abigail Schwartz, please contact your local police department."

Brody shut it off.

Thorp's cheeks were red, his eyes narrowed to watery slits, and his hands kneaded the air. "That fucker. Jesus Christ, I've been reading about that freak for years. He's wanted for all kinds of shit, but somehow he keeps opening these clubs and every time he opens one—*this* shit happens. I hope they catch the son of a bitch."

Thorp slumped down into the seat. He stared at the empty bin of Nectar's files and forms. All that was left inside were a few crumbs, motes of dust, and a single strand of hair.

Brody returned to the kitchen, the house silent. He folded his arms, leaned against the counter, stared at his friend. The snow had stopped falling outside, and the sun had started to break apart the clouds. A mass of half-melted white slid off the awning over the back deck, cascading to the ground in a heavy whomp. "Do you want to leave it to the cops, then?"

"No. I mean, if we could get the guy ourselves— that'd be great. If he killed Abigail, there's probably a chance he's got Nectar somewhere, too." He put his face in his hands, the light smattering of hair on the crown of his head wagging back and forth as he vigorously ground his face against his palms. "But if they couldn't catch him those other times," he said, voice muffled against his hands, "they probably won't be able to do it this time, either."

"There's a lot of red tape."

Brody remembered Detective Pierce giving him the backhanded compliment of saying that, yes, he was a vigilante and it was wrong—but at the same time, Brody was getting results where he couldn't. Probable cause wasn't a good enough reason to be granted a search warrant anymore. People were allowed to keep their private lives kept private unless there was an insuperable pile of evidence against them. Going on names and addresses like Brody did was the old-fashioned way. And in a day and age of scanners, cars preinstalled with tracking bugs, people getting followed all over the globe just by a piece of laminated plastic in their pockets—the willingness to beat the pavement and a keen sense of observation obviously still worked.

"How would we even begin to look for him? It's not like we can go door to door and ask for the guy. He's probably not even in Illinois anymore. Hell, he's probably your next-door neighbor." Thorp laughed, a heavy desperation lodged within it.

The mood definitely could be lightened, but Brody couldn't see any possibility of that happening for quite some time. "So, is that it?" he asked, arms still crossed.

"What do you mean?"

"I mean, are we doing this?"

Thorp counted the laces of his boots, then met

Brody's eyes. He nodded, waggling his chin so subtly it was as if he were giving cues to Brody, his pitcher on the mound. "Yeah," he said, his voice just as soft and barely perceptible as the nod, "we're doing this."

Thorp pinched out the single strand of hair by one end. It caught tiny breezes cutting through the house only it could feel, swaying, stretching out, and recoiling slightly into its soft, natural bends.

Watching Thorp, Brody said, "This will be different, going after Titian. This . . . shuffles the cards."

Watching the strand's slow crawl through the air as it stretched, then curled once more, he said, "Yeah. It does."

"And you still want to go through with it?"

Thorp set the hair down in the corner of the container, nodded.

"All right." Brody unfolded his arms, but the weight of them still being knotted across his chest remained. He swallowed, and it got stuck somewhere behind his Adam's apple. The back of his head burned slightly, as if he had just drawn in a breath of air-conditioned wind after being out in the heat for weeks. It was the same sensation he got every time a woman with a black eye said, "Yes, I want you to do this for me."

And as he always did in reaction to hearing that clink of the hook being freed from the chain about his neck, he took immediate stock of what was available to get the job done. Brody looked at Seb's Fairlane parked behind the house. The driver's door still hanging open, the dome light shining a sickly yellow. The monitor set into the dashboard was also on, displaying the map of the local area, the grid of Illinois farmland. Thorp's house mapped as a beige square. The surrounding farms marked in red, denoting private property. The fiercely green triangle in the dead center representing Seb's car itself, parked and angled due east—back toward Chicago.

It couldn't be helped; his mind was already set in motion on how to take the next step.

Brody buttoned his filthy coat and said, "Come outside with me."

18

They sat in the Fairlane, Brody poking at the touch screen and keying through the personal settings menu.

Thorp looked around the haggard interior. "Whose car is this again?"

"It belongs to an asshole named Seb," Brody answered distractedly.

"Seb? What kind of name is Seb?"

"I think it's short for Sebastian." Brody tapped onto the security menu and swiped his finger down the monitor, scrolling the list of options. With all the smudges and grime and overlapping finger-prints, it was hard to see the small, white text. He cupped his hand over the monitor to cut the dome light's glare and found the setting that he was looking for. He smiled, elbowed Thorp in the ribs to get his attention off the junk heaped in the backseat.

"What?" Thorp said, squinting at the dashboard monitor. "I can't read that."

"Okay, so here's the thing. This car has a security feature. If it's ever stolen, the owner can track the car with their phone."

"Well, don't turn it on," Thorp cried, slapping Brody's hand away. "Any guy that has someone's nuts hanging from his mirror, I sure as hell don't want him here. Besides, you stole his car. You don't exactly want him to find where you're keeping it, do you?"

"It's not *me* I want *him* to find. *I* want to find *him*."

"Why? You have a car now. Fuck the guy. Let him take the bus."

"Listen to me, would you? I don't know any criminal types out here. I need a card-carrying member of the Chicago underbelly. And Seb is all I've got. I'm positive a shithead like Seb and Titian Shandorf have at least crossed paths or Seb can lead us to someone who has."

"And you think letting him find you with his stolen car is the way to do that? Imagine you take the car back to Chicago and turn that thing on. Okay? Imagine you're hiding in the backseat ready to jump the guy when he gets into his car. Now imagine that it's not just him but every one of his goddamn friends piling in and they rip you limb from limb right there in the McDonald's parking lot and throw your pieces to the seagulls."

Brody stared at Thorp, completely stunned at the degree to which his morbid imagination could plunge. But he had to admit that Thorp had a point. What if

Seb came to fetch his car and he wasn't alone? It was a possibility that he was glad Thorp had explored, since it hadn't crossed his mind.

Brody looked at the slider on the car-finder feature waiting to be moved from Off to On. He took a deep breath and patted Thorp on the shoulder. "I suppose I'm going to need to visit that stockpile you have in the basement, then." He got out.

Thorp stood, talking over the battered roof of the Fairlane. "I *meant* I should go with you."

"Out of the question. You on a crowded street with a gun? No offense but I don't think that's a stellar idea."

"Fuck you, man. Do you recall how our scorecards compared from the practice range? I can shoot. Besides, when was the last time you picked up a gun?"

Brody rolled his eyes. "Ten years ago."

"When do you suppose was the last time *I* picked up a gun?" Thorp asked, thumbing his chest.

"I give up. Yesterday while I was sleeping you had one to my head?"

Thorp's expression hardened. "Not funny."

"Sorry, sorry. I don't know. Tell me. When *was* the last time you held a gun?"

"Once a week without fail, I go down to the bog and set up a row of bottles and take them out, all down the line. Fifty yards out. And I do *not* go back inside until I have them all down." He mimed firing, even providing the imaginary gun's kick, scanning left to right, ending with pointing the invisible rifle at Brody. "I was in the top of our class. And not to dig up the past or anything, but I did pull the trigger in one incident when it really counted."

Brody felt jarred by being forced to recall that alleyway, the bear trap, the prosthetic limb, the kid at the end of the alley, the look on the kid's face—terror accompanying his softening determination. Brody's rifle butt to his shoulder, ready to fire, but his trigger finger: frozen. The three-round burst directly next to his ear—everything ringing now—turning slightly and seeing the snaking twist of gray escaping the gun in Thorp's hand. Thorp's face tight and shiny with sweat, his eyes bulbous, mouth hanging open. A thousand things happening at once.

"Fine," Brody said and headed toward the house. "We'll leave in an hour."

They didn't speak for a majority of that time.

Brody made himself a ham sandwich and cut up an apple and, on his way to the back porch with his plate, took another cigar from the countertop humidor. He watched the sun dissolve into the horizon. The farthest clouds vibrantly purple surrounded by an otherwise gray sky.

He savored the sandwich and ate each quadrant of the fuji slowly. He was doing so because he considered Thorp's suggestion about Seb having friends. And in doing so, he couldn't eat without taking into account that this could very well be his final meal.

00:59:59.

He'd enjoy seeing the moon, when it could be glimpsed, while it lasted. He'd recharge the lenses as soon as they died out, and once they were recharged, they'd depart for the city.

Abigail Schwartz. Brody tried drawing a line between her and Nectar, imagining them as friends, having a night out on the town. Perhaps they were lovers. After tiring themselves out with a protest, their arms sore from holding up hand-painted placards all day, maybe they would sit and stare at the sky like he was doing now. He wondered if they spent time together at Mother Nature's Womb for any other reason besides planning their next protest. He whispered their mantra aloud again, and at the end of the third recitation, he tugged the collar of his shirt. They needed to visit the gardening shop, if merely to cross it off the list of possibilities.

Brody bit off the end of the cigar and spat it away. He watched the chewed nub sail over the railing into the yard, and that was when he noticed again the dangling wires looping in inverse arches from one tower to the next across the width of the land. He studied the three wires running in parallel from one derrick to the next, heavily contrasted in their thick black housing against the sky beyond. He stared and pondered.

The connection between Nectar, the Probitas letter, and Titian just wasn't fitting together. He had the different tectonic plates of clues and people, but no matter which arrangement he put them in, nothing comprehensible could be distilled—no clear Pangaea could be found.

The sliding glass door opened, and Thorp emerged with a small leather pouch and a gathered tangle of clothing in his hand. He sat down in the Adirondack chair next to Brody, the old wood creaking under his weight. He unzipped the leather pouch and spread it out on the small table between them.

Brody glanced over and saw a few spools of thread and needles arranged in their individual holders. He recognized the wad of filthy clothing as the pants he had been wearing earlier that day. They were stained with pink patches of commingled blood and drywall dust.

Thorp untangled the pants, handling the garment gummy with dried blood bare-handed as if it were fresh from the dryer.

"Never figured you for much of a tailor," Brody commented, taking a puff from the cigar.

"When you live alone and work a field without a wife, it's a skill you pick up pretty quick so you don't have to run to town for a new pair of pants every week," Thorp said with a grin and threaded the sewing needle with one eye closed.

"Thanks," Brody said after a moment. He finished the cigar and ground it out on the heel of his boot. He set the cigar butt on the table next to Thorp's sewing kit. "About before. I'm sorry."

"For what?" Thorp looked up, harpooning the thread at the edge of the ragged gap and then pulling it out, up, and away. His expression was quizzical; the question wasn't meant to be sarcastic in the least.

"For saying that shit to you. It wasn't good. About the crowded street and not trusting you with firearms. I know you're a crack shot. And the whole thing in that alleyway. I've been meaning for a very long time to call you and thank you for that."

Silence for a moment. Then, "It's all right. But for curiosity's sake, why didn't you?" Thorp asked without looking up from his sewing this time. "I mean, I'd do it again if I had to. Wouldn't bat an eye. But I could've called you too. Never mind. That was a dick thing to ask."

"I don't know why I didn't call. I suppose there was a kind of . . . hesitation to connect with anyone after I went on to Alexandria. I wanted to push it back as quickly as I could and just move on to the next thing in life, and . . . I never considered that you were stateside probably looking for someone to talk shit over with."

"I coped," Thorp said, nearly finished mending the pants. "I pretty much did what you did. Put it behind me, got out of Chicago. Started over with a clean slate, tried to stay busy. Little did I know that only a few months later I'd start buying these things off the Internet." He nodded at the military crafts congregated on the lawn. "When you're done with the past, that's when it's finally buried, but until you are you keep building monuments to it whether you want to or not."

Brody stared at one of the decommissioned Darters. The gentle angular shape of it, the cluster in its abdomen where supplies were housed, the thorax where the passengers sat—where the two of them had sat, strapped in, on several occasions in a different Darter.

"I'll get rid of all this stuff someday. When I'm ready. I'm going to bury all the guns in the field or melt them down and make horseshoes out of them. Maybe I'll donate these rust buckets to a museum. I don't know. Check it out," Thorp said, holding up the mended pants and giving the sutures in the material a tug to test its integrity. "Good as new."

Brody dropped his feet off the railing. "If picking

up the gun and going through this shit will disturb the peace you've carved out for yourself, I can go it alone. I just want a gun to use as a threat, anyway. I don't even want it loaded."

Thorp skirted the question. "Do you really think that if we get this Seb guy to come and get his car that he'll be able to lead us to Titian Shandorf?"

"If not directly to him, to someone who knows him."

"And you're sure of that?"

"Pretty sure."

"Do you think Titian was involved with Nectar disappearing?"

"I can't be certain until we get closer and ask some questions. But there might be a connection with the similarities in records that Abigail Schwartz and your sister had, plus they were in the same activist group. Nectar has an outstanding tab to Titian's nightclub—she's been in his orbit at one point or another."

Thorp looked at the Darter, the snow-capped Fairlane, the barn, then finally Brody. "In your honest opinion, do you think Nectar's alive?" He raised a finger. "Wait. Don't answer right away. Don't give me the half-cocked positivity that you do. Give me your honest-to-God gut *feeling* on this. Give it a second, think it over, and *then* tell me what you really think."

Brody considered The Mothers, Abigail's headless body, Nectar's debt to The Glower, every other piece of information, foggy trace, and weak clue he had collected over the last set of days. He closed his eyes, letting the answer come to him and roll over his tongue. "Yes."

"I *told* you to tell me honestly."

"I have no reason to believe she's dead."

"Then where is she?" Thorp snapped. "Where the fuck is she?"

"She might be hiding out, waiting for it to cool down. You don't know."

"No, *you* don't know. I've taken a life; you haven't. That kid is *gone*, and I robbed him of possibly getting straightened out, living a normal life free of the terrorist cell crap and—"

"What does that have to do with finding Nectar?"

"I've killed. I know how easy it is. And if I can say it's easy, someone like me who never had any interest in killing nobody, someone like this Titian motherfucker, who probably looks forward to the next neck he can get his hands round—I can't imagine what kind of state Nectar is in, wherever she is."

Even in the failing light and Brody's vision at the very beginning of dissolve, he could see a thick tear rolling down over the cusp of Thorp's cheekbone, hang for a second, then drip onto the mended fabric where it soaked in and vanished.

Brody took a deep breath and placed a hand on Thorp's shoulder. "We'll find her."

19

Once the sky was dark and Brody's lenses had charged, he put the case in his pocket and tracked his way through the accumulated six inches of snow to the house. Thorp had set off for the basement armory under the declaration "to find something appropriate for the situation at hand." Brody pictured stepping into the armory to find him in full flak gear, grenades and automatic rifles hanging from every available inch on his body, crowned with a bandanna haloing his thinning hair, which Brody imagined cut into an attempt at a mohawk.

Instead, he found Thorp atop a stool at the workbench, tinkering with a disassembled pistol. Thorp glanced over his shoulder and waved Brody over.

Brody looked over the individual components of the pistol, the springs and the tiny intricate folds of metal and firing mechanism, the hammer and pin. He assembled the gun in his mind and saw it whole: the same make and model as the one they'd been issued in combat training. Brody remembered it being clunky and of cheap manufacture, loud, but incredibly precise. It had been the Army's favored sidearm for a dozen years ever since the gun's inception.

"The Franklin-Johann," Brody said.

He could hear his drill instructor shouting the name of the gun to the platoon after they had fallen in as well as the informational spiel that followed as a way to hammer home the Franklin-Johann's role. "This is your sidearm. This is for when Old Bessie, your assault rifle, is not appropriate to the situation at hand. The Franklin-Johann semiautomatic pistol will lovingly provide you with ten rounds of stopping power at medium to close range. It is the fallback weapon, your second lover that you keep in your back pocket for lonely nights when the situation at home has gone sour. Love her, respect her, and she will always be there to help you through any shit storm."

"I got one for you, too. I'm just cleaning them. I haven't pulled them out in a while. The last thing we need is to fire one of these things and it doesn't work." Thorp probed a brush through the inside workings of the pistol. When he was satisfied the gun was clean, he reassembled it with a blur of motion. He slapped in the magazine and chambered a round. He clicked on the safety and flipped the gun around. Holding the muzzle, Thorp pushed the grip toward Brody.

Brody's hand remained at his side. He blinked at it, hesitating.

"It's not going to bite," Thorp said. "The safety's on."

Brody wrapped his hand around the rubber grip. Thorp released his grasp, and the familiar weight of the gun pulled Brody's hand toward the floor. He had forgotten how much weight the Franklin-Johann had. He let it hang there in his hand for a moment. All the training and the countless hours on the range firing at hay bales with painted-on targets cascaded over him— the ear protection, the shooting glasses that tinted the world gold, the muffled sound of everyone in line firing in turn, and that faraway pop the shots made.

He had lived a full decade blessedly free of guns, only to be holding one again. He felt permeated by the nauseating authority and tingly danger that holding a weapon of such unmasked lethality carried with it.

"Are you okay? Because if you don't want the Franklin—"

"It's fine. It'll do." He slid the gun into the back of his pants where it would be concealed beneath his peacoat. Even back there, the trigger guard looped over the top of his belt—the gun causing the buckle to dig in against his abdomen. The gravitas, even without the weapon being in hand, was sharply ubiquitous.

Thorp thumbed rounds into a spare magazine, one at a time. At this sight of quiet and practiced preparation, Brody felt his stomach give a slight heave. His throat had run dry long before he'd come down into the basement. A nagging hollowness of terror and doubt had wormed its way into his chest. Watching Thorp load the clip with one brass-jacketed bullet after another, that click-click it made with each new addition being filed in, Brody had to think of Nectar to chase off the slow trepidation that was climbing atop him. He thought about her as the kid she was when he met her all those years ago. And in her first jigsaw photo, smiling, and then when she was a teenager and very much not smiling. It was worth it. He buttoned his coat and repeated the notion again in his mind. *It's worth it*. Wrestling with that bullshit, carrying a gun again—it was all for Nectar.

"I'm going to start the car, let it warm up." Brody didn't wait for Thorp to respond. He passed through the basement, cleared the stairs, and hadn't even fully closed the back door before he had the pistol removed and the magazine ejected. He yanked the slide back to kick out the chambered bullet.

He put the gun in one pocket and the magazine in another as if afraid the thing would reload itself on the drive if neglectfully stowed in the same pocket with its ten little friends. He sunk down behind the wheel of the Fairlane, started the engine, and upon feeling the hot air from the vents, sighed. He had another one of Seb's cigarettes and attempted some closed-eyed breathing exercises between drags. It helped.

A few moments later, Brody heard the jingle of keys and looked through the empty windshield frame to see Thorp locking the farmhouse. There was no bandanna tied around his head, no ballistics gear, but the simple sight of Thorp's rucksack—which looked full—set Brody's teeth on edge.

Thorp got into the car and shoved the bag into the backseat, where it landed with a profound metallic clatter.

Brody put the car in reverse without asking about its contents. He didn't want to know.

For the entire ride, Thorp kept his hand up to block the roaring gale pounding directly into the car. He'd peek out at Chicago looming ahead, all its lights and traffic making the backs of his eyes ache. It reminded him that it had been a long time since he actually left the house. He had spent too much time there alone with his thoughts and theories and an overactive imagination that sometimes found in its stagnancy a way to twist back around on its owner. In its bite, he felt as if he were the sole perpetrator in his own misery. That he was the solitary mason setting up the bricks around him, the digger of his own moat that encircled his life.

Beyond the rumble of the Fairlane's engine, he could hear the imagined thrum of the Darter as they were being taken to a new location with a new slew of problems. He remembered guys in their unit kissing rosaries, hands clamped together in prayer, others sitting quiet and stoic, thinking of home. Some took to bad habits like rituals, doing a complicated hand jive before taking a pinch of chewing tobacco, or rubbing their disposable lighters like a lucky charm or rabbit's foot before lighting up. Some deliberately put the peril that waited for them out of their minds and sat by the open ramp door, the city of blond stone passing beneath them, looking as indifferent and bored as a man biding time at a bus stop. Thorp tried to be like them, to give an air of being effortlessly and blandly composed, even though beneath the surface he was anything but.

To calm himself, he removed his Gizumoshingu from his rucksack and felt with his fingertips in the darkness for where the car's audio input was hiding. A moment later, Thorp treated Brody to the Ramones' "Commando" at top volume. He sought approval in Brody's face and was treated to a small smile developing beneath his squinted, orange eyes.

"Remember this?" Thorp cackled, trying his best to shoo out his worries.

"How could I forget?" Brody said, his face washed white in the monitor's radiance. "What else you got on there?"

"All the good stuff. I got 'Flight of the Valkyries,' Zevon, Intrepid Hound Dog, JSBX. You remember how we used to listen to this stuff heading in?"

"Yeah, I'm surprised they never heard us coming, all of us singing together like that."

For the song's minute and fifty-one second duration, they were quiet.

When it abruptly ended, Brody leaned over the middle seat and shouted, "That was great, but do you know where this Mother Nature's Womb place is?"

The slight bend in the road caused them to turn so that they were driving directly into the wind. The frozen current rhythmically pulsed through the car so aggressively it made their eardrums feel boxed. Neither man said anything while Brody negotiated the bend, ice on the road catching the car's headlights with flares of dull white.

When they began going along the straightaway once more, Thorp lowered the volume on the music. "I thought we were going to nab this Seb guy."

"We are, but there might be something at this gardening supply place where Nectar met up with those other protestors. Worth checking out, anyway."

"But I thought it was closed," Thorp shouted over the wind.

"It is but there might still be something there."

"What about Seb?"

"We'll do that afterwards. I know going past the gardening place is kind of a reach, but I want to eliminate all loose ends. Can you look up the address for me?" Brody gestured at the monitor set into the dashboard.

Thorp leaned forward and poked at the touch pad, entering Mother Nature's Womb in the search query just as "Worrier King" began.

Located on a barren street on the north side of Chicago, Mother Nature's Womb was still standing—in some definition of the word. Even from halfway up the block where they parked, the earthy tang of potting soil could be easily identified. It was a narrow two-story brick building that visibly leaned, with a closed pharmacy to one side and a burned-out storefront on the other. The windows of the gardening supply shop were taped over with old newspapers on the inside. The sign had been pulled down, leaving chains hanging above the front door.

Some hallmarks of The Mothers remained: a faded painted marijuana leaf on the mailbox. A smiling, round face set into the brick that watched over the sidewalk and resembled what a female counterpart to Buddha might look like. Mother Nature corporeal, Brody surmised.

05:59:59.

That would be sufficient, he hoped. A quick look around, moving onto baiting Seb once they found nothing, just as Brody suspected. But it felt good to be here, to be thorough and kick over every rock, even the ones that didn't seem worth the time or the gas.

They went to the front of Mother Nature's Womb and peeked in through the spaces between the newsprint pages quilted across the glass. Nothing could be seen inside, only the reflection of their own peering faces. Brody wasn't surprised to find the door locked. He gestured to Thorp, a whirling display of dactylology for "go around back," utilizing the hand signals they had learned at Fort Reagan.

They crunched through the tall weeds that ran alongside the building and got to the rear. Dozens of plants spilled out of their pottery prisons and grew unbothered in wild tangles. A greenhouse with every panel of its glass shattered. Beyond was the back door of the shop. Seeing how large and sturdy it was, Brody immediately thought of The Glower's refashioned meat locker door. He threw an arm in front of Thorp before he stepped up to the door. Brody pointed two fingers at his own eyes, then at the ground at the back door. Congealed mud resultant from melted snow. Tramped through the puddle were recent footprints.

Thorp pulled the pistol from the back of his pants and clicked the safety catch off.

Brody studied the prints. They were from large feet, probably around the same as Brody's own. Shoes, with a decorative tread that was molded to look like a woman cradling a child, both of them adorned in flowing dreadlocks.

"Looks like it's just one person," Thorp whispered.

"Either way, keep 'em peeled," Brody said.

Brody tugged on the door handle. The door made a metallic snap and opened with a tortured groan of rusted metal. Thorp clicked on a flashlight and entered. Brody came in behind him and shut the door. Again, just like the door at the nightclub, there was no way to lock it from the inside. He noticed an aluminum tray that was used to line the bottom of a rectangular pot and jammed it up inside the door. From the way the tray was bent, that was apparently how the door was normally secured.

Inside the back room of Mother Nature's Womb were more planters on several shelves reaching to the ceiling. Every plant was dead, brittle as ancient bone. In the corner, a desk with reams of paper upon it, a clear plastic tarp thrown over. On the wall, held in place with thumbtacks, a burlap banner matching the one in Nectar's own in-home greenhouse.

Using the flashlight mounted to his phone, Brody glanced down to see if the muddy footprints went anywhere, but the entire shop's floor was covered in a soft carpeting of spilled potting soil. The moment the prints crossed the threshold of the back door, they were lost.

Before going through the papers on the desk under the tarp, they moved into the main room and looked around. This was where the shop did transactions. There was a display of different gardening tools and bags of potting soil that had deteriorated and spilled their contents onto the floor. The tang of potting soil, with its heady mix of environmentally conscious chemicals and minerals, was intoxicating. It conquered everything else. There could easily be a dead body in here somewhere, and they wouldn't even smell it.

Remaining quiet, they walked carefully and deliberately. Thorp kept ahead of Brody, aiming his light over anything of interest, his gun at the ready in his other hand.

Brody spotted a partly ajar door behind a beaded curtain. He made a soft click with his mouth, like signaling a horse, to get Thorp's attention. He pointed.

They approached the door, crossed the earthen floor as silently as they could. Brody eased the door open, and Thorp went first, bobbing his head around the corner for a quick peek, then stood at the bottom of the stairs, moving the flashlight up the risers to the landing above.

A frantic scrambling moved from one side of the upper floor to the other when they had climbed halfway up the stairs. Both Brody and Thorp instinctively ducked and pointed their guns to the top of the stairwell. They waited for the noise of clumsy fumbling to stop, then continued up the remainder of the narrow stairwell.

Thorp turned off his flashlight and tucked it away since there was a suitable amount of light pouring in from the street. He held his pistol out with both hands and scanned the various open doorways.

Brody crept into the first room, saw that it was just an empty space, with peeling paint on the walls, the floor sinking in the middle of the room, further evidence of the shop's dilapidation. He glanced up at a hole in the ceiling that went out directly to the sky.

Brody joined Thorp in the next room and found a mattress, stained and old, in the corner.

They turned to the remaining room with their sights trained on the closed door.

They were within inches of the door when they heard it. A single electronic chirp. They stopped, listened. The two men kept their breathing as calm as they could, their nostrils flaring with every breath. They took another step forward, and the chirp came again, this time two notes.

Thorp suddenly shouted, "All right, come out. Whatever you have ready to blow, just put it on the floor, okay?"

In reply came a scared yelp. They heard a metallic clunk of something heavy dropped on the floor.

Thorp lurched forward and shouldered the door aside, his gun held out.

At the back corner of the room crowded with empty aluminum shelves and decorated with more burlap banners was a young man with a mangy beard dressed in a destroyed trench coat. His hands shot above his head, his face screwed up into tearful fright, and he yelped again. His hair was long and matted and mostly contained within a baseball cap, the bill of which was threadbare.

Brody looked down at the thing resting on the

warped wooden floor. It was a large device painted a cautionary yellow, a dial with its needle flicking from zero, then clear across into the red every few seconds, in sync with the mechanical bleats. It looked hodge-podge, with new electronic additions spliced in with wires knuckled with black electrical tape, naked circuit boards clotted with dust that were hot glued in place.

"What is that thing?" Brody snapped, pointing.

"It's a Geiger counter," the man said, his voice shrill and alarmed. "Please don't kill me. I haven't done anything. I'm leaving town tonight. I won't say anything to anybody about anything. I swear to God. You already torched the files. You already got Abby and Nectar—"

"What did you say?" Thorp pushed an arm against him and ground the barrel of the Franklin-Johann to the man's temple. "Do you know what's happened to Nectar? Did *you* kill her?" He leaned in, using the length of his forearm to bracket the bearded man against a fiberboard filing cabinet.

"Stop," Brody said, putting his gun away.

"Do you know where she is?" Thorp blasted.

Brody had never seen Thorp look that way. He rested a hand on Thorp's arm, and, as if hit with a poisoned dart, Thorp immediately calmed.

He released the man, who took a step backward and straightened his duct-taped lapels.

"Well?" Thorp said.

"N-no," the man stammered. In the light filtering in through the thick, dust-choked air Brody could see that the man was in his early twenties. "All I know is from the news—about Abby, about Alton. Now you want me?

I fucking work here part-time. I was just an associate member, basically an assistant."

"You must know something." Thorp raised his gun. "Tell me."

"I don't care if you aim your *dick* at me. I'm still not going to say a single thing." The man leaned close to Thorp's face. "I don't know if you can see me, you assholes." He produced his middle finger.

Thorp batted the man's hand out of his face and shoved him.

He stumbled, stepping into an empty file box, his decorative sneakers getting caught in a tangle in torn, wet cardboard. He kicked it away. "Fuck the *both* of you. You think you can do this shit to people and get away with it and—fuck it, I'm *gone*."

"We're not here to hurt you," Brody explained. "We're looking for Nectar."

"Funny, that's the same thing they said." He skipped sidelong toward the door.

Brody blocked his path. "Who said they were looking for Nectar?"

"I'm not saying shit," the man hissed. "Abby said that if and when they come, the Geiger counter will go off. You guys showed up; it went off. It means you're playing for the other team. So, with that, I bid you assholes adieu." He tried to bolt for the door.

Brody caught him across the chest with his arm, dragged him into the room, and closed the door to remove the temptation. He flung him back with ease. The man couldn't weigh more than a hundred and twenty pounds.

Desperate and clearly feeling trapped, the man

shrieked, folding at the waist to press out maximum volume as he screamed, "I'm not going to say a goddamn thing. I made an oath to The Mothers."

"We better quiet him down," Thorp suggested. "He's making a lot of noise."

The man went on screaming, his belting call of refusal reaching an unspeakable pitch as it dissolved from words into one long peal as if he were duetting with the Geiger counter.

Thorp growled and raised his gun again. "Shut up. Just shut the hell up."

"Thorp, come on," Brody said. "Enough with the gun."

The bearded man suddenly fell silent. He cleared his throat and asked, "Thorp? You're Thorp Ashbury?"

Bending down and clicking the Geiger counter off, Brody said, "Okay, let's hear it. Who are you?" His voice echoed now that the screaming machine—and people—were silenced.

"Mateusz McPhearson. I always asked Nectar to bring you by, so we could show you everything we were doing, but I never thought I'd actually get to, like, meet you." He shook Thorp's hand.

"What are you talking about?"

Mateusz stretched out his arms to showcase the room of empty shelves, as if each one held a magical treasure that one had to have an ironclad belief to see. "A lot of this is for you. Well, when this room was worth seeing. But, yeah—you were a big inspiration to continue the fight."

Brody moved forward. "Listen, let's cut to the chase here. You trust us now and that's great, but we need to know if you can tell us what's happened to Nectar."

Mateusz consulted Thorp. "Is he cool? He's got a fixer's eyes."

"They're carotene lenses," Brody said through gritted teeth. "We came here because we read her jigsaw profile, saw she was affiliated with a group called The Mothers. We put two and two together from another jigsaw profile and saw Abigail Schwartz owned this place. Wasn't much of a stretch figuring it out, the name of the shop and the name of the group."

He laughed brusquely. "Yeah, Abby never was much good at shit like that. The woman had a cat named Meow for crying out loud."

"Are there more of you here?" Brody asked.

"More of who?"

"The Mothers."

Mateusz smiled. "That's funny, but no. It was just the three of us."

"You said you were an associate member."

"It just meant I was only allowed to get *half* the inside jokes."

"Wait, wait." Thorp said, hand held out, his other arm clutching the Franklin dangling at his side. "What do you mean this is all for me? I don't really like the sound of that. What fight?"

"All the shit they were doing to the troops and everyone else and hiding it all." Mateusz brought out a shrink-wrapped pastry from his trench coat. He unwrapped one end and sniffed the thing before biting into it, his hands shaking. "Sorry, but I've got to do something about my blood sugar—otherwise I'll keel over."

"What the hell are you talking about?"

"I'm prediabetic, I think."

"No." Thorp groaned, "What you said. About the shit they were doing to the troops, the hiding—*what* were they hiding? How does it involve me, exactly?"

Mateusz held his thousand-yard stare, talking into the bitten end of the jam-filled crust. "You sign the waiver: you're a candidate for their tests. We brought in dozens of guys who just got back from overseas. We found out that a good half of them have it, one version of the wavelength or another, still ringing around in them like a bell. We had all kinds of records, test results. Guys going on tape telling us what it was like. That being, you know, before." He gestured at the space around him again, albeit this time with less dramatics.

Brody noticed that each aluminum shelf held the outline in dust where a box had been. Each shelf on ten different racks filling the entire length of the room had once held an awful lot of information—packed boxes, judging by how bent the shelves were in places.

"Maybe you should start at the beginning," Brody suggested.

20

After Mateusz swallowed the final mouthful of his prepackaged pastry, he took a seat on the floor. "Last July. Some of the soldiers from the area were allowed to come home, and everywhere you looked there they were. They kind of stand out in a crowd, with those tragic hairdos they inflict you guys with. Anyway, we were here. That being Abby, Nectar, a few others, and myself. The air conditioner was broken, and it was, like, sweltering in here.

"So, we decided to go out for drinks. We piled into the van and headed down to Brentley's Pub up the road apiece. Even though it's only two in the afternoon on a Wednesday, I think, the place was just crammed with soldiers. All in their uniforms and shit, drinking and carrying on. We decided to stick around, despite it being crowded and loud—and that's when our little Abigail fell in love."

He paused to light a cigarette. "So, it was Abby and Alton, Alton and Abby—day and night with those two. We still did protests, but it often ended up being me and Nectar and a few of the others going instead. Abby was spending more time away. And when she did spend time here, progressively we began to see a sort of—you know, *way* about her. Nectar and I took her aside and asked if her new soldier-boy boyfriend was hitting her or something. She said he was sick all the time. Headaches, nosebleeds, violent outbursts. Never toward her, mind you, just wrecking his apartment and stuff.

"I talked to him, and he said he couldn't quite put a finger on what was going on. He mentioned he had done some bad shit overseas, and I suggested he might have post-traumatic stress. Well, Abby got wind of that and made it like her life's mission to fix him, bought him a holo-camera to document his thoughts and work shit out. Anyway, he wasn't getting any better so she started watching his tapes. Shitty move, I know. But she found out what was really eating at him."

"What was it?" Thorp asked, his voice dry.

"Nectar was the one who told me, who had heard it from Abby. I never saw his holo-videos."

"Well, what did she say?" Thorp urged.

Mateusz flicked ashes, wrapped his arms around his knees, and said, "He moved out of his apartment to live in the basement at the Y, because he claimed it was 'safer that way.' He recorded the videos more often, and Abby kept watching them. He was antsy, feeling like he was being watched all the time. Abby couldn't take it any longer, so finally she confronted him about what he had said on one of his videos: he had worked as an information technician while on tour in Malaysia. He'd been assigned to set up equipment for the base."

"What sort of equipment?"

"That's just it." Mateusz grinned. "What Nectar described to me sounded like it was just a hub for wireless networks. Probably so the troops could use their ordis in the barracks. Malaysia still doesn't have the blanket yet. She wouldn't go into much more detail because she was freaked out. It wasn't like Nectar to be so direct, but she said that you"—he pointed at Thorp with his cigarette—"were stateside and, no offense or anything, you had kind of . . . changed."

"She thought I had changed?" Thorp said. "I'm the same guy I've always been."

Mateusz frowned. "I hate to be the one to tell you, but Abby rigged up that Geiger herself, specifically for the wavelength that Alton had in him. And it rang the same way with him as it did when you walked in here."

Brody's gaze fell upon the hodgepodge Geiger counter. He wondered if it would make that same trill if he was alone in the room. He had been getting a lot of headaches lately, but he figured it came from switching from lenses to sonar so often. And back home, he chalked up the occasional nosebleed to allergies or the notoriously bad air of downtown Minneapolis.

"What happened to him?" Thorp asked.

Mateusz and Brody both looked to the floor.

Mateusz muttered, "Apparently you don't watch much of the news."

"Why? What happened?"

Brody filled him in. "About a month ago he shot ten people at a shopping mall in Minneapolis. Then himself."

Mateusz ground out his cigarette on the floor. "We did some scans on him as we did more research. We asked him if he knew or remembered anything, but he'd get in this really weird, hostile way. We could ask him questions for only fifteen minutes max before we had to stop and let him cool off."

"Nectar received letters from Probitas, a security team, saying they should stop making a fuss with their clients," Brody said. "Do you suppose it could be connected to Alton?"

"What do you mean?"

"Maybe Alton told Nectar something that sent them on the trail of people they shouldn't have been chasing, the ones who'd used Alton."

"I can't say. They kept me in the dark about a lot of what they did. Whatever they'd dug up, they knew they had to take it underground, keep it quiet." Mateusz glanced at the empty shelves. "This room used to be where Abby made her flower arrangements. Obviously, you can see she ended up devoting more time to digging into stuff other than her business. When the place went belly-up, the building got condemned. I figured whoever they'd pissed off was behind it, and I offered to use my own savings to keep the joint alive, but Abby insisted they take it as an opportunity to go off the grid, become squatters in a building she used to own."

Mateusz stared at an old green and red plaid sleeping bag in the corner. "She used to sleep over there. Nectar, that is. She had your stuff—the research specifically for you, Thorp, over there. She didn't have as much as Abby had collected, but she was trying."

"What happened to it?" Thorp asked.

"We were getting groceries one night. Came back, everything was gone. The place next door? I'm sure you saw that. Yeah, same night our place gets broken into, a fire just 'accidentally' starts. We picked through it, and, sure enough, some of our shit was in there. We got a couple of sheets, though, nothing major. Here."

Mateusz got to his feet, dusted himself off, and stood on the seat of a chair. He reached into the bare rafters and brought down a shoe box, then brushed the yellow powder from its lid and opened it. Inside, a few half-melted CT scans printed on transparencies. As Mateusz fanned them out, Brody could plainly see the progressive degeneration. The first looked normal. The colors in the second were a bit shifted, the black and gray swirling slightly. The third looked like a twisted mess, a grayscale tempest lodged within the cross-sectioned head.

Mateusz held the first transparency at arm's length against the light. "Alton. Good old Al Christmas. Never had I seen such a bad case of the world totally fucking someone over." He shook his head and put the transparencies away. "Shame. He was an all right dude."

"Why'd he do it?" Thorp asked, his voice quiet.

Mateusz scoffed. "If Abby was here right now, she'd slap you silly talking like that."

"Why?"

"When you were in this room, talking about Alton and what happened in Minneapolis, you were to strictly say: 'What he was *made* to do.' But sometimes they'd get on a roll and forget I was around. They had code for everything, but there was one person they never used a code for."

"Who?"

"Elizabeth Lake. The wife of Thomas Lake, the president of DRN Engineering. She was one of the people Alton shot. Abby and Nectar fixated on the idea that she was the key to everything. I mean, Minneapolis was kind of a haul for Alton. Why not shoot people here in Chicago if he was so compelled? That's one. And then have some engineering bigwig's wife killed, two. I have to admit; even to me it sounds fishy."

"So you think Alton was being blackmailed or something?" Thorp murmured. "Was he a moonlighting merc and you guys just didn't know it?"

"If you knew Alton, you'd know he joined up because he didn't know what else to do with his life. He never had a shred of interest in hurting anyone. He wanted to learn a trade, get married, have a mess of kids. I think Abby and Nectar found out the exposure to the shit he worked on overseas was associated with the shooting."

"The same stuff that I was apparently exposed to?" Thorp asked, glancing at the Geiger counter. "I honestly don't remember feeling anything."

"You don't feel it," Mateusz said. "It gets in you and

that's it. I saw the CT your sister got from your medical history. That's why I was so surprised to see you here."

"What's wrong with his—?" Brody asked.

"So that's what I can expect," Thorp said, cutting him off. "That I'll be going about my way, minding my own business, and suddenly I'll become hypnotized and feel the urge to shoot a bunch of people?"

"See." Mateusz gave a miserable laugh. "This is where I always end up losing my audience. They take what I'm trying to tell them and throw it back in my face. It's a whole lot different from hypnotization—they're creating tumors in the brain to shift things around, crush certain things out while amplifying others by adjusting the brain's topography, the hardware itself. They're promoting cancer growth in order to—"

Thorp took a weak, shuffling step backward. "My fault. It's my fault my sister's dead." His knees buckled, and he caught himself against the wall. He withdrew the stubby butt of a cigar and lit it, shaking his head and pinching the bridge of his nose. "If I hadn't been such a kook and jumped down her throat whenever she told me she was going to tour Europe or take night classes to become an auctioneer or whatever . . . My sister's dead. Because of me . . . Nectar is dead. She got somebody pissed off by poking into shit thinking she was helping me."

"I blame it on Alton," Mateusz said. "Not to speak ill of the dead or anything, but if it wasn't for Abby hooking up with him and becoming interested when he got nosebleeds all the time—all this could've been prevented. We could've all just been cruising along, none the wiser. But you know. C'est la vie."

"Do you know where they may've had another Mothers hideout?" Brody asked. "Any mention of where they may've kept a backup of research?"

"Abby couldn't keep the lights on in this place. I doubt she could front the rent for a hideout. They worked strictly on hard copy, no backups. With nothing digital, there'd be no risk of a hack."

"What were they planning before they went missing?" Brody said.

"They were going to sign up—that's the last I heard from them. They'd decided right out there on the sidewalk after Alton's funeral." Mateusz paused, the hollow in his cheek flexing in and out as he ground his teeth. "The release, the waiver. That's what it all hinged on."

Brody recalled when he had decided to join the Army. He had gotten arrested, and his father gave him an ultimatum the morning he picked him up from jail. Either he could join the service or take the Greyhound to his uncle's in New Orleans and work on prefab houses, every one of his paychecks coming back to his father to recoup for court costs and bail.

Brody chose the Army. He remembered the recruiter's office in St. Paul, and it was there he met Thorp, who had decided to sign up in Minnesota on a whim after a particularly bad road trip Brody never got the full story on. He was standing outside in the summer heat, running hands over his freshly sheared scalp, when Thorp walked up to bum a smoke, commenting that Brody didn't have to cut his hair himself, that they had someone to do it. Brody laughed, said he thought it'd look like he was taking things too serious. They shared a chuckle and were called inside a moment later to start the filing process. They sat down at separate desks, and the sergeant handed them each a pen and a phone book–sized tome of forms to fill out.

As Brody flipped through the forms, the sergeant put his hand atop the pile. "This is just saying if you get hurt in the line of duty, you want your organs donated."

Did he want his organs donated?

"Sign it," the sergeant said. "There's about fifty more of you goons I have to get through here today."

Brody signed, flipped to the next page. The title of the next form was something about deciding to waive any ill will toward a third party group that wished to—

"This is just saying that you don't mind being exposed to certain plastics that have been discovered in some rare cases to cause cancer. You're young and strong; you'll be fine. Sign it."

Brody clicked the pen twice and jotted his signature.

"Yeah," Brody said, blinking back into the present, "they make you sign all kinds of forms. A lot of forms."

"Right," Mateusz continued, "and Abby and Nectar wanted to get far enough through the process that they'd be asked to sign the waivers, then they could snatch the sheets and bolt. They had a lawyer. All he needed was proof—a copy of that release—showing that this certain unnamed third party wanted to test the effects of microwaves on the human brain during the recruit's duty. In the really fine print it said that even after the recruits were retired from active service, they permitted the Army to test on them even further."

"Did they get them?" Brody asked.

"No. What I just told you is all Alton could remember from what he'd read."

"He saw that and still signed?"

Mateusz shrugged. "Needed the bread." He turned to Thorp. "I'm really surprised she didn't say anything to you, let you in on the plan."

Thorp stared at the floor, watching the smoke curl from the end of his cigar.

In his silence, Mateusz added, "It's honorable what she did, and it's honorable what you did, you know, signing up initially and everything. It's . . . it's kind of fucked up, how it all turned out. I'm sorry. If I could make it different, I would."

With that, Thorp walked across the room, turned the corner at the door, and headed downstairs. He called over his shoulder, "I'll be in the car when you're ready."

Brody waited until he heard the back door of the shop below close. He turned to Mateusz. "Do you think Titian Shandorf might have any direct involvement in this? Abigail's body was found in his club."

"Who's to say? They—and I do mean *they* in the classic conspiracy theorist definition of the word as nefarious persons unknown—may just as well be trying to pin something on him by *putting* Abby's body there. Clear any possible ties between them and us by throwing a wanted serial killer in the mix." His face twitched. "But when some scrawny dude with the nastiest teeth I've ever seen on a living person comes wandering off the street and says he hears it from a good source that he should circle the block every couple of days, check up on us, make sure we're playing *safe*—one has to wonder."

"You think it was him?"

"Sure as hell looked like the sketches they got up everywhere online to me," Mateusz said.

"Any advice on how I can find him?" Brody asked. "I really think he's our best lead."

Mateusz sighed, peeking out from underneath his messy tangle of hair, one strand twitching every time he blinked, the lashes snagging against it. "I'll tell you how it is. This whole deal is one big fucking machine. And you and I, we don't even get the credit of being a cog—no, we're not even cogs in the machine; we're the fucking particles of shit stuck in the teeth of those cogs. And my best advice is to *make* like shit and go stink it up somewhere else where they can't find you. Because whoever they are, they'll just roll right over you. They saw to it that Abby and Nectar aren't making any more noise. You should consider yourself lucky *you* haven't gotten their attention yet."

"Do you think Titian is working as a hitter?"

"The only one who would have any knowledge of that is six feet under."

Brody grimaced. "Who?"

Mateusz took the gritty shoe box and shoved it to Brody's chest. "Alton Noel," he said as if he were handing over the man's ashes.

Brody held the box and noticed it was astonishingly light. "You want me to have this?"

Mateusz leaned forward and whispered, "You want to continue the dig, you're going to need the map. All you can do is check for an online diary or something. Maybe Alton kept one in the service. Maybe he put those holo-videos online. Maybe he was an astute notetaker in the classroom of life. Who knows. But he understood what was going on, and it's a serious wonder how much of it he took with him, you know, to the grave. For what it's worth, I hope you guys at least find her body. Nectar was a cool chick and her brother deserves closure." The surviving member of The Mothers got four steps in the direction of the door.

"Wait," Brody said, holding the shoe box. "How many? What's the percentage?"

"Of what?"

"The soldiers they used."

"What, you're worried you might be one?" he asked. Brody nodded.

"One way to find out." Mateusz nodded at the Geiger counter. "Abby got that thing perfect. You click it on, and you'll have your answer once the capacitor warms up."

Brody looked at the ramshackle machine on the floor, the leather-wrapped handle, the frizz of wires sticking out all over. Had both of them set it off when they walked in or just Thorp? Headaches . . . nosebleeds.

"Only way to know without a body scan." Mateusz checked his watch. "I'd hang out, but my bus is leaving in a half hour. Take care of yourself. I wish I had the balls to stick around and see it through . . ." He turned and left.

Brody listened to him walk down the hall and descend the stairs. He heard the door shut and the cadenced, squeaking tramp of ornate sneakers on the sidewalk. Brody looked out between the wooden slats and watched Mateusz cross the street, moving quickly like a mouse, and vanish into the shadows when he reached the end of the block.

03:59:59.

Brody surveyed the contents of the room. The scattered, empty folders in autumnal shades littering the floor, the yawning accordion files, and the stacked, bent columns of cardboard boxes unloaded of their cached information. The Geiger counter. He pulled his flashlight beam away and left it where it lay on the floor in the dark. He navigated his way downstairs, taking only the shoe box with the transparencies with him.

Walking through the disarrayed shop, he thought about Thorp and his frequent smile, dirty limericks, and trademark laugh. He knew his friend hadn't hardened with age, that his personality hadn't turned dour due to war. Instead, the inside of Thorp's head probably resembled Alton Noel's CT scans he now carried under his arm and deposited into the backseat of the Fairlane.

With his head dropped back on the headrest and his eyes closed, Thorp appeared to be utterly drained, pale. He was breathing with slow, deliberate inhales as if fighting just to keep from vibrating to pieces.

After lighting a cigarette, Brody flung the pack onto the dashboard, where it skidded across the ice that formed around the vents. They sat in silence, staring through the open windshield frame at the deserted street ahead. There was nothing to see except the snow.

Brody started the car and rested his hands on the wheel. "Still on board?"

Thorp drew in a breath and sighed. "Yeah."

21

The coffee at the truck stop tasted like highway runoff. Brody set the polystyrene cup down on the metal ledge of the MetroTab phone booth and gave it a dirty, distrusting look. From inside the enclosure, where one could upload new versions of GPS that included up-to-the-second address listings, Brody watched Thorp tape Saran wrap to the edge of the windshield frame, then pull the roll across. He carefully walked around the car holding the roll at arm's length so it wouldn't tangle, and, after biting a strip of duct tape, he secured the other end. He did this until there was a new shrink-wrapped windshield installed.

As the bar glacially filled on the MetroTab patch download, Brody glanced away from his phone to watch Thorp carry the empty roll to the wastebasket.

While dusting off his hands after a job finished, Thorp seemed to feel his friend's gaze and looked up. Brody saw in Thorp's eyes a mounting worry that the man was swiftly trying to cover by busying himself.

Thorp took a seat on the trunk of the Fairlane, folded his arms, and waited, watching the interstate's gold and crimson lights ebb and flow. A second later, he popped up and went to the front of the car again, this time to lift the hood and check the fluid levels. Understandably, he was seeking busywork.

The download booth with the key-scratched fiberglass windows told Brody, "Thank you for using MetroTab. Every listing in the Chicago, Illinois, area has now been downloaded to your mobile phone and/or handheld device."

Brody stepped under the pump awnings that buzzed with a million watts of fluorescent white. He queried *Alton Noel* on his freshly downloaded program.

"We're about half a quart low," Thorp said.

"We'll be sure to tell Seb when we return it to him," Brody chided.

"I'm just saying," Thorp complained, "if we're going to drive all over Chicago, we might as well have one thing marked off the list that *won't* go awry on us. In most cases disaster can be prevented by keeping equipment in decent working order, you know."

Brody turned his phone around to show Thorp the display. He stared at it. Brody narrated for what the program was displaying, "Al Christmas has an online journal."

"Who the hell is Al Christmas?"

"I searched for Alton Noel and got no results. Mateusz mentioned Al Christmas, and lo and behold, I dropped it in a search engine and got a hit."

"Well, what's it say?"

"Can't access it."

"Suppose it's them." Thorp squinted. "Blocking it."

"Possibly," Brody said.

"It's still up, though? You can see the address is operational, yeah?"

Brody nodded.

"That means it hasn't been shut down all the way; it's just been blocked. Could probably access it if we could get to whatever he used to create the journal. Most people don't bother ever signing out of things like that because—who would? It's only a blog. I mean, how often does this shit happen to a person, right?" Thorp snorted. "It's probably under his reader application's Favorites folder. One click and you'd be right in."

"Are you suggesting breaking into yet another person's home?" Brody asked, lowering his phone.

"You never know what he might've put on there. The guy hadn't been back long. He probably needed a way to vent. I'm sure if something was up, he wrote it on there. You should see this box that I got out in the barn chock-full of composition books."

Brody raised his phone to examine the page again. "Just like Mateusz said, his last known address was at a YMCA."

"Nothing surprising about that. I shacked up there for a while when I first got back."

"Suppose it's even worth checking? He's been dead for over a month. Wouldn't they throw out his stuff?"

Thorp grinned. "You see this coat I'm wearing? Courtesy of the YMCA lost and found. Those people don't throw *anything* away. What the police didn't take following the shooting without a doubt ended up in the lost and found bin. And if Alton was using an ordi or some other device to write the journal, it's still probably there and transmitting especially given the fact that there *is* a journal to deny you entrance *into*, right?"

For a second, all that could be heard was the ceaseless hum of the interstate and droning of the fluorescent lights above their heads.

Brody unbuttoned the collar of his coat. "What do you want to do?"

"What do you mean?"

"We have two leads here. We have Alton Noel's place at the YMCA; there's only one in town with rooms for rent. And we have Seb. With one simple flip of the switch we can have instant access to a potentially in-the-know criminal. Which way do you want to go?"

"Hell, I don't know. You're the gumshoe. Say you're on the trail of some . . . person or whatever. Which leads do you follow?" He paused. "We could always split up and see what that got us." Thorp looked at Brody, at the interstate, back at Brody. He chewed his lip, twitching and flexing his pinkies back and forth, back and forth, the orchestra of actions seeming wholly unconscious.

"You all right?"

He groaned, a trumpeting that signaled all his jittery mannerisms to cease. He looked down his nose at Brody. "Just stop. Come on, man. We get some news about the wires over my house potentially making me weird, and now you're going to look at me sideways every time I say anything. Trust me. Fit as a fiddle. I'm good. I think we're finally onto something. On the drive over here, I was giving it some thought and . . ." He nodded, never finishing his sentence. "Yeah, I feel fine. Why?"

"Never mind. And no, by the way. Splitting up: bad idea. You don't have a phone."

"Fine. We can stick together. No big deal."

"But which do we do first?"

Thorp leaned to one side to get his hand into the back pocket of his jeans. He withdrew a quarter. "Heads we go and pay this Seb fella a visit. Tails we go take a swing past the YMCA."

Seb's phone issued a couple notes of music. He had it flipped open before the song finished. He was out with his dudes at a bar, trying to rid their minds of a particularly sour day they had just experienced. Their boss was in no uncertain terms a slave driver. Working in the yards was a killer. A man could feel like his ass would bond to the seat of the forklift after what felt like days without a break. Sure, he had the Slavic cunt and her sow daughter to count on for bonus finances, but a man of appetites needed a lot of dough to fund not only overhead but a means to go out and have the big fun sometimes, too.

They were about to split for another locale to continue their night elsewhere since the she-beast behind the counter decided they were already lit enough and denied them another round. Seb found it fortuitous, since now out of the bar he could hear his cell ring—something that would've been drowned out inside the last watering hole. He smiled. The text informed him that his car's tracker had just been turned on. After the dry cleaner bitch had boosted his ride, he'd kicked himself for not having the thing on all the time. Now here she was probably in the parking garage of whatever dump she lived in, fiddling with the settings of her newly procured ride, trying to find a way to turn on the windshield auto-tint, but she had tripped the tracker instead.

He grinned. "Silly broad," he said, the cotton ball in his cheek partly slurring his speech.

"What's going on?" Spanky asked.

Seb showed him his cell, the map displaying downtown and the flashing arrowhead in the middle representing his ride.

"That your whip?" Spanky inquired.

Seb nodded.

"Well, what you gonna do?"

"I'm about to get my ride back from a very, very silly little bitch. Let's get moving before she realizes what she's just done to herself."

Spanky ground his gaudy Zäh—the SUV that was famously only available in a pearlescent paint job—to thrumming life. The Zäh growled out into the freshly plowed street, ignored the red light, and thundered due north.

They approached the parking lot of a closed-down porno theater and among the flickering streetlamps saw the lonely Fairlane sitting by itself. Spanky angled his vehicle behind the stucco-colored car. The piercing blue-white of the Zäh's twelve headlights bounced off a rust-barnacled bumper, the license plate nearly hidden under a chalky layer of road salt. The running boards were splashed with dirt and more salt, evidence that the girl had really made use of her new ride and taken it all around town.

Seb sat forward, anxious.

"That it?" Spanky asked.

"That's it," he said. "Cut the high-beams on."

The Fairlane was washed in even more brilliant blue light. The Zäh's high beams passed easily through the rear window into the car. There were no silhouettes occupying the seats.

He motioned for his friend to pull forward. They crunched ahead cautiously, the massive tires roped with chains clinking and grating on icy tarmac.

They nosed up directly behind the Fairlane. Spanky flopped aside the stained floor mat and withdrew a matte black submachine gun from a compartment in the floorboard. He pulled back the slide, hard. Seb knew this trick; the double slap of metal striking metal with the first round being chambered would be heard by anyone stupid enough to try to hide within the Fairlane, a warning. Seb put out a hand to his partner. *Easy does it. Approach the car slowly.*

The men narrowed in on the car parenthetically— Seb on the passenger side, Spanky on the other. Seb drew his Colt and trained it on the passenger door. He took a breath and lurched forward quickly to peek inside, ready to pull the trigger. Through the frosted glass, he saw the front and back seats were empty. No one in the car. He noticed the windscreen was shimmery, oddly shiny.

He moved to the front of the car and bellowed, "What the fuck?"

"What's up?" Spanky whispered.

"The windshield. That fucking bitch broke my windshield. Look at this plastic shit, this sandwich wrap bullshit she put in its place. I'm going to put a fuckin' brick through that bitch's head."

Even though Brody was coming up behind the slurring lug, he knew his presence had been detected while he was still a few strides off. He leapt forward just as Seb was starting to about-face and put the barrel of his unloaded Franklin-Johann to Seb's neck before he could turn all the way around.

Seb froze, his posture going rigid. From behind, Brody could see Seb look to his friend for assistance. In profile, the one eye he could see was bugging from its socket. *Do something*, that eye screamed.

"Don't look at him," Brody scolded. "Just put down the gun, Seb."

Brody glanced around the giant to see Thorp had done his part, had come up behind Spanky. With the clearest rendition of "okay, you got me" Brody had ever seen on a human face, Spanky cast his submachine gun to the asphalt with a loud clatter.

"Your turn," Brody instructed his own captive. "You too."

Seb had his arms raised, but his hand was still folded

around the gun, nearly burying it in his impressive mitt. "You're pussy-whipped by that fat bitch? Tell me it ain't so. You can get all kinds in this city, man, and you're going to go for that bitch—do her dirty work for her? Jesus H."

"Get rid of the gun," Brody said.

Seb reluctantly tossed the Colt away. "What's this about? Is it because I roughed up your girl? If you knew her like I knew her, you'd do the same thing—she got a mouth on her. A bitch should know her place. A bitch should be seen and not heard. You do this, and you're in for a world of hurt. Spanky, can you believe the stupidity of this dap son of a bitch?"

Spanky didn't look to be in the mood to shoot off at the mouth like Seb. He kept his hands raised, his expression woeful defeat. "Daps be dumb," was all he managed, and even that was barely audible with his downcast face partly buried in the fur collar of his coat.

"Get in." Brody shoved the barrel of his pistol harder against the back of Seb's thick neck. "And cut the chest thumping. You're not fooling anyone here."

Seb moved obediently toward the passenger door.

"No, you're going to drive." Brody glanced at Thorp, who was staring at Spanky. He had a weird air about him, both focused and indolent. Brody had to try twice to get his attention.

"Yeah?" Thorp asked, blinking out of his trance.

"You take him, have him follow us in his car," Brody said.

"Okay," Thorp said and ushered Seb's pal back in his Zäh with a wave of his handgun.

Brody kept his pistol trained on Seb as he got in

the driver's side, the suspension creaking beneath the man's considerable heft. When sliding into the passenger seat, indigo cubes of safety glass and snow crunched beneath them.

Seb surveyed the interior of his car, the broken glass everywhere, and when he met Brody's gaze, there was no shortage of hate in his eyes.

"Start it up. Let's go," Brody ordered.

"You really expect us to get far with my car looking like this? We're going to get pulled over. They'll find you with that piece, baldy back there with a gun on my buddy. Let's just call it even. You can keep the car, give it to your woman if that's what you want. Just leave me the fuck out of it."

"Let's get moving," Brody said, ignoring Seb's pleas.

Seb double tapped the power button on the Fairlane, and after a second of protest the engine rumbled to life. Seb crushed the steering wheel, the rubber creaking under his grip. He cocked his head toward Brody, smirking. "Well, where would you like to go?" he asked, parroting an auto cab's pleasant greeting with a sneer.

Brody broke his stare on Seb for a moment to look back at the Zäh. The two men both watched, waiting for what came next, the windshield wipers thumping back and forth. Thorp gave a weak thumbs-up, his expression remaining flat.

Brody turned forward. "Take me to whatever shit hole you live in. We'll start there."

"So you're going to not only boost my car, but you want to *rob* me as well?"

"Not at all. I just want to get out of here before, as you suggested, the cops come sniffing around. Drive."

Chicago was arctic, deserted.

The only traffic were the snowplows grinding up one street and down the next, amassing dunes at intersections and burying cars whose owners hadn't bothered to move them. Flashing amber lights, cascading over the cityscape. The hiss of the salt being scattered in the plow trucks' wake, like it was attempting to hide its scent trail from predators.

Seb drove like a gentleman. Kept it well below the speed limit, stopped at lights as he should, and even used his turn signal.

When one panel of the cling wrap broke free, the snow and wind pounded in over the hood and into their faces. Squinting through it, Brody held the gun with one hand, resting it on his lap. There were cameras at every major intersection, but they were too close now to get stopped for having an illegal weapon in a moving vehicle on a public street. He kept glancing at Thorp and Spanky to make sure they weren't lagging too far behind. Getting split up because of a poorly timed light could prove disastrous.

During a wait at a painfully long light, Seb adjusted the heat, screwing the knob all the way to the hottest setting, but the vents couldn't compete with how much cold was seeping in. Seb, despite his size, was visibly shivering, his gap-toothed jaw rattling at inconsistent intervals. "You're not even with that dry cleaner chick, are you?"

Brody pulled his coat collar up. "Just a friend."

"And her errand boy, taking out the trash. Is that it?" Seb asked.

"It's not even about her, if you want to know the truth," Brody said. "But for the record, when we get through here, if I ever hear you saying a fucking *word* to her—I swear to Christ Himself I'll come and find you." It was an honest threat, but at the same time, Brody felt like he was doing the chest thumping now. Still, he left the caveat out there in the chilled space between them. For whatever reason, Brody felt it had to be said.

"This is the face I make when I'm scared." Seb laughed a single high-pitched note through his nose.

"Just drive."

Brody wished he was home and away from all this. He wanted to put on some music, sit by his row of windows, and watch the sun come up. He wanted to buff the floors of the community center—work off the remainder of his debt—and never get involved in anyone's problems ever again.

When they came to the next red light, Brody watched in the side mirror as Thorp gazed at Spanky as if he were weaving a long and altogether boring story. But Spanky wasn't speaking. The weekend gangster, with the eyebrow ring and tattooed cheekbones, held the wheel in both hands and stared directly ahead, his pierced lip unmoving. Thorp dabbed his upper lip with the back of his hand. When Thorp pulled it away, despite his view being divided by a mirror and a pane of glass, Brody could see a bloody streak across the lower half of Thorp's face. A nosebleed.

Brody watched Thorp dab again and again, checking his hand each time he pulled it away. He'd glance at Spanky to make sure he wasn't using the opportunity to pull a fast one but kept dabbing at the slow escape of red from his nostril. Thorp looked up, found Brody's gaze, and held it. With a red-streaked hand, he made the A-OK gesture that denoted "clear for takeoff."

Brody nodded and Thorp smiled but not with his eyes.

"Go," he told Seb. "It's green."

Not much to Brody's surprise, Seb lived in a cubie, an underground extended-stay motel. The living area was a ten-by-ten cement cube that came with a Murphy bed, no TV or refrigerator, not even a toilet or a sink. The cubie tenants shared a couple of bathrooms upstairs that doubled as the public restroom for the bus depot. Cubie Apartments, a place for the discerning criminal—as even the commercials subtly stated in not so many words. The mascot for the place was even a lamb seen in mid-leap over a fence. Undoubtedly, its look of mischievous delight was meant to convey someone dodging a cop, parole officer, or bounty hunter.

Seb turned down a slush-littered back street and up to a garage door painted in the candy cane stripe, fought with the electric window to get it to shimmy down just far enough to allow his arm out, and punched in a ten-digit code at a panel. From there, Seb drove the Fairlane down the ramp into the dank underground area where the lighting was sparse and the entire place reeked of exhaust and human filth.

He wedged the Fairlane into the parking spot of

his apartment and killed the engine. Spanky carefully maneuvered his ostentatious pearl-on-wheels sport utility vehicle into the next spot over. The attached cubie was currently vacant, its door laced with police tape. Seb sat with his hands in his lap, looking ahead at the dented metal door of his miniscule home.

To Brody, it appeared that he was preparing himself for death—his face was back to the solemn frown that made Brody think even more of those Easter Island heads. The fire in his eyes seemed to have guttered out to a weak smolder sometime during the drive.

"Go ahead," Seb said. "Do me in. God will understand I was just a misguided fuckup."

Next to them, the engine of the Zäh silenced.

Brody looked beyond Seb to see that Thorp still had his gun trained on the friend. But Brody was unable to make out Thorp's expression. He could see only the side of his face, a smear of dried blood hooking around from his nose like lipstick that had been applied during a sneezing jag.

Brody returned his attention to Seb. "I'm not going to kill you."

"Then what do you want? I don't have much. I already blew my whole check tonight."

"I don't want your money, either." Brody tried to find a way to word his request. He took a deep breath and shifted in his seat. "I want to find Titian Shandorf."

"The goddamn serial killer? What in the fuck do you want to find that animal for?" Seb gasped.

It surprised Brody to see someone as hardened as Seb cower at the mere suggestion of Titian Shandorf.

"It doesn't concern you. If you don't know him, maybe I'll just change my mind about killing you and move on to your friend over there, see if *he* knows anything."

Seb remained silent. He gazed at his cubie door.

Brody squeaked on the cracked seat as he turned. He thumbed back the hammer on the Franklin-Johann. "Giving me the silent treatment isn't exactly a wise tactic at this particular juncture. Time is an issue here, and I need to know what you know if you want to continue to be able to live in this dump."

"I say anything about him, he'll find me," Seb said, his sturdy bravado obviously spent. "He's a ruthless motherfucker. He cuts people up, fuckin' keeps people locked in *cages*, tortures them, *does* shit to them. Rapes them and makes them eat shit and drain cleaner and forces them to kill themselves. Records it, sells the tapes. He gets off on it."

"Well, by the look of things, you're not a stranger to cutting people up, either." Brody knocked the barrel of his handgun against the plastic-encased testicles hanging from the rearview mirror.

"Those are bull nuts. I just hustle money. I say a few choice words to that chick and her mom, they cough up dough, and I go about my merry way. Shandorf and his crew are into some *other* shit. Human sacrifices. Satanist stuff."

"There's a rumor that he can also be bought, despite being such a sick fuck."

"You can't buy someone like that. He's a volcano with rabies. He gets his hooks into something and that's it. You get in his crosshairs, your days are numbered."

"Do you know anything or not?" Brody pointed the pistol directly at Seb's cheekbone. He didn't let the metal touch his flesh, didn't want to scare him that much, but he wanted to make a more thorough threat, a mortal promise hovering in his periphery. "Because, and I'll remind you, this is important."

"The Glower is the only place I know you can find him."

"Nope, I checked there already. The place is dead. A few knives, a dance floor, some sound equipment. Besides, the place got raided and it's on lockdown, under constant surveillance. He wouldn't go back there, and I won't waste any more of my time with it, either."

"If he's not at The Glower, I don't know where the fuck he could be. If you were some psycho killer, do you think you'd make it easy to be found? I hear the guy burned his jig years ago, owns no electronics—making sure there's no way to trace him. The motherfucker probably doesn't even have fingerprints anymore. Maybe he used a laser pointer or some shit to screw up his retinas so that not even *those* would scan and injected himself with other people's blood so it won't test right. If the cops can't find him, you sure as hell won't be able to."

Brody weighed the conjecture and the facts. Like so many urban legends, the truths just sounded like truths, whereas the bogeyman stuff didn't hold up when analyzed logically.

Brody put the grip of the pistol against his forehead, as if he were attempting to break a fever with the aid of the cold metal. He had his eyes closed to think for just one second. He heard the creak of Seb shifting on the split vinyl seat. Out of the corner of his eye, Brody saw Seb's palm and the five stretching towers of his outspread fingers reaching toward him, a hand big enough to crush a planet.

He turned the pistol at him. "Hold it."

"Sorry, pal. Holding your piece like that, it was almost like you *wanted* me to see your shooter has no clip in." Seb clutched a twisted handful of Brody's coat, pulling him closer and driving a fist into his face at the same time.

22

Brody took the hit, his head lashing back and colliding with the passenger side window—the glass crunching and spiderwebbing.

Seb seethed, hissing and foaming as he crushed Brody down into the seat and struggled to get a solid hold on him. His callused hands fought past Brody's frenzied thrashing and found their place around his throat.

In a fit of self-preservation, Brody tried pistol-whipping the man, but the swing was weak in the tight confines of the Fairlane, Seb easily slapped the gun aside. Brody next tried clawing at Seb's hands. He could feel the pressure of backed-up blood in his face, his skin tingling with the first indicative bites of suffocation. With Seb putting his entire body weight into the choke hold, there'd be no way to peel him off.

Brody wriggled his fingers into the pocket of his coat to fetch the knuckleduster. He found it, accidentally looped his fingers into it backward, flipped it around, and got it onto his fingers properly. He connected with Seb's jaw and his hold loosened slightly. Brody drew back and jabbed at him again and again, but the giant was unwilling to let go of his prey. Brody had made him lose face tonight, and that obviously wasn't something the man took lightly. Seb's sweat-greased face formed a wicked sneer of victory.

Brody punched him a third and fourth time, the metal singing out against Seb's skull. His head was turned with each strike slightly, barely nudged, a divot of skin pocked in. Seb's smile was as unwavering as his apparent determination to throttle the life from Brody.

There was a change in vacuum within the car—the cling wrap spanning the windshield frame sucking in like a sail facing an unexpected wind change. Seb's clench slackened, and the winning simper on his bloodied mouth turned solemn.

Thorp ducked into the Fairlane, his pistol pressed to the back of Seb's head. "My friend may not like to carry loaded weapons, but I assure you this one *is* loaded. Get out."

Seb struggled backward out of the car.

Brody rubbed his throat and barked the dead air from his lungs. When he stepped out of the car, he did it with unsure legs. The world was filled with streaking comets and the glittering aftereffect traces of nearly having been strangulated.

When Brody came around to where Thorp held Seb at gunpoint, he noticed Spanky had been brought out as well. Both of the men stood before Thorp's sights.

"What now?" Seb asked, shrugging, casually bleeding.

"You're going to give me your keys, phone, and your jigsaw," Brody managed, his voice wracked and hoarse.

"What? Do you have any idea how much it costs to get a replacement jig card? And my phone? What the fuck? Get your own."

"Just in the event that you're lying to me, I don't want you to call Titian and tell him I'm asking about him. Jigsaw and your mobile. Now."

Seb wedged his cell out of his pocket with two fingers, then his keys. He handed them over, then took out his wallet and removed the laminated card and handed it over as well. They both went into Brody's hand still wearing the knuckleduster.

Thorp asked Brody, "What are we going to do with them?"

Brody pointed at Seb's cubie door.

Thorp needed no other word. He waved the gun at Seb and kept it trained on him as he walked over to the door.

"You dumb shits," Seb commented. "Doing this to us, thinking you're some kind of heroes. Gonna clean up the big bad streets of Chi-Town huntin' serial killers?"

Brody ignored Seb's opinion, turned to Spanky who continued to stand idly by, hands raised. He could now see what was inked into the man's wrinkled lids whenever he blinked: *Never. Dead.* "You too. Jigsaw and phone."

Brody glanced away from Spanky for a few seconds

to watch Seb struggling with his cubie door.

A shot rang brightly throughout the parking garage.

Brody whipped around and saw Spanky crumpling to the concrete between the parked cars. Bits of shattered skull and pink crumbs of brain tumbled out onto the fur collar of the man's puffy satin coat.

Thorp, with a sweaty strip of hair pasted across his forehead, switched his gun's safety back on, impenetrably indifferent.

Brody stared at the corpse, unable to form words.

Seb got one look at Spanky facedown on the floor, a majority of the back of his head made into a crater of ruptured pink and red, and gaped at Brody and Thorp. "You . . . you said you weren't going to kill us."

"Get back in," Brody ordered, deciding to take care of the matter at hand before asking Thorp why he had murdered Spanky.

Clearly rattled, Seb ducked into his apartment. Brody pulled down the door before the giant's sorrow had a chance to shift into anger. He threw the lock on the cubie door and turned back to Thorp who stood with his gun at his side, glancing up the shadowed corridor.

"What the fuck is wrong with you?" Brody snatched the gun from Thorp's hand.

Thorp let the Franklin-Johann go without a fight, seemingly too mesmerized by the slow river still pumping from Spanky's vacated head and crawling toward the storm drain to get upset.

Down the way, Brody spotted some figures at the far end of the parking garage looking toward the source of the gunfire, inquisitive but keeping their distance.

"He was going for this," Thorp said, pointing at a pearl-handled pistol tucked into the waistband of Spanky's boxers.

Brody grabbed the derringer and held it in his palm, unable to avoid noticing that the metal was still warm from being pressed against Spanky's flesh. "It's not even a .22. If he shot it at us, it'd probably hurt your ears more than anything."

"How was I to know?" Thorp shrugged.

The sight of death before him, the smell of burned cordite on the already stinking air—completely unnecessary. He pocketed Spanky's pistol, as well as Thorp's. When he dropped the Franklin-Johann into his pocket the barrel was still hot, the heat easily soaking through his coat's wool to his side.

"Get in the car," Brody said.

With nonchalance, Thorp went around the back of the Fairlane, got in, and closed the door.

Brody looked at the body, the widening pool of blood under the dead man's face.

A series of heavy bangs came from the door of Seb's cubie accompanied by muffled and unintelligible shouting.

Brody popped the trunk on the Fairlane and, with some difficulty, gathered the overweight thug in his arms and dropped him in. Getting some blood on his clothes was unavoidable. There was a metallic splash as the keys fell from Spanky's loose grip.

You killed him. You fucking killed him. The sound of a bolt snapping in the cubie doorframe sang out like a rock falling into a metal pail.

Reacting to the sound like it had been a starter pistol,

Brody slammed the lid on Spanky, unsuccessfully avoiding his inert if still accusatory gaze, and got in. He double tapped the ignition, but before putting it in reverse he turned to Thorp.

He was still blandly indifferent. The blond hair atop his head rode the gentle breeze, undulating like a dozen golden and miniscule antennae. He blinked down the length of the hood at the cubie door and its series of metal bubbles popping up across its surface, unaffected. "Shouldn't we go? I don't think that thing will hold him for very—"

Brody interrupted, "Tell me. Did you get anything out of him at least *before* you killed him?"

"We didn't talk," he muttered.

Brody dropped the Fairlane into reverse. "Well done. Really. Good work."

23

"Why did we bring him with us?" Thorp asked.

"The better question might be why the hell did you shoot him?"

Thorp dropped his hands to his knees. "I told you—he was going for that gun. Would you have preferred that I just let him fucking kill you?"

They drove a few blocks and came to a red light. A plow came thundering the other way, washing the two men in the haggard Fairlane with pulses of yellow. The salt crystals being thrown from its rear as it passed rained against the side of their car, a momentary hailstorm.

"What now?" Thorp asked after the truck had passed, his voice meek.

Brody checked the rearview mirror. He caught a glimpse of the bull testicles hanging from the mirror that were perpetually swaying into his line of sight. He ripped them off and tossed them out. They hit the asphalt with the clack of two billiard balls colliding. "I don't know."

"He didn't know where we can find Shandorf?"

"Nope," Brody said.

The light turned and they pulled forward.

"And where are we going now?" Thorp asked.

"That last cup of coffee at the truck stop didn't cut it," Brody said. "And as you pointed out before, we should probably try to avoid disaster by keeping our equipment in decent working order. My brain doesn't work for shit without some caffeine in it."

Brody had to look closely to make sure the server behind the counter at Noodle Shack was actually breathing. When she caught him leaning forward and leering at the collar of her uniform, she gave him only half a cup of coffee before backing away to the kitchen. He tried to apologize, but she was already out of earshot, too far back into the steam and Latin music that filled the kitchen to hear it.

"Maybe I should be the one asking you if you're all right," Thorp said from the stool next to him.

"I'd rather not speak right now if that's okay with you."

"Is this because . . . ?" Thorp received a withering look, nodded, stared at his hands cradling his coffee mug. "At the time I thought it was the right thing to do, and I just figured—"

"Stop. Just stop. Just . . . no." Brody looked around them again, glanced at the kitchen door. "What's done is done." He lit the final cigarette from Seb's pack, then crushed the cellophane packaging and deposited the crackling knot onto his plate. He didn't remember smoking an entire pack today.

For a few moments, they said nothing.

"Tell me something. Do you think it would be hard for someone like me, who isn't exactly what you'd call simpatico with gizmos and gadgets, to break into Alton Noel's ordl?"

Thorp folded a piece of buttered toast in half and said before biting into the corner, "Do you mean like a hack?"

Brody glanced around the dining area. Save for an octogenarian couple in a far booth, they were alone. "Yeah."

"I can do it," Thorp answered. "No problem."

"I think we really need to put the pedal down here. It won't be long before word gets back to whoever has Nectar what we're up to. We need to cover as much ground as possible. We need to get proof and get it quick. Especially now with that cargo we're carrying."

02:59:59.

"I take that back," Brody added, "We *really* need to make use of our time here."

Thorp, chewing: "Should I just go back to the house, then?"

"No, I think we should do what you suggested before—split up, get more done, and regroup, say, in a couple of hours. The YMCA is right up the street." On the counter between them, nestled against the chrome napkin dispenser, was Thorp's ordi. Brody navigated the holo, seeing the blue dot denoting where they were on the map and where they had to go.

"Is that where you want me to go?"

"I'll go there."

"So where do you want me to go?"

"Take the car and find a suitable place to deposit the contents of the trunk, if you know what I mean. Because that junker out there is already a magnet for the cops, and I'd hate to try and explain what's back there."

"Excuse me but you can't smoke in here," the waitress curtly informed them, giving both men a start. She pointed to a No Smoking sign above the counter.

Brody apologized and got off his stool. "I'm going to finish this outside. You settle up; this one's on our friend." After depositing Spanky's jigsaw into Thorp's hand by disguising the exchange in a handshake like he'd seen people do in several movies, Brody headed outside.

There was still some light traffic, even around midnight. The same sodium lights found in every city lit up the entire strip of road that the Noodle Shack was on.

Brody stood outside smoking with the cigarette tucked into the corner of his lips so he could keep his hands in his pockets. It was then that he inventoried all he had on him, just to make sure he hadn't lost anything in the scuffle with Seb. The lens charger, the sonar in its case, two cell phones, Seb's ring of keys along with his own ring of keys, the knuckleduster, his lighter. And, of course, who could ignore the presence of not one, not two, but three guns? One in each side pocket and one tucked into the interior pocket by his chest. It was the heaviest his coat had ever been.

He glanced through the tinted glass of the restaurant. With his wide back posted atop the stool, Thorp continued to finish his breakfast, hunched over his plate.

Brody took a stroll down to the end of the restaurant, then around the corner to a Dumpster. When he lifted the lid the carnivalesque stink of fryer grease jumped out at him. Brody let the pearl-handled derringer and the phones that weren't his fall in with a hollow bang. After he removed the key for the Fairlane, Seb's ring of keys went in as well.

He gave pause, for he still felt as if he hadn't unloaded it all. Where were Spanky's keys? He had heard them drop out of his hand at the cubie lot, and then . . . He looked at the Fairlane. Of course, Spanky's keys weren't the only thing of his that required dropping off. Brody zeroed in on the trunk.

Never. Dead.

He turned away.

Into the Dumpster went Thorp's handgun. He was going to throw his own in too but thought better of it. They still had a while before the end of the night. Nonetheless, he had it in his hand, trying the slide time and time again to ensure it wasn't loaded. He took the magazine out of the left pocket and checked it against the streetlamp glow. He put it away and checked the chamber of the handgun—everything was in its place.

The front doors of the Noodle Shack jingled.

Brody returned his gun to his coat and eased the lid of the Dumpster shut, wiped his hands off on his pants, and headed back, nearly running into Thorp as they crossed paths at the corner of the restaurant.

Thorp let fly a yell and clutched his chest. "Don't *do* that."

"You snuck up on me," Brody said.

"The hell were you doing back there, anyway?"

Think fast. "Taking a piss."

"They got bathrooms inside, you know."

"I was out here already, and with our waitress yelling at me I wasn't about to go back in just for that."

Thorp watched him, nostrils flaring, still riled. "Whatever you say. Let's get going. I don't want the sun coming up while I'm still driving around."

Thorp drove without flipping on the wipers—or wiper, since only one worked anyway. The patchwork plastic on the windshield developed sinking pockets where the snow collected. Each time a pocket threatened to pull the whole thing down Brody gave it a push to empty it, sending the snow out ahead of the car in a brilliant puff, but soon another spot would begin to fill.

"I really wish this thing had auto drive," Thorp complained when he had to slam on the brakes at a stoplight.

They slid halfway through the intersection, saw no reason to stop when they were pretty much already on the other side anyway, and kept right along.

Brody turned the dome light on.

"What are you doing?" Thorp asked.

Brody reached into the backseat for the shoe box with Alton's transparencies. He held the swirly, grayscale sheets of plastic—some were warped and crunchy from only partly surviving the arson attempt—against the light with one hand, and with the other, he used his phone to photograph them, utilizing the dome light so all the detail could be captured.

"I've started e-mailing myself what we've collected so far," Brody said, taking a second and third snapshot of the transparency. In the second one the image was more skewed, the gray matter within the oval of Alton's head a fraction more warped. "I've got Abigail's fingerprint analysis sent to myself and now a copy of all the scans."

"Good thinking."

They made a turn where the Fairlane's GPS suggested.

"All right, so there's no easy way to ask this," Thorp began.

Brody took another photo of the third transparency, his neck craned to get a clear shot of the plastic sheet held directly on the dome light's bare bulb. "Ask what?"

"Can I have my gun back?"

"I don't think that's possible," Brody said. He returned the transparencies to the shoe box and replaced the lid—all photos taken. "I threw it away."

Thorp kept his gaze on the road as they crossed the North State Street Bridge. "You threw away my gun." It wasn't a question. "When?"

"Back at the restaurant, along with that peashooter that cost Spanky his life and their other stuff. All I could see was future exhibit A when I felt it move around in my pockets."

"That gun was a collector's item."

"I don't know what you're complaining about. You

already have an entire museum's worth of guns back there. You could go to war against a few dozen of Seb's friends with what you have in that bag."

"Yeah, but that Franklin-Johann was an antique."

Brody groaned. "You know as well as I do that the Franklin-Johann was a terrible weapon. Cheaply made, more often than not the sights were off—swing by the Two-For-One after you drop me off, I'm sure they have a bargain bin dedicated to the Franklin-Johann semiautomatic."

Thorp made a sharp whistling sound through his nostrils. Brody had heard the noise only once before when Thorp had fallen victim to a prank on the barracks in Cairo. Someone had filled every one of the handyman's socks with cheese from a can.

"Look. You like to go into things unprepared; that's fine. You want to bring brass knuckles to a gunfight, fine. That's you. But as long as we're in this, running against dangerous people, one of us needs to be armed at all times. *Needs* to be."

The GPS informed them, "You have reached your destination."

"I don't think what you're going off to do requires a gun. He's not dangerous anymore." He looked over at Thorp, cast under the harsh, unshielded glare of the dome light. Anger still polluted his eyes.

Thorp had no response.

"One hour," Brody said. "Meet me back here in one hour."

Standing on the slush-strewn sidewalk, Brody couldn't help but check the address on his phone against where he stood. The YMCA on Dearborn Street wasn't like any Brody had seen before. It was tall, for one, and set centrally in the city, clearly visible from the sidewalk. Most he had visited as a youth for swimming lessons were in tucked away, old-looking buildings. Even the community center in Minneapolis was off the beaten path—across the street from the recycling center and up the block from the meatpacking district.

This YMCA had a definite art deco finesse to its architecture, and inside it smelled like a comfortably musty old hotel. He was expecting a throat-blanching chlorine and locker room reek.

Approaching the front desk while shaking the snow from his hair, Brody asked the T-shirt-clad young woman, "Excuse me, but would you happen to have a room for the night?"

"Do you need it just for the night?" the girl asked. She had fiercely red hair that was bunched into angry, defiant curls. Her face was a scattershot of freckles. When she smiled, it made Brody think of motherboard innards—so much metal.

"Yeah, just one night," Brody said.

"Do you happen to be a member of the armed services?" she asked.

"Yeah. What gave me away?"

"This is a pretty frequent stop for veterans," she said, "and I've sort of worked it into my routine whenever anyone comes in asking for a room."

He handed her the military ID.

She looked it over and blushed. "Uh, I'm sorry but this is expired."

"I don't have any money," Brody deliberately blurted

as if having this room for the night was a matter of life or death. He imagined when Alton came here, he probably thought it was. "I've got probably a buck to my name at best. I just need a place to get out of the cold for a while."

The girl bit her lip. "The lock on room number eight is broken. If you don't mind the lack of security, you can stay in there . . ."

"That's fine," Brody said.

"It's perfectly safe. Everyone here gets along really well. A few months ago, someone got into trouble and . . . long story short, he locked the door before he left and took the key with him, and since he was in no shape to bring the key back . . . Never mind. I'll just show you the way before I freak you out any further."

"Try me." He smiled. "I love a good horror story."

She bit her lip again. It was plain to see she wanted to tell him but was hesitant. "You heard about that guy who shot all those people in a mall in Minneapolis last month?" She cocked an eyebrow, apparently in complete rapture over divulging the lurid details of horrible events.

"Yeah?"

"This is where he stayed while he was apparently planning the whole thing." She leaned back in the afterglow of the story being told. If you want to change your mind, I can give you a different room."

"No, no. Call it a morbid curiosity. I want to see it."

She came around the counter and escorted him to the head of a staircase but didn't accompany him down it; she simply pointed and said it was down there on the left. Then she clicked on the stairwell light and handed him a few folded tissues.

He accepted them, and he must've had a confused look on his face because she added as she walked away, "You're bleeding." She jammed a finger into the mass of red curls at the back of her head.

"Thanks," he said, dabbing his head with a bare hand and then the tissues and pulling out crusty smears of half-dried blood onto the soft paper. He felt something dig against his palm and pinched a square of broken glass from his hair. He headed downstairs, still dabbing.

Each one of the rooms had a tall, narrow window set into the door. Most of them had the curtains drawn, but a few shameless men slept with their doors open, sprawled onto cots and cocooned, snoring, in stained sleeping bags.

Brody reached the room he had been appointed, finding it easily since it was the only one in the well-lit basement hall that was missing its doorknob. He turned on the light and saw it was as expected. Kind of clean, linoleum floor, a folded cot standing in the corner, a milk crate for a nightstand with a brand-new Bible resting on it. Brody had to admit it wasn't far from what he came home to every night. There was a closet, and he found nothing but a blackened, holey sock. None of it seemed to be Alton Noel's belongings. All of what remained appeared to belong to the Y.

He returned to the hall and traveled to the end where it bent and went deeper beneath the building. He could hear the pumps for the pool going, that expected smell of chlorine now coming to him. He came to a classroom of sorts, flipped on the light, and examined the décor. It was where a GED class apparently met, with the electronic chalkboard still displaying a snapshot of the periodic table of the elements.

In the far corner of the room, he spotted a handwritten sign on a jagged triangle of cardboard: *Lost & Found.* He went over to the canvas laundry bag of items and sifted through. Most were strange-smelling garments, a forsaken toddler's shoe without its mate, a well-thumbed video game strategy guide, a handful of loose ceramic hair curlers.

At the very bottom, Brody found a flip-top ordi, with its silver case chipped to reveal the bland black plastic underneath. Emblazoned on a peeling manufacturer's decal was *Mediapurisu*. He took a seat at one of the classroom desks and opened the device. Inside, the keyboard was so well worn that only the *Q* and *X* still bore their paint. He wiggled his finger on the touch pad, and half the monitor came to life. He moved the cursor around and read the different links available. He wasn't sure if the other half, the half that remained black, had anything available.

Nothing on the surface indicated this was Alton's ordi. No personalization by way of stickers on the lid, and the file marked Photos didn't have a single image saved to it. It was difficult navigating the broken screen, Brody felt there were other icons waiting to be clicked on just on the other side of the dead half of the monitor. He pushed the cursor over into the murk and clicked here and there in the blind spot, but no programs opened.

Of the program icons not within the dead half, Brody found a hologram-video editing program. He tapped on it. The program loaded, and Brody watched as dozens of entries were listed in the recorded videos dubbed *confessions*. Each video, each confession named Al Christmas as the author.

Bingo.

He closed the lid and took the damaged ordi back to his room. He closed the door and remained at the window for a moment to ensure he wouldn't be interrupted. He pulled the gauzy curtain over the glass slot in the door and took a seat on the cot with Alton's confessions.

He pressed play, and a numeral three made up of translucent white light floated in the center of the room. It became a two after a beat, then a one.

A male voice came from the Mediapurisu's tinny speakers: "We're sorry. The holo-video you want to watch was recorded in a space much larger than the one you are in now. Would you like to continue, even with dimensional irregularities taking place during the presentation?"

"Yes," Brody told Alton's ordi.

Then Alton Noel was there in the room with him in holo. He was dressed in a gray T-shirt, a pair of loose-fitting jeans, work boots, his hair still cut to stubble. While to the untrained eye, someone might be convinced that it was actually him standing there, Brody had seen many holos in his day, even sometimes being taught by one in school when the regular teacher couldn't make it. It looked like a genuine person, but if the lights weren't dimmed, he'd appear ghostly, foggily lucent as an unpolished gem, and outlined against the background a bit too heavily. It almost looked like the holo had been plopped into this world and superimposed onto it, and in a way that was exactly what happened. Alton appeared this way now to Brody, stammering to find his words for his first entry.

"I don't really know how to use this thing." His voice was timid, soft. He was muscled, baby-faced, fidgety. He held his arms at his sides as if he were standing in a strong wind, afraid of being blown over.

Another voice came. "Just say what you want. Whoever sees it won't be someone you know." A woman stepped directly through the wall toward Alton—the dimensional irregularities of not watching a holo-video in the same place it had been recorded, Brody gathered.

She was svelte and tall, wearing her hair half in braids, half loose. The coloring of the holo-video was a bit off, but Brody could tell it was Nectar.

She pointed to approximately where Brody sat, guiding Alton's gaze, where the camera had stood when they had made the holo-video. "Right there. Just imagine someone you really love is right there." For a fleeting second, she seemed to be making eye contact with Brody.

Alton sighed, rolled his eyes. "Why did you guys buy me this thing?"

Another woman entered through the opposite wall, came up beside Alton on his other side. Abigail Schwartz. It was remarkable how much she and Nectar resembled one another—cherublike cheeks, bright eyes, even a similarity to their voices. Throaty with an affected accent of SoCal infused with a suburbanite's attempt at sounding Latina.

"I hope it's me you're picturing over there," she jibed.

"When did you get here?" Nectar asked.

"It was slow at the shop, closed up early. Wanted to see if you were able to talk Mr. I Hate Ordinateurs into *finally* using his holo-cam." Abby dropped her purse and removed her jacket. Both disappeared; apparently the holo-cam registered them unimportant after they'd left her person.

"I am," Nectar said, "but it's not going so well."

"What, it's on right *now*?" Abigail squealed.

"Right there." Nectar pointed toward Brody in a different place and—according to the time stamp—a little over a month in the future.

Now Abigail looked into his eyes. She fixed her hair, pumping it up with her palms like an old-time starlet. "Why didn't you say something?"

They all laughed.

Brody allowed a smirk.

She curled an arm around Alton's back, guiding his gaze toward the camera. "Well, go on then, honey. Tell the good people everything you want them to know."

Sandwiched between the two women, Alton looked ahead . . . and stared.

They both elbowed him and giggled.

Finally, the young veteran spoke. "Okay. All right. My name is Alton Noel. I am—was—a private in the United States Marine Corps."

"That's good," Nectar said, nudging him. "But keep going."

"And this is my post-traumatic stress disorder recovery

diary."

The girls applauded, hugged him on either side.

He smiled, visibly embarrassed.

The video ended.

The next holo-video began immediately. Two supine nude figures floating two feet off the floor made love. Abigail straddled Alton as she grinded against him and made small, chirping whines. "*Yep,*" she said between moans, slowly gaining momentum . . . "*Yep, yep.*"

The highly private moment made Brody avert his eyes immediately. It wasn't prudishness, but he knew it wasn't intended for him or anyone else to ever see.

"Next," he said.

Alton was dressed again and sitting in an invisible chair in an empty room. Brody assumed that the holo-cam knew not to waste disk space by uselessly measuring and recording the spatial arithmetic of furniture and other objects unless told to do otherwise.

"Hey," he said, elbows on knees, bent forward and fiddling with his fingers, picking at a hangnail. "I'm not really sure what to say. I mean, talking about shit and opening up and all that—I was raised to keep your insides inside and crying is for pussies, but I think I have to talk about this. It's, you know, important."

Brody listened, watched.

"I started this thing as a way to talk about my feelings. But I think I have to—no, let me start over." Alton disappeared, then reappeared less than a millisecond later, this time a few inches closer.

"When I was on the base in Malaysia, we had to sign up for duties when we weren't at war or active. So some guys got mess hall duties or vehicle maintenance—by luck of the draw, I got information technology. Like some kind of joke. Me in IT? I did it, took the classes—the whole bit.

"Anyway, one day they call me to the mess hall and it's just me. It's Gunnery Sergeant Dobbs and some brass, guys I don't recognize. They tell me to install these new transmitters all over base for the wireless. I say we already have wireless, and they tell me this is different. So I set up the wires in the barracks, in the mess, even in the rec and weight rooms. And that night, everyone's puking. They're running to the shitter, getting sick in the sinks, right there on the floor, shitting themselves—all of it. I think it must be food poisoning, but that night—it's weird—we had leftovers. And I can't imagine something we had already eaten could make us that sick, right? But it keeps happening. I get called into the mess, all alone, and Dobbs is there and the brass—who never say who they are—and ask me to install more transmitters and routers and shit and just like before everyone gets sick."

When he spoke again, it came out reedy. He was wringing his hands, shaking his head, and sniffing back tears. "I don't know what I did. I don't know if it's my fault everyone started getting sick. But then it just kept getting worse, and guys would have to be airlifted out to see a medic at another base, and they'd never tell us what happened to 'em or anything. *Fuck.* Did I do this shit to them?"

00:59:59.

Brody sat forward. "I'm going to need more than that."

And as if he had heard him, Alton looked up in the direction of the holo-cam at Brody and said, "They told me not to take copies of the instruction books. They told me not to tell anyone about any of it. They said I could get court marshaled if I did. But for everyone out there online who wants to know the truth—fuck it—I don't care anymore. The name on the packages all said 'Hark Telecom.' Yeah, that's what I thought—the fucking phone company? But it was them. If any of those soldiers died, I want it to be known to God and everyone else that it wasn't all me and I didn't know what I was doing, okay?" He paused. "That's it."

The video ended. Brody began lowering the lid of the ordi when the next one started without warning. Alton was directly ahead of him, so close that if he were physical, Brody would've been able to feel his breath.

"I'm not a bad person," Alton said. "But I went with them. They came to my fucking job, where I make a living. Said they were the government. I thought, *This is it; I'm done.* So I went with them. They drove me out to this place, and all I can remember is it had dirt floors. And, yeah, I'm here again at my place. Just woke up, no idea how I got home. I'm moving out of here today, going to the YMCA to stay, lay low." He shook his head violently. "I don't know what to do. I don't know what to think. All I know is this fucked-up-looking guy with a braided beard and the worst breath I've ever smelled walked right up to me at work the other day and told me if I'm not able to be found on ten-twenty, I'm through."

Ten-twenty. October 20. The day Alton shot Elizabeth Lake and the nine others. Brody inched forward on the cot's canvas. "Come on. Give me a name."

"He opened his coat real quick, showing me he was covered from head to toe in knives, and walked off. I have no idea if that's part of it or . . ." Alton sniffed. "I had enough, though. I wasn't sure how he'd react, but I shoved him. I told him to tell me who he is, and he smiled that shitty smile at me and said, 'I'm just your uncle Titian, kid.' Fucking freak."

"There we are," Brody said.

"He said that with my experience I was the ideal candidate. But he wouldn't tell me for *what*. Maybe it was because of what went down in Kuala Lumpur—I just did as I was told. Kill or be killed, right? I tried to kick his ass, but he ran off, got into a car with some guys."

The azure ghost of Alton Noel took a deep breath, and when he continued it was with grit. "I'm going to hide this ordi somewhere. I don't know what's going to happen—if the shit about ten-twenty is true, if the things I'm hearing are real, if the shit I hear myself saying sometimes means anything . . . I just . . . I just want this shit to be heard, and I pray to Jesus it makes sense to you—whoever you are—watching this. Please don't judge me. Please."

Alton broke down into a blubbering wreck, still seated on his invisible chair. From the collar of his T-shirt came a metallic jangling. His dog tags fell and snapped together at the end of his lanyard. They clinked, muffled, as he squeezed them in a fist. Alton's close-shaven head bobbed up and down as he quietly wept. "I don't know what to do . . . I wish time would stop. I don't know what's going to happen on ten-twenty, if that's even a date or a time or . . . I wish someone would *tell* me what's going to happen—"

Brody struck esc, killing the video.

24

Every park Thorp drove by, there
was a rent-a-cop posted. Every lot
he passed, he accidentally met eyes with
the attendant. Even the boardwalk was
under electronic surveillance. It seemed
there wasn't a single place in all of Chicago a
man could go to rid his trunk of a dead body.

Deciding to take a break, Thorp angled
the car alongside the curb, killed the engine,
and sat back with his fingers crossed
on his belly waiting for the answers to
come to him.

The clock on the dash told him he had
already burned up twenty minutes driving
around. There was no way he'd regroup
with Brody in another forty minutes,
tell him he still had Spanky in the trunk,

and have him *not* get mad. He had to make progress on something, even if it weren't the job he had been tasked to do. He brought up the Gizumoshingu from the backseat and logged in. If Brody could play detective, so could he. That is, if the vendor selling that hack app had gotten back to him . . .

Thorp kept a dummy account online for separate finances, none of which were tied directly to the bank his jigsaw was linked to. This he used for the type of online shopping that might raise some eyebrows. The decommissioned Darters had been bought this way, as well as a good percentage of his armory's contents. The vendor had accepted Thorp's fake name and address, probably ran the account through an app of his own to double-check him for a possible undercover cop, and approved the transaction. Thorp installed the hack tool and went to work.

He got onto the Probitas website, where employees could enter a password and access time cards and such. Thorp bit his lip, staring at the monitor with bleary eyes. A bar filled, the log panel riffing by with endless computer talk, code, numbers, symbols. Evidence that his ordi was working hard. The fan even kicked in, further evidence that this sucker required some serious labor.

After burning up another ten of his remaining forty minutes, the app finally allowed Thorp access to the Probitas employee portion of the site, the firewall effectively chiseled. He read a few memos and a couple of pieces of news, one being that Lucy in reception was due to have her baby in a week and everyone should wish her well.

He moved on.

He came to a tab labeled *client news* and opened it.

Hark Telecom was listed at the top of Probitas's clients. He bristled, his hands even more numb than they already were, but he forced himself to click on it. He entered the company profile and went through the records of their prior requests and the people who Hark had personally asked Probitas to intervene on the behalf of.

What appeared before his eyes made his throat run dry. Suddenly feeling the need to retch, he threw open the driver's side door but nothing came except a squiggling long white line of spit that clung to his bottom lip. He spat and glared at the ordi displaying the news and spat again. He couldn't believe it. What it meant, if it distilled the truth—he couldn't bear it.

Nectar Ashbury had been issued a behavioral discontinuation packet from Probitas, per the request of Hark Telecom. Going through the PDF copy they'd kept, he confirmed it was the same letter Brody had found at her apartment.

No one knew about the news he had received. He hadn't told Nectar or anyone else about his trip to the doctor. Apparently, he didn't need to tell Nectar anyway. She had scooped his medical records online. He knew that it was a reason why he was feeling strange a lot of the time, why he felt light-headed every morning, why for no reason he'd need to quickly find a place to sit or risk clipping his head on the kitchen counter. The nosebleeds, the out-of-nowhere headaches that didn't ache so much as erupt. The others that weren't so bad but still made his eyes water and ears ring.

Thorp always thought it was the first sign of old age coming up around the corner. Most of the time he looked and felt like hell, and now—on top of that—he had been deceived. Maybe he would have been healthier if this hadn't been going on. Maybe he would have avoided drinking at night, every night. Maybe he would have had years free of anxiousness, serious lows and soaring highs, and all those terrible times in between when he wasn't even sure what he was feeling.

He'd been able to live this life of quiet comfort, buy decommissioned vehicles and firearms over the Internet, not have to work, and if he managed to sell a bushel of apples at the farmer's market, well, that was just a bonus. Hark Telecom had kept a roof over his head, but now Thorp knew it was merely a safeguard, packing his bank account so full of money that the idea of asking questions would never cross his mind. The roof provided a curtain for what hung beyond and above it, the wires suspended over his house that were making him sick.

He took the ordi in his hands and asked the Hark Telecom company profile still on screen, complete with picture of their glass and granite lobby, "What, only a matter of time and you'd phone me up too?" He wiped away tears.

His fingers took a moment to cooperate, but when they did, he continued to dig. The Probitas packet had been requested by Hubert Ward. The name rang no bells to Thorp, so he quickly closed down the hack window and jumped online.

He dropped Hubert Ward's name into the search engine, and fifteen pages of the man's life came on screen, mostly accolades for his technological achievements. He'd worked with several well-known companies, had been a developer of many now commonly used products, having gotten his start in Silicon Valley. He was relatively new to Hark Telecom, an online article from *Popular Mechanics* read, and barely upon being hired as the head of research and development, he caused a stir by having his entire department brought up on charges of corporate espionage. The accuser was Thomas Lake, president of DRN Engineering, who claimed that Hubert Ward and his team had planted employees inside DRN to steal prototype schematics.

Nectar and Abby were right. Elizabeth Lake was the key to all of it.

The article had been expanded last month in October when Elizabeth Lake had been slain. Thomas Lake, in the wake of his wife's death, was labeled by his colleagues as emotionally compromised and was subsequently removed from his position. They feared he'd make a wrong call and end up driving profits into the ground. His final request before his involuntary sabbatical was shocking: drop the suit against Hark, despite the fact that he was the one who had initially launched it. He was asked why he wanted to drop the multibillion-dollar suit against Hark if he and DRN had good reason to believe they'd been the victim of corporate espionage. His cryptic reply was that he had to think about his son, Joel. When asked if he thought his wife's death and DRN's lawsuit against Hark were connected, again Thomas said he had to think of his son, adding only: "Family comes first."

Thorp started the engine, dropped it into gear, and tore off.

Fortunately, the drive to Hark Telecom took him a while. He had time to cool off and collect his thoughts. Just because Nectar had gotten cease and desist letters on behalf of Hark Telecom didn't necessarily mean they were behind it. He had to take things one step at a time like Brody was always telling him. Jumping to conclusions could only lead to unfavorable results, but he couldn't turn off the investigative part of his brain now. He glanced at the Fairlane's clock. He had time, if he made it quick.

At red lights, he navigated the Gizumoshingu's list of programs until he found the one called Freq-finder, an application that promised to pick up mobile phone activity or CB radio chatter anywhere in a square mile's vicinity. He'd downloaded it after seeing a late night infomercial, sure there were people on the edge of his property, crouched like insects, watching him from the dark, and hadn't used it since.

Of course, now that theory didn't sound so out there.

The program patched itself, started, began checking the area.

Hitting another red light, he pulled the ordi into his lap. It was picking up a bevy of activity from a place just up the street. He looked. Despite the snow and natural distortion of the sandwich wrap, he could still see Hark Telecom's tower that stood noticeably taller than the other structures, the gleaming, white spire jutting to the sky. It seemed to bend and loom over the car, like a smirking colossus watching a challenger race toward its feet.

Glass and steel, occupying the entire block. Massive in the other bearing as well, stretching up beyond the low and heavy snow clouds, seemingly stabbing into the heavens themselves. A dagger big enough for God killing, rising out of the crust of the city, a proud proclamation of mankind's uncontested victory over everything on the earth—and soon—everything above it.

He had to admit it was quite the sight, but he had work to do.

Thorp parked on the opposite side of the street, nuzzled up behind a pickup that had been left out to suffer the wrath of the snowplows. The brown slush and fluffy white had been shoved, like a glacier through hills, up around the truck. It made for a decent hiding spot.

He slid down in the seat of the Fairlane, adjusting the dials of the radio until all the squelching white noise was removed from the nearby signal he was picking up. Thorp glanced across the street to the watch station. The security guards, two young guys with greased-back hair, stood languidly, leaning on the counter, laughing occasionally. Neither watched the security camera feeds just off to their right. They seemed to be swapping stories that involved drinking—or women— or both, guessing by their gestures.

Thorp adjusted the radio some more, getting a hit on a conversation between two guards in the upper floors. They were too far away, so it came out garbled and rife with crashes of static. When he looked up to ensure he wasn't going to get made, Thorp spotted one of the guards at the kiosk right inside the Hark Telecom entryway staring directly at him.

The guard cocked his head and spoke into the radio clipped to the shoulder strap of his bulletproof vest. Thorp heard the guard through the Fairlane's speakers. "Dispatch. Got a vehicle here. Light brown Ford Fairlane—older model. Appears to be a white male inside. Want us to do anything about it?"

Thorp's first instinct was to flee. But he knew as soon as he got a block away, he'd lose the signal and possibly some information. He could have firsthand experience of how the Hark Telecom security team dealt with a possible threat. All he would have to do is know precisely when to leave. Here was an opportunity to give Brody good news, evidence he could serve a purpose, not fuck things up. He forced himself to wait, to listen. He slid down farther in the seat.

"No," another guard answered. "Unless they stop or come in to ask questions, there's no reason to leave your post. Mr. Ward wants us to keep the lobby top priority."

Thorp dared a glance.

"Roger." The guard lowered his hand from the radio but continued to watch Thorp.

Thorp faced forward and wondered how long it would take before the ground-floor guard asked the other unseen guard if he was positive that he shouldn't do something about the man across the street—sitting in his thirty-year-old beater at this ungodly hour.

The second guard, speaking in a way that said he was in charge, continued. "Once he's gone, make your rounds. Don't bother with the upper floors. Keep your squad on the lower half. Floors one through forty only until further notice. I'm going to take my dinner break."

"Sounds good. Over," the second guard answered.

"Good enough." Thorp started the Fairlane. He had gained a tidbit of information about the Hark Telecom building and could report back to Brody with it. He wasn't sure how much use it could be, but when it came to recon, any knowledge gained was a step in the right direction. He attempted to pull forward and felt a slight slippage under the front tires. He braked, paused, wrung his frozen hands. *Be casual*, he reminded himself.

"You know, something about this guy's face rubs me the wrong way. I might hop outside for a sec, see if I can spook him off. Jake is down here with me. No need to worry."

"Go ahead," said the second guard, who was upstairs or miles away.

Thorp could stand it no longer. He put the car into reverse. He backed up and felt the back tires rise over an incline in the snow—and then the whole back end of the car slammed down, successfully finding a deep rut in the snow. He dropped it into gear and mashed the accelerator, but all he got was the constipated whirring of the tires spinning, unable to find decent grip.

On the radio in the passenger seat, "Okay, so I think there is something of a genuine concern here. I'm heading out there."

Thorp cursed, swinging the wheel left and right to try and get the car to dislodge from the snowbank. He began narrating for himself as he often did when he plunged into an anxiety attack. "I know now that they're only guarding the bottom half of the building."

"The facts," one self-help TV guru once said during an hour-long advertisement for his set of book and audio lessons, "are always something good to list to yourself when feeling uptight or frightened. The things you know for sure."

"I think he's stuck," the guard still inside commented with a chuckle.

Into third gear, the Fairlane's engine screamed. Thorp downshifted, tapped the clutch, pumped and shifted with all four of his limbs in a frantic dance.

The security guard, dressed in a heavy black jacket and cap with the Hark Telecom logo stitched into it, clicked on a flashlight. He was halfway to Thorp, walking the ice-slick asphalt in short, eager strides.

"I know they have only two men watching the front doors overnight."

"Sir?" the guard shouted over the Fairlane's agonized shrieks. "Can I help you?" He tapped on the window with the end of the flashlight. "Sir, this is private property. It may look like just a street, but Hark Telecom owns this corner here to that corner down there. You're in violation of—"

"I now know they *own* the fucking street."

"Sir?"

The tires had ground down far enough into the packed snow and ice and found traction deep within. The car leapt out of the spot, Thorp twisting the wheel to avoid running headlong into the back of the snowed-in pickup, and skidded and squealed down the blacktop. He turned to give the guard one last winning sneer and saw he had something in his hand. There was a flash and Thorp convulsed as if shot. From the bulb at the end of the device in the guard's hand came a spiral of what appeared to be a pitched fistful of chopsticks, all glowing white, darting toward his face.

Momentarily blinded, Thorp swore and fought to see the path ahead of the car around the clustered streaks spiraling before his eyes.

The radio in the passenger seat called triumphantly, "I got a face-map of him."

Driving with eyes blasted blind, he left the guy standing in the middle of the street, growing smaller and smaller in the rearview mirror.

Thorp realized he was safe. All they had were the results from the face-cartographer, and since he rarely spent any time in the city and hadn't been arrested in a while, there was a good chance there wasn't a current face-map on him anywhere. His self-disappointment leapt away, and he hollered and punched the roof of the car.

He'd done something, possibly been of use.

"We'll find you, Nectar. Just wait and see. We're coming for you, Sis."

25

Brody stood on the corner outside the YMCA, having watched the traffic lights go through ten revolutions. He shifted Alton's ordi under his other arm and checked his phone for the time. Thorp was fifteen minutes late.

Across the black asphalt that looked oiled in its reflectivity, the first car in some time approached. Brody identified it as the Fairlane by the shape of the headlights. He stepped onto the curb. As it pulled up, Brody heard the car struggling, the supple rumble of the long-in-the-tooth engine now issuing a shrill whine.

Brody opened the door. "Everything all right? And why is the car making that sound?"

"I know who did it." Thorp made eye contact with Brody. "I know who got Nectar."

"All right. One thing at a time. Hop out. Let me drive."

Thorp and Brody orbited around the car to switch sides, then set off.

"What do you mean?"

"I hacked the Probitas website and found that Hark Telecom is their leading client. The letter sent to Nectar had been requested by Hubert Ward, the head of R&D at Hark. She was onto something, the whole bit about Elizabeth Lake being murdered. Her husband was trying to sue Hark for stealing his ideas. And it just so happens that Alton drives four hundred miles and kills her of all people? It's not solid proof or anything, because as Mateusz said, she and Abby had protested at a lot of different places over the years and . . . and with Alton, who knows if that's why he did it. Hey. What's with the face?"

With both hands gripping the wheel, Brody said, "I pretty much came to the same conclusion. Alton Noel installed electronics on base while stationed in Malaysia. Electronics from Hark Telecom."

When the car sounded like it might call it quits, Brody halted his story. He pulled over to let the Fairlane work out whatever bout of discomfort it was suffering and pleaded with it to delay its death rattle until they at least got out of the city. It agreed, the engine returning to a normal idle. After a couple of backfires as loud as gunshots, they continued.

"And that's not all. The guy was in one hell of a

ANDREW POST ● KNUCKLEDUSTER

334

hard place. He was wracked with guilt over what he'd done." Brody glanced at Thorp, whose expression had darkened faintly. He ground his teeth and scrambled for a way to move the subject along quickly. "But what we have here is proof that he was a decent person that didn't want to murder those people but he had been put up to it."

"He could've just been saying that stuff for the benefit of the camera," Thorp pointed out.

"No one's that good of an actor," Brody said. He highlighted the videos from top to bottom with one pass of his finger and copied them to the e-mail he was preparing. "Not only does he say it was Hark that had him install the base's tech that made everyone sick, but when he got back stateside, he was visited by someone who carried a lot of knives, cautioning him to be available on ten-twenty. Said he shoved the guy down, demanded his name."

"Titian Shandorf?" Thorp asked.

"Called himself Uncle Titian."

Thorp blew all the air from his lungs. "Christ." And, "It's green."

Brody handed the ordi over to Thorp.

He took it, peered into the monitor to see the two-dimensional version of Alton's video freeze-framed. "What's ten-twenty?"

"The twentieth of October."

"Shit." Again, he exhaled in a quick puff. "Well, that clinches it, then, right? If some guy came to him and said something about ten-twenty and that was the date he killed those people—and Elizabeth Lake, the wife of

Hark's enemy. He must've been put up to it. Doesn't that make sense?"

"It does to you and me, but we really need some good honest facts, genuinely solid evidence. We can't take what we got so far to the cops and expect them to do anything other than point us in the direction of the bughouse. We've got to link Hark and Titian."

They turned onto the interstate. Morning commuters surrounded them on all sides, and despite Brody trying to dodge around them before the inevitable jam was encountered, they weren't so lucky. Thankfully, the accident that had occurred up ahead was quickly shuffled to the shoulder, and shortly after the blinking cones and the cops in their reflective vests were out of the way, traffic continued unabated.

While passing the wreck and the crowd of officers, Brody noticed Thorp sink down in his seat. He was about to ask what was the matter, then pieced it together on his own. Through gritted teeth, Brody gave his opinion on Thorp's failure to get rid of Spanky.

Thorp apologized profusely, quietly, and when they got beyond the flashing red and blue lights, he sat up in his seat and checked his mirror. The cops were preoccupied with the wreck, and besides, out of all the cars on the highway, how could they possibly know one of them had a dead body in the trunk? This was Chicago. There were probably a few cars out this morning with bodies in the trunk.

Thorp broke his stare with what was going on behind them and asked, "Anything on Nectar?"

"She was in the first video," Brody said.

"How'd she look?"

"Good. Pretty." He added, "She got tall."

Thorp nudged a pocket of snow in the plastic wrap to the edge. It scattered away alongside the windows as a flashing, pitched handful of glittering white. "Yeah, she always was quite the beanpole, wasn't she?" He started to say something more, but his voice tapered off into a squeak.

Before Brody could scold him about what tense he should be using when talking about his missing sister, Thorp grabbed his Gizumoshingu from the floorboard and said, "Would you mind some music? I could use the distraction."

"Go for it."

Thorp started a playlist and muttered the lyrics.

Brody watched the road ahead as the jagged city shapes fell away in favor of storage units, sports bars with dead signs, boat and RV outlets, and hunting supply shops. The emporiums people who lived out in the sticks came in for but far enough from the urban fringe that they'd never have to set foot in the city proper.

The streetlights became less frequent, just a dotted line spaced far enough apart that the circles they painted on the asphalt barely touched the edges. He yawned, watched as one of the farthest lanes melded in with the others. The traffic thinned out to a trickle, and before long they were alone on an empty two-lane road once more.

Snowflakes began charging the shine of the Fairlane's headlights in an antagonistic flood. Brody was suddenly very glad Thorp had been so resourceful with the plastic wrap and tape. Haloing everything that dared to glow, Brody noticed, was the same constant flow of passing flakes. For a splintered fragment of time, he dreamt of sandstorms.

"This takes me back," Thorp said after "Commando" had come around for the third time on the shuffled playlist.

Brody invited conversation to keep himself awake, even if it meant talking about the old days. He said, "Oh yeah?" and forced his orange eyes open as far as they'd go. "Listen, you might have to drive in a minute because I think I'm just about out on a—"

00:00:59.

"—charge."

They pulled over, switched places. Back on the passenger side, Brody hoped that the stop had sidelined Thorp's desire to talk more about the past, but it wasn't so. Thorp had barely dropped the car into drive before he started again.

Thorp said, "Do you remember when we did Operation Ceramic Groom?"

The three words stirred their hearer. "Sure, the largest hospital in Cairo taken over by revolutionaries, a suicide bomber standing watch in the children's burn unit wing while another sat beside an innocent woman who was being kept alive by machines. Good times."

It took a lot to slather some sarcasm across the recollections of that particular day. He now knew what Thorp meant, though. Hearing "Commando" at top volume, sitting strapped into a seat. The Darter passing over the city, eating up the distance from the base to the hospital in seconds—seconds

Brody begged to double, triple. Setting down on the hospital helipad, rushing because never would they think to post a man on the roof—they were all on the ground floor, watching the lobby, using the nurses' kiosk as a makeshift foxhole.

Thorp jolted Brody from the memory by speaking over the song. "It worked."

"Yeah," Brody admitted. "They never saw us coming." He got it. He glanced at Thorp, who raised his eyebrows.

"We have an idea that Titian is working for Hark, but like you said, we need hard evidence. We know they're only watching the bottom floors closely. It's an idea. And there are no bad ideas in the planning phase when thinking about stopping the bad guys."

"True," Brody said, "but we're not planning anything."

"I'm just spitballing here."

"You're talking about hijacking," Brody said, screwing the lid on the lens charger and withdrawing the sonar, "because there sure as hell ain't any way we're going to get a pilot to take us to the Hark Telecom roof voluntarily. And if you remember, a whole lot of what the bad guys did involved schemes very similar to that one."

Thorp shrugged, broke eye contact with the road long enough to run his finger over the touch pad to find the next song that suited his mood. "All I'm saying is that you can't deny the fact it worked. We'll do what you think is best, but that's all I'm saying. Direct access to whatever Hubert Ward has on his hard drive might be useful and—"

Brody glanced at Thorp and noticed he was looking ahead about half as often as in the rearview mirror.

Some more textures bled into Thorp's face, and Brody could detect that he was squinting. "What's going on?" he asked over the wind roaring through the car.

Thorp didn't respond.

Brody turned around in the passenger seat and looked, even though there was little to spy because the rear windscreen was still intact. He listened instead. He could hear the engine noises, the Fairlane's wheels crushing snow under its tires, but beyond that . . . the sound of another engine, a bigger one. He spun around to face the car's touch screen. "The tracker. We never turned it off."

Thorp freed one hand from the wheel to swipe through the car's menu, found the tracker option, and turned it off.

"What a relief," Brody scoffed. "He'll never find us now."

Thorp ignored the remark and removed the Franklin-Johann from Brody's coat pocket. He attempted to eject the magazine to check it, even going so far as to thumb the button three and four times in rapid succession. But Brody kept the gun unloaded. Eyes on the road, gun, road. "I'm going to need bullets, man."

"Give me a second." Brody took out the magazine and handed it over.

In a daring move, Thorp took both hands from the wheel and reloaded the gun with a clatter. He engaged the safety and set it on the seat between them but kept a hand upon it.

Twisting in his seat, Brody listened to their pursuer's engine get louder and louder, the vehicle giving all it had to eat up the distance between them.

"Can't this piece of shit go any faster?" Thorp shouted, giving the wheel a series of openhanded strikes.

In a moment, the Zäh punched through the sheet of falling snow and was on them, bumpers colliding. The closely trailing vehicle eased off a few yards and then lurched forward again, the bumpers hitting a second time with a shriek of buckling metal.

The Fairlane was rushed forward, the front wheels momentarily losing traction. A tiny bark of friction sounded when the Fairlane found bare asphalt beneath the snow and dug at it. The other side was still in the slick stuff, and the steering wheel was violently kicked against Thorp's hands.

Brody shouted, "Shoot at him or something!"

Thorp shoved the handgun at him. "I'm trying to keep us on the road. You shoot."

Three reports came just as the last word left his lips, the glass collapsing into the car into the backseat. Through the new opening, Brody watched in horror as the sonar painted the Zäh into the diorama. It was rudimentary in shape, as blocky as a bad special effect, but altogether terrifying knowing who was driving. Brody was frozen this way, literally caught in the headlights he couldn't actually see.

When the bumpers collided again, Thorp snatched the gun from Brody, rolled down the side window, and fired backwards, gouging out one of the Zäh's headlights.

The plastic wrap mask that the Fairlane wore gave way without warning. It became a twisting, shining braid and detached, soaring into the snowstorm's winds. Wind and ice kicked freely into the car once more. Brody raised a hand to divert some of its bites, but it did little good. He turned his face away from it, the sonar's ping finding its way into the Zäh, since one of the windows was being rolled down. In polygon, he saw Seb reloading his weapon with one hand on the wheel.

"Now," Brody urged.

Thorp fired and the Zäh reacted at once: the front end wiggled.

Seb angled his body up into the open window. Another volley of shots into the Fairlane.

There was a solid punch against Brody's spine, a slug striking his seat. He touched his back and felt no blood, no warm ache. But now, added to the snow blowing freely and tearing about within the car, came the toxic stench of melting foam.

Thorp glanced around. "There's a curve coming up. I've got to slow down." Again, he tried giving the gun to Brody. When he didn't take it, Thorp merely let it drop, his hand racing back to the wheel.

The crook in the road came up, and Thorp tapped the brake. The move had been miscalculated and they lost too much speed, nearly coming to a full halt in the outermost portion of the curve.

Seb barreled up on them. All Brody saw was the vehicle's grille slam into them.

The impact sent the Fairlane into a spin. They were on the road for a few more seconds before flying through the ditch to the other side. By momentum alone, the Fairlane crossed the field, easing into a slow crawl—the engine clunking and wheezing. Thorp stomped the gas, but the car didn't kick ahead along the snow-covered dirt. The engine didn't respond.

Brody heard the click of the dashboard monitor dying, that muffled pop akin to a lightbulb filament throwing in the towel, as well as the series of small clinks as the instrument panel's needles dropped back to zero.

And lastly, a metallic cough sputtered and spat steam, belching up and around the lip of the hood—the Fairlane's final white flag.

26

Out on the road, the one-eyed Zäh executed an awkward four-point turn. Once aimed in their direction, it carefully dipped into the ditch and came up on the other side with just a small grunt of acceleration.

"We have to kill him," Thorp said. "There's no way around it."

"Let me see if I can talk to him," Brody said.

"He was shooting at us not even a minute ago. Do you really think he's going to have a chat?"

The sport utility vehicle edged closer, crunching over frozen dirt.

"I have to try," Brody said. "I mean, we're kind of in a spot here."

"He's not going to let us go," Thorp

pressed. "Don't get out."

Brody opened the Fairlane's door, the metal creaking. He presented his bare hands as he stepped into the path of the slowly approaching Zäh.

The engine died. Seb got out. His breath wisped about his large head as he began laughing. He put his hand on the steaming hood of his friend's vehicle and said, "Look at this."

"Just let us go," Brody said. "We're in the middle of something here. Something big."

Seb drew a simple black handgun and looked at it as if he were sharing a wordless inside joke with the firearm, then took a step forward. "So you think murdering my best friend, robbing me, stealing my car—all of that is small change to you? Not worth your time? Me and him went way back, you know. Way back."

"All right, I get it, but—"

"Why don't we get *him* out here?" Seb rumbled. He called to the Fairlane, "Hey, baldy. Yeah, you trigger-happy motherfucker, come on out. I want a word."

Brody sighed. "How'd you do it?"

"What's that?" Seb said.

"Find us."

Seb grinned, stuffed a hand inside his coat, and came out with another phone identical to the one he had given Brody at the cubie apartments. "Burner phone, baby. Never leave home without it."

Thorp approached with his arms held out, the gun in his grip—his eye centered over the sights. "Drop it."

Seb snickered. "No. *You* drop it." He glanced at Brody. "Where'd you find this piece of shit, anyway?"

Brody kept his hands raised. "Thorp, come on. Put it down." He noticed he had the rucksack on his back, both his and Alton's ordis sandwiched together and bound with a bungee cord dangling from his side. "Give him something and maybe he'll let us off the hook."

"Oh no you don't," Seb said. "You ain't giving me nothing, and you ain't buying your way past me. This is Illinois we're in. And we have a little thing called the you-fuck-me-I-fuck-you clause that goes exactly as it sounds. So, I'll tell you again, killer. Drop the gun, your bag of goodies, and get down on your knees."

Thorp kept the Franklin-Johann trained on Seb. "No."

"I don't remember asking," Seb said. He got half a step toward Thorp before he seemed to change his mind. While staring at Thorp, he pointed his gun at Brody.

"Shit. Do what he says. Just put the bag down."

"He deserved it," Thorp said. "Your friend."

"Excuse me?"

"Spanky, or whatever his real name was. He deserved it."

Seb's forehead collapsed in a profound display of stupefied disbelief. "Are you really saying this to me when I have your friend on the business end of this thing?" He kept his gaze trained on Thorp, sidestepping closer to Brody.

Brody watched the barrel of Seb's gun, a perfect black circle, widen by a few more degrees as it approached his face.

"You care to elaborate on how you came to this conclusion about my friend of thirty-two goddamn years?"

"*Thorp.*"

"When I was in his truck, I saw he had a syringe in the ashtray. He is where he is now and it's for the better. You ask me, one less smack head in this state is an improvement."

Seb pulled the gun from Brody's forehead and fired at Thorp. He missed, instead hitting the fender of the Fairlane directly to Thorp's right. It was close enough, a good scare.

Thorp lowered his gun.

"That's it. On the ground. Kick it over." Seb glanced at Brody while he was bending down to retrieve the Franklin. He deposited it into the inside pocket of his coat. "It seems now you're getting an understanding of what you're in for."

The gun barrel returned to Brody. "But first shit's first. While I do take my friend being murdered serious, I take the personal affront you shamed me with to be of precedence." The hammer was drawn back in a double click. Steel touched his forehead.

Brody couldn't bear it for another second and looked away from the gun. He gazed across the plains, all of this year's crop harvested and gone, the soil underneath immaculate white. The snow fell in large, tangled clumps, seen to him as individual pixels, too small to waste the sonar's processing power in giving their intricacies detail. He watched the flakes glide past, felt them alight on his face for the last time. He wanted it to be a surprise when the end came. Perhaps, if he had a guardian angel, he or she might swoop down and sweep his spirit away so he wouldn't have to feel anything or even hear the crack of gunfire.

And that was when the sonar picked up something

in the distance, a solitary figure in the far reaches of the field, walking up in a composed gait.

He was too afraid to shout, to alarm Seb and make him accidentally squeeze the trigger prematurely. He wanted to see what would happen, his final wish. He watched as the gauzy silhouette became two, then three. Then a crowd of ten or more identically sized people, all matching strides.

At once, he understood. Even though he could still see them afterward, Brody closed his eyes.

He wouldn't be simply shot in the head. He would be twisted into a pretzel by viciously territorial Arties. There it was, the two ways he would be unceremoniously expulsed from the world. "Son of a bitch," he whispered.

"What'd you say?" Seb snapped.

Brody trained the one blind eye that wasn't being crowded with a gun barrel toward Seb, more out of habit than anything. He swallowed. "Something I just saw troubled me."

Seb formed a half grin. "And what's that? You saw a vision of me dancing on your fucking corpse, me tea-bagging your buddy over there for shits and giggles after I do him in? Tell me. Oh, wait, I know. You saw your name on that bullet inside the barrel of my *guh*—"

Hot viscera sprayed into Brody's face. He ducked aside, Seb's finger squeezed, and the gun discharged inches above his head. The Artificial stood behind Seb, its arm elbow-deep into his back—a mud-clotted hand gripping a twisted, slippery mass of his intestines sticking out the front.

Seb looked over his shoulder. "What . . . the fuck?"

Thorp moved back but kept the gun raised. "We need to go."

"Where's the property line?" Brody asked as the other Artificials drew near.

Seb turned, angled the gun against the closest Artificial's head, and pulled the trigger. It flinched, retracted its arm back through Seb, the tangle of guts going in again. Seb moaned. It cast the mass aside and stepped forward, seeing that its job was not complete.

Seb slapped a hand over his gushing wound, but it still left a trail as he staggered toward Brody and Thorp. "Please," he gargled.

The robots followed. One grabbed him by the forearm and Seb's face twisted. He turned and fired into the robot again and again. Another seized him and turned his wrist, bones breaking, the gun landing in the snow with a fluff. Seb screamed, and it was quickly snuffed out when a metal hand of rubberized fingers was placed atop his skull. It wrenched backward until his head touched the small of his back. Sudden silence then as he sunk down among the feet of Artificials and into his ignominious end, a twisted heap.

Brody pushed Thorp in the direction the car tracks led. They ran through snow, skidding on unsure feet, stumbling and yet managing not to fall. Behind them, the whine of servos and the steady tramp of spiked legs punching through the frozen earth, cutting the distance between them effortlessly.

The ditch, and the end of the property line beyond, was still a distance. They weren't going fast enough. Brody pushed as hard as he could, throwing his arms and legs and charging through the ankle-deep snow.

Thorp clanged along, his overloaded rucksack weighing him down. He was lagging behind.

"Get rid of the bag," Brody shouted.

Thorp yanked it from his shoulder, spun with it, and heaved the heavy bag of guns at the robots. One was bowled over by it, but the others gracefully dodged their waylaid companion and continued the chase without it.

They ran on, but the road was still too far—the Artificials coming up on them too fast.

"We're not going to make it," Thorp rasped. He was still carrying stuff, jangling as he ran, bogged down.

Brody noticed the set of ordis and ripped them from Thorp's belt. He tucked Thorp's under his arm and still running, still fighting his way through the snow both on the ground and blowing into his face, he opened the lid of Alton's Mediapurisu. He had left the holo-video player running. He could hear servos behind him, feel hands trying to snag the woolen fibers of his peacoat, missing—but getting closer. He slapped the touch pad with an open hand. "*Come on.*"

"We're sorry. The holo-video you want to watch was recorded in a space much smaller than the one you are in now. Would you like to continue, even with—"

"Yes, yes, yes," Brody screamed.

Unseen to Brody, Alton Noel appeared floating beside them, gliding along the snow in a seated position. He narrated the chase: "I don't know what to do . . . I wish time would stop . . ."

Brody took a chance and with a flick of his wrist flung the Mediapurisu ordi away. It sailed through the air, Brody imagining Alton Noel riding within its orbit like a seated, weeping god. As Brody wanted, some of the Artificials gave chase. A few remained on them, but it was enough of a distraction that there was a moment's indecision among the horde of robot farmers when they weren't sure what to pursue. It bought Brody and Thorp time to make it to the ditch and leap over to the road beyond.

The robots stopped at the property line, dogs hitting their invisible fence, all with the same fixed stare on their fleshless faces, watching the two men walk off into the blinding rush of snow.

One called after them in monotone, "This is private property. Please do not trespass on this land again."

Behind them, the ghost of Alton Noel asked for mercy, snowflakes passing through his skin of light.

They walked with their heads bent forward into the fierce wind, hands pulled into sleeves, collars turned up, and each letting loose uncontrollable frozen grunts each time they got blasted by another salvo. The farm was still a couple of miles off, and before they were even a mile away from the field, they had lost feeling in their hands and feet.

"This isn't really what I had in mind when you asked me to come out here," Brody said. "I haven't dropped a line into a single pond yet."

"To be honest with you, it wasn't what I had in mind, either." Thorp laughed, his voice muffled, half his face tucked into the collar of his coat.

Brody wanted to bring up his idea just to have

something to discuss to make the face-first march into the snowstorm more tolerable, but survival training came back to him. Talking while being pelted by lake effect snow and subzero temperatures was not only a great way to waste heat but also a handy way to develop pneumonia. He decided not to vocalize his idea until they got closer to the farmhouse. He was pretty sure Thorp was thinking the same thing, anyway. Operation Ceramic Groom.

With a backyard full of military aircrafts, all they needed were some time and elbow grease and know-how and they could have a Darter pieced together, up and possibly running in a matter of days.

27

Brody took the front steps two at a stride. He was at the door, hand on the knob, when he realized Thorp wasn't behind him.

He looked back and saw Thorp standing in the yard, gazing up at the trio of wires looping directly over the house. He stood casually, arms at his sides, face serene. He seemed lost in thought, as one could easily be found on a day much warmer than today. The snow was already filling in his tracks leading to the spot where he stood.

"Hey. You got a key?" Brody asked with his shoulders scrunched up in an attempt to save his already purple ears from further frostbite.

"Yeah," Thorp said, breaking his trance. He got out his keys.

Thorp was reluctant to step through the front door of his own house, even after walking what felt like a hundred miles in below-freezing temperatures.

When all this was said and done, what would it mean when he had the wires cut down? Would he have to return to working a regular job, going into Chicago with the rest of the commuters? How would he get there? He was unable to get a driver's license, so would he have to take a cab every morning? But that would prove expensive with no longer receiving a steady income from Hark. He'd have to move back into the city into a cramped apartment sandwiched above, below, side to side by noisy people. He dreaded everything ending and changing.

He wanted to find Nectar—by any means necessary—and if he had to live in the projects after all of this was over, he'd do it. If she were alive and well, he'd do it. If not, he considered fleetingly—if she were dead, as his suspicions itched, what then? A shot of brandy, a trip out to the barn one night once he'd talked himself into it. Rope, a chair. A quick beg for mercy upon arrival. Tip.

Thorp felt Brody watching him and met his friend's gaze. In Brody's pumpkin-hued eyes, he could detect a thick sympathy piled there. Thorp went up the rest of the stairs of the front porch and unlocked the front door. He would figure things out later. He'd cross that bridge when he came to it, if he survived that long with a pan of scrambled eggs for brains, that is.

Nothing looked moved or altered in any way. Living alone, Thorp was able to keep close tabs on every object's proper home and nothing looked askew.

Thorp and Brody didn't say anything. They filed into the house, went about their way, but it was irrefutable.

It crept in.

The bleak anticipation that at any moment the front door could blow off its hinges, booted feet pouring into the house. Gunfire before any question could be asked or begged. A battering splintering the front door as easily as it would a house of cards. Or the more hands-off approach: bunker-buster shot straight down the chimney, bull's-eye. Or the more hands-on: A man good with knives who had absolutely no qualms about wet work so long as he could do it with his own personal flair—*stop*.

Thinking it was not sufficient, he said, "Stop." Thorp shook his head—those cloying, horrible thoughts, they weren't his own. In a strange way, it felt all right now, knowing he didn't own these quick diversions his mind made by the hour every day. They'd been manufactured, installed, whatever the term was. But fear of the next nosebleed, the next pounding headache only alcohol could soothe absorbed that momentary peace he found in the realization. He needed to busy himself. Do something. Anything to just stop thinking for even just a moment.

He went to the kitchen to make coffee, had the pot's lid open and the coffee ready to be scooped in, but couldn't concentrate. He left a trail of black crumbs from the coffee can to the waiting pot, the measuring spoon empty upon arrival. He threw it back in and threw his coat back on. Despite his fingers not being entirely thawed yet, he went outside into the cold.

Brody sat by the potbelly stove, watching the snow blow in through the back door Thorp had left open in his quick escape. He got up and closed it. He didn't need to go out there and chase him down to ask. Brody knew.

Before closing the door and severing the reach of the sonar, he watched Thorp trudge to the corner of the barn and around it to the shed at the far edge of the property to get away from it. Even out there, he'd still be under the net thrown down by the wires. Was it possible to be more affected by something knowing it was happening?

He, too, could feel it.

Lips at his earlobes chanting an inexhaustible string of nonwords, none of them pleasant.

He thought about home. Not his apartment but the home he had grown up in as a boy. He could feel tension ease out of his shoulders and neck. His limbs all felt a foot longer when it all had gone.

Brody emptied his pockets onto the dining room table and took over making coffee. He liked how it felt, doing this simple task, so he watched the coffee percolate up into the glass bubble of the pot. Hovering his open hands near the warm metal of the pot, he thought more about home, zeroing in on the minutiae of that cornflower-blue two-story house on Hennepin Avenue.

The square painted onto the backboard fixed above the garage door. It was the same shade of oxblood left over from painting the doghouse. Him and his dad, shooting hoops. Dad in his overalls, the ones that had his name still legibly stitched to his chest. Grunting jump shot—pockets jangling full of keys, a box cutter, coins, nuts, bolts, washers. Jangling when he made the shot, jangling when he landed on work boots so worn the wink of chrome of his steel toes shone through.

"Got me again," he'd say, proud.

Brody smiled to himself as he held the backs of his fingers near the speckled metal of the coffeepot. They were so numb he could probably lay them directly on the heated metal and not feel anything initially. He felt miles calmer now, though. He let the coffee continue to brew and journeyed back further through his youth.

Coming home from church on a humid summer Sunday morning in the family car. Resting his chin on his mother's seat back, complaining that he was so hungry he could eat *two* horses. She offered to make waffles, and she got a stunned gasp from the backseat in reply. Brody wouldn't end his list of the things he loved about waffles until they were on his plate.

Once home, there she'd be, Mom in her Sunday best, pouring waffle batter into the waiting metal mouth of the press. "I should've waited until I could change before I said anything." She pinched his nose. "My little bottomless pit."

Tweaking precisely until the press's knobs were meticulously set, she flicked a dab of butter onto the metal as a test. If it sizzled, it was ready. She poured in the batter, lowered the handle, and waited with one hand holding it in place—as if the batter might try to spring free. In the amount of time it took that only she knew, she looked down at Brody and winked.

He watched with fascination—she knew just how long to keep that handle down so the waffles would come out perfect. He recounted the trial and error after Dad bought her the press—lifting the lid and seeing the smoking black wreck inside. "Ah, nuts." But she'd developed a sixth sense for it. Counting to *x* with "steamboats" after each number? A poem that took the exact amount of time to mentally recite as a waffle to transmogrify from batter to a square of golden goodness?

Mom turned and lifted the press, scraped out the square of fluffy perfection onto a plate. She hesitated. She kept the press lid open, the metal mouth yawning. She adjusted the knob, dropping the arrow down into where the number ten, set in a bolder typeface than the other numbers, waited. Immediately the metal reacted, creaking as it expanded and grew red. Holding the lid open, she turned to Brody. "Can I ask you a favor, sweetness?"

Brody, at nine years, nodded.

"Let me see your hand for a second."

No.

No, that's not—that never happened.

Brody took the coffeepot from the burner and went outside with it. He was making a beeline for the barn when he nearly ran into Thorp. Brody held the coffeepot, steam billowing out of the fluted spout. He noticed that Thorp held an axe and faced the south corner of his property. He wore a crown of vapor rising off his shiny pate that shattered whenever a breeze tore by but would always foggily materialize again.

Through the wall of snowflakes, Brody could see it

was the wire guide derrick Thorp was facing. He was at a careful distance, as if lying in wait for the derrick to spring from its moorings and dart away—at which point he'd give chase.

"Probably not a good idea," Brody said. He adjusted his grip on the coffeepot; the handle was a bit warm where it met the pot itself.

Thorp sighed. "I know. But remind me anyway."

"They'll know for sure that we know. They'll be out here in a heartbeat."

After a moment, "Is it the same for you?"

"Ugly thoughts?"

"Yeah."

"Yeah."

"Not sure if I can take it. I'm really not sure if I can take it." Thorp slid his hand down the length of the smooth axe handle. The head buried itself at his feet. He raised his other pink-fingered hand and clutched his temple, mussing his hair. "It's terrible. I keep thinking these things about Nectar, about them showing up here—killing me. Killing you."

Brody couldn't deny it; it seemed doubly worse. As if Hark had dialed it up to eleven. Before he considered it to be merely an infectious paranoia, but now it seemed clear that something was looming about them, gremlins unseen. Invisible sharks just below the glassy surface of everything—not even so much as a shining wet glimpse of a fin to let you know, yes, it's something outside doing this *to* you.

"You have to try and shake it," Brody said, knowing it sounded as useless as telling a gunshot victim to walk it off. "Focus on something positive. It worked for me kind of. We'll get this shit out of here soon enough, but we can't risk attracting their attention until then."

"They saw me. Tonight when I went to listen in with the radio. The car was stuck in the ice, and they got a good look at me."

"How?"

"What do you mean?"

"Well, was it one of the guards, or were you caught on camera? Kind of a stupid question. You were probably on camera before you even got a hundred feet from that place." Brody sighed. "Did you let him see your jigsaw?"

"No, but still—I fucked up," he said.

"Come on. You didn't fuck up."

"They *know*. It's only a matter of time before they come out here and *find* us and . . . I mean, hell, I'm on their payroll. It sure as shit won't take much for them to figure out where I live." He dropped his head back and gave the wires a long, exasperated sigh. He shook his head. "And there it is again."

Although Brody wished Thorp had waited before going off to Hark, he couldn't really fault him. He'd gotten a lead, and just like him, once that first piece fell into your lap, it was hard not to spring up looking for others. "What's done is done. It's not like you did anything, did you?"

"A security guard came out, told me to leave."

"Big deal, he probably thought you were just sleeping it off before heading home."

"He told me it was private property, that I was

trespassing. He didn't see my jigsaw, didn't even talk directly to me—he said it from the other side of the window. But he got a face-map on me."

"If that's all, then there's nothing to worry about. I'm sure we're still under the radar—"

"They were probably waiting for me to do something like this, get curious, go asking questions about why it was after they put these things up I've been feeling so goddamn weird all the time and . . ."

Thorp pulled the axe from the snow and, accompanying the effort with a shout, heaved it toward the tower. It ate up the distance in plunging sweeps and collided with a hollow bang, not damaging a thing. The echo sang for what felt like a full minute.

Thorp made no move to retrieve the axe but instead set off toward the barn in a lopsided jog.

After the barn door slammed and all Brody could hear was the droning hum of the wires above his head and the occasional shove of blustery wind, he returned to the house. He knew it would be as bad in there as it would be in the barn or standing in the yard. But at least he'd be able to feel his toes.

He was sure to let the warm memories of his childhood home roll to the forefront before passing through the threshold of the farmhouse. He closed the back door but left it unlocked for Thorp.

Slumping onto the couch, Brody removed the sonar, rubbed away the residual stickiness on his forehead, and watched as the last echoes of the wire-frame world about him collapsed into darkness. Operating by feel alone, he opened his e-mail attachments from the messages he had sent himself, absently flipping through them and requesting the ones his blindly guided finger happened to fall upon to be read aloud. He listened to the messages, the strings of numbers and medical jargon that he didn't really understand, detailing Alton's brain scans. Then he listened again to the copy he'd made of the Probitas letter.

It'd been a red-letter shit day. He asked his phone to tell him what time it was out of morbid curiosity. It felt like they'd been out for weeks instead of just all night. It was nearly 8 a.m., the day before Thanksgiving and two days before he was due in front of Chiffon's desk.

As if a personal request in concern for his personal well-being, the phone requested, "Please recharge." He obliged and found the charge-by-vicinity area built into the face of the coffee table, that spot slightly warmer than the rest of the grain. He set his phone upon it and decided to take the phone's request personally so he went and poured himself another cup of coffee—knowing it was full by pouring into the cup with his index finger looped down inside—and carefully returned to the couch, minding his steps.

No lenses, no sonar, his thoughts were a mélange of black and white unbidden by any distraction besides the crackle of the wood-burning stove and the sharp twinkle of snowflakes being thrown against the windows. He saw images of his parents and home. Then he imagined the Minneapolis law successfully redacted, cutting short his effort to find Nectar. He was hauled out of prison and stood blind in a courtroom as an ad hoc PR representative from Hark Telecom questioned him in court: "Yes, he is the man on our surveillance tapes, the one who tried to commit corporate terrorism against us."

For a minute, his mind got the better of him, and he imagined slow demises for Nectar, for Thorp, for himself.

From the vicinity of where he'd left his phone on the coffee table to sponge up some volts, Thorp's ordi issued a soft two-note chime.

Glad for the interruption, Brody ran a hand over its lid, clearing away the flakes of snow that had melted down to cold, wet hemispheres. He flipped it open and grunted, "Read."

The ordi began reciting its latest e-mail. Brody's frustration and worry mounted with each word, but shortly before its end the electronic narrator cut short.

"Read from beginning."

Nothing.

"Read?"

Unlike his lenses, Thorp's Gizumoshingu had unrivaled battery life and seldom required a charge. Still, he set it alongside his phone on the warm spot on the coffee table and tried it again, figuring maybe putting his phone so close to it messed something up connection-wise. He tried the ordi's power button a few times and heard no vent fan whir to life, no string of music denoting a successful powering on. He reapplied his sonar to get a better look at what he was doing; even if he couldn't see anything on screen at least he could find the ordi's power button easier.

He held his breath to listen. The fan for the wood-burning stove was off. The persistent thrum of the refrigerator in the kitchen was gone. He put his hand on the coffee table and felt for that warm spot but found none. Had the power gone out?

Power or no power, what the e-mail was in the middle of telling its intended recipient, Thorp, wasn't good news. Brody got to his feet and nudged open the door with his foot since he was carrying the Gizumoshingu, two coffee cups, and the steaming coffeepot. He crossed the lawn and was surprised to find Thorp wasn't in a panic with the entire property's power off.

He was at the backmost wall of the barn, filling troughs and murmuring to himself. Was he doing this in the dark, perfectly content? Had the wavelength finally etched in that deep?

Thorp turned, keeping one hand on the snout of the horse Brody knew to be Carol, and gave a smile that the sonar pegged for embarrassed. Embarrassed for his earlier display with the axe, Brody assumed. Thorp stared at the Gizumoshingu under Brody's arm. His apologetic smile turned to a frown.

"Something wrong?"

There was a distinct rumble coming from somewhere in the barn. Before the sonar found the boxy, vibrating shape by the far wall, he smelled the generator's acrid smoke.

"The barn's lights, they're hooked up to the generator?" Brody asked.

"Yeah," Thorp said. "Why? What's up?"

"You got a space heater?"

"Right over there. What's the matter?"

He set the coffeepot and cups aside, pulled the ordi out from his armpit, and held it out for Thorp.

He reached for it with both hands. "What is it?"

"Just read it," Brody said.

He opened the ordi, the e-mail still on the screen, and read aloud, "'Mr. Ashbury, it has come to our attention that you trespassed on our property at 12:52 this morning. While you may be one of our cherished customers, we regretfully inform you that Hark Telecom is discontinuing your service effective upon our receiving automatic confirmation that this message has been opened. Please note that any further similar behavior on your part will be met with legal action. Thank you.'" He lowered the ordi. "Think we should be worried?"

"If they were going to raid the house, I'm pretty sure they wouldn't send you an e-mail beforehand."

"True. Still, though. Wish I had known. I would've gotten a gallon or two pumped out earlier when we were in the basement because the goddamn genny is right about in the E—"

In that second the generator made a defeated thud, silenced.

The horses whinnied nervously.

"Great," Thorp grunted.

Brody clicked on his phone's flashlight for Thorp's benefit. "You mentioned something about pumping gas?"

"I had a reservoir installed in the side yard. I'll go get it." Thorp retrieved his own flashlight and tested its beam against his palm, grabbed a metal gas can from the corner, and set out across the yard.

Brody stroked Carol's face, scratched behind her ear. He told her it would be all right, that Thorp would be back in a minute.

When Thorp returned to the barn, he found Brody standing outside. His hands were buried in his pockets and his eyes were closed, but he still seemed to be facing something. Thorp saw him twitch, his head cocking like an alarmed doe. Apparently, despite only being a few yards away, Thorp had gotten within range of the sonar. Just as quick, as if trying to pass off he'd been startled, Brody settled. Thorp assumed it took a second to recognize someone through the sonar. That or Brody was better at hiding how jumpy he truly was.

Thorp stood under the barn's awning with him, setting the gas can down. Aligning himself with his back against the barn door like Brody, Thorp could tell where he'd been sending the sonar's ping to see, to map, to calculate. "I don't suppose we even need to say it." He clicked off his flashlight. "Do we?"

"That entirely depends," Brody said, sipping coffee. "On?"

"To what end we are doing all this."

"What do you mean?"

"What we're thinking with Ceramic Groom. It's not very likely we'll walk away from that. If it works, great, but if it doesn't, what is our objective?"

"To stop Hark."

"What about Nectar?"

Thorp choked. "Well, of *course* we want to find her. But being pragmatic and all . . ."

"Yeah? Go on." Brody opened his eyes, and they shone milky, catching the glow of early morning sky. "You're being pragmatic and what does that mean, exactly?"

"What the fuck is this all about?" Thorp snorted. "You act as if she's your sister."

"Do you believe she's alive?"

"What does it matter?"

"It matters. Do you, though?"

"Sure," Thorp shrugged. "On a scale from one to ten it was like a seven or eight before and now after meeting that Mateusz guy . . ."

"Yeah?"

"Well, I'm just not as convinced as I was before, okay? Finding Nectar, stopping Hark, finding Nectar's body, finding the piece of shit that Hark hired to kill her—it's all one and the same, isn't it? But let's be real for a second. You really think they'd *kidnap* Nectar? What, for money? It's Hark. Come on, man. Despite that, I still believe she's alive. Never mind, back to the point you were making. I'm being cooperative. *I'm* the one who suggested we do our own version of Operation Ceramic Groom, aren't I? I want to find her."

"You want to get even; that's different."

"Again, what the fuck difference does it make?"

"It *makes* a difference," Brody shouted, his voice drumming throughout the farm.

In reply a sylvan resident howled far off.

"What's in your head when you go into something is what's important. You and I, we get a Darter pieced together and fly it into the city and we manage—somehow—not to get shot down, then we get onto the roof of Hark Telecom and we encounter some minimum wage security guard who wants to play hero. How you'll react to that is entirely dependent on what's in your head, your motive, right now at this second."

"You want me to tell you what I'm thinking?"

"Yes, yes, I do."

Thorp crashed two open palms against Brody's chest. "I think you're a fucking Boy Scout. *I* think you're going through all this shit because you believe you owe me. *I* think you're keeping such a fucking sunshine-and-lollipops attitude because you're scared if Nectar turns up dead, I'll go even *more* off the fucking rails— and *then* what will you do?" He took a double handful of Brody's coat. "I think you potentially see yourself becoming like this. I think you're praying to God that you weren't one of the ones they picked for this shit, and you feel bad for me." He wiped his nose, looked at his hand—red—and wiped again. He released Brody's coat and stepped back.

"You finished?" Brody grunted, adjusting his collar.

"Am I right?" Thorp asked and sniffed, his eyes downcast toward his blood-smeared fingers.

"I'm not even going to say whether or not—"

"Am I *right*?" Thorp roared. "Tell me. Am I fucking right?"

"Who the fuck *wants* brain cancer, huh? Of *course* I hope I'm not in the same boat as you, but I'm not doing this out of pity or a guilty conscience. I'm doing it because you fucking asked me to."

Thorp paused, then decided to say what he felt—no sugarcoating here. "You fucking liar." He pulled back a fist.

But Brody was quicker. He took Thorp's halfhearted hook, pulled him in, and delivered a punch of his own to his belly. Thorp made a surprised bellow of pain.

There was a small clink of something colliding with his belt buckle. It was the sound that let Thorp know that Brody didn't have preternaturally hard fists but had in fact used the knuckleduster on him. Thorp doubled over, one hand slapping the barn door for stability, and coughed—laughter slowly came into it after the third or fourth hack.

Brody stood by and said between labored breaths, "I'm sorry. It was a gut-reaction kind of deal."

"That thing really fucking hurts." Thorp cackled. "Man alive. No wonder those girls pay you so much. Christ." He stood, putting his hands on his hips to retain a straight spine. "I honest to God think I may've gone and shit my pants."

"I apologize. It's just a reflex. You can hit me if you want."

"No," Thorp said, blew the air out of his lungs, refilled them. "I deserved that. Yep. I did." He leaned back, hands on hips. "Jesus." He gave Brody a puckish look that he hoped he picked up on, even with the sonar. "I wouldn't hit a blind guy. That's not very . . . neighborly."

They stood outside the barn amongst the scattered footprints in the snow, a record of their tiff like numbered dance steps. Both of them gazed out from under the awning toward the military vehicles—all of them wearing a coat of white. The two Darters were the closest, and their glass bubble cockpits were half-mast with eyelids of snow, staring and judging the two men still heaving from their argument that came to blows.

"Do you have a mag scope here?"

"One that works? No."

"Going to need one if we're going to sustain lift over Chicago."

Thorp sighed. "I know."

"What about an aircraft registration number? Can we get one of those online?"

"That one"—Thorp nodded to the Darter on the right—"still has an active number."

"How much would it take?" Brody asked.

"To get it to fly?" Thorp snorted. "Just let me bend over and pull that million bucks out of my ass."

"I don't mean money. I mean the actual labor," Brody said.

"We could make a whole one by scrapping the one next to it for parts. Of course, there wouldn't be much of a rider compartment, but I guess we probably won't be needing it, with it just being us two."

"Could end the fuselage right behind the cockpit," Brody suggested. "Cut down on weight."

"Faster," Thorp added, eyebrows raised. "Yeah, that's good."

They both gave pause.

"Are we really considering this?" Thorp said.

"If they pass the thing they're trying to pass state-wide, the first time I use my jigsaw in January, the cops will be called. I'm going to jail. They want me there. And to tell you the truth, I'd rather crash and burn than spend the next ten to fifteen in prison."

Thorp was finally able to stand without feeling as if his abdomen would split open. "If we do it right, that won't happen. I don't want you to do any time, either, but you know what I mean. In the big house is better than the one upstairs, right?"

"With the friends I have in there, unfortunately I think I'll be relocated to the other one in no time at all." Brody smirked.

A beat passed. Thorp continued to wipe at his nose and peel the ruddy crust from the rim of his nostril. He flicked a flake of it away. "Brass tacks for a minute, okay? Whether I believe Nectar is alive or not isn't really that important. You may think it is but it's not. I mean, in my head I'm looking for justice. Not revenge, mind you, but justice. It's different. If she's gone, we have a good reason to believe it was Titian Shandorf who did it. Whether or not he was working for Hark Telecom because of what she and Abigail and Mateusz found out—I don't know. I'm not sure what point I was making here, but . . . you don't owe me shit. What's going on with me is my bullshit to manage. You and I will crack this thing, and in the end, however it turns out, I just want to say thank you for putting up with me. I think that sock to the gut you gave me shook my common sense loose."

"Anytime." Brody cuffed him on the shoulder.

"I'm serious. I mean, this could go south real quick. And . . . I don't think either of us will likely walk away from this unscathed, odds are. Putting this thing together"—he gestured at the dead aircraft—"and putting her in the air, excuse my math, but probably just a few *thousand* felonies. And that doesn't even count the landing her on the roof of a downtown building, breaking in, and all of that. From what you said, you're already in deep shit back home, and if you don't want to go through with this, now's the time to say something."

Brody nodded. "I'm still in."

Thorp brightened sarcastically. "And on the other hand, if we *do* manage to get in there and snag what we're after, who the hell knows *what* we'll do with it."

Brody didn't smile. "I have a friend in the St. Paul Police Department."

"He the one who wants to put you behind bars?" Thorp chuckled.

"Well, maybe he's more of an acquaintance. I know a guy; let's say that. And I'm sure Nathan will listen if we give him something concrete enough."

"What are we after? Before we even break open the toolbox, let's have that out in the open."

"Hubert Ward. It was him who had Probitas send the letter to Nectar. He's the only major name that's come up in all of Hark's personnel so far."

"And what do we aim to get?"

"Evidence that he has Titian Shandorf on payroll. Even if the stuff The Mothers were trying to expose has to wait, we can at least start the process by getting proof that they've hired Shandorf to kill people they'd like to see dead."

Thorp scoffed. "You think they'll just have pay stubs sitting around for us to find?"

"Think about it. Hardly anyone uses cash anymore. They practically don't even print the stuff anymore. Any payment, any movement of money from one account to another needs to use one kind of jigsaw or another. And since Ward was sending the letters to tell The Mothers to stop sniffing around, his database would be the most likely place to find the starting line of the paper trail. We get some kind of record and send it to Nathan, and we get Titian, Hark, everyone in one whack."

"You say 'we get this' and 'we get that.' Don't get pissed off, but I have to ask how."

"Well, I'll just keep my fingers crossed that accessing his ordi will be as easy as playing Alton Noel's videos."

"Wait a minute," Thorp said. "You mean we."

"We can't both go," Brody said. "You drop me off, circle round, come back, and pick me up in fifteen or twenty minutes. We can't risk them surrounding our ride on our way out. No, no way. I'm going alone."

"You're not going alone. I can write a program to have the Darter circle around on autopilot, drop us off, and pick us up. You got lucky with Alton's ordi. He didn't have it encrypted. Hubert Ward's tech is going to be just a *wee* bit different, especially if he was up to the shit we think he was." Thorp picked up the gas can and opened one of the barn doors, drawing it out wide.

"All right," Brody said, following. "But no guns."

Thorp upended the gas can into the generator. "Guns but no live ammunition. How about that?"

Brody scowled. "What, rubber bullets?"

"Got a whole box of them down in the basement." Thorp started the generator with one kick, and the lights hanging from the rafters of the barn came on.

Brody pulled the lens charger out of his coat pocket and handed it to Thorp. He plugged it in and the device beeped; the unit immediately began boiling with a soft trickle. "Speaking of which, we have to go back to that field, pick up the guns, clean things up a little, and . . ."

When he looked up, Brody's head was thrown back, as if preparing to sneeze. "What is it?"

"*Listen*," Brody hissed.

Thorp heard it, too. The monotonous screech of aircraft engines. He shut the generator off, though it hadn't even had a chance to warm up. The lights above faltered, died out.

Shielding themselves from above with the barn's awning, they stood in the backyard, watching the two Darters pass overhead. They moved at a steady clip, their narrow bodies barely perceptible in the overcast morning.

"Tell me what's happening."

"They're circling around the property," Thorp answered.

They listened, watched.

It was almost easier to tell where the aircrafts were just by sound. They'd drift ahead of darker clouds and disappear for a moment until their running lights winked. Thorp caught a better glimpse when one of the Darters moved across a lighter patch of sky where the sunlight managed to break through the dense cloud cover. It appeared bulky, swollen. As if the mechanical insect was pulling along a pregnant belly.

"They look different, not the same model as the ones we know—not like these here." He gestured at the decommissioned vehicles.

"What are they doing? It doesn't sound like they're getting any farther away."

"They're coming back around."

"Should we run?"

"They're not even at half-speed. They're not chasing anything."

The Darters descended gently along the copse at the rear of the property and down over the hill. Perfectly timed, the first Darter halved its girth when a large, flat object tumbled from its underside, falling heavily. Then the second Darter released its cargo. This time, Thorp could make out a flash of color—a creamy hue or off-white—as it fell into the bog.

Brody cocked his head in the direction of the violent splashes.

Thorp pulled him under the eaves of the barn as the Darters crossed the yard. Brody ducked when the Darters screamed overhead. With their loads severed, they ascended sharply—their engines blaring with the effort—and punched up through the clouds and were gone within a moment. Stillness returned to the Illinois countryside.

"What was that all about?" Brody asked.

"I think they just dropped something in my cranberry bog."

"It sounded enormous. What the hell could make splashes like that? It would have to be the size of a . . ." Brody's shoulders dropped. "About the size of a Fairlane and a Zäh."

28

The Fairlane had sunk, and the battered grille of the Zäh stuck out of the muddy water defiantly. Brody and Thorp stood on the banks of the cranberry bog, Thorp saddled atop Maribel. Thorp had offered to allow Brody to ride Carol, but he had never ridden a horse in his life and thought it wasn't exactly the appropriate time to learn.

"We have to get out there," Thorp said.

"How deep does the bog go?" Brody asked.

"Four feet mostly, but it gets up to about eight out there in the middle." Swinging his leg up and over, he dropped off the horse and guided her to the water's edge. "We can't have the car sticking out of the water. It's obvious they put them here to drop the dime on us. When the cops show up, if the vehicles are hidden at least it'll buy us some time while they're looking."

Thorp threw Maribel's reins on a leafless branch of a shrub and waded into the water. He took in a quick gasp through his teeth once the water had spilled in over the top of his boots.

"Get out of the water," Brody said, hands in pockets.

"What?"

"Get out of the water," Brody repeated, harsher.

Here and there a sheet of ice had developed, forsaken, shriveled cranberries suspended within. Even with the sonar, the water was clearly cold—it didn't move like the lakes and rivers of Minnesota when it was warm. The wind passed over the bog's surface and the water didn't move freely; it moved as if in slow motion. It was on the edge of freezing over, a mere half-degree change from crystallizing.

"It's not worth it," Brody said. "Let them call it in. Let the cops show up."

Thorp stepped out of the water, groaning with his numbed feet, his pant legs darkened halfway to his knees. "Okay, so who is it that needs the pep talk, me or you?"

"I'm most likely going to prison. And you said yourself that you can't even *make* a cop arrest you. You couldn't do any time if you asked. So, fuck it."

"Fuck it?"

Brody waved his hand at the leering, broken mouth of the Zäh. "I'm not going to waste my time with this. They want to plant evidence on us, let them. Let them fucking rain down a hundred dead cars on us. We're going to start working on that Darter tonight." He walked away.

Thorp untangled Maribel's reins from the shrub and guided her along, following Brody up the dirt path.

"I'm glad you have the fire going in you and everything, but I don't think it's the dead cars they wanted in the bog."

"We both know what happened to them happened because it had to," Thorp said. "But we have to think about what happens *after* all this. What if Hark is planning to report us to the cops?"

"There're no tracks," Brody shouted. "They dropped the cars out of the fucking sky. It'll be inadmissible in court, not even evidence. How did we get them out here? Neither of us even owns a car. They can try to incriminate us all they want; we can get around this one no problem. It'll take time, but what they did here tonight is just plain sloppy. You got money. We can get a decent lawyer."

"I had money coming in, but that's a thing of the past now. And we don't have time to go to court for this. Tomorrow will make it twenty-five days that Nectar has been missing."

Brody sighed, launching a burst of steam into the air. "If Hark calls it in, if the cops show up and start poking around, it *looks* bad; that's for sure. But there won't be enough linking us to them. They'll see that there wasn't time for us to get the vehicles from the field down here, and with no tracks, yeah, their trying to get one over on us is completely shot full of holes."

"My gun," Thorp said. "The one Seb took from me at the field."

At that, Brody's stride halted.

Brody groaned. "Your goddamn Franklin."

"Afraid so." Thorp nodded. "I'll get a saddle on Maribel, and maybe together the horses can pull the cars out and—wait, what are you doing?"

Brody threw his coat aside, stomped down to the edge of the bog, and kicked off one boot, then the other. He tossed Thorp his phone, wallet, and lighter. He pressed his thumb against the sonar to make sure it was going to stay stuck. He splashed only three steps out into the water before the temperature hit him. His steps became slower. Each time his socked feet landed on half-frozen mud at the bottom, it was like his soles were struck by lightning. Radiating agony that reverberated through him—up his shins, to his knees, and into the muscles of his thighs, awakening the newly notched flesh in the crook of his crotch.

His voice jittered uncontrollably. "Any idea where the Fairlane might've ended up?"

"I saw some bubbles a second ago over to your right."

Brody moved that way, the black water crawling up to his waist. His exhales came out in contracted jerks, puffs of steam washing over his face in the wind—the smell of his own breath, musty with tobacco and sweet from the last coffee he'd had. His teeth chattered fitfully like a malfunctioning typewriter.

"Do you want me to come in?" Thorp asked.

"No point in both of us getting hypothermia," Brody managed to say.

The ping played over the surface of the bog. In wire frame it became a colorless checkerboard. He trudged another couple of feet, the half-developed sheet of ice cracking as his chest pushed through. He kept his arms high, let out little snarls and grunts he couldn't help as he stepped farther and farther, deeper and deeper. Again, he thumbed the sonar. The water, rife with rock-hard cranberries, was at his armpits.

His knees hit the bumper.

"Is he in there?" Thorp asked from the bank.

"Hold on."

When Brody lifted the trunk lid, Spanky drifted out and bobbed to the surface. Brody saw his head push through the white gridded bog, close enough to the sonar that the minutiae of Spanky's face could be found—the texture of his dead, sunken cheeks, the five-o'clock shadow poking through like cactus quills. The bumpy, swirly road map on his eyelids like subdermal worms bending themselves into cursive: *Never. Dead.*

"Yeah," Brody said, "he's in here."

He pulled Spanky around and shoved him through the water. The corpse pushed a wave of water out ahead of him and drifted languidly toward the bank. Brody watched to make sure he wouldn't change course and go in the wrong direction, then watched Thorp crouch to receive the corpse. He looked disgusted.

Brody stepped around to the side of the car and opened the door with some difficulty. Seb bobbed out as well. Brody dragged the giant man along by the hood of his jacket onto the muddy shore.

Upon pulling himself from the water, Brody flapped Seb's waterlogged coat open and retrieved Thorp's handgun. "Here." He shoved the ice-cold thing against

Thorp's chest and walked up the hill, fighting with his coat.

The wind tore across his damp clothes, and his body felt as if it were imploding, bones telescoping down into themselves, his flesh crawling like it was recoiling from the muscle, folding up and racing to the core in a frantic dash of self-preservation. Each step roared. "I got to get to the house. I can't be out here."

"But the power's off. There won't be any heat."

"We'll handle that in a m-minute. I need to make sure I'm not going to lose my f-fingers." He tottered along with everything numb, socks squishing with each step. "You said you got a space heater, right?"

"Pretty much confirms that they're onto us, huh?" Brody said, driving the shovel down to take another bite out of the frozen dirt. It came away in chips, splinters—frosty brown sheets. He cast the shovelful aside. He stopped for a moment to flex his hand and slap his palm against his knee. He wondered if the loss of sensation would be permanent.

"Let me take over," Thorp said.

Brody stepped aside and picked up his coffee from the ground, finding it had gone cold. They were in the trees, about half a mile within the more forested and far-flung portion of Thorp's property. It smelled to Brody like Mother Nature's Womb—if the gardening shop also happened to be a place to store dead bodies. He glanced down at the corpses. The discharge they had let loose when their souls were shoved from their bodies was palpable on the air. He turned away.

His face warmed suddenly. He must've come out

from behind a tree trunk's shadow. The sun was up but was about as useful in warming them as saying the name of the distant star over and over, but he could feel it on his face faintly, knew it was there—and stared into its assumed location with clouded eyes with no fear of it damaging anything. He and Thorp had been at this all night, and now it was threatening to eat into yet another day.

Thorp pressed his foot atop the shovel blade, driving it in deep. "I always hated this part."

With the sonar, Brody examined the depth of the rut Thorp was finishing. "Let's not talk about that now," he said, setting his coffee down. "That's good. That's deep enough. Here. Get his legs."

They slid Seb over and placed him in the hole, then Spanky next to him. The top of the burlap sack was open, and an arm splayed out. A hand with the fingers squeezed tight in a bloodless fist. Thorp edged it back in with the side of his boot.

The grave was shallow. It took only a few minutes to fill it back in with icy dirt.

Brody stood, leaning on the shovel handle, eyeing the mound as Thorp kicked some half-rotten dead leaves over it. He bent and gathered up a load of sticks, leaves, tore some green underbrush from the earth, and dispersed it on the heap. He took a small bottle from his coat and poured its contents around and over the grave. Brody detected the odor: ammonia.

When finished, Thorp asked, "Suppose we should say something?"

"Like what?"

"I don't know, man. They're dead. Just because we weren't on the same side doesn't mean we shouldn't show them some respect."

"We buried them in bags that horse food came in," Brody said. "I think we're a little bit past the showing respect portion of this ordeal. If it were them up here and us down there, I'd understand. Can't exactly give a proper burial when all of this other shit is going on."

"But look at it," Thorp said. "It's like they were a couple of dogs or something."

"Don't," Brody said. "It only makes it worse."

Thorp swallowed. "This isn't right."

"No, it's not. But, you know, shit happens."

Thorp shook his head. "Wow. I know you were always cool as a cucumber, water off a duck's ass and all—but even for you that's pretty cold. They were people."

Brody scattered the dregs of his coffee aside into the carpet of dead leaves and snow. "Like you pointed out, Spanky would've shot us if you hadn't stopped him—and Seb, well, that was just a case of trespassing gone awry." He took up his shovel, coffee cup hooked on his index finger.

"You think it was . . . something else that made him come back?"

"Who?"

"Him." Thorp nodded at the mound. "Them."

"What do you mean?"

"How they dropped him off. You think it was all just them trying to pin it on us or . . . something else? I deserve to have to deal with it, I guess. I did kill him after all." He coughed once, raspy.

"It's done," Brody said. "You threw down the ammonia so if the cops bring dogs they won't find shit besides the cars. We got your gun, these two're buried, and scents are covered—it's *through*." He waved his hand. "Okay? Through."

"I got to answer for this," Thorp said.

A beat passed. The last of the crickets tuned themselves down, then out.

"I'm going inside. I still can't feel certain parts of myself, and if they were to fall off I'd be rather upset." Brody walked away, shovel handle resting on his shoulder.

"I told God I'd never kill anyone ever again," Thorp shouted after him.

Brody's strides faltered. He hesitated, then continued walking. He didn't answer because he didn't have an answer to give.

29

Late in the afternoon, Thorp woke to the sounds of toil. He roused from the couch, and the Gizumoshingu fell to the floor. Immediately, he was rewarded with an onslaught of unpleasant images and ringing ears. It was verbatim to the previous night's bad dreams. He didn't allow them any more time to sink in: he got on his coat and headed outside with his ordi in his grip.

He paused upon taking one step onto the back porch. The Darters were gone. Just two dark craters where they had been, two dirty trails where they'd been dragged through the yard, digging up the grass en route to the barn. They were mostly fiberglass but still weighed well over a ton each—how the hell did Brody do it?

Thorp opened the barn door and stepped inside.

Brody was at work with his eyes closed and his forehead pushed toward the open hull of the Darter, elbow-deep in the craft's mechanic innards. "I got coffee over here," he said.

Thorp saw the horses were breathing heavily, lapping up water in turns. They were still wearing their bridles. A network of ropes and pulleys were strewn all over the empty space above the aircrafts. He noticed a simple machine had been made utilizing the net Thorp used to bind stuff up and store it in the rafters. It was filled with nearly the entire pile of old electronics as a counterweight. Still, apparently the medieval-style vehicle relocation hadn't been enough; the horses looked exhausted. He gave Brody a smirk. He thumbed at them. "Did you?"

"I apologized afterward and gave them a couple of carrots. I couldn't have dragged these things in here on my own." Brody wiped a rag down the length of his blackened forearms and tossed it onto the workbench cluttered with parts, butted cigars, coffee cups, and a half-eaten bowl of shredded wheat. He'd also brought out a hot plate Thorp hadn't seen in years and wired it up to the generator, alongside the space heater he'd apparently slept in front of, indicated by the rumpled horse blanket.

He saw that the more damaged of the two Darters was dismantled most of the way, the other wearing its companion's parts. The ridged gray scars of welding looked decent, and the wings were folded up together on the aircraft's back neatly. Brody had gotten a lot of good work done throughout the morning.

"I hate to admit it, but she's looking pretty fine," Thorp commented, running his hand along the more complete aircraft. He never thought he'd see either Darter complete again, as he saw one the first time on that airstrip out behind Fort Reagan. It was both a consoling and thrilling sight.

Brody turned out the pocket of his jeans, and what looked to be ten pounds of nuts and bolts tumbled onto the workbench. "Pretty much good on this. Just have to get the airfoil working and reinforce the manifold over the engine compartment. I'm missing a few pieces, but I've managed to fabricate some of it together out of sheet metal. May not be airtight and it looks rough as hell, but it's passable."

"Have you even attempted the circuitry and stuff yet?" Thorp inquired, ducking his head in through the open cockpit door. "I can start in on that if you want."

The instrument panel was a mess of broken dials and thousands of frayed ends of wires sticking out like begging hands. When the Darters had been delivered by flatbed truck he had considered them more or less complete. But now, looking at them with the mind-set of reassembling them for actual flight, countless hours of work and frustration stared him in the face. He said to Brody as much as himself, "I think I have a few of the old books lying around somewhere on that stuff."

"That'd be great," Brody said, putting his coat back on.

"Flight computer's gone," Thorp said. "No autopilot."

"Suppose we might have to touch down after all, then, huh? Can't exactly send this thing on a quick loop around the city without it knowing how to fly on its own. Do you know where we can get one of those? The black market or something?"

"Oh, come on now. You're talking to the handyman, remember? I'm better than that." Thorp smiled. He poured himself a cup of coffee. It tasted good, if burned. "I'll just need a few things." He nodded toward the dangling pile of electronics, still captive in the net. "There's probably something in all of that I can use."

"But doesn't the autopilot function operate with an AI?"

"A basic one, yeah. It's just a map system and a series of preprogrammed flight patterns. Basically a whole slew of code and a timer. Hell, I could have the thing take off from here, fly us all the way to your apartment in Minneapolis, and get us back without either of us ever having to touch the controls except for the go switch."

"Then what are you waiting for? You get cracking on that and I'll get the tail fin going. Before dinner we'll have this thing in the air."

They worked throughout the remainder of day and well after the sun descended again. Thorp had discovered an old boom box in his pile of forsaken electronics and had it tuned to a classic rock station. It was the same music he preferred when in the service, stuff that had been popular long before his time, but music he felt the most connection with. He found himself humming when his thoughts steered into dark territory and openly singing along when they veered off completely in an attempt to counteract them.

As the songs passed one to the next, the men labored

at their separate stations within the barn. Brody used the torch to tack the dual tail fins onto the end of the passenger shaft, never having to shield his eyes from the welding flare. Thorp's fingers danced on the keyboard, creating a long series of code on his ordi that would be the autopilot function.

The men didn't speak for hours, never even went into the house to relieve themselves. They yellowed the snow outside and returned with unwashed hands to their respective jobs.

Around the same time both men's work grew quiet, finishing touches were applied. Thorp emerged from the cockpit, Brody from the nose of the craft where he'd attempted to bend some sheet metal, and they met at the workbench wearing matching looks aimed at one another.

"Ready?" Thorp asked.

Brody nodded. "You?"

"Yep."

The craft squealed, and the four wings spread out on its back and began to violently beat the air, kicking powdery snow away in surging, rhythmic bursts.

Thorp buckled his four-point harness. Brody slid on a pair of headphones and adjusted the microphone before him. He could see nothing beyond the windshield but felt the lurch in the well of his stomach as the Darter lifted off. The magnetic gyroscope within the beast's belly twisted and turned and scoured the earth beneath it for any sort of metal to push off of—scarce in their rural setting.

Nonetheless, after a few tired barks from the Darter's engines, the aircraft took flight and hovered a good thirty feet over the top of the barn. Brody clutched the worry bar and imagined seeing the shingled roof of Thorp's house and barn far, far below. Thorp plunged the aircraft forward through the icy wind over the cranberry bog and surrounding forest and then back again.

Thorp pointed at the nose of the Zäh still sticking out of the iced-over bog. "I wonder if they found my rucksack."

Brody was too terrified to answer, so he just shrugged.

"Let's take a look," Thorp suggested, and they began following the road to the scene of the other night's carnage.

"Well, I think that's about where we were," Thorp said, filling in for what Brody couldn't see.

"Yeah?"

"Snow's covered it all up. Can't even see tracks or anything."

"They probably took care of that, too," Brody managed. His stomach gave a quarrelsome twitch.

Thorp pushed the stick forward, and the Darter obediently started to descend. He cocked the craft forward enough that the nose was pointed straight down. It remained hovering like this, Brody feeling the bite of his harness in his chest.

"What is it?" Brody asked. Holding the bar ahead of him and his legs straight out, his body bracing for impact all on its own, he imagined the nose of the Darter was a mere fifteen feet off the ground, if not less. His confused equilibrium settled, and he could feel the craft was entirely vertical, its tail stuck straight up in the air. The engines gave a low whine, struggling to keep it upended.

Thorp narrowed the Darter down closer. He leaned forward in his seat. "I don't see it."

"It snowed last night," Brody said. "Are you sure this is the right place?"

"Yeah, that's the corner of the Hanson farm over there, so this must be it. This is right where Seb bumped us and sent us through the ditch. We were about *here* when I chucked the bag at that Artificial, and now I don't see anything."

Brody felt the vehicle fighting to keep itself straight. He gripped the worry bar so tight he thought his hands might lock that way permanently, the sonar feeling around inside the cockpit but unable to see anything beyond the tempered glass. The rumble bouncing off the ground ahead of them changed, grew closer, telling him Thorp had just inched them a bit farther down. He muttered, "Maybe you should pull up."

Thorp gave the joystick minor corrections, nudged the Darter forward, and Brody's stomach responded by mimicking the sensation of what it might feel like to house a bag full of displeased snakes inside his body. Without breaking his gaze, Thorp reached over and hit the double-time function for the wings. The vehicle responded at once, and the four wings started beating furiously at twice the rate.

"I'm trying to blow some of this snow out of the way. I think I got some tracks here."

"*Pull up*," Brody said, sure he was about to hear the

nose of the Darter scrape dirt at any second. "We need this thing in working order. Pull *up*."

"There it is," Thorp said. "Hold on. Let me see if I can grab it."

The sound exploded into the cockpit. Out of Thorp's side of the cockpit, with the glass hatch open, the sonar threw out its ping—rumpled, flat land. Brody could see the shape of the rucksack lift out of the snow as Thorp carefully kept one hand on the joystick and leaned out with the other to grab the bag from the ground.

"Okay, if we haven't landed, I'm *sure* we shouldn't be this close to the ground."

There was a heavy slap and a shatter of glass.

Brody whipped around, and the sonar felt at the break in the glass at the cockpit window directly beside him.

One of the farmer Artificials, clinging to the side of the Darter, twisted its arm into the cockpit through the new opening. Finding nothing, it retracted, craning back and throwing its fist against the cockpit window again to widen the gap.

Thorp wrenched back on the stick. He gave the Artifical a side-to-side shimmy, and it was pitched off. It hit the ground below silently in a puff of white.

"Fuck off, robot."

He closed his cockpit hatch, but snow still rushed in through the jagged hole on Brody's side accompanied by the deafening shriek of the Darter's engines. Thorp switched off the double-time setting, and they lowered their pitch to just tolerably loud. Angling back on the stick, they ascended more, rotated in place, and veered toward the farmstead, the soggy rucksack crammed between them.

They barely had the wheels down before Brody had his hatch open and was walking away from the Darter in quick, short strides. He suddenly recalled copilot training as well as how much time he spent in the restroom following each lesson.

A thick cable ran from the open panel on the underside of the Darter into the barn to the generator. The generator now had a hose running from its tank, out of the barn, across the lawn, into the house, down the stairs, and to the basement where it was hooked up with a coupling to the buried gasoline reservoir.

"Ironic," Thorp said, looking over the various hoses and cables, some of which had been patched with tape or rubber swatches and epoxy.

"What's that?" Brody plugged in his lens charger at the only available outlet. The generator had been busy, powering not only the radio but the hot plate and now the Darter.

"When it first came out, the Darter ran on gas. Like everything else. And this one was refitted with a battery. So we're taking gas, putting it through the generator to make electricity to fuel an aircraft that used to run on gas."

"Speaking of charge," Brody said, "I'm going to run in and get a pot of coffee made."

Thorp tried every square inch of the property, crunching the legs of his lawn chair down into the snow until they hit more solid earth, taking a seat, and listening to the ether. He'd shake his head, the straps of the flight helmet swinging back and forth, say, "Nope," and move on to a new spot. He returned to a section of the side yard that seemed to be less bad than the rest, and that was where he wheeled the steel fire pit.

After getting the fire started and taking a seat, sudden movement at the corner of the house startled Thorp to the point that his hand nearly went to his hip.

Brody came around, holding the coffeepot fresh from a spell on the hot plate in the barn. He took a seat next to Thorp and admired the fire.

Poking at the balled-up newspaper to wedge it under one of the logs, Thorp asked, "Feeling any better?"

"Yeah, stomach's doing enthusiastic somersaults now instead of triple axels." He poured them coffee, the stream of black stuff hemorrhaging steam. "How cold do you suppose it is?"

Shrugging, Thorp said, "Twenty-five, thirty tops."

"You really think it's better out here than inside the house?"

Thorp propped the log up on another one. "I'd like to think it is." He could feel Brody looking at him.

"Does that help?" Brody asked, knocking on Thorp's flight helmet with the visor screwed up, the loose straps, leads, and connectors draping his shoulders. It clacked inside, loud.

"Hell, I don't know. Go get yours and see."

Without another word, Brody sprang to his feet, his strides confident despite walking face-first into pitch black. Sometimes Thorp envied Brody's sonar. Never need to buy another flashlight again with that thing around.

A moment later, Brody returned to the orange glow of the fire with his helmet on. He took his seat at the steel fire pit and threw back the visor to let the sonar do more than what it probably could in there, ringing about inside the helmet, only mapping the contours of his own head.

He must've felt Thorp watching, because he turned toward him. "You know, we might as well break out the Reynolds Wrap." He glanced over his shoulder at the road. "It's probably a good thing not too many people drive by this place. I'm sure we look like a couple of loonies right now."

"I'm surprised the cops never came by," Thorp said. "I kept pausing between code lines to listen for cars coming up the driveway."

"They're probably busy," Brody said, easing down in the lawn chair, the rubbery noodles that made up the seat squeaking like hands aggressively petting balloon skin. "That law reform coming up, a lot of people are probably out trying to take advantage of stuff they won't be able to do in about a month."

"What exactly is going to happen, anyway? What're they changing?" Thorp asked, watching as the intricate palace of ash that the newspaper had become crumbled soundlessly under its own weight.

"Besides rewording what is technically theft and what's sometimes argued as just 'pre-apocalypse emergency ration-gathering,' a law that had been passed that says if a couple has a dispute and there's a third party involved and something should happen between the couple, violence or otherwise, the third party cannot be held accountable."

"Are you saying you're some kind of gigolo, too?"

Brody smirked. "It was written that way so governors and mayors and councilmen could steal whoever's wives they wanted and not get in trouble when the other guy found out and attempted to get even. Government guy throws a punch in self-defense, maybe ruins a carpet while being chased out—no harm can come to him so long as he's the third party in an extramarital affair. Of course, with me, that loophole meant that as long as I said in court that I was merely an unknowing adulterer who gave the husband or boyfriend a shiner in self-defense, then off the hook I remain."

Thorp paused. "So, again: you're a gigolo?"

"I never *did* anything with any of the women. It was just a way to knock some sense into the guys they were shacked up with and—you know what? Never mind. They're changing the law, and I'm going to be taken by the coattails and thrown into the pen by an all-too-enthusiastic, old-fashioned-headwear-enthusiast detective I happen to know. That's it."

"I thought he was the one you're going to e-mail all this stuff to."

"I am," Brody said. "Just because I trust him with our research doesn't mean I'm best friends with the guy."

Thorp nodded, poked. "Oh, I almost forgot. Happy Thanksgiving. We missed it yesterday." He produced two tin cans and a crank-operated opener. "Making today Friday."

Thorp tossed Brody one can, and Brody laughed when he saw it was cranberry sauce. "Sure was."

"You were supposed to be back today. For your probation thing."

Brody accepted the can opener, wedged the cranberry sauce between his knees, and cranked the can opener around the perimeter of the lid. "That I was."

"Oh shit, man."

"It's all right." Brody waved him off. "My probation officer's a very understanding woman."

"Really?"

"No. I'm screwed." He pried off the jagged lid of the can, dabbed three fingers into the shiny mass of burgundy gelatin, and tried it. "But at least we have cranberry sauce. And I'd rather be sitting here having cranberry sauce any day of the week than dealing with my probation officer."

A moment passed.

"Thanks. Really. I mean it."

Brody's reply was a grin.

They both went back to their cans of cranberry sauce.

Quiet hours went by, more logs were burned, talk only occurring when one man thought of a possible snag in their plan. Each snag that arose was worked out among them, a plan would be set, and they'd go back to being quiet and watching the fire once more.

Brody retrieved cigars from his torn and dirty coat. They took turns using his lighter, puffed for a moment, and sat watching the fire. Brody toyed with the raw plugs on the end of his helmet's leads.

A scream broke out of Thorp's lungs, shrill and sudden. He flung himself out of the lawn chair and tore the helmet from his head, swung it high, and spiked it down against the snow where it bounced and rolled away. Thorp looked up at the three black-encased wires running directly above them. In the quiet night, beyond the crackling fire and the wind, their gentle humming din could be heard. Even more so now that Thorp had his helmet off.

"Why don't they just do it and get it over with?" he screamed. "We can't go anywhere, and they probably got us on satellite."

Brody stared at the fire, arms crossed. "They're not dumb. They're doing what they did to Thomas Lake. Cut off the power, up the dosage in those things"—he jutted his chin at the wires—"and just hope we take care of ourselves."

Thorp's labored breath slowed. "You too?"

Brody nodded without looking up from their sad excuse of a fire.

"You think they can make us do that?"

Shrug. "Probably."

Thorp raised his middle finger at them, and if that weren't clear enough, explained what the gesture meant. When he turned back around, partly ashamed, he felt his nose running profusely, but after he touched it and looked at his fingers, he saw they weren't bloody. "When can we get a move on? Can we leave tonight?"

Brody tossed the cigar butt into the fire pit. "We can't just cowboy this thing."

"That's fine, but I don't want to sit here under this shit anymore," Thorp said. He stepped so that he was under the edge of the house's roof, but it made little difference. It wasn't so much an out-and-out sensation but just a niggling tease—like someone tickling the very back of his brain with the feathery end of a wheat stalk.

"Do you think you can get some blueprints of the Hark building online without picking up any suspicion?"

"I doubt it. That kind of activity screams red alert." Thorp smoothed down his hair. "Getting into Probitas's site was one thing, but Hark actually *develops* spyware protection software. I can't imagine they'd leave anything to chance. Especially if they're up to no good."

"How high of a priority do you think research and development is within Hark?"

"Pretty high. It's their bread and butter."

"Do you suppose that would have any influence on its placement *within* the building?"

"It's hard to say. There're a lot of places now that have substructures and subbasements with walls that are ten feet thick to prevent remote hacks. So, if Hark plays stuff close to the vest, stuff they don't want anyone to know about, they'd probably keep it down there. Hubert Ward's a big cheese; he was the one who gave the order to keep the lower floors under a closer eye, according to the night watchmen. So maybe that's where his office is. But then again, up higher is where they often keep the important people. I don't know. It could be almost anywhere."

To Brody, the logs were just throwing off heat as they slowly dissolved. The sonar saw no fire outside the pixels rising, the drifting cinder flakes. Ten minutes had passed when neither man had said anything. Brody sat, hunched, staring into the fire and running through endless scenarios on how their plan would turn out.

He didn't have to keep a tally of outcomes where they failed, were killed. It was obvious that an unfavorable result was better than likely.

"So, suffice it to say, we know absolutely nothing," Brody said, breaking their long, pondering silence. "We're going to be taking an illegal aircraft into city limits, parking it on a privately owned structure—which I guess could be considered trespassing, even though it sounds like there should be a term scarier than that—and we have only fifteen minutes to get in and find what we need in a building ninety stories tall with no idea where to start."

"That's more or less it, yeah," Thorp said.

"We'll have to wing it, then. We can't risk any more time." He turned his head to ping the road for oncoming squad cars. Nothing. He took a second to give the wires crisscrossing the yard like shoelaces a sneer for putting the momentary focus-stealing thought in his head.

"We'll have to work fast and try to get as much as we can while we can. We have the Darter, we have you and what you can do with hacking, and we have me and I'll be timekeeper and lookout and run interference if need be." He fingered the metal loops of the knuckleduster in his pocket like an old man worrying change.

"So that's it? We're going to head out soon?" Thorp plucked his helmet from the snow and upended it to empty it.

"Yep. We'll leave tonight and grab what we can." Brody drained his coffee to give himself a second to think of an appropriate way to word what he wanted to say next. "I don't mean to be an asshole, but we can't have you going off the rails again. What happened at the cubies . . . Spanky may have been going for a gun and you saved my life and I appreciate that, but—here's the thing—we absolutely cannot hurt anybody this time around. Okay?"

Thorp nodded with downcast eyes. "Look, man, about that—"

"I understand," Brody interrupted. "I do. But a bonk on the head, maybe a bit of the close-quarters stuff we learned back in the day, all right. A little diplomacy goes a long way. We can't give Hark anything more. It'll just make shit worse."

"That's suicide," Thorp said. "If they find us, *they'll* be armed. We need a way to protect ourselves."

"Riot control stuff only," Brody said. "They'd like us to shoot their employees. Then we'd be out of their way rotting in jail while they kick the dirt over everything."

"Fine but I'm telling you it's a bad idea. If Hark Telecom is aware of what Hubert Ward is doing, they aren't going to fuck around with security. They're going to have stopping power and then some."

Brody said nothing. The fire continued to throw off tapering heat that in order to feel he had to lean his chair on the front legs. Everything inside the pit had now been reduced to what the sonar saw as latticed hills of powder.

"What time do you want to go?" Thorp asked.

Brody listened for the grumbling generator in the barn. "Whenever that thing shuts off."

"Okay," Thorp said quietly, "I'm going to get packed up."

"Rubber bullets," Brody reminded him.

After Thorp went around the house beyond the sonar's reach, Brody heard the rumble of the sliding glass door followed by the slap of the rubber gasket when it was closed.

The lawn chair let out the rubbed-balloon sound again as he sat back. The aluminum frame of the chair against his neck burned it was so cold, but he kept it there anyway. He couldn't help but notice the wires swaying in the chilled wind. He glared at them and listened to their innocuous thrum for a handful of minutes before he gave up and dropped the visor down on his helmet.

30

They passed over Chicago smoothly, one building after another sweeping underneath them. Brody felt his stomach turn each time another structure glided under his feet beyond the glass of the cockpit. The Trump International Hotel and Tower came and went. They had gotten nearly to the heart of the city, almost over the river. Angling around Aon Center, Hark Telecom came into view in front of the cockpit. Reflective glass threw their running lights back at them, as well as every other light surrounding the tower as if it were trying to remain invisible, even at ninety stories in height.

Almost as if it had been timed, as soon as Brody looked at the radio, it screeched once followed by a collected voice asking them for their call sign and destination.

Thorp, hand on the stick, spoke into the microphone, his voice sounding in Brody's headphones, "This is X-Fifteen, headed to O'Hare for VIP drop-off."

No response.

They were nearing Hark's illuminated roof too quickly and Thorp cut the engines slightly and the Darter's wings slowed a fraction. They hovered level with the seventieth floor of the Willis Tower. Brody watched a cleaning lady make quick work of a high-rise office, shoving a vacuum around a desk and under it, none the wiser to the man watching her.

The control tower still hadn't responded. Brody glanced at the radio set into the Darter's instrument panel. He muted his microphone from outside communication, so only Thorp could hear him. "That's an awfully long pause. Maybe we should just get moving before they send their buddies up."

"It's fine," Thorp reassured. "But we'll have to hop out when this thing is still moving. I have her programmed to head to the private airstrip at O'Hare, touch down there, and then immediately take off again before the recharge team gets to her. She'll pick us up in fifteen minutes."

"And we can't have any longer?" Brody said.

"This is O'Hare International Airport," a different voice called. "We do not have any scheduled landings at our private airstrip. Please return to your place of takeoff and reroute your destination accordingly."

Thorp took his microphone off mute. "Afraid I can't do that, O'Hare. We're running on E up here, and unless you want me to use the Dan Ryan as my emergency runway, I'd suggest you give us clearing for a quick recharge. We have approximately half an hour left in our tanks."

There was another lengthy silence.

After Thorp switched his microphone on mute, Brody said, "We're going to need more than fifteen minutes."

"Afraid that's all we're going to get. They see this thing is landing on autopilot, they're going to be suspicious. If it touches down, that's all the time we'll have before the team can get to her on the strip. It'll need to be airborne before that."

"What happens when it takes off without them getting a chance to refuel it? Won't *that* look suspicious?" He saw in Thorp's face a smear of realization forming.

He turned forward, facing approximately in the direction of the control tower. "Change of plans, O'Hare. We'll turn it back around. Instrument panel is a bit glitchy. We got plenty of go-juice after all. Making the circle and turning back to point of takeoff. Thank you. Have a nice night." Thorp turned to the ordi plugged into the instrument panel of the Darter, lifting the Gizumoshingu's lid. Brody watched as his fingers danced across the keyboard and a green cube of light jumped out and he pushed his hands into it, moving his fingers assiduously as a seasoned puppeteer, pulling cursors across the displayed map.

"Make sure to actually have it land so we have time to get on board," Brody suggested, watching the skyline.

As he typed Thorp said, "She's going to take a quick swing around the city. I'll stay on the com as if I were still piloting to try and chat with them, to stall. She'll be back in fifteen minutes to pick us up. But she'll only set her feet down for ten seconds before dusting off for the house again."

"You do what you need to, and I'll keep an eye on the time," Brody said. The stopwatch on his phone was programmed for fifteen minutes. Brody held his finger over the start button as they crept in closer to the glowing white disk of the helipad.

Thorp typed feverishly and swiped his fingers through the holo panel framework. He double tapped the floating cylinder that represented Hark Telecom within the map, then hit execute.

Without delay, the vehicle charged forward, pitching Brody back into the copilot seat. Thorp's hands were no longer on the controls. He undid his harness and grabbed his rucksack. He detached the ordi from the control panel, and the hologram map immediately winked out. He shoved it securely down into the mouth of the rucksack and cinched it closed tight.

"Get ready," Thorp said as the Darter rapidly narrowed the space between them and their destination.

Brody unfastened his harness, pulled off his helmet. He patted himself down to make sure he had everything he'd need. He gave the knuckleduster a quick pat for good luck.

His throat parched as the roof came into position. The Darter automatically descended, drawing in close as it was programmed. Thorp opened the hatch on his side of the Darter's bulbous head, and Brody reluctantly did the same. The terrible screech of the engines, the steady thrum of the wings drowned everything else out. The distance that remained beneath the Darter after it finished its descent still looked like a lethal drop. From this height, it would be hard to miss the helipad directly beneath him, but Brody knew a sudden gust of wind could push a free-falling human body several meters off course.

Framing the edges of the building on all sides was the vertigo-inducing fall to the street below. It looked like it would take an entire week to plummet the distance. He saw a silver snake dart along a black line, the "L" making its hourly pass around downtown.

"On three or what?" He turned to see if Thorp was ready and instead glimpsed Thorp's back as it cleared the open door of the cockpit.

Brody let go of the seat restraints, kicked forward, and let gravity do the rest. Air thundered past his ears; his eyes were immediately blown dry. The helipad jumped to meet him. His boots struck, and his impetus pitched his body ahead. Brody rolled twice and stopped himself and surveyed his surroundings. Even though he was dizzy, he had the mind about him to press the button on his cell to begin the stopwatch.

He heard the impact of something solid and plastic. He watched wordlessly as Thorp chased the scattering ordi. It broke free of the rucksack in the fall. The battered Gizumoshingu was swiftly ushered across the cement by the cleaving high winds. Thorp leapt for it, managing to snag it before the wind could coax it off the edge.

The din of the Darter's engines raised in pitch, the

dragonfly turning and gliding away.

They made their way into a labyrinth of air filtration units for cover and got securely concealed among the steam-belching units, their backs pressed against the warm sheet metal.

Brody noticed Thorp cradled the Gizumoshingu as he traced the rim of the glass projector lens to clear away any shards. A jagged line ran across its face. Any holo the ordi would produce from now on would be smeary, inaccurate to gestures passing through it or unresponsive altogether.

"Do *not* tell me that thing's broken."

"It's fine," Thorp said, replacing it in the rucksack.

Brody watched the distant Darter move out, beginning its wide pass to turn around. Its white and red lights flared in the night sky, the only indication it was still there, soaring pilotless. "Are they saying anything?"

Wedging a finger against the bud in his ear, Thorp listened for a moment, eyes closed. "Nothing. They must be fine with letting her circle around."

"Let's hope."

Thorp took out his Franklin-Johann and slid in a magazine of rubber bullets, advanced one into the chamber.

Brody peeked over the unit throwing rancid chemical-treated steam in his face to get a glimpse at the security camera. It could be avoided by hugging the wall, but getting directly under it and picking the lock into the building would be another story. Already things were becoming more complicated than he had anticipated. "Camera."

When he turned back around, he saw Thorp, bent

on one knee, tying a paisley bandanna behind his head, the front triangle obscuring most of his face. "Are we planning on robbing a train?"

Thorp tossed a second bandanna to Brody. "We can't avoid all of them, and they already got a face-map on me," he said, gesturing ahead to a security camera.

Brody put on the bandanna, tucking the loose end into the collar of his shirt. He charged around the row of air filtration units and approached the maintenance door. Once beneath it, he pushed the camera away on its pivoting neck so it angled toward the sky. Undoubtedly someone would notice, but he was too busy kicking at the door to dwell on the notion.

The door opened and the men scrambled inside.

They found narrow metal stairs that led down to an enclosure that seemed to be where the elevators were maintained. A storeroom set off to one side with its door hanging open and an old office chair before a dead monitor.

Brody scanned the area. There were double wide doors off to the side by a row of long water pipes. "The cargo elevator. Probably no cameras in there."

"And a great way to get boxed in," Thorp said. "This way." He turned before Brody could agree and briskly advanced toward the stairwell door.

They went down two floors and decided to see where they had ended up. The bandanna did little to help his breathing, before long Brody's nose and lips were wet from perspiration, but still he kept it on, even taking a moment to tighten the knot at the back of his neck. They slowly entered the office area, finding an expansive cubicle farm sprawled out before them. Tall, carpeted walls in the shade of sea-foam green and identical workstations, every monitor's screen saver the Hark Telecom logo—a radio antenna with radiating thunderbolts set atop an exaggerated arrangement of the solar system in which all the planets were the same general size.

Separate offices were set around the perimeter with glass walls and desks constructed with genuine wood. Great views of downtown.

"This is probably just where the number crunchers work," Brody said. "Let's go down a few more floors."

Thorp kept his back to Brody, steadily walking forward with quick heel-toe steps. He stopped at the corner following a long wall of cubicles and stole a glimpse around it. "You never know. Engineers might do casual research and development shit in here. I mean, it's not like the movies—there's not going to be a lab with people in clean suits."

Brody looked out the windows. There were all kinds of aircraft lights slowly flashing along the horizon. It was impossible to tell which one was their Darter. He was afraid to see how much time they had already used, but he checked the phone's stopwatch anyway. "Eleven and a half minutes. We need to get a move on."

"Down here," Thorp said and advanced along a row of cubicles. He ducked into the first one and went to the monitor and tapped on its display to wake the machine up. The screen saver blinked away, Thorp selected the interoffice phone directory from the options, and the window fanned to all four corners of the screen. He touched the research and development tab and then the green icon of a phone to begin the call.

Without a second's hesitation, there was an answer. "If you'd like to make an appointment with Mr. Ward, please leave your name and number. If you want to schedule a meeting, please use the company's scheduling program. If you want to make the appointment in person, please feel free to visit research and development located on the eighty-first floor. Thank you and have—"

Thorp cut the prerecorded message off. "Eighty-one," he said and they headed to the stairs.

Unable to resist checking how much time they had remaining, Brody groaned when he saw they had already killed six minutes. "If we run out of time, is there any way you can call the Darter back?"

Thorp was quiet for a moment. Brody already knew his answer even before he explained that once the Darter was programmed there was no way to remotely cancel the autopilot.

They got to the landing and when they opened the door to the eighty-first floor, Brody's expectations of a research and development department were proven to be just so.

Everything, floor to ceiling, was a peerless white. Long, white tables with instruments and complicated machinery stood on every square inch. Monitors and hardwired ordis were everywhere. The lab was divided up by glass walls etched with *Hark Telecom* and the company's symbol.

"There," Brody said, spotting a door on the far side of the lab. The plaque read: Hubert Ward, Department

Director, Research and Development, Technological Innovation Division.

The door was locked. Both men scoured the lab for something that would break down the sturdy-looking door. While Thorp was quick to give up and pound the door with his foot and then his shoulder, Brody continued looking. He lifted his bandanna to steal a quick breath of fresh air. "Give me a hand with this," he said.

The rolling stainless steel table, once cleared of the equipment piled upon it, made for a great battering ram, especially with four legs behind it propelling it forward. The far end of the table hit true, but the door held and both men nearly flew over the tabletop. They wheeled it back to the far side of the room, and when Brody ordered the charge, they ran a second salvo against the door with all they had. The door broke free, snapping off the dead bolt and one of the hinges.

Inside, the modestly sized office was in severe contrast to the clean room aesthetic of the lab. Everything was wood grain—the walls, the parquet tiles on the ceiling. The only touches of modernity were the black lacquered desk and the ordi set atop it, which was equally new and shiny.

Thorp connected the Gizumoshingu to Hubert's desk unit and set to work immediately.

Brody kept an eye on the time and repeatedly checked out the circular window set into the far door for any security guards or straggling workaholic Hark employees who might be coming into the lab. "Eight minutes."

Thorp said nothing. He tapped the function to pop the image out, and the projector wavered for a second, giving two false starts. When it cooperated, the holo came out tilted and folded. Thorp tried to navigate the image, trailing his fingers through the lines of light to physically scour the files of Hubert Ward's computer. Again, the app he'd bought to break into Probitas was put to use.

Brody looked away from the window overlooking the lab to inspect the walls of Hubert Ward's office. Certificates issued from Hark for various money-saving deskbound heroism, one decreeing that Ward had single-handedly made Hark Telecom one of the most profitable companies in the world with some piece of circuitry Brody had never heard of.

He studied the series of framed photos Hubert Ward had on his wall and sought a pattern until he found one man appeared in all of them. Ward looked like most professional men over the age of fifty. Confident, hands in pockets, smiling for the camera with that subtle expression that said he had better things to do than get his goddamn picture taken. Medium height, neatly parted silver hair. Strong cheekbones hilling the sunken cheeks beneath them. Gray eyes set behind a pair of rimless glasses. His skin leathery, as if he spent much of his free time outdoors. In every picture Ward was dressed in shades of gray or black—the only snatch of color ever found on the man was in his ties, and they arrayed blandly from gunmetal gray to a pastel green to one picture where he wore one of creamy white for a wedding.

In the last photo Hubert was shaking hands with another man with silver hair and glasses, except this other man was dressed in camouflage and wore markings of a four-star general. He looked like every other career brass, except for a recessed purple scar running down the side of his face from the outside corner of his left eye to his chin.

"Huh," Thorp said softly.

"You got something?" Brody asked, taking one final look into the lab before crossing the office. He glanced over Thorp's shoulder and saw the display of files as Thorp thumbed through them, tabbed with the various projects that Hubert Ward was overseeing. At the end, the final tab was suspiciously placed out of alphabetical order with the others, labeled *Project Silver Fox*.

"What is it?" Brody asked, unable to hide the hollowness in his voice.

Thorp waved his hand through the tab to open the file. There, a slew of disorganized information fell into the room above the desk. The holo-projector had a hard time displaying it all with his freshly cracked lens, and Thorp had to scroll through it to project the information clearly from end to end. Its contents had familiar snippets, regarding wavelengths, frequencies, fleeting images of brain scans, CTs, magnetic resonance images.

"This looks about right," Brody said. There were image files of brain scans. Photos of walls broken open displaying thick tree trunk–sized columns of bound-together wires and cables.

There was a small video clip of a diapered chimpanzee thrashing against its cage, rolling over onto its back, picking up a rock from the floor of its enclosure, and beating itself over the head with it.

Thorp moved on. He got to the very back of the file and found a roster of names and numbers, tabulated amounts that the men immediately assumed were in the value of dollars. The first few dozen names were none they recognized. Another file was on display at the end, labeled *contacts*.

Brody didn't need to see its contents before saying, "Send that to me." He took his phone from his pocket.

Thorp told the Gizumoshingu to send to Brody Calhoun, and the contents of Project Silver Fox folded into an envelope shape and vanished.

A second later, Brody's cell beeped confirming the message had arrived in his in-box.

Thorp scrolled down until reaching a name they were anxiously seeking: Shandorf, Titian H. Next to his name was: *$100,000—consultant.*

"So there it is." Thorp sighed. "Evidence that a known serial killer and rapist was under the employ of none other than Hark Telecom as a *consultant* of all things."

Brody opened the new e-mail just to double-check he had the same information, complete with the entry with Titian's name. He slid his phone away and checked his stopwatch. Four minutes. He slapped Thorp on the shoulder. "Let's get going."

"Wait," Thorp said. "I want to know how they got him the money. Maybe they still have his jigsaw on file. Maybe we can get his jig number, look it up on your reverse directory thing on your phone—"

"We're going to miss our bird," Brody said, using the military terminology in hopes it would grab his friend's attention more effectively.

It didn't. Thorp continued to run his hands through the hologram to direct it through the project's file. Brody could see the reverse of the hologram from across the room. Thorp was no longer even in the correct file anymore. He was going through Hubert Ward's Rolodex of associates.

"Just copy it to your drive and let's go. We can look through all that later. We got what we came for. You sent it to me, and when you save it to your ordi's drive, we'll have it saved in two places. We've got them."

"Maybe there's something deeper that won't copy, hidden files or something—a location on Nectar, a place where Titian keeps people. I want to get through this shit tonight. I've waited long enough. We're close. We're close. We're *close* . . ." With frantic, flitting eyes, Thorp stared into the hologram, rummaging through Hubert Ward's files haphazardly and going through things at a breakneck pace that only a keenly trained eye could keep up with. All at once he stopped.

When Brody didn't hear the trademark click of holographic pages being turned, he looked to Thorp. "Something wrong?"

Thorp pointed to the digital page.

Brody came around the desk to see the image better. Despite the holo being bent and the text disjointed, he could make it out. His stomach turned when it all fit together and he understood.

Under the project file's list of candidates were Thorp's and Brody's names.

Brody bent forward, reading the list again and again. Dozens of names. The only ones familiar were his, Thorp's, and Alton Noel's. "So that's it. There it is."

"After all this is said and done, you should probably see a doctor."

Brody stepped away from the desk. He checked his phone. The stopwatch displayed three minutes remaining. They'd have to move with almost superhuman speed to get to the roof in time for the Darter. "Let's go."

"All right, just let me—*shit*." Thorp sprung out of Hubert's high-backed leather chair and crushed himself against the window.

Brody rushed over. "What is it?"

Thorp, his face illuminated by the light pitching in through the city beyond, melted of expression. Slowly, he shut off his earbud. The Gizumoshingu's speaker took over, announcing what the Darter was picking up from the O'Hare tower.

"—or we will be forced to shoot you down. I repeat, remove yourself from Chicago airspace or we will be forced to shoot you down."

Brody looked east to Lake Michigan. There were innumerable sets of blinking lights, all creeping across the starlit sky. But only one blossomed suddenly with a white flash, then a second. Even from the great distance, a soft thud carried in the air and rattled the glass against his palms. The glowing ball of white sharpened, shifting to a more fiery shade as it became smaller, streaking as it descended and was snuffed upon hitting the water.

31

The surveillance program hesitated before allowing Thorp to pull it up onto his ordi's screen. That or the ordi was doing the hesitating. But after a moment, Thorp had the surveillance camera feeds— all one thousand and fifty-six of them—on his monitor, fanning out like the million-lens eye of a bug. He twisted his hand in a peculiar way and placed it on the keyboard to hit six radically spaced keys at once. In a blink, all the feeds were dead, gone to fuzz.

Thorp gathered his ordi and wedged it into his rucksack. While his arm was still submerged in the bag, he withdrew an assault rifle. He snapped in the clip and extended it toward Brody.

Tearing his gaze from the smoking

wreckage burning on the glassy surface of Lake Michigan, Brody stared at the butt of the gun. A gun he had known so well. So many days spent with an identical rifle, sleeping with it in the bunks, carrying it from place to place—it was like a steadfast companion through his years in the service. He knew the weight of it, the feel of it. He could tell if it was loaded or not just by holding it in his arms. He didn't make a motion to take it from Thorp.

"This is going to get hairy," Thorp reminded him. "You need this thing. If we're going to get out of here alive, you have to do this with me."

Instead, Brody took up the Franklin-Johann Thorp had resting on Ward's desk. He looked into Thorp's eyes and said nothing, forcing himself to keep his fingers wrapped around the grip of the pistol.

"Fine," Thorp said. "But you better be good with it."

They went to the office door. Beyond, in the stark white lab, there was still no activity. The security team may not have been alerted yet. They could be in the break room, swapping stories and downing coffee just as well as they could be donning their flak jackets and stop-gel-equipped vests.

"What's the plan? Try to make it out the front?"

"Well, we could go up to the roof and jump, but I don't think that will get the results we're after," Thorp said. His cold and distant demeanor had shifted yet again. Here he was, like he'd been when Brody knew him in Egypt. A secret second personality waiting to be swapped in when needed, Jekyll and Hyde with no serum required.

"I don't want to kill anybody," Brody said.

"You probably won't even *hurt* anybody with rubber bullets," Thorp commented. "These guys will probably be wearing some high-grade stuff. Rubber bullets are just going to bounce off them like tennis balls. I have another rifle if you change your mind. Armor-piercing rounds, a few clips with incendiary rounds—"

"No," Brody said firmly. His still-swirling guts from the Darter ride reawakened, and he felt the urge to get sick again. No matter how he held the gun, no matter which hand it was in—it felt uncomfortable.

As they crossed the lab, Thorp pulled the assault rifle to his shoulder and walked with the barrel pointed out ahead of him, peering down through the scope with one eye. As he trod softly across the polished white floor, he said, "We don't want to get boxed in. We'll keep using the stairs. You keep the rear, and I'll make sure we don't get stuck anywhere. With any luck, we can just scoot right on out before they even know we're here."

Brody followed, his heart a shuddering lump in his throat. He felt like he had those first few weeks on the training course. Running up staircases that led nowhere. Doing drills. Firing with only the laser target at cardboard men that'd pop up in windows of plywood façades, receptors in their chests and heads, flashing their eyes like a midway game when hit with a "kill shot." Those kill shots, his only ones.

He couldn't help but shake his head as he followed Thorp to the stairwell. It had all gotten so fucked up so fast. He compared now to the original Operation Ceramic Groom. Going up to the roof and lifting off carefree, jubilant and high-fiving the men in his squad for a job well done. This was the alternative it could've easily taken all those years ago. Stranded, having to go down, diving headfirst, unsure as to what lay ahead, praying that everything would turn out okay. But the overwhelming knowledge that it wouldn't be all right was as present as the knot in his guts.

They made it down to the seventy-eighth floor without altercation.

They took a moment at the wide landing and listened to the infinite stairwell spiraling down to the ground floor. No noise, no commotion, no banging boots on metal stairs coming up to meet them. Nothing.

Just the sound of their own labored breaths.

Brody checked the stairwell behind them and saw no flitting shadows, heard no sounds at all.

Growing suspicious that it was all too easy, Brody reached out for the door of the seventy-first floor to make sure it was unlocked. It opened freely. The thought that they were being bottlenecked subsided. But still, it was too smooth; they had made nothing but noise since arriving. Someone should've come along by now, or some indication they'd been detected as a presence within a building that needed to be purged. "This seems strange, doesn't it? There's no one here."

"Oh, they're probably putting up blockades and trip wires in the lobby," Thorp said. "They'll start to move up this way when we don't show in the next half hour or so."

And with that last two-letter word having passed through Thorp's bandanna, every light in the stairwell shaft darkened.

Thorp went to his rucksack for the flashlight. Brody

retrieved his phone and was clearing the flashing stopwatch to select the flashlight when the shaft lit up again, except instead of the soft white it'd been casting before—it was a harsh red akin to that of a darkroom.

Brody looked to Thorp.

"It's for their infrared. The red light cuts the flare and makes us easier to see."

"So they're onto us," Brody said. "Great."

"Looks like we'll just have to do what we can to get out of this shit." Thorp pulled the rifle stock in tighter against his shoulder. He clicked on a flashlight attached to the muzzle of his gun.

Brody had a sudden thought. "The train."

"What about it?" Thorp said.

"It runs right past this building. I remember seeing it on the way in."

"Those trestles are three stories high. We'll have to get down to at least the fifth floor." He shifted the rifle. "Is that what you want to do?"

"I don't see many other options. Break out a window and jump for it," Brody said.

"All right, here we go," Thorp said and charged ahead.

They began their descent. Being quiet was impossible, so they decided to make up for their volume with speed. Brody couldn't resist but aim his pistol every time he caught his own wide-shouldered silhouette running up alongside him on the stairwell wall. The nerves were mounting, and his heart hadn't slowed since they had made the leap from the Darter over fifteen minutes ago. He held his phone out in front of him, a train schedule on the screen. "The 'L' goes by here at one thirty."

"What time is it now?"

"Ten to one."

"Guess we might have to hole up somewhere and—wait, wait. Stop, stop, stop." Thorp choked, Brody nearly running into the back of him.

On the landing for the sixty-third floor, they stopped, listened.

Foggily, ringing hollow and distant—barely audible—rhythmic, heavy footfalls.

Brody laid his hand on the landing railing. It gave a faint tremble. "How many do you suppose there are?"

Thorp closed his eyes. "I don't know."

"They're down there a ways," Brody whispered. He leaned over the railing, and in the red light nothing could be seen beyond a few floors down.

The rabble of boots was increasing an octave every second—they were moving quickly.

A sudden screech sounded, a ragged breath, and then a voice overamplified to a deafening volume came across the tower's loudspeaker system. "Please put your weapons down. We will not use deadly force if you are cooperative. When our task force comes upon you, if you are facedown with your hands behind your head and your weapons down, we will *not* use deadly force."

Thorp grunted, shook his head. "Right. Sure."

Brody nodded at the door for the sixty-third floor. "Dodge?"

Thorp yanked the door open.

They found another sea-foam green cubicle farm, a carpeted cavernous space with every inch packed with empty workstations.

They cut to the outermost wall facing south, pressing their faces against the glass to see straight down to the elevated trestle below. An eight-car train had just careened the bend out of sight, allowing them a glimpse of its chrome rear.

"That's the one o'clock," he said.

Beyond the hum of all the idle work space machines, they heard the security team in the stairwell drawing near.

Leaning against the warm plastic hull of a copier, Brody ducked inside a cubicle. Thorp did the same across the aisle—after noisily advancing the first round.

Regretting every cigarette he'd ever had, Brody pressed his palm against his chest to force his ragged breathing to quell—each sharp intake through the nose pulled in the smells of burned coffee and dusty electronics. He coughed, sputtering, lowering his damp face covering to spit. When he heard the approaching clamor against the stairs ringing hollowly, his breathing seemed to snuff itself.

Beyond the plain white door with the stick figure placard walking on the zigzagging serrated blade of stairs, the guards moved by.

After it had quieted, Brody slowly stood up, watching the handle of the door. "How secure was that hack you did?" he whispered.

"It was an ugly one. I'm sure it set off their firewall. But that was when we were just going to be fifteen minutes." Thorp stood as well. "We should get a move on while they're still heading up there."

They crept out onto the landing and listened to any sound permeating the cherry-colored chamber. Soundless. They looked up and saw no flashlight beams, nothing at all. It was as if the guards had materialized to give chase, and once they knew they had been foiled turned back to a cloud of microscopic dust to make the return trip more expedient.

Moving as quietly as their boots would allow, Brody and Thorp subtracted another ten stories. Then another and another. They paused when Brody thought he heard something, held their breath to listen, and then continued.

The handgun's grip became loose, slick with sweat in Brody's hand. Sweat dripped from his chin, the tip of his nose, his elbows, darkening the collar of his shirt. Another flash of basic training came to him: running the circuit in the summer sun and collapsing at the end. He never considered the taste of water so fantastic in his life. The chants that without fail began, "I don't know but I've been told . . ."

The fourth floor came upon them. Carefully shouldering the door aside, Thorp walked in staying low. Brody followed, scanning the cubicle farm with his pistol equipped with rubber bullets, still not having looped his finger over the trigger yet. All clear.

"We're good," Thorp said and let the rifle dangle by its strap across his chest.

They went to the far side of the floor and looked down. The trestle was there, but it looked like quite a fall. Not like the one they had done in the not-so-recent past but still a daunting distance. And this time, there'd be the chance of landing on an electrified rail.

"We have to time it pretty good," Brody said. "Don't want to jump too late and miss it."

"Or too early and land in front of it," Thorp added.

Thorp ducked out of his rifle's strap and turned the gun around to ram the butt against the window. He had it wrenched back in both hands when Brody stuck out a hand.

"What time is it?"

Thorp lowered the rifle.

Brody withdrew his cell. It took a second before the phone cooperated, bogged down as it was with the massive e-mail waiting in the in-box. A warning prompt informed Brody that the duplicate files copied from Hubert Ward's ordi tipped the scales at four zettabytes, putting a major strain on the phone's processor. It was doing all it could to keep itself from crashing. Brody okayed the warning and waited for the main screen to load, the display coming in one quadrant at a time jerkily.

"Seventeen past," he said finally, tucking the noticeably warm phone away.

"We got thirteen long minutes." Thorp threw the rifle strap over his head.

A deep pounding noise in the stairwell caused both men to drop to all fours behind the walls at the edge of the maze of carpeted cubicles. Blood charged into Brody's face, a twin set of fat veins leaping up in his temples. The world fluttered before his eyes in a wave of grainy streaks—the lenses were starting to falter. He'd get the red digits in a second, he knew.

Across the aisle, Thorp positioned onto one knee, the rifle in his arms. He leaned forward and peeked out beyond the corner of the cubicle, pulling back quickly. Making a V with two fingers, he pointed them at his own eyes, then the stairwell door.

Past the rushing of blood in his ears, Brody listened. The door to the stairwell's hydraulic made a soft moan of unlubricated metal turning on a hinge. He heard the muffled sound of the first guard stepping onto the office's carpet with caution.

More entered. The sound dispersed. They spread out, not communicating with any means Brody could overhear. He stole a glance as one rounded the corner at the far end of the office.

A man turned automaton, featureless and high-shouldered in matte black armor covering every inch of him. Adorned with a complete face mask, a high collar that was thick, unbending, like he was wearing blinders, the man had to turn his whole body to look in any direction other than forward. Wholly packaged in titanium-weave flak of top-shelf manufacture, stuff typically reserved for generals, unpopular politicians, or religious figureheads. He held his weapon casually with both hands: a new model rifle, its muzzle busy with devices, scopes, a louvered suppressor that made the barrel nearly double in length, electronic eyes, computer-aiming assistants—a peerless instrument of lethality.

Just as Brody glanced, 1:19 became 1:20.

He looked up to see Thorp across the aisle, readying his assault rifle in reaction to the approaching, if meandering, tread of a security guard. Brody held his breath, kept clutching the pliable rubber of his pistol grip. It took every ounce of him to force his finger through the trigger guard. The soft pad of his index finger met the steel. It was cold.

The guard stopped inches shy of their cubicle

openings, spun on his heel, and walked back.

Brody sighed internally, never making a sound aloud, but relief crashed on him in a deluge—until he saw Thorp standing, rifle to shoulder. Brody watched, paralyzed, as Thorp disengaged the safety with a flick, took aim, and let three rounds shatter the silence of the office.

His ears responding by singing along with their own squeal, Brody remained low and went for the south-facing window. Thorp covered him, letting a few more shots go in the direction of the three security guards. They were well concealed, and in the commotion of the gunfire, Brody could hear a guard frantically summoning backup on his walkie-talkie.

After putting his pistol away, Brody hoisted a desk printer and threw it toward the glass. Thorp provided cover fire. The printer shattered, leaving only a scuff in the tinted surface. He took out his pistol and hammered the bottom of the grip against the glass. A sizable crack splintered from one corner of the pane to the other. He focused on it, digging out chips of laminated glass, when he heard the whistling patter of a silenced assault rifle.

He ducked, the rounds hitting the glass above him. Broken glass rained down, but when he looked, the window was still intact. On the floor, in his hair, and in the collar of his coat were tiny bits of broken glass. A sudden heady smell, sweet like caramelized sugar, enveloped him.

Brody was baffled until he noticed among the glinting chips bent hypodermic needles and pinheads of clear liquid soaking into the well-tread carpet. *Anodyne. They want us alive.*

Thorp gave no answer, rose from his hiding space, and fired bursts of gunfire back at the guards.

Brody snatched the pistol up again when Thorp fired, striking against the glass as if hammering a nail. The two-inch-thick pane came down in broken, laminated sheets, flakes the size of his thumbnail. He swung again and again, another volley of tranquilizer rounds hitting and shattering upon the window frame beside him, one even puncturing the sleeve of his coat and left dangling, not striking him.

"Throwing lachrymator," one of the guards shouted to his compatriots.

As Brody had expected, there it was—the sound he dreaded. The snap of a pin being pulled and the heavy thud as the tear gas grenade was tossed in their direction. The canister burst and spun on the floor, spewing a thick gray fog.

Immediately, that smell of burned sugar of the broken darts was replaced for Brody—to that of cayenne pepper, of melted tires, of spoiled fruit. He hammered at the window, but each grunt was becoming heavy. He yielded fits of violent hacking instead of another inhale. Pulling the bandanna back up did precious little to keep the choking gas out. The hole to the outside world he'd made through the glass—perhaps big enough to fit a pinky through—became a blurry dot before his eyes. The carotene lenses reacted to the gas, his vision stacking doubles and triples.

"Keep with the darts. I'm changing to slugs," one of

the guards said.

Brody took this as his cue to duck behind a cubicle wall. He heard the guards switching their magazines, slapping in clips that had actual bullets.

Thorp ignored the gas, popping up to fire, with tears running down his cheeks and off his chin, the flesh circling his eyes a deep ruby. He wiped at his eyes with the length of his arm.

"They're switching to live fire," Brody shouted to Thorp. The smoke grenade spun in his direction, and he kicked it away where it bounced, gliding across the floor, hissing angrily.

The muffled whistle of the fire was now different, a denser, meatier sound. The bullets smacked into the cubicle walls with more punch to them. The air over his head was filled with sawdust, bits of semiburned cubicle upholstery.

Brody remained in his hiding place, feeling useless, still holding the Franklin-Johann.

Thorp noticed him trying to bat the sting of his weeping eyes. "They're going to fucking kill us. You've got to shoot back."

Brody, his eyes teeming with bloody spider legs reaching from one corner to the other, shook his head.

Thorp dropped down into cover, yanked his bandanna from his face, and shouted at him, his voice rising to a desperate shriek, "You take out your fucking sidearm and you *shoot*, soldier."

"I can't."

Thorp snarled and stood up to fire.

There was a clap of sound when a shot connected

with Thorp, hitting him in the chest. He was thrown back, stumbled, and dropped. He let go of the rifle to grip the wound. Brody noticed the vial of glass, the miniature plunger within pushing forward, the clear liquid being shoved into his bloodstream. Thorp tried to pluck it out, but the drug took effect immediately. His head lolled forward, and his fingers loosened on his assault rifle.

Brody started to crawl across the aisle when the carpet came alive at his fingertips with fire. Three smoldering holes where the guard using live fire had taken divots out of the carpet, digging into the cement floor beneath.

Remaining in cover, Brody watched as Thorp attempted to fight the drugs, pushing his eyes open wide, even though they were slowly curtaining closed on their own. He fumbled around for the gun.

Brody took out his cell and checked the time, saw that it was exactly half past one. The train would be coming at any moment. He could very well escape with what he had in his in-box.

The guards filed down the aisle.

But he thought about finding and rescuing Nectar on his own only to have her come out of her bonds to freedom and discover that her brother had died in the struggle—she would surely blame herself. Most likely carry an unspoken resentment toward Brody for not doing more. He'd be doing plenty of that himself to make up for any animosity she might have toward him.

What would be worse?

Brody looked at the envelope in the corner of

his cell's screen denoting the new massive e-mail, all of Silver Fox waiting there, ready for viewing. He highlighted the e-mail and selected Nathan Pierce from his contact list as the addressee. The phone momentarily halted, all activity on the screen freezing. Brody tapped send over and over, and just as the armored men stepped into view, training their muzzles on him, the e-mail vanished, sent.

And not a moment too soon. A boot swung in and knocked the phone out of his grasp, and by the feel of it, broke one of his fingers as well.

Brody slumped to the floor, and he could see across the aisle as Thorp finally succumbed and spilled backward with his limbs splayed out.

Standing, Brody put out his hands, leaving the handgun on the floor.

The guards lowered their weapons. One went for a zip tie looped through his belt. Another telescoped a baton with a swing. The closest planted the toe of his boot on the Franklin-Johann and sent it skidding away behind him.

The guard who had been using slugs stood over Thorp's motionless form. He kept his back to them and flicked Thorp's rifle from his hand with his foot. "To the van," he said, his voice muffled from inside the goggled mask.

They closed in around Brody. A hand gripped the lapel of his coat, as well as his wrist.

"Easy now," one said.

Brody drove his free hand into the pocket, and when it was pulled free, it was armored across the knuckles with black metal. Squeezing the knuckleduster directly before impact, Brody sunk a punch into the closest guard.

Mayhem cut loose in immediate reply. The armored men turned the butts of their rifles on him, swung at him with batons, punched him with gloved fists. Brody swung and connected with another one's neck, aiming for the provided slot in the high Kevlar collar. The man let out a panicked wheeze.

Another stepped forward, swinging his rifle like a bat. Brody ducked, let it pass over his head, and threw a jab at the man's belly. He cast the rifle aside and caught Brody's fist. They grappled, falling to the floor in a scrambling heap.

The one with the baton took Brody's open back as an invitation, the steel ball on the end of the telescoping club easily finding his kidneys, his spine, glancing off his shoulder blade, and in the same pass colliding with the back of his head. Pinning the man beneath him with his knees, Brody struck repeatedly with the knuckleduster—got a solid seven hits in—when he felt the suppressor-equipped muzzle kiss the back of his neck. He was in midswing when he heard the muffled thwack.

He sunk the final punch, the man's head twisting away in the impact—and everything grew a shade darker. He raised his arm again, having to consciously pull the arm up and away. The motion caught gravity, and he felt the world sucking at him, pulling him back. He had no choice but to let it.

In the plunging tunnel of shade that enveloped him, as Brody sunk to the floor beside the guard he had knocked unconscious, he saw it blinking there, like a divine spark being cast over a fog-throttled gulf. Six digits and two colons, all in red: *00:59:59.*

Flat on his back, he could feel the faint vibrations as well. The "L" passed below, rumbling over its trestle without its new passengers. The digits blinked two more times and were gone—and he with them.

32

A rapid series of metallic clicks and an abrupt slam jarred Brody awake. Naturally it made him think of his many visits to county lockup.

He blinked a couple of times and saw nothing before him, just limitless black. He heard scraping steps all around him, treading on dirt floors. He surmised; the charge on the lens died when he was out and now he was completely blind.

Brody struggled as much as his drug-fogged brain could perform. The cuffs were warm; he had been wearing them for a while. He twisted in the seat, metal biting into both wrists. Rope or tape or a combination of the two bound him at the ankle, knees, elbows, across his chest and waist.

Not just blind but blind and tied to a chair. Peachy. *00:14:59* lanced out of the dark.

No, blindfolded.

He heard a croaky voice. "Hey, man. Dude, hey. Look. He's up."

He felt the heat radiating off a feverish body and then the mirthless tug at his eyebrows as a band of duct tape was ripped away. In the action, the tape dragged his eyelids along, far enough to allow his lens to drop out. He saw it go, a flashing transparent disk tumbling away. He blinked and blinked, but his sight in the left died.

He still had one lens.

Brody looked up at his captors. A pair of young men, both with messily shaved heads. Patches of blond spiked off their skulls in places while a majority had been buzzed to pale flesh. They stood dressed in tattered jeans, threadbare T-shirts, and one of them wore Brody's peacoat and his bandanna. Brody recognized the look in their eyes: a partly erased dullness. Something clearly was missing.

It took a moment, but Brody recalled seeing one of them before. Bait & Tackle, the rat-faced kid cutting onions with the nametag that read *Rice*. He decided it better not to say anything in case it set them off. They looked like the types that could easily switch from tepid to scalding.

Brody looked around him as far as his neck could crane. There was no sign of Thorp in the room. The walls were corrugated steel, weakened and patchy with rust. The ceiling low, also rusty metal with naked bulbs hanging from frayed wires. A barrel in the corner had a fire burning in it. The unmistakable reek of burning hair loomed in the air.

He looked down and saw two dirty, rubbery wheels astride his hips—a wheelchair. He was bound to a wheelchair.

On the dirt floor before him was a display of everything that had been in his pockets. The knuckleduster, his cell, his wallet, the sonar case, the lens charger, his cigarette lighter, his ring of keys—on which was still Nectar's spare he had gotten from Paige.

One of the emaciated thugs held Seb's jigsaw card. He was peering into it, his twig-like arms trembling from cold and/or withdrawal or just the excitement of the prospect of hurting someone. "Hey, hey," he said, elbowing his partner, "I *know* this asshole."

The second thug took the jigsaw and held it within an inch of his right eye. "Yeah, that's the motherfucker hustled me one time. Said I'd get higher than I've ever been. I went home and packed the pipe and didn't feel a goddamn *thing*." He brought the picture of Seb's unsmiling mug close to Brody's face. "I was going to feel a little bad about killing you, but if you're friends with this asshole, that changes shit."

"He's dead," Brody said, hoping it would put him somewhat in their favor. If he had to die, he at least wanted it to be quick. He didn't want to spend hours suffering, smelling junkie sweat, and listening to them slaughter the English language as they took turns sticking him with screwdrivers and sharpened pencils.

"Yeah?" the thug asked, looking at Seb's face again. "Did *you* kill him?"

"No," Brody said. "An Artificial killed him."

"An Artie, huh? That sounds like bullshit. Doesn't that sound like bullshit to you, Rice?"

Rice nodded.

"Yeah, it sounds like bullshit, man. Seb being taken down by an Artie. You know them plastic-faced bitches at AFA won't lift no finger to *nobody* about *nothing*. They ain't allowed."

"Not in their programming, chief," Rice added. "Want to try again?"

"Not an Automat Artificial, a farmer Artificial."

"Shit damn," Rice said, taking the lead in heckling Brody. "I didn't realize there was *farmer* Arties. I always wanted to be a farmer. Raise cows, goats, pigs, chickens, ducks, and shit. Yeah, man. I'd *love* to be me a robot, no emotion and shit, no need to eat or shit or drink or get high—just do and do and do and do and do my goddamned job *forever*."

"That actually sounds kind of shit to me," the other thug confessed.

"Yeah." Rice sighed, staring at Brody. "It does kind of sound like shit, doesn't it?"

They lost interest in that notion and returned to Brody's pile of belongings. They opened the lens case, poured out the enzyme water, cast it aside. Rice picked up the knuckleduster and slid it down onto his knuckles, fanned it out before him like he was admiring a bejeweled hand, then moved on to other things while continuing to wear it.

When they got to the sonar case Brody winced slightly, trying to keep his extreme discomfort under wraps.

"Denny," Rice said, picking up the sonar case, "what in the hell do you suppose this thing is? His diaphragm or something?"

"His what?"

Rice chuckled. "Nothing. Before your time." He opened the case and looked at the white disk inside. He turned it over, and since it had no buttons to push, he took it out of the case and started spinning it end over end, stopping when he realized the underside had a ring of adhesive on it. He applied his finger and peeled it off with fascination. Rice looked at Brody. "What *is* this thing?"

"Helps you concentrate," Brody said.

"Oh yeah? How does it—*work*?" Rice touched the sticky pad, pulled away, stuck his finger back on, pulled it away—the sound a gummy thhhk with each pull.

He must've known or had seen something on TV about it, because after turning it around to look at the sonar's plain front—Rice slapped it to his forehead. He stared straight ahead for a few seconds, blinking. A light flashed on the side of the sonar, and Rice's posture shot straight. Crackles could be heard from the vicinity of Rice's head. Synapses by the million overloaded and burst. He was dead before he hit the dirt floor.

Denny dropped Brody's phone and scrambled over to Rice, patting him and shaking him as if trying to rouse him from sleep. He screamed his name into his lifeless face.

He sat back on his haunches. "Ah, man. You overdid it again. I knew you took more than just one, you fuckin' liar. Stupid fuck." After a few halfhearted slaps to his friend's chest in an approximation of CPR, Denny stared into Rice's somber face, defeated. "That sucks."

Denny peeled the sonar from Rice's forehead and examined it, angling it around and pinching it between two fingers. He glared at Brody and held out the sonar accusingly. "Did this do it to him? Did this *fucking* thing do this to Rice?" Anger swelled in his voice with each question. "Did you *fucking* do this to him? What the *fuck* is this thing, anyway?"

"I think your friend is just tired." Brody looked at Rice brain blasted on the floor, his fiercely bloodshot eyes at half-mast. "Let him sleep it off."

Denny reapplied the sonar to Rice's head. "Come on. Wake up."

Getting no results, Denny sneered at Brody. He slid the knuckleduster off Rice's fingers. Approaching Brody and making a fist, Denny hissed, "I think *you* did this to him." He was nearly impossible to understand; the teeth remaining in his head were tightly clamped together. "I think you fucking did something to him to make him die. What was it? Was it that thing?" He pointed at the sonar stuck crookedly to Rice's greasy forehead. "Some kind of other brain-mixer trick that Mr. Ward can do? Tell me, you fuck. Tell me what made Rice go dead."

Brody swallowed, preparing himself for the inevitable blow. "I did it."

"*How?* Tell me how you did it." Denny punched Brody in the face. He had surprising strength in his ropey arms, and the strike genuinely stung.

Before Brody could say anything, Denny hit him

again, this time in the nose. The crunch of cartilage and bone beneath the metal was as audible as the fireworks that had gone off in Rice's head. The knuckleduster bit into his upper lip and made his head snap back. He groaned, letting his ringing head loll to the side. He spat blood. He hadn't been punched with the knuckleduster before—he now understood why it staggered the biggest of men.

As Denny pulled back to punch him again, the door behind Brody rumbled open, causing the junkie to pause his swing.

Brody glanced up and saw Denny shrinking back, apology rapidly spreading on his face toward the person standing out of view. He shook his hand, and the knuckleduster flopped to the floor. He tripped over Rice as he backed away, slinking to the corner of the room and reducing himself to a stooped ball with his knees held to his chest. His eyes transfixed on whoever was there—with esteem, trepidation.

"What happened?" a gnarled voice asked.

Denny pointed a crooked finger at Brody. "*He* killed him." His voice was small, childlike.

"Take him out of here," he said.

"Who, him or him?"

"That one." A long-fingered hand, the nails caked in black, pointed at the corpse on the floor.

Denny did as he was ordered and got to his feet. Brody noticed when he stood, the crotch of his pants was dark. Ignoring it, Denny obediently took his friend by the arms and dragged him out of the room. As he drifted by, Rice's body shifted and the sonar fell from his forehead to the floor, back among Brody's other belongings, landing with its white plastic facedown.

00:07:59.

Eight minutes and he still had no idea whether or not Thorp and Nectar were alive. The place didn't echo, and no sound came through the doors. He figured the walls were thick and they were being kept in separate rooms.

He watched as the man came around to stand in front of him. Blood dotted the man's hairy belly and droopy chest, and his hands were slathered in red, dripping from the fingertips. On his belt hung a collection of long, rusty blades among other mundane cutting implements: a utility knife, a scalpel, a pair of hook-nosed shears intended for pruning tree branches.

Titian Shandorf searched Brody's face, a small pink smile tucked into his bushy beard. He took a deep breath that hiked up his shoulders and let it out, as if bored. He surveyed the different items Denny and Rice had taken such an interest in and regarded them with indifference, all except for the lens charger. He picked it up and turned it over until the coiled cord that Thorp had grafted onto it unraveled. Titian looked at Brody. "You're blind?"

Brody nodded. A steady stream of blood was pumping out of his flattened nose. The pain made his already burning eyes water all the more. He felt a steady drip land on his lap, falling from his collapsed nostrils.

"Can you see me right now?" Titian asked, stepping forward. The lens charger slipped from his hand and hit the floor with a dry thud. He leaned down and peered into Brody's face, so close Brody could smell the sharp rancor of Titian's breath. A bloody finger nearly touched the surface of Brody's right eye—Brody felt it brushing his eyelashes. He didn't allow himself to flinch.

"This one, right? This one you can see out of right now. Not the other one." Titian's right shoulder moved as he waved a hand in front of Brody's blind eye.

Brody nodded.

Titian stepped back. "Ironic, you being the sightless sleuth and all with that whole thing about justice being blind. I suppose when they fish your body out of Lake Michigan, that'll be what they put on the newspapers and everything. 'Blind Detective Found Dead—Major Injustice' or something." He ran a hand through his salt-and-pepper hair, flattening it down with a pomade of blood.

"Where's Nectar?" Brody asked, his voice slurred from his torn lip and his mouth readily refilling with blood each time he swallowed. "Is she dead? Did you kill her?"

Titian looked at Brody as if he wanted to answer. He walked past him, then behind him and out of sight.

Brody expected to feel the hefty chop of a machete going through his neck. He closed his eyes so it would be a surprise, possibly instant and painless.

But instead of a rusty blade singing through the air, he heard the creak of wheels. He opened his eyes and saw Titian rolling an ancient TV set in front of him. It was one of the CRT variations, encased in wood with frilly fabric hiding its speaker.

Brody glanced at Titian standing next to the dead TV.

"Oh, this?" Titian said. "I don't have anything to show you, but Hubert does. I just got it ready for him. I have to keep things busy up here." He waved a hand next to his bushy head of wild gray hair. "Otherwise, I lose focus and I forget my orders and, well, I could forfeit a lot of money if I do that." He found a folding chair across the room and sat down, his elbows on his knees, leaning forward, staring at Brody.

Brody gazed at his reflection in the gray TV screen and saw the door behind him, a long workbench of sorts with a variety of large wrenches and other tools. At the far end of the reflection, he could make out what appeared to be a mannequin head. It wore a dark and curly wig. He turned and glimpsed a flash of chestnut hair but couldn't identify the face.

"Can you see that behind you there?" Titian asked from the shadowed corner.

"Is that Nectar?" Brody asked, fighting to keep his tone even.

Titian got to his feet with a grunt and paced noisily across the room, all the knives and metal about his waist jangling loudly. Brody watched Titian in the reflection of the TV as he picked up the head and brought it over to him.

Brody felt cold flesh pressed against his cheek. A soft lip, hanging loose, was mashed against his cheekbone next to his eye on his blind side. Brody twisted as far as he could away, but Titian held the rotting, grayed head of Abigail Schwartz against him. Titian laughed, made kissing sounds, and then set the head on top of the TV on its ear, where he rested a hand on the upturned, blood-spattered cheek.

Brody's stomach lurched. Abigail's face looked drawn tight, the skin beginning to give way to decomposition. The cheekbones jutted and eyes hung open, dry and lifeless. Her jaw was slack, and it was evident that insects had taken up a home within. A tiny yellow worm made slow progress up the bridge of her nose.

"She was a real fighter. Boy howdy did she kick. Man, that was an ambitious struggle if I've ever seen one. Most of the time you tell them what's going to happen and they freeze, get that OMG look, and just lay there like they're drunk on prom night and don't make a peep until you have the knife actually *in* them. But her . . . she really did not want to die. She must've had a lot to live for, something important to do, a purpose. And I think that's why a lot of these girls don't put up a fight. They think, 'This is the end of me and my sorry existence' to themselves and they let it happen to them because, well, what else do they have going on? They'll be a celebrity on a small scale for a while when the news folks run their picture and all of that—and what girl doesn't want to be someone famous?"

He picked up Abigail's head by the ears, held it out before him, and stared into her lifeless eyes as he made his way to the corner of the room. He paused as if bidding her a silent farewell, then let the head fall into the burning barrel.

The barrel had a few jagged holes formed into it from rust. Through its side, Brody could see Abigail's cheek and bottom lip. Draped across her face, the hair curled and burned up in individual trailing embers like a thousand tiny fuses. He had to look away. He *had* to look away.

"Burn them," Titian commented blandly, watching. "That's the rule. Yep. Have to burn them or break them up. Anything to get rid of the brain. The brain is where the fingerprints are, so to speak."

"You too?" Brody said. "I thought you were just a consultant." He dared a scoff. Even to his ears it sounded pithy, his bravado sullied by his swelling disgust.

"You have them, I'm sure. I have them. I know that. The girl, she has them. Yep, when Hubert's through with you, that's where you go—right in there." Titian motioned to the barrel. "Got to clean up behind oneself. Can't leave anything behind, got to stay tidy."

"Is she dead?" Brody managed, unable to keep his voice from shaking. "Just fucking tell me that much. I don't care what you do to me. Just at least give me that satisfaction and tell me she's dead."

Titian folded his arms. "Do *you* think she's dead? If you're playing detective with soldier boy out there, you must think she's still alive and kicking. Did you lie to your war buddy and tell him you think his sister is alive?"

"Yes, I told him that—and I do think she's still alive."

Titian swooped down in front of Brody. He spoke so quickly that all his words ran into one long jitter. "That's it. Hope. Bright, shining God-deliver-me-from-evil-please-oh-please-not-me *hope*. That's what I want to see on someone's face when I put them away—a glimmer of blind hope. No pun intended. Miss Schwartz had it. She really thought she could fight me off and make it out. *Wrong*. I took her by the hair just like *this*."

Titian wrenched Brody's head back by his hair. "And I took out this little beauty right *here*." He removed a utility knife from his belt, ratcheted the corner of the razor out, and held it to Brody's throat.

Just from the tiny fraction of pressure being applied, Brody felt the blade gliding easily into his skin.

"And I'll tell you what I told her. 'Thanks for playing but good-*bye*.'"

33

Titian released his grip on Brody's hair, but the razor remained in place.

A voice, nearly so quiet it was inaudible, posed a simple request: "Titian, if you wouldn't mind, would you go and assist your colleagues upstairs? They're having trouble getting the other gentleman to fit into the garbage chute."

Titian nodded at Brody, still under the blade. "You got a handle on him? He has an attitude issue."

"It's fine. Go and help the young men upstairs. I'll call you when I'm ready."

The knife, much to Brody's relief, moved away from his neck, ratcheted closed, and was clipped back onto Titian's belt. Titian clattered out, slamming the door behind him.

A man with neatly parted gray hair walked in front of Brody with his hands in the pockets of his suit pants. He looked as if he had been called from a night on the town following a harrowing day at the office: no suit coat, shirtsleeves rolled to his elbows, tie partly loosened. He inventoried the room, then finally acknowledged Brody as if it were easy to miss the sight of a profusely bleeding man cuffed to a wheelchair.

"Hubert Ward," Brody choked, red spittle flying.

"I am."

"Mr. Ashbury must be a very dear friend for you to risk violating your probation to come all the way out here just on a plea to find his missing sister."

Brody remained silent.

"You and him share a pretty ugly past. Well, your record is shining, but that one incident in an alleyway in Cairo—a moment like that really defines a person, doesn't it? You didn't shoot that child soldier but Thorp did. You witnessed it, and you *wanted* to shoot him to protect yourself and your friend. But you hesitated. Thorp went through with it, committed himself to an atrocity that would define him in order to save you. And moments like that, events where we have to go left or right, is what makes us who we are."

Hubert pulled his cell out of his pocket and pointed it at the TV. The screen hummed to life showing a test pattern featuring the United States Army emblem. A blast of static and Brody's full name and military ID number appeared for a moment. Then, in an unceremonious edit, the viewpoint flashed to a gun barrel aiming across a muddy field of a firing range.

At the end, paper silhouettes of armored men. Gunfire overloaded the speakers of the television as the camera watched the barrel flare with a muzzle flash, the target at the range splintering apart at the torso and head.

"We have every single second of what your barrel-mounted camera saw while you were in the service. Every time you disengaged your rifle's safety, the camera began rolling. On the practice field, you were a crack shot. But out in the real world, we saw a different man entirely. One who resisted, who was gun-shy, who may have knowingly or unknowingly hesitated. Of course, *knowingly* hesitating is the same as restraining, desisting."

The viewpoint from the assault rifle shifted to the cramped streets of Cairo and a handful of men they had assumed were insurgents. They were being held at gunpoint as one of Brody's fellow soldiers patted each one down for explosives, detonators, weapons of any sort. Brody's assault rifle shifted from one man to the next.

Then it ended—safety reengaged—and the viewpoint switched to a man talking on a cell phone in front of an electronics repair shop. Brody remembered that day. They had gotten a call that a bomb maker was setting up a meeting place with a buyer, and they thought they had him. The guy turned out to be calling his grandchildren in America on a foreign exchange student program.

The perspective switched again. To the man in the alleyway caught in the bear trap—the would-be ambush. The crowd at the mouth of the alley under the scrutiny of Brody's barrel-mounted camera, not perturbed about a gun pointed at them, their curiosity too great.

"You never fired upon anyone," Hubert commented,

standing beside the television set sizing up Brody as he watched his own gun-mounted footage roll by. "Not a single person. Not even here, when this young boy emerges with his full intent on killing you both."

The footage displayed the boy, stepping from the crowd with the assault rifle bundled in a blanket. Unwrapping it and struggling to raise the heavy thing to his shoulder. The boy, one eye closed, took quick but careful aim.

A three-round discharge but not from the muzzle of the camera's eye they were currently watching—from next to it, from Thorp's assault rifle. The boy's chest: a bursting blossom of red.

The boy falling.

The gun clattering to the ground.

Thorp charged ahead to tend to the dying boy he had just shot. The footage went black. Brody's safety had been reengaged.

"There it is, the reason you won't be going any further in our project, Mr. Calhoun. You see, to be a part of Project Silver Fox, one has to have had the experience we need *before* the wavelength was given to them. You can't ask a chimpanzee to go onstage and play Mozart without a few piano lessons. I would've gladly let you continue to give the police someone to chase in Minnesota, but since you sniffed around and found some things out, I can't let you go." One eye clouded over with a gray streak of cirrus, while the other watched the dead screen of the TV, staring at his own warped reflection.

"You look unconvinced. Let me show you something

else." A click on his phone's screen made a CT scan arrive on the TV. "Every one of us goes to someone else for advice. Guidance is important, and with its hand on our backs, we feel comforted by making decisions on our own if that push is gentle enough.

"Take this man here, this being Mr. Ashbury's brain we're looking at, by the way. You see this tomography image and how everything looks normal. This was when he first enlisted in the armed forces. He was making terrible choices with his life, floundering. And then . . ." Ward clicked his cell, and the fuzzy screen changed to a more colorful scan. It appeared the brain had been partly shifted around like that of a Doppler radar with a thunderhead moving in. "We rearrange some things, make more activity flow to one part of the brain. We helped him become a better man by changing the way his brain worked. He became a better soldier, and because of it he made quick decisions as a means of survival. You, on the other—"

"That's bullshit," Brody said. "When we enlisted, it was before scans were done. All we had were physicals."

He turned to Brody, blinking behind his frameless lenses that flared in the harsh light. "Just because you didn't stand in a plastic box doesn't mean we never got your scan. You were a pacifist from the very beginning. Your personality test proved that you would hesitate in order for someone to pull the trigger for you. You had a hard time committing to anything, let alone doing what needed to be done to save your friend's life. We decided on a different approach for your retirement."

Ward clicked the phone screen, and the TV display

changed to an exploded schematic of what Brody recognized immediately as the intercom radio headpiece he'd worn underneath his helmet.

"This, you surely know, is the Beacon headset, a product of one of Hark's sister companies. It was the conduit to which you and your unit of soldiers were first exposed to the wavelength that would help you become better men and women of the armed forces. At least that was the intent until we realized we had the opportunity to do something different with Mr. Ashbury. The incident in that alleyway was a stroke of luck for us. We had just started tweaking the frequencies to adjust Mr. Ashbury to be more aggressive. We wanted to mold you to have more restraint. The impromptu test validated our decisions. Thorp was to be more forceful, a go-getter, self-aware, and confident—while you were to be inward, introverted, and cautious. Since adjusting brain waves isn't an exact science, we not only got what we wanted but a healthy dose of other quirks as well. We got crippling paranoia from Thorp and a pugilistic misanthrope—albeit one that knows his limits—out of you. It was interesting how you both went in different directions than we expected but wholly interesting ones.

"I was inspired by an article I read while in college about Dr. Lyudmila Trut of the Institute of Cytology and Genetics. She took over where Dmitry Belyaev left off with the astounding progress made over twenty-six long years. Their goal—to see if silver foxes could be domesticated. Similar tests on wolves had been performed by other scientists but with no progress.

Taking the one percent of foxes from a group that showed neither fear nor aggression, they nurtured the animals to see if they could get a wild animal to become as docile as a common neighborhood dog. Over more than fifty years, this went on.

"Dr. Trut and her team raised one generation after another in two separate groups. One to be tame, the other to be more aggressive. With the group meant to be more docile, a wondrous thing happened. The foxes developed dog stars in their coats, their tails and legs became shorter, the level of adrenaline—the hormone that's most directly associated with aggression—was substantially diminished. They even began to have curly tails. They took wild animals and made them into run-of-the-mill dogs.

"And the other group came out becoming even *more* vicious than those of their brethren living in the wild." Hubert smiled briefly. "And naturally, I was interested if the same methodology could be applied to people. But I was a man who knew technology, nuts and bolts, and I wanted to see what I could do with that present knowledge of mine."

"Alton Noel never wanted to hurt anyone."

"He was our first and never before was there a man more perfect for a job. A man who had fired upon his enemies, who was strong and dedicated. And he exacted what we wanted out of him perfectly."

"You made him kill people. You made him shoot Elizabeth Lake—why? She had nothing to do with anything. She was innocent."

"An innocent woman associated with a very dangerous man," Hubert corrected with an upheld index finger. "Thomas Lake would've ruined Hark Telecom, me specifically, if he could've proven I had sent moles to be hired at DRN." He paused. "But that's neither here nor there. Thomas Lake is ruined and Alton had his funeral—that's all in the past. Let's talk about the reason you're here."

He clicked a keypad button and the TV woke up again, seeing through the electronic eye of the surveillance tape from the armed forces recruiter's office. Two men in uniform, doing work at their stations, some tinny pop radio playing in competition with the white noise being stirred up by an oscillating fan. They both looked up in response to a chime signaling someone entering the front door.

A woman dressed in a paisley sundress entered, sunglasses propped in her forest of strawberry blonde hair like a black plastic tiara. She approached their desks, flip-flops slapping her heels with each stride. "Hi, I'm, um, interested in signing up," Nectar said, sounding as if she were speaking from a script she had neglected to memorize thoroughly.

"Great," the recruiter said enthusiastically, gesturing to the seat in front of his desk. She sat and he produced a clipboard of forms and a pen. "I'll just have you take a look through these and—you are graduated from high school, yes?"

"Oh yeah," Nectar said. "Quite a while ago. I'm twenty-four. I hope that's okay."

"Just fine. We turn people away at twenty-seven."

"Oh, good," Nectar said and went to filling out the papers.

A moment later when she was halfway down the page, a large man entered the recruiter's office. Nectar looked over her shoulder, and her shock was clear.

Despite the footage being grainy CCTV, Brody could see her face drain of color.

Titian stepped into the frame. "What are you doing in here, dear?"

"H-how did you—?" Nectar stammered.

Titian approached Nectar, put a hand on her bicep, and lifted her out of the chair. He took the clipboard out of her hands and set it down on the desk and leaned toward the recruiter. "I'm sorry about this, but my daughter is under the impression that the military is a good way to get out of taking care of her family. My apologies."

Nectar struggled against Titian's grip until she seemed to notice something that made her calm down all at once. With Titian standing behind her, using her body to block the knife he had to her back from the recruiters, he shook his head at them as he backed out of the office with Nectar in tow.

The two recruiters stood, ready to take action. But once the double chime sounded again, they looked at one another and slowly took their seats and returned to work. "Sit. Stay."

The TV went dead, the screen crackling with static electricity. A few motes of dust tumbled around on the screen's glass surface, chasing one other.

"Where is she?" Brody asked.

"Here," Hubert said. "Getting prepared for what she'll do for us. She's like you. She never actually fired a weapon on anyone before, so we're taking a different tack with her—the same we would've eventually taken with you. Of course, this means longer exposure to the wavelength, more possibility of ruining her, but possibly worth it, even if she just ends up yielding data for us."

"She never technically joined. She never got sent anywhere or killed anyone. What the hell will you have her do?"

Hubert grinned. "Don't need a lot of training to press a button."

"You're going to have her . . . ?"

With an indifference Brody had never heard from human lips, he said, "Everyone has their uses."

Brody was stunned to the point of muteness. He began three times to form a pithy retort, but nothing came to him. His mind tumbled end over end, never grasping any semblance of logic. He spat at Hubert, his words coming to him fumblingly: "I e-mailed all your project files to a friend of mine. He'll take one look and start tracking my phone. I'm on probation, and they tend to keep close tabs on me. They'll find me, find us."

Hubert regarded Brody's phone on the earthen floor. He bent down and touched the screen to wake the device and went into the e-mail out-box. The change in Hubert's demeanor was easily recognizable, his expression dropped when he had seen the enormous e-mail that had been sent to Detective Nathan Pierce.

Holding Brody's phone out so he could read from it, he placed a call with his own. "Again, relying on someone else to fight your battles." He brought the phone to his ear. "Hubert Ward to speak to Mr. Axiom, please."

He waited, continued to scroll through Brody's e-mail. "I have some troubling news . . . We need to dispatch an individual to Minneapolis. Seems one of our silver foxes made a call for backup. A detective, Nathan Pierce. Yes . . . Last night, so it probably hasn't gotten very far yet . . . A local one will do it, I think . . . Okay, thank you, sir." He hung up and sneered at Brody.

"Axiom, huh? Even *you* have a boss. What is he, Hark's CEO?"

"Quiet," Hubert said and stepped to the door. Opening it a crack, he called out, "Denny, would you mind assisting me for a moment?"

There was the sound of scuffling steps approaching, and Denny entered.

Hubert pointed at Brody. "Would you mind wheeling him into the main room? I want to show him something."

Denny went behind Brody, switched off the wheelchair's brakes, and spun him toward the open door.

Across the dirt floor, Brody felt himself glide on the rubber wheels. There was a slight bump. Brody glanced down and saw that the chair's right wheel had just run over the sonar. He watched, despite the rapidly reducing digits in his eye, as the sonar swung past again and again with each revolution of the wheelchair wheel, held in place by its everlasting adhesive.

Into the next room he was carted, this one a wide-open space with thirty feet of air above them. The entire dank factory lit solely by one enormous arc light, its brightness tangible on Brody's skin. Looking around, he saw this was a place where freighter ships would be worked on and then immediately run down the massive ramp into Lake Michigan's waters. Rusty steel on every wall, unused catwalks, and temporary walls made of two-by-four frames sheeted with clear plastic pulled as tight as drum skin. Makeshift laboratories, complete with worktables and instruments and miles of cords and cables running from monitors to databases.

They continued through the factory, passing numerous defunct pieces of machinery. Denny struggled when they came across a thick band of cables, tipping Brody back in the wheelchair from its front wheels for clearance. The addict grunted, his arms too weak to be pushing around anything heavier than his own weight.

Brody didn't fight. He took the tour through the shipyard to survey his surroundings, to try to estimate a means of escape. He didn't see a lot of options.

A long hallway stood off to the side, made of the same patchy, rusty wall of the room they had just brought him from, except the metal looked a fraction newer and haphazardly thrown together, stitched at the edges with bolts and haphazard welds. At the end of the hallway, an open doorway shone to Brody's bleary eyes as a flashing rectangle. After his eyes adjusted he saw an array of parked vehicles, mostly ruined and ancient cars from the last century and one nestled among them, gleaming black and immaculate. Ward's, without a doubt.

Beyond, Brody caught a glimpse of Titian Shandorf standing back as a group of men tried to wedge Rice's corpse into the narrow slot of a slag smelting stove, intense black smoke boiling out from around the body's dangling legs. Wheeled along, the sight was cut short. Brody faced forward.

Denny pushed Brody to the middle of the central room alongside two rows of large spools of black wire and parked his wheelchair at the end of the aisle. Something struck him and made the world feel tilted, as if vertical had suddenly shifted. Vertigo stirred in his head, and his ears began to ring. His head suddenly felt heavy and hard to keep balanced upon his neck, as if he were suddenly missing multiple vertebrae; his limbs fell slack in their bonds. He felt his bowels loosen. Like hands under his skin feeling about, the sensation permeating from the spooled wire gripped and caressed him like a drunken lover. In his neck, in his skull, fingering his brain.

At the other end of the aisle Brody spotted two wheelchair-bound people sitting side by side. Both figures were secured with tape, and their faces were bloody. More tape was wrapped messily around their heads holding their gags in place. Thorp and Nectar.

Brody couldn't bear the sight of his friends bleeding and weakly struggling, but he felt looking away would seem like he was giving in. He continued to stare, making himself hold eye contact with each of them in turn. Another rush hit him. Nausea and ears ringing made him involuntarily let his head roll on his neck. He looked at the dirty rubber of his chair's wheel. The sonar was stuck facing him on the apex of the tire, camouflaged under a fine layer of rusty red soil.

"I will prove to you," Hubert Ward said, coming around in front of Brody, "that a candidate can never do anything outside of his bounds of experience. A double-edged sword. In one way beneficial because none of the subjects can ever do anything unpredictable—and yet it *limits* them as to what you can *ask* them to do." He turned to Denny, who still gripped the handles of Brody's wheelchair, and gestured at Thorp. "Cut him free."

Denny approached Thorp, drawing a small key chain knife from his urine-soaked pants.

"Oh, and your sidearm, please."

Denny switched the knife to his other hand and removed the Franklin-Johann and held it out for Hubert.

Hubert took the gun in one hand and flipped the lid on a nearby ordi resting on a plastic storage barrel with the other. He set the gun aside to type with both hands.

A second later, one of the giant spools of humming wires began sending out a different, higher pitch of white noise.

Parked in relative proximity to it, Brody felt a strange heat come over his mind—as if a funnel had just been jammed through the top of his skull and warm milk was slowly being poured in.

Denny cut the last of Thorp's bounding tape from about his ankles. Brody was surprised that Thorp didn't immediately spring out of the chair. He sat there, released, staring ahead with a tepid look on his face. Eyes dull.

"Mr. Ashbury?" Hubert asked.

Thorp focused on Hubert.

Nectar went into a riot of thrashing. She screamed, muffled beneath the band of tape across her face. She stared at Brody, urging him to *do something*. The metal parts of her chair brattled.

He could make out only some of her words. But it didn't matter. There was nothing to be done. He looked away.

Hubert turned the gun around until he held it by the barrel. He extended the grip toward Thorp. With some duct tape still clinging to the sleeve of his nylon coat, he took the gun, looked at it for a moment, then at Hubert.

"Stand up so Mr. Calhoun can see," Hubert suggested and Thorp obediently did so. Hubert smiled at Brody as he whispered in Thorp's ear.

Thorp listened with his eyes half-closed. Then he pointed the barrel of the pistol at Nectar's face.

"*Stop*," Brody howled.

"You see what happens when you interfere, girl?" Hubert shouted at Nectar. "Try and challenge innovation and this is what happens." He faced Brody. "Pliable and docile and *tame*. Securely on the leash, with absolutely no threat to anyone that his handler does not deem dangerous."

Under the barrel of the gun, Nectar stared at her brother with tears steadily streaming down her face. She had ceased fighting and pulling at the restraints, trying to work her jaw to loosen the gag. She was quiet. She begged with her eyes and her eyes alone.

00:03:59.

"Don't make him do that. Please. Stop. I get it, okay? Just stop." Brody pulled with all his strength at the tape wrapped in thick bands around his arms, his wrists, dug in deep into the crooks of his elbows, across his knees and ankles, even across his waist and neck. He squirmed and fought and roared, but the tape wouldn't give.

"Draw back the hammer."

"Make him stop. Make him stop!"

"Now flip the safety catch."

"Wait, wait, wait. Stop. Please. Just stop."

Hubert stepped away from Thorp, but the gun was not lowered.

"It's all about the journey the signal makes. Entering right through the layer of bone encasing the brain." Hubert felt around on Thorp's head as if he were pointing out locales on a globe. "Through the external acoustic meatus here"—he tapped behind Thorp's right ear—"the signal goes right in, finds the memories of experiences best suited to the command, and—just like that—it's all pinched, set, *usable*. In your case—without a confirmed kill, without that experience for the signal to find and utilize—you're condemned forever to throw punches. You are Early Man, using your fists, whereas Mr. Ashbury has evolved." He patted Thorp on the shoulder. "What do you think? Have we had quite enough of Mr. Calhoun, or does he need another example?"

Thorp said nothing, stared languidly at his sister at the end of the barrel.

Nectar had her eyes closed, head bowed resolutely. Her face from the cheeks down were soaked with tears.

"Denny, cut Mr. Calhoun's right arm loose." He met Brody's eye that was rapidly counting down the remaining minutes and asked with a winning smile, "That is your dominant hand, right? You are a righty, yes?"

Brody just sat there.

"Are you sure about this?" Denny asked, sawing through the threads of the duct tape with the inch-long blade of his key chain knife.

Hubert didn't answer. He rested his hand on the back of Thorp's head, gently stroking the shaggy hairs that hung over the collar of his shirt. "Please give me the weapon."

Without hesitation Thorp reset the safety on the pistol, turned it around, and handed it to Hubert in the same way it had been handed to him.

Nectar gave no indicative change in her sunken posture that she felt better having the gun taken away—she was limp, possibly unconscious. Brody couldn't tell.

Hubert took the slide of the handgun and worked it back repeatedly until he realized the safety was on. He clicked it, jerked the slide, and then reset it. Taking one long stride toward Brody, he extended his arm and placed the loaded gun in his now-free hand.

Hubert was illuminated by the buzzing arc light directly above, his peaked face creating deep, strange shadows in his cheeks. He threw out his arms to his sides as if he were about to break into a joyous song. "Go ahead, Mr. Calhoun. Shoot me. Shoot Denny behind you. I will show you that your inability to kill goes beyond the puppet strings of conscience. Your restraint isn't just what makes you a great pugilistic thug, but what I have done for you has made you into someone who cannot pull the goddamn trigger."

00:01:57.

00:01:56.

00:01:55.

Maybe it was the exposure to the pounding

amounts of Hark's signal within such close proximity or the beating Brody had endured by Rice with his own knuckleduster—something stirred in Brody. The layers of dust covering his memories of that day in the Cairo alley cleared in one gusting blow. With the weight of the loaded gun in his hand, he felt pulled as if it were not just a seven-pound piece of metal and plastic in his hand but something far heavier. He was being dragged down by it, mile after mile, straight down where no light had ever traveled, into impenetrable darkness. He held the gun. He remembered.

34

It was nearly time to return to base to hit up the mess hall for the meat loaf promised every Thursday. It had been an uneventful morning doing patrols, steering the wide Terrapin through the narrow streets of Cairo and trying to avoid bowling over people on bicycles, which were more common than cars in the parched desert city—only to turn around and do it again.

Brody remembered adjusting the vent on the air conditioner above him. Inside the Terrapin, it only took seconds after pulling the back door ramp up for the space to grow sticky with humidity.

"So this is it?" Across the aisle, strapped into his seat and his helmet sitting low on his head, gloved hands on the controls, Thorp took his eyes from the road and repeated his question when Brody didn't answer.

"Yeah," Brody said. "A few more of these runs and that'll be it."

"They'll be lucky to have you," Thorp said.

Brody chided him for his momentary show of sincerity, something commonly sought by fellow soldiers but stamped out at once. First you said you cared about someone or liked having them around, and the next thing you knew they were dead. So it was better to keep stuff like that to yourself.

"And what about after that?" Thorp asked.

"I'll have level three clearance, and I'll be able to be part of the sweep team instead of doing *this* shit the rest of my life."

Steering the Terrapin through a wide turn—it wasn't exactly what you'd call nimble—Thorp brayed incredulously. "And what's wrong with doing patrols with your good buddies, huh? Ceramic Groom was just about the most fun this old boy has ever fucking had in his whole fucking life. You calling that *boring*?"

The rest of the unit joined in heckling Brody.

Brody put up his hands in mock defense. "All right, all right, it's not so bad with you guys, but being stuck in this damn thing with the heat and the stink—*that's* what I can't stand." He adjusted the vent to blow the air away from him.

Everyone laughed.

That was when the call came in. Their unit was to report to the edge of the market district to help a man who was caught in a bear trap. This incited a laugh from most of the men, Thorp especially.

"Please repeat," Thorp told dispatch.

"Market district, east end. A man is caught in a bear trap."

"We're on our way," Thorp said and hung up the receiver. "Bear trap. That's a new one."

"Think it's Tanner's unit trying to prank us?" Brody suggested.

"Might be," Thorp said, throttling down. "But we better go have a look just to make sure."

They made a quick turnaround in a vacant lot and rumbled east, the dry pavement scratching and crunching beneath the massive tires.

Two dozen people in flowing loose garments stood bunched together at the mouth of the alleyway; the men watched with unabated curiosity while the women peeked between fingers.

Someone had to remain in the Terrapin, and of the six in their unit, Thorp and Brody were among the ones to get out. They pushed through the crowd and went to the man at the end of the alley, doubled over with his lips peeled back from his teeth, sweat dripping from his bearded face, howling in agony. The translator in Brody's ear couldn't keep up with what the man prattled—only pinches of interpreted pleas came through in deciphered monotone: *help, tricked me, it hurts.*

"You're going to be okay," Brody said. The metal maw had swallowed half the man's arm, the teeth biting in on the front and back of the elbow. Brody tried to pry the jagged jaws with his free hand, but someone had added screws, broken glass, razor blades, nails, and inch-long lengths of barbed wire inside. He looked at Thorp. "I have to put down my rifle."

Thorp nodded and took a knee next to them, keeping the gun in the crook of his arms, watching the morbidly curious spectators crowded at the end of the alleyway.

Brody pressed his boot heel beside the man's pinned arm and pushed down with his weight, the hinges of the trap creaking. Nearly as soon as the serrated jaws were open wide enough Brody realized the man's arm wasn't bleeding at all. The chewed divot glinted with alloy—there were wires, half-crushed servos, and whining electronic muscles. The man seemed to be washed of his pretend agony, and he reached up into the sleeve of his shawl to unbuckle the bionic appendage.

The demeanor of the crowd shifted—they seemed to understand. From them: gasps, alarmed cries. The concept was a contagion and it took the longest to reach Brody. He pulled his rifle to his shoulder and disengaged the safety. He held it on the crowd, watching. They all shifted, startled, scared, expecting . . .

"What's going on?" Brody murmured to Thorp.

"No clue," Thorp said.

Brody glanced at the man, still working at the limb's straps inside the billowy sleeve. He'd be brought in for questioning, probably slapped with a fine for wasting their time, detained over a weekend at most. He turned around.

Gasps, shouts.

A boy emerged. He stared at them with an assault rifle pointed in their direction. He lifted it to his shoulder; the gun was probably as tall as he was.

Brody saw the boy push through the trigger guard.

Brody mimed him, reaching, applying pressure but unable—absolutely unable—to *squeeze*.

A noise as loud as thunder sounded next to him.

The boy fell, his gun sliding from his limp hands and across the cobblestone street.

Without a word, Thorp charged down that way.

Brody crumpled into a seated position right there on the alley floor, gun across his lap, ears ringing. Everything was muddled, far away. His head swam at the sight before him: Thorp pulling the bloody boy to his chest and screaming into his headset, "Immediate assistance." Tears In Thorp's eyes. Blood smeared on the boy's face and pumping freely from his cratered chest. Screaming. People running away. Some onlookers even threw rocks at Thorp. Brody remembered the boy's face—eyes frozen saucers, skin ashen, soul gone.

Beyond the confusion and noise, he heard the hollow clunk of an empty aluminum can glancing off concrete. He turned to see the one-armed man going through a collection of wooden boxes.

Brody stood, approached the man's back. Through the thin material, Brody could see the man's muscles working feverishly. He used the nub of his remaining right arm to clear away debris. The man hoisted something out of the trash and shook browned lettuce from it. A revolver.

Launching himself forward, Brody caught the man just as he turned with the gun in his hand—already taking aim at Thorp.

The two wrestled. Despite the man having only one arm, he gave quite the fight, trying to wrench the gun out of Brody's grip. Brody pushed the man against the alley wall, the rifle barrel shifting under his own chin. He shoved it toward the one-armed man.

The translator in his ear gave a monotone rendition of what the man was saying through his gritted teeth: *murderers*, *son*, *interlopers*, *my boy*.

They fought until the gun cracked and the man, half his face peeled from his skull, crumpled to the ground. He lay, struck dead immediately, next to his discarded limb still in the bite of the bear trap.

A violent jerk in Brody's hand—the flash snapping at the dusty gloom.

Hubert fell back with a gasp.

Nectar screamed out beneath her bonds.

Thorp remained stock-still, catatonic and indifferent.

Hubert slapped a hand over his chest where Brody had shot him. His eyes were wide, so much surprise. He looked to Denny, who stepped forward with the knife in his hand.

Brody turned the gun as far as he could angle his wrist and fired. A black dot appeared on Denny's forehead directly above his right eye. A riot of colors—pink, red, white, gray—sprang out and hit the wall behind him. He lurched forward in midstep and collapsed quietly. "Hey," was his final utterance.

00:01:21.

Again, Brody aimed the pistol at Hubert. The man was now on his back, weakly kicking, trying to get to his phone. With each kick, Hubert began to slow. Halfway to the dirt-covered device he tried to roll over onto his front, still clutching his chest, but he made it only partway. He returned to his back, looking upward. Hubert grew still at the feet of Nectar, dying before he could reach his phone.

00:01:17.

Brody tugged at the thick band of duct tape over his elbow. He heard not the tape's fibers breaking but the wooden arm of the wheelchair splintering. He kept pulling, never relinquishing the death grip he had on the pistol. The arm of the wheelchair made a solid snap, then came away from the metal body of the wheelchair on the next pull. His right arm was free.

He set the gun in his lap and yanked the tape off his left arm. He broke the other armrest and pulled the linked cuff out. He began working on his legs, yanking and tearing as quickly as he could. Mind racing, the overwhelming deluge of nausea upon him. The warmed milk sensation clung. He felt both serene and anxious at the same time—scared mindless and yet perfectly in control.

His mind was still in Cairo. He had never reported shooting the one-armed man in the alley. The event hadn't been recorded on the barrel-mounted camera, never put into his file as a confirmed kill. As soon as Brody shot the man, he ran to check on Thorp. The sunglass lens put under the boy's nose fogged. It was impossible to tell where the bullets had struck him; his rough-textured garment was heavy with blood. Brody helped load him into the back of the Terrapin, where they laid him on the floor. Someone else drove, because Thorp refused to let go of the boy's hand.

00:00:59.

Brody looked at Hubert, the bullet hole right over his heart. He pointed the gun into the old man's face. He inched back on the trigger. Hubert Ward stared at him, his eyes lifeless and empty. His mouth a perfect *O* filled to the brim with blood.

00:00:45.

The Terrapin rumbled on. The intercom was alive with distress signals. Similar surprise attacks had happened all over the city at the same time—an organized attempt to weaken the military presence. He sat at the Terrapin's rear glass, watching the city slide by them, the general populous unsettled—pitching rocks, sticks, and hunks of spoiled meat at them as they passed. Everything bounced off the metal skin of the armored vehicle. Brody watched, disquieted. The sun was going down. He focused on the colors.

He returned to base and the mess hall. He had the table to himself; everyone else was on their shift or out in the yard discussing what had happened. Brody ate meat loaf, drank coffee, smoked cigarettes, and let things go into the boxes they needed to be put in.

It stayed gone for a long time.

00:00:30.

Brody turned the gun from Hubert's slack face, pointed it at the screen of the man's phone, and fired, the device shattering.

He looked to Thorp. He still stood, seemingly frozen in place, staring into the empty middle distance.

Brody pushed through the plastic curtain to one of the makeshift laboratories, going to the several ordis and their holo-displays. None of what the monitors

displayed—endlessly scrolling numbers and icons and levels and fluctuating scales and dials—made sense to him. There was no clear way to shut any of it off.

He took the handgun by its barrel and hammered the monitors, keyboards, open places where disks or drives could be inserted. One by one, the spools of wire beyond went silent. The ozone in the air seemed to fall away, and the tingly sensation Brody now realized had covered every inch of his exposed flesh was gone.

Thorp fell forward onto his hands and knees, becoming violently ill, barely having time to peel the tape from his mouth before a flood of vomit rushed out.

Brody went to Nectar, took the tape off her wrists. He studied her face as he worked, saw she had gone flaccid—her head had rolled back and her open eyes displayed nothing but the whites.

Both Brody and Thorp pulled the wires from her body and removed the restraints. She was limp, malnourished, and pale. When they lifted her from the wheelchair, the sheet covering her lap fell away. She had been put into a chair equipped with a bedpan. A catheter tube ran to a hanging, swollen bag clipped to the seat back. She moaned, pawed at the fallen sheet.

Shouts, whispers—Brody listened as Titian and the other men approached.

00:00:15.

"Get her to cover," Brody said. "Stay there."

00:00:14.

There was shouting, the clatter of guns. Titian and his men filed back into the main room of the shipyard. Brody glimpsed them in the distance, a flash of an arm or a set of running legs, the approaching march, dodging defunct machinery and pillars of dead wire, trying to make their way through the rusted metal labyrinth.

00:00:10.

"Are you sure?" Thorp asked.

"Go. Now."

Thorp removed the lock from his sister's wheelchair and carted her away, holding one hand to her shoulder to keep her from tumbling out of the chair.

00:00:02.

Brody turned and saw the men. They all matched Titian's general description: haggard and dressed in tattered clothing, wild, feral eyes, and unkempt looks. They charged, slapping and moving around and between looped wires—everywhere, wires.

Brody hid behind a half-completed hull of a freight liner. He pinched the lens out just as the final second counted down. Blind, he listened for the buzz of the arc light above—aimed toward it—and fired.

The factory was thrown into darkness.

Brody, operating strictly on short-term memory as to where everything was, crept over to the wheelchair and found the sonar where it had been stuck against the tire. He slapped it to his forehead and the ping shot out.

Confused shouts, blind fire ringing. Titian's friends stood perplexed and blind, mapped in geometry. Puzzled polygon men. Even though they were behind cover, lying in wait, hiding, the sonar found each one of them in one ringing sweep.

Brody stepped out from behind the rusty hull and opened fire.

35

Brody made his way through the first few men before they assumed where he was and their accuracy increased. He sought cover behind a massive reel wrapped in chains, feeling the tremble of bullets striking against its opposite side. Once there was a lull of silence, he immediately fired back and continued forward, shooting at them individually. Each shot expertly placed between their eyes, the sonar and his gun arm co-ordinated harmoniously.

But they began to understand what was happening and trailed back to the hall to find more secure cover.

Brody fired once more, missing the last one as he sprinted around the corner. He got to the entrance of the long corridor and saw they had thrown themselves into the doorways lining the passage. Brody could still see them, crouched boxy figures holding boxy guns standing within other, larger boxy shapes.

Titian shouted, "He's using sonar. Close it up. Close it up."

They heeded the command and one by one the men vanished behind closed doors to kill the sonar's ping.

Brody hunched down behind a tree trunk-sized mass of cables and let the sonar feel what it could. Despite the shipyard factory being rusty and dilapidated, the walls were in good shape and he could detect not a single man. He could hear panicked shouts and weapons reloading. He ejected the clip of his own gun and let the sonar feel down inside. Three bullets remained. He pressed a boot against the shoulder of a nearby thug to roll him over. Beneath the corpse was a gun, sticky wet with blood. Inside the magazine remained ten rounds.

He waited not a second more. He rose from behind the crushed car and fired through the wall of the closest room.

The sonar's ping filtered in through the hole, and the men inside could be seen ducking in what looked like a coordinated reaction.

Squaring up his aim, Brody fired through the wall again. The man fell and his companions in the room with him stared in awe. He fired two more times, taking them out as well. None inside had time to fire back.

He advanced down the hall to the room where the first pack of men had been hiding. Entering, he surveyed them there, with their guns still gripped in their dead hands. He took up the closest one's weapon, a combat shotgun with a snub-nosed barrel. As he turned it over, the shotgun's inside lit up in his mind's eye. The interior of the load was full—the previous owner had never gotten a single shot off.

Wasting no time, he stepped into the hallway, estimated where the men were with the sonar, and fired into them before they could make it to the door.

He fired into the opposite wall, found that room empty. He listened, everything still and silent.

Down at the end of the hall, Titian came into view but out of range for the shotgun to do any sort of serious damage. Regardless, Brody brought the shotgun up and fired, Titian slamming aside to dodge the spray of buckshot. He pumped and fired again, moving forward. Titian raised his pistol, and Brody ducked into a doorway to avoid the fire. The shots rang off and came through the steel wall, one muffled thwap after another of the silenced pistol being hastily emptied.

Both men took pause in cover.

"Fucking Hubert," Titian said as he reloaded. "What a spectacular mess this has turned out to be. Course, I can't really be that surprised. If something sounds too good to be true, it probably is. One day with enough adjusting, I could've been an upstanding citizen with a new name, placed somewhere else. That idea had its appeal. Just imagine. You and me, walking side by side on the street, a couple of regular joes going to work, practically living like a goddamn Artie. Normal folks with all our desires put away—submissive and on the *leash*."

Brody leaned the barrel of the shotgun out the door and fired.

Silence a moment. Then Titian continued. "Even though Ward had a pretty good argument, I always doubted there was a way, outside of a well-placed bullet, to fix bastards like us. We're dyed in the wool. Our daddies beat us, we grew up on Tom and Jerry blowing each other up with sticks of dynamite, and he thinks he can take all the bad shit out as easy as unloading a dishwasher—"

Brody jumped out, attempting to catch him off guard. He fired, dropped to one knee, pumped, fired again. The shots ripped through the steel wall of the room where Titian was hiding.

The sonar slowly mapped the room Titian stood inside. His gnarled head of hair matted down from melted snow, his heavy belt of blades. Titian stood motionless, the pistol pointed upward.

Brody remained crouched, holding the shotgun, ready to fire from the hip once the sonar settled. He had to be standing completely still for it to get an absolutely perfect fix on everything. He could miss with a gun just as easily as sometimes he missed his chair when sitting down too quickly.

Titian stepped out with a machete in hand, pitched it outward, the blade turning end over end in the air, reducing the space between the two men with deep, plunging cuts.

Reaction forced his hand, and Brody pulled the trigger on the shotgun and blasted the space before him. The machete was kicked back, where it hit the wall and slapped to the dirt floor, the blade perforated end to end. Brody pumped the next shell out and lunged forward, striking while Titian was choosing his next weapon from among his generous collection.

The killer bounded out of the room and slapped the shotgun barrel aside just as Brody pulled the trigger, but it wasn't fast enough. Although not a direct hit, the close proximity to such a sound and blast gave Titian an immediate burn across the side of his face, the flesh rendered red and black. Howling, he took the second of disorientating carnage to remove another blade from his belt and bring it down at his target.

Brody turned the shotgun to try to block the blade, catching Titian's wrist. The blade, a long curved knife intended for cleaning fish, sank into Brody's shoulder. He shoved back, but the blade had already sunk in deep, nearly to the handle. Titian came forward low and grabbed at Brody's middle to pull him to the floor. Brody kept his balance, and the two were rushed back to the wall, Titian grabbing the handle of the knife and driving the remaining length of the blade in. With the shotgun pinned between their bodies, Brody scrambled to grab a hold of anything he could.

Titian's black-and-white face, mapped for shape and minor calculable detail, showing his rotten teeth protruding from the gums. Their faces so close together, Titian's breath, the smell of blood and cordite and violence.

"I know that I am what I am, and if it means I don't get to do shit like *this* to people like *you* anymore, I don't ever want to change. I don't know why I ever wanted to give it up, honestly. But with Ward dead, I guess it doesn't really matter. That right there is enough proof that God wants me to be a putrid bottom-feeder forever. And I will not argue. I can accept it. I will happily be what I am, play my part, do what I do, with a new skip in my step till the day I die."

Brody brought up a knee and managed to get the snub-nosed shotgun freed. He yanked it away, pumped in the next shell, and swung it, jamming it hard under Titian's chin.

Titian caught the barrel before the trigger could be pulled, pushed it aside, and simultaneously plucked the blade out and drove it again, this time into Brody's abdomen. There was a distant pop when the tip broke flesh. Brody's body came alive with pain, and a gasp escaped him. Along with it, his grasp faltered on the shotgun. Titian, with a quick sideways wrench, freed it from his hand and drew in close, pushing the blade in a fraction deeper. It was hitting bone, the blade grinding against a rib—the tip seeking something inside, thirsty to puncture more.

"This is the part in the movies when my guy would say, 'We're just alike, you and I.' And your guy says, 'We're nothing alike.' But we both know that's bullshit. In this case, we both know my guy's right. The two-headed Jack, connected in the middle, one end up and the other down. Flip us around and it looks the same. Just a matter of perspective, where you're standing."

The agony flared as the knife dug in another inch, then was angled up, where the hand driving it sought to find the bottom of a lung or something else vital, soft, and waiting. Brody tried backing up to get free of it, but his back was firmly against the wall, the length of Titian's forearm pressed against his throat.

"I could be you. I know a guy who can rewrite jigsaws. Take a dab of my blood, wipe your information off, and just like that, I could be you. Easy as that. And this is better"—Titian nodded at his knife—"because if you do get out of this and you're no longer getting what you need to be the upward Jack, well, that card would flip around pretty damn quick. And before long, your rap sheet would resemble mine."

Brody could barely take a breath. He wasn't even present enough to think about a retort, the pain in his belly so immense that it felt like he might break apart entirely, and left in his stead would be a Brody-shaped mass of nothing but agony.

"Nobody wants to see the hero go bad. So, let's take our little eraser here." Titian swiveled the knife. "And rub you, the mistake, out before it becomes too much of a sob story."

A shot rang out—and Titian's chin evaporated from his face in a burst of red. The knife withdrew and he stumbled back, clutching his partly broken face.

Brody threw a hand over the wound in his stomach, the blood hot against his palm.

Up the hall Thorp advanced, pistol in two hands. He moved into position over Titian, sitting up with the geyser of red pouring from the rat's nest of his beard. Thorp aimed down at him. His mouth hardened, his lips tightening and then flattening over and over. He said he'd never kill again, and Brody wasn't about to have him break that promise yet again.

Brody peeled his hand off his wound and struggled

to his feet. He reached for the weapon.

Thorp glanced at Brody now standing next to him. "I can do it."

"Give it to me."

"I'll do it. Just let me do it."

Titian looked at the two men arguing over who was going to kill him. He seemed indifferent to what they decided. He closed his eyes, the realization that he'd been bested settling on his features. It was a bad wound—his bottom lip was gone and with it a few of his teeth—but he'd survive. Everyone present knew that.

A dry scuffle, bare feet on dirt. Nectar stood at the end of the hallway, draped in her soiled sheet, pulled tight and held at the neck. Nectar's voice, bouncing off the metal walls, came like a song, so soft and delicate, barely a voice at all. "Thorp."

Thorp glanced at his sister, then at Brody, then at Titian. The gun was handed over.

Brody took it in his hands, drew back the hammer, and extended the barrel down at Titian, who struggled to breathe, sputtering. When the barrel was on him, he didn't close his eyes. Brody and Titian gazed at one another wordlessly for a few moments, the killing implement between them.

Titian's hand fell away from the wreckage of his face. He drew a breath to say something, but it was cut short. The shot rang out, the flash, the bullet was propelled, and Titian was silent. The gun was thrown aside, and the hand holding it returned to tend the wound.

Every few miles Thorp asked Brody how Nectar was

doing since the roads were too bad for him to steal a glance. Hubert Ward's vehicle had a full tank, and once the engine warmed up, the heat was a blessed thing.

Groaning with the pain still screwed in deep in his belly, Brody put his arm over the seat and looked into the back, seeing Nectar sound asleep, coiled up on her side, knees pulled to her chest. The ping sent across her cheek displayed a peaked look about her, the sockets surrounding her heavy-lidded eyes concave, her wrists spindly. Her hair looked lifeless and hung in one greasy banner from her head. She had her brother's nylon jacket folded and balled up under her head. The ribs, showing even through the thick material of her sweatshirt, rose and fell evenly.

He reached into the backseat and carefully adjusted the stretched out, billowing neck of her sweatshirt, looping it onto her bony shoulder. "She's good," Brody answered Thorp each time.

They drove out of Chicago and onto the highway toward the farmhouse.

Thorp swore under his breath.

Brody didn't need to be able to see through the windshield to know what was going on; he could hear the gentle thrum of the police Darter hovering over the farmhouse.

They didn't evade what was waiting for them, didn't punch the gas and tear off farther into the frozen night. They were all hurt, and even if it meant going to the hospital and lying in bed cuffed to one of the rails, it was better than bleeding out in a field somewhere. Thorp parked in the driveway behind the collection of police cruisers. Brody noticed Thorp looking out the passenger window.

The passenger door was yanked open, and Brody's sonar felt the person's face and body standing there—and saw it to be wearing a duster and a fedora.

"Nathan," Brody said, even managing a tired smile. "I guess you got my e-mail."

"As well as an anonymous tip." Nathan Pierce gestured to the side yard. The Fairlane and the Zäh were being towed out of the bog by chains, both letting loose a flood of water from their interiors. "Why don't you do me a favor and step out? Let's take a minute to get this all squared away. What do you say?"

Brody obliged and watched as paramedics rushed over to the vehicle, shoving Thorp aside, and helped Nectar onto a stretcher. Thorp went into the ambulance with them but not before looking back at Brody and searching his face.

Brody nodded.

The vehicle turned across the lawn, its shrieking siren sounding to the world ahead to make way, and began its charge toward the nearest emergency room.

When Brody turned around, Nathan had his cuffs out.

"Really?" Brody said.

"It isn't me doing this."

Brody smirked. "Chiffon."

Nathan nodded. "When I started making calls about this thing you sent me, apparently word spread and she threatened to bring *me* up on charges if I didn't arrest you. You missed your appointment."

Brody watched the ambulance speed along the country road until the sonar could no longer detect it, the pixels jumping away, the ambulance seemingly dematerializing.

"She won't come all the way out here to bust your balls. She'd likely miss choir practice. So, what do you say? Couple of days in Chicago's lockup instead of in Minneapolis? A week behind bars in a jail that's not so loaded with friends of yours? Call it even? Given the circumstances, it's honestly the very best I can do."

"Sure. But no cuffs this time, okay?" Brody said.

"Deal." Nathan put the cuffs into the pouch on his belt. He guided Brody to his unmarked Lincoln parked at the edge of the property and opened the back door. Brody got in and let Nathan close the door.

Once inside, Nathan adjusted the mirror to get a look at his new passenger. "There's going to be a lot of red tape to sort through, one big rigmarole."

"Yeah," Brody said. "Should I mark anything off my calendar for the rest of the month? Ask my landlord to call Goodwill to empty my apartment?"

Nathan removed a pack of cigarettes from his khaki duster and pushed one through the plastic-coated mesh dividing the front from the back. "For the road?"

Brody took the cigarette and cracked the back window as far as it would go: two inches. It was far enough to allow not only the smoke out but the signal of his sonar. It felt all around the property of Thorp's farmstead. The barn where they had put the Darter back together, the craters left in the dirt from when they had been pulled back into unorthodox service, the house itself, where so much of the desperate search and planning, including the sleepless nights, for Nectar had been done.

And above all of it, even over the roof of Nathan's

Lincoln, the wires—thick as wrists—still hanging there. The low drone, detectable even beyond the hovering Darter's gentle din—the wires still coursing with the frequency, searching for a host to sink its influence into.

Brody dropped his cigarette out the window and pressed the button to roll the window back up, shutting out all the noise. He sat back and listened instead to the electric engine of Nathan's car hum as they tooled along the country road, a few miles behind the ambulance, back to Chicago.

36

Word had gotten to Chiffon as to
what the detective had done, and
she was none too pleased. She made a
few calls, even going so far as to send
Brody an e-mail explaining what was to
happen. While everything that had come to
pass with Hark Telecom was getting sorted
out, he would remain in county after the day
and a half he spent in the hospital being
treated for his various injuries. He
could write his statements behind
bars, and if things matched his story,
he would be transferred via prison bus
back to Minneapolis where all his remaining
community service hours would
transfer directly, hour by hour, into
prison time, with an additional three

hundred for missing their scheduled appointment.

Brody could say nothing in protest; it was a fine deal. He was confident that everything with Hark would come to light—all the evidence was still in place at the shipyard, and the contents of Hubert Ward's files contained the nefarious goings-on that the company had been behind. It was the Fairlane—which was full of evidence, even with some of Brody's blood—and the Zäh that kept him behind bars.

"Things aren't quite tallying up in a savory way in *that* particular department," Chiffon wrote in her e-mail, complete with italicization.

For three weeks Brody remained in his cell, except for two hours a day to go to the gym or walk the chain-link cube in the courtyard. He navigated the world with his sonar, stared at the TV mounted to the wall behind metal grating in the cafeteria, unable to see its picture—but heard Hark Telecom stock was, no big surprise, plummeting.

What was happening to Hark was the talk of the entire country. The company was divided up and sold off in massive chunks. The endless cubicle farms were cleared out, the office furniture sold in the corporate equivalent of a sheriff's sale, held in the employee parking lot. The number of jobless people was higher than it had ever been in Chicago. The more talented employees were hired at various companies the world over, once they had been determined to have not worked anywhere near research and development of course. Soon the Hark building that presided over downtown was empty and at night, all the other high-rises around it would be lit up here and there with late-night workers and cleaning crews, but that building became a stoic black monolith, wholly unlit and unoccupied.

The police chased as many leads as they could. The only one that had an easily sniffed trail was the one involving Hubert Ward, the shipyard, the six thousand miles of cable, the computers that pumped out endless streams of a broadcast-ready frequency that, once tested on laboratory rats, offered a plethora of results. Some rats became hostile to certain frequencies and exposure to the radiation within the wires—others more docile, tame. Some of them grew antisocial and never left their plastic hutch in the corner of their pen.

Stephen Marko, the CEO of Hark Telecom, made a public announcement claiming he had no idea what had been going on in his company. The man who had built up Hark from a telephone repair company started weeping on live television, telling the world that he was deeply remorseful for those affected. Since the company was essentially dead and all the funds were dried up, he couldn't offer any compensation. All he could offer was an apology.

Brody heard footsteps enter the cafeteria that weren't from prison-issue foam flip-flops. The sonar pinged the man standing in the back of the room searching the prisoners as they ate loose mashed potatoes and wheat toast, determining it was Nathan Pierce. Brody remained in his seat since getting up—or even so much as preparing to stand up—before they'd been excused by the guard wasn't just frowned upon but often resulted in a broken rib.

Nathan found Brody at the table, gave him a nod. He met eyes with the nearest guard and pointed at Brody, then jutted a thumb over his shoulder.

The guard, not breaking his stoic stance at the end of the buffet line, gave him permission with a wave.

Nathan and Brody left the cafeteria for the reception center. He was given a cardboard box with his belongings—his ruined clothes and wallet and keys and even the knuckleduster.

When he was finished getting dressed, Nathan took Brody's phone and replaced it with a small box.

"For me? You shouldn't have."

"Go ahead," Nathan said, flipping Brody's phone around to open the panel on its reverse side.

Brody couldn't see what was printed on the box, so he shook it next to his ear. By the sound of it, a new contact lens charger with a set of fresh batteries.

"On the house," Nathan said, fiddling with Brody's phone.

Brody and Nathan were alone in the locker room with benches and lots of yellow lines painted on the floor that prisoners, by no means, were to cross before being told to do so. They stood on either side of that line, Brody at the mirror and the row of sinks carefully putting the lenses into his eyes.

His reflection spiraled out ahead of him, the digits blinking: *29:59:59*. He saw the detective behind him, looking at Brody's dead cell phone. "What's wrong?" Brody asked.

"I don't want anyone to hear what I'm about to say,"

Nathan said, giving Brody his slumbering cell, then going into his own pocket to do the same to his own. He glanced at the corners of the ceiling. Brody noticed that was where black domes were set up, just as they would be in any square inch of the prison.

Nathan sighed. "We're releasing you today."

Brody turned around. "You make it sound like a bad thing."

"You kicked over a pretty big rock. Consider the can of worms officially opened. That e-mail was like the one piñata string that once pulled makes everything fall out."

"That's a lot of metaphors."

"Bear with me. I haven't slept. Just *listen*, okay? I'm trying to tell you, even though Hark has been splintered up and sold off, we couldn't keep up with everything— stuff got away from us. When our tech guys tried to pry into certain sensitive files, they'd vanish. Self-destruct. Poof, gone. But we were able to chase it back out through the firewall and see that it was e-mailed in enormous chunks to an address, an overseas registry."

"Any idea who it could be?" Brody said.

"We're asking for a search warrant to get into that account and find out who was stockpiling Hubert Ward's files. But it's going to take a good deal of time and patience before we're going to see any progress."

"Why are you telling me this?"

"I want you to forget about all this once you're released. You did your time. You won't have to report to Chiffon anymore. The slate has been wiped clean. Take this as an opportunity for a fresh start."

"What about January? The reform. Wasn't that a week ago?" Brody had been keeping track of the time by moving a pile of matchsticks from one pile to another, but at some point his count got screwed up, and now he wasn't sure if it was a week into January or New Year's Eve.

"It was, and since you were out of state it didn't apply."

"What?"

"I pulled some strings for you. In exchange, I want you to tell me right now you're going to leave it alone. That's all I want."

"Do you expect me to go after whoever is stockpiling Hubert's files?" He shook his head. "Explain it to me again. Why the hell am I being released? You tell me I have a clean slate, but if I go walking out the door and get arrested the minute my jig gets scanned at a convenience store, I'm going to be kind of ticked."

"You got a Get Out of Jail Free card. The judge ruled to change the adulterer's law, but since there were so many cases, he took the unpopular route and had them all thrown out, claiming they were just misdemeanors anyway."

"So I have a clean record now?" Brody laughed. "Haven't had one of those in a while."

"Don't get too ahead of yourself. There're still a few marks on there but nothing I can hold you for. The investigation with Hark is ongoing, and you can't leave the state or much less break wind without my preapproval—so once you're home: stay there." Nathan stared at Brody, his mouth a single flat line cutting across his face like it had been scored there.

Brody scratched his beard. "There's something else. Just go ahead and say it."

"We don't know what to do next," Nathan said. "There's no way *to* know. Until we get the clearance to chase this thing overseas, we'll just have to keep our eyes peeled. But with you and Thorp being under this shit for years—I mean, I know you told me you don't use a gun, but there was an awful lot of dead bodies at that shipyard . . ."

"I did what I had to do."

Nathan sighed. "I'm going to leave it at this. Make it a onetime thing. Keep all this under your hat and don't consider this bullshit something for you to take care of. Put it behind you. Move on. Get a nine to five, meet a girl. Just don't go round thinking that Hark is going to come and get you again because—trust me—they're through."

Brody thought about the shipyard and the violence he'd cut loose on those men. Titian Shandorf in particular. Hubert Ward. After replaying the scene over and over while lying in his cell, Brody determined the number of men was eleven. Twelve, if you included Rice—which Brody did. He thought about those lives he had ended, shoveled together in the same pile with the one man he had killed before that night, the man in Cairo. He'd ended thirteen lives. He considered what Hubert Ward had told him about self-control, about being a pugilistic misanthrope—and how that wasn't by choice, just an unanticipated effect of the silver fox signal.

He shook his head as he put the rest of his belongings into his pockets. He held the last item, the knuckleduster, in his palm and thought about how many men he had hurt or maimed. It ranked into the hundreds. One or two a week for all those years since he got out of the Army. Hundreds of fractured collarbones, knocked-out teeth, flattened noses, broken arms. Same deal following: red and blue, flashing. Metal cuffs on the wrists, stale coffee and stale air of the interview room, Chiffon's office with the horrible gospel music playing on an endless loop—all of it, none of it—was it him or was it an unconscious influence?

Brody put the knuckleduster in his pocket, shook Nathan Pierce's hand.

"We'll probably need to call you in to clarify a few things. Thorp volunteered information about Sebastian Calloway and his friend Anthony 'Spanky' Ellis."

"And?"

"The courts are so backed up—trying to put away Hark's people who knew what Ward was up to—that they've decided to look the other way. Calloway and Ellis were both pretty high on the DA's list, and a few of the judges I mentioned their names to said they were practically on a first-name basis with them, and, well, as far as they were concerned, two less faces they have to see a dozen times a year is a good thing."

Nathan sighed. "And besides that, I've still got a notebook full of questions for you. Naturally, without said notebook with me, I can't remember a single one of them for the life of me." He looked at Brody for a few seconds, his eyes bloodshot. "I called Thorp. He's coming to pick you up."

"Thanks." Brody turned on his heel and walked to the reception center door and waited to be buzzed through. "See you back in Minnesota?"

Nathan nodded.

The metal door slid aside and natural light flooded in, the sound of snow falling in a whispery, wet hiss. Brody faced the cold and went through the three layers of fence—all topped with razor wire—to the outside.

He blinked at the cold, his eyes sensitive to the new lenses, and saw an idling cab on the corner with a couple of familiar faces looking out the back window. Brody couldn't help but smile as Thorp and Nectar got out and rushed over to him.

Thorp hugged him, nearly squeezed the breath out of his lungs with a bear hug.

"Easy now," Brody said. "I still got some stitches."

Nectar also hugged him but it was much weaker. Brody patted her back. Her spine was still easily felt through her shirt, but it wasn't to the degree it had been when he'd last seen her. She looked much better.

She winced, tucking her hands into her jeans pockets. "I hope you didn't get in too much trouble."

"No, it wasn't because of this—it was because of previous convictions. Nothing major." He watched Nectar sweep a band of hair behind her ear. "Just some old stuff that had to get squared away." He said it and a moment later it caught.

Nectar naturally missed it. As she thanked him, Brody looked to Thorp who looked back at him with an appreciative smile. They nodded at one another.

"It was really great of you to do that for me," Nectar continued. "I don't normally take pills unless I know what they are. And you know how it can be, you're in Tokyo having fun with your friends and one thing leads to another and you don't want to be the one not getting high—and, well, I just have to ask: How did you know to look for me at the bus station of all places?"

Brody turned to Thorp. His friend shrugged, stared at the sidewalk. Brody glanced back at Nectar and smiled as genuinely as the whirling confusion in his head would allow. "Lucky guess, I suppose."

Thorp still peered down at the sidewalk, his face screwed up tight.

"Lunch?" Brody suggested.

Thorp smiled. "Yeah. Sure."

The three sat in the back booth at America's Favorite Automat across the street from Nectar's former apartment building.

Nectar kept looking out the front window at her stoop, where she used to call home. "I can't believe those assholes evicted me. I was just a couple of weeks late on rent. People go through hard times, right?" She looked to her brother, then to Brody.

Neither of them said anything.

She went back to glaring out the window for a few more seconds, then slid out of the booth, claiming, "I'm going to go look at the pies."

When she was out of earshot, Brody turned to Thorp across the table and leaned forward. "She doesn't remember anything?"

"Not a thing."

"What happened in the hospital? Did she wake up talking about going to Tokyo and accidentally taking a bad pill and you and me finding her at a bus station?

Where did she get all this?"

Thorp shrugged. "I never left her side. No one ever came into the room except for the doctor. He told me that sometimes the mind will build a story for itself to fill in gaps, that the narrative of memory needs to be continuous and all blank spaces need to be filled in with something, even if it sounds ridiculous to other people."

"So no one supplied this Tokyo story?"

"No."

"Jesus, that's strange."

Thorp scoffed. "What *hasn't* been strange about this past month?"

"Do you suppose it was what they wanted her to think?" Brody asked after a moment. He waved a hand next to his ear, "So if she got free or something she wouldn't actually remember where she was or anything?"

"Beats me." Thorp watched Nectar over Brody's shoulder. "Beats the hell out of me."

When Thorp grinned, Brody turned to watch as Nectar twirled in front of the slices of pie, doing some sort of ballet with hands raised and spinning on her toes. She caught her balance on the plastic wall of the pie display case, looked around, then went back to dancing.

Brody turned back around and hunched over the table. "Detective Pierce, the one I e-mailed the information to? He told me to leave it alone and move on with my life."

Thorp sipped his coffee. "That's a good idea."

"I think you should do the same."

Thorp took his napkin and wiped the coffee foam from the tip of his nose. "Not to worry about that. After we got home, I wanted something to do with my hands and started working on the Terrapin . . ."

Brody lit a cigarette to hide his displeasure with the direction Thorp's story was taking.

"The lawyers said I could keep all the money from Hark they had given me over the years. I said I wasn't planning on giving it back, anyway. And then they told me someone was going to remove the wires at my house. Apparently, even though they had shut down the source at the shipyard, more units might still be sending out the signal and they didn't want to chance it. They don't want me to sue is what it sounds like. Either way, I got the Terrapin running. Me and Nectar did, actually. And we ripped that tower out of the ground ourselves."

Brody smiled, pleased to see the story ended differently than he expected. "So, it's over. You won't be getting your checks anymore. Is that fine with you?"

"Yeah," Thorp said. "I could stand to return to the hustle and bustle of the city, get out among people again. No man is an island, right? Got a job interview downtown Monday, crane operator and maintenance."

"Handyman."

"You know it."

Nectar approached the table, picked up the cigarette Brody had in the ashtray, took a deep drag, and released the smoke slowly. "Good Lord, that's wonderful." She sighed.

She caught Brody looking at her and took another drag, her eyes lighting up. She pulled out the collar of his shirt and blew the smoke into the material. As the smoke drifted up between their faces, she stepped back, looked at her handiwork, and laughed, giving the mark a swipe with her thumb to ensure a job well done.

She sat down. "I'm sorry. Don't worry about it—it'll come right out. It's just something I do to people on a lark."

"It's fine," Brody said, smiling. He studied the oval-shaped nicotine stain on his shirt, the death kiss, and looked at Nectar. She had selected a piece of blueberry pie.

The Artificial server came to the end of their table and sized them up. She kept her gaze on Thorp, her expression flat. "Sir, will you be paying today? It seems that within your party, you are the only one with a bank account currently in the positive. You can pay at the counter when ready."

Thorp leaned to one side to retrieve his wallet, took one last sip of his coffee, and left the booth.

Brody watched Nectar eat her pie, one large forkful at a time. He continued to look at her until she met his eyes. She set the fork down and plucked some napkins from the dispenser. "What?"

Brody pointed at his collar, the death kiss, and raised his eyebrows.

Her face remained flat. She folded the napkin in half, set it aside. "Not in front of him, okay?" she said, keeping her voice low and subtly cocking her head in Thorp's direction where he was struggling to insert his jigsaw into the nautilus. "If he knows I know, then he'll never let it go. This way it's a clean break."

"You remember everything?"

"Yeah. But as long as I say I don't remember any of it, he won't talk about it. And if he won't talk about it, then we'll be able to move on and just . . . live our lives." She glanced Thorp's way, and so did Brody. He was getting his receipt for the meal. Speaking fast, "I want him to go to the doctor, get on some kind of pill to fix whatever they did to his head." She smoothed the napkin's folds out to its original square shape. "And be done with it."

Thorp began walking back, scrutinizing the receipt.

He had to ask. "What about Axiom? Did you hear anything about—?"

She stared at him. For a moment, it was hard to read what her eyes were telling him. Was she surprised he knew the name? Did the mere mention of him frighten her? She held that strange look for a few more seconds. Just as Thorp's shadow fell across their table, she nodded, nearly imperceptibly, even going so far as to scratch her ear as she did it. But she did nod; Brody saw it. She had at least heard him say Axiom, whoever he was and whatever role he had played in all this.

"All right," Brody said. He had a bevy of questions, but this wasn't the time or place. He wasn't about to screw up what Nectar was already doing, this stellar job of playing ignorant in front of her brother. The whole bit about Tokyo and the bus station, he had to admit, was convincing.

Thorp put his hand on Nectar's shoulder after he'd sat down beside her. She leaned into her brother's chest, closed her eyes, and seemed to go to sleep immediately. Thorp shifted a strand of hair out of the corner of her eye. He looked up and saw Brody watching them and gave him a grateful smile.

Brody returned it.

37

It took some finagling to get Amtrak
to let Brody use his old ticket when
he had missed the scheduled return trip by
well over a month. He assumed they caved
because of his limp and the condition of
the right side of his face, which was green
and purple. Despite getting passage for the
12:10, the train was late, delayed heading out
of Chicago due to ice on the tracks. He sat on
their uncomfortable benches, closed
his eyes, and thought about nothing but
sleeping in his own bed.

He got to his private car and carefully
eased into the seat. The cot in the county
jail had done his bruises and aches no
favors. After the doctor had referred
Brody to a physician in the Twin Cities

who could remove the stiches in his gut, he informed Brody that the gouge in his shoulder had gotten infected and the tube of antiseptic salve he gave him would make the pain stop. The opposite was true. Brody shouldered off his coat and applied the cream, cramming his hand down the collar of his shirt, gritting his teeth against the burn the salve created. He paused, feeling something land on the back of his wrist. He pulled his hand out: a single red dot.

He sniffed and dabbed at his nose, then looked at his fingers. A smear of red.

The collar was loosened, stretched out from trying to get his arm inside. It didn't stop him from hooking two fingers and tugging at it, though.

On his home voice mail in Minneapolis, Brody had close to seventy-two messages. Samantha at the community center expressing worry. Chiffon trying numerous times to get a hold of him. His bank notifying him of severe overdraft charges. A few possible clients sobbing and saying, "I heard about you from a friend. Do you think you can help *me*?" His landlord reminding him that it was past the first of the month when rent is normally paid.

Brody went to his couch and sat down with his coat still on, looked at the dead face of his TV screen. He tugged at his collar and let his gaze trail up and down the walls, looking for any sign, any mismatch in the color of the polished cement, any irregularity at all.

He splashed cold water on his face. He looked into the expanse of glass making up the entire wall of the bathroom and in it he could see nothing, even with the new lenses from Nathan. Staring back at him: a face. A man. Bruised flesh and battered bone, a newly crooked nose. And as much as Brody didn't want to admit it, he saw a puppet. The strings were cut, but he still bore the eye hooks, screwed in tight. Titian's words came back to him. He slapped off the light.

In the living room he found his peacoat on the floor, lifted it just enough to get what he sought from the pocket, and dropped it again.

His fingers found their way into the knuckleduster with ease.

He wasn't sure where to start, so he decided to just pick a place.

Looking up toward the wall next to his TV, he saw the smooth layer of new cement, a smooth-cornered square. It had been patched a few times when pipes froze or something needed fixing. He knew something had been altered whenever he came home and smelled the lime and congealing agent of the cement. Never even so much as a note regarding a work order from his landlord.

No reason to be suspicious, then.

The first punch resounded against the cement with a clang. The vibration trailed up his arm and dug into the fresh hole in his shoulder—the antiseptic cream that was supposed to subdue any pain proved yet again to be a bunch of bullshit. Brody punched once more, a puff of gray dust breaking free. When he twisted in order to throw a clean jab, the delicate flesh still held together by stitches screamed. A hairline crack an inch long formed in the wall. Another strike and the crack grew by two more inches. Another, the first crack lengthened and a new one started—a rough divot began to take form.

Wiping the grit from his forehead and nose, he peered into the hole he'd made. There, a dense collection of wires—most of them small and narrow—electrical, more electrical, a water filtration line, electricity. Brody sorted through them all, grunting, coughing at the dust.

He plunged his hand deeper into the hole and found it. Rubbery, thick as a wrist. He pulled it out of its nest of fellow wires. No markings or laser-etched codes at all, entirely black.

Brody let the wire hang there, the long loop nearly touching the floor, while he got a knife from the butcher block. He returned with the knife and stared at the black snake, ashy in a patina of cement dust in most parts and fiercely dark in dots here and there from his sweat.

So many years doing it, unaware. The community center, all the battered women he had helped. The urge to go out and act upon it, that persistent pecking to exact, settle, solve, fix. And the restraint he considered his biggest asset—the ability to stop once they'd had enough.

What if he had never learned of the wires and their frequency, of the project at all? Would he have continued to carry on, getting healthy doses of the stuff every minute he was in his apartment, forever solidified as an involuntary vigilante? Would he continue to be able to stand firm, knowing when to stop *without* it? Would he accidentally go too far and kill the next wife beater he got hired to rough up? He was certainly capable of it, he now knew. Titian's words again. Not what Brody could be but what he *would* be, without it leashing him.

Brody held the knife by its handle and rolled it around in his grip, looking at the waiting belly of the black snake. Despite it being freed from its cement enclosure, he could hear the gentle thrum of the energy still coursing through it, droning. A cold prickle on his skin. A tug at the collar of his shirt.

He stared, standing in his living room with the knife in hand, resisting.

A very special thanks to Dr. Lyudmila Trut, whose research I came across through the *NOVA* documentary "Dogs Decoded."

MEDALLION

P R E S S

Be in the know on the latest Medallion Press news by
becoming a Medallion Press Insider!

<u>As an Insider you'll receive:</u>
· Our FREE expanded monthly newsletter, giving you more insight into
Medallion Press
· Advanced press releases and breaking news
· Greater access to all your favorite Medallion authors

Joining is easy. Just visit our website at
<u>www.medallionmediagroup.com</u> and click on
Super Cool E-blast next to the social media buttons.

medallionmediagroup.com

MEDALLION